BENT TREE COTTAGE

The Tanners, Book 4

Pamela Ann Cleverly

CLEVER INK, LLC,
Mentor, OH

ISBN-13: 978-0-9970522-5-1

*This book is dedicated in memory of Dana P. Talcott,
my loving partner of twenty-six years. He was my inspiration,
my best friend, my lover and the champion of my books.*

Rest In Peace, My Love.

ALSO BY PAMELA ANN CLEVERLY

<u>The Tanners Series</u>

In The Shadow Of The Lighthouse, Book 1

A Beacon In The Dark, Book 2

It Started With Besse, Book 3

CHAPTER ONE

Fairfield, Charles City, Virginia
Early April 1993

He'd sit, back resting against the ancient bent tree, sucking on a blade of grass. The young lad fantasized about the gloomy old mansion perched on the lonely stretch of Long Point. He'd been old enough to understand the words "Never go near the Whitaker land; you'll catch the polio," yet young enough to believe he'd never get caught. In all those years, he never saw a light behind the lace curtained windows, never saw a car under the porte-cochere, never saw a boat moored to the sturdy dock, and never saw anyone except old man McTavish who tended the grounds. He'd made a promise to the bent tree, back then, that someday Bent Tree Cottage would be his. Even though the whole island knew the Whitaker family would never give up their land--the lawyers said so. But Travis Tanner always kept a promise.

⇒┼⇐

"Travis, are you listening?" Olivia Bentley Tanner waited for an answer. Her husband stood before the large Palladian window in Fairfield's library. His hands grasped behind his back. She'd spent the last few minutes giving him a rundown of her schedule for the day. She'd be home late after a day of planning meetings at the house on Freemason Street, in Norfolk, for a new charity she was working on. He hadn't nodded, shrugged, or given any indication that he'd heard her. "Earth to Travis." No response. "An alien spaceship landed on the lawn, sucked up the twins, and took off over the James."

"Huh? Oh. Good idea." He sounded a million miles away.

Olivia set her daily planner on the arm of the closest sofa. She padded across the room and wrapped her arms around her husband's waist. In a tight hold, she rested her head on his shoulder. "Want to share it with me?"

"Share what?" He bent down and kissed the top of his wife's head.

"Whatever it is that has you engrossed in an empty courtyard."

"The Whitakers are going to lose Long Point."

Whitaker. Whitaker. Why couldn't she place the name? Whoever he, she, or they must be, they were significantly important. Her mind raced in a million different directions. She was pretty good remembering names—she had to be when dealing with a multibillion-dollar industry, not to mention the slew of government names and faces that changed with every presidential election. Long Point. Long Point? Olivia pulled back her head. Why was he thinking about the Lake Erie Islands? They wouldn't be returning to Ohio for another month or two. She dropped her arms to her side and took a couple of steps back. "Long Point? The Long Point on Kelleys Island?"

"Yeah." Travis turned away from the window and faced her.

His eyes had taken on a serious look. Like he was about to tell her their parakeet died, only they didn't have a parakeet. Ohio was a long way away from Charles City, Virginia. Whatever was troubling him, it couldn't be that bad. "If I remember correctly, Long Point is tied up in trusts and legal red tape. It can never be sold. Never leave the Whitaker family."

Travis took her hand and guided her to one of the over-stuffed, floral-print sofas. He motioned for her to sit. "Not sold—taken—by the Feds."

Olivia settled against a raspberry-colored silk throw pillow. Arching one eyebrow, she still couldn't fathom what that had to do with them or why it seemed to trouble Travis. "Okay?" She motioned for him to continue.

"I've kept an eye on the property and made it known to anyone who would listen that I'd be interested at any price." He paused a beat. "I think I was ten when I made a promise to the bent tree."

Olivia searched her brain for anything that would trigger a memory that could possibly explain what he was talking about. She remembered, years, actually decades, ago, cruising past Long Point on her boat, the *Lovely Lady*, and seeing the gloomy old stone mansion called Bent Tree Cottage. But what did that have to do with Travis today? What could possibly have put him in such a funk? "What bent tree?"

"Native Americans would take a sapling and bend it over and tie it down with a vine. Then when it grew up straight, it would have a bend at the bottom. They used them as markers—kinda like the first road signs."

"You made a promise to a tree? When you were ten?" Olivia gave him her sweetest smile. Boyhood memories were important. She could imagine the young Travis with blond tousled hair playing around a crooked tree. "Promises are important—no matter when they are made. But sometimes it's impossible to keep them. You shouldn't feel bad."

"I got a call from a buddy of mine who works in the IRS. Young Jimmy Whitaker hasn't been keeping a very good eye on the family finances. They're about to lose everything. Everything. The whole kit and caboodle."

"Long Point?"

"Yes. They have until Wednesday at noon to come up with the money. After that, our Uncle Sam becomes the new owner."

Olivia scooted next to her husband, taking both his hands in hers. "I'm sorry." Childhood dreams were sometimes the hardest ones to let go. She'd had more than a few—only one survived—the *Lovely Lady*. Even that died a horrible, fiery death in the end—just off the shores of Kelleys Island. She squeezed his hand in sympathy.

"I offered them ten times what it's worth," Travis answered in a monotone. Like this was something he did every day and not a big deal. "I'll know something by Friday."

Olivia's heart jumped—then jumped again—and again! Then it finally leapfrogged into her throat. "What?" she croaked.

"I put a cash offer in. They'd be crazy not to take it. I'm saving Long Point."

Olivia pulled her hands back and folded them in her lap. Where did this come from? She'd met Travis eleven years ago— the year she and the *Lovely Lady* moved to Marblehead, Ohio. In all those years, he'd never mentioned the Whitakers or Long Point. At least not in the context of owning it, which was legally impossible. She was missing a piece or two of the puzzle. "You mean you're buying *more* land on Kelleys Island? The island isn't that big, Travis. How many properties does that make now? You do remember we own the Captain's House on Marblehead—our summer home? Just a twenty-minute ferry ride away from the island."

Travis leaned forward, resting his forearms on his knees. He stared at the toe of his Nike, clasping his hands together into a tight fist. "Four. Three vacation rentals and a lot next to the airport." He paused a beat. "Well, five, if I get it." He opened and then closed his fist. He gnawed his lower lip and scrunched his face, as if a battle of emotions were raging inside. Then all went calm. Travis glanced over his shoulder locking his eyes with hers. Giving her that little boy smirk she could never resist. "If *we* get it!"

Olivia jumped up, standing before him with her hands firmly planted on her hips. "Oh no, you don't, Travis Tanner. You're not pulling me into one of your schemes. I want nothing to do with that huge pile of Gothic stone! Besides, everyone on the island believes it's haunted."

He lifted his hands in a supplicatory gesture. "I made a promise."

"To a *tree*!" Olivia's voice rose to a decibel that could rattle the three-hundred-year-old windowpanes and then she shook her head. This was definitely the dumbest thing he'd ever done. "And the tree isn't even there anymore!"

"It *was*—when I was a kid." Travis knew his wife's temper wouldn't last long if he kept calm. It never failed, that is, as long as neither of them was in danger—and those were memories he'd rather forget.

Olivia threw up her arms. "I give up." She could feel her cheeks turning red in anger. "I give up." She felt defeated and lowered her arms to her sides. "Do what you want. But count me *out*!" She turned to leave the room. "I'm late for the meeting in Norfolk. Don't wait up for me." She reached the archway and turned back to face him. He looked beaten. Like he'd just lost his team the championship. She forced an encouraging smile. "Maybe take the boys for a sail? Looks like a beautiful day."

⚓

It was early that afternoon when Travis steered the *Livy V* through the yacht club's channel and into the James River. He and the boys waved as they passed Fairfield's acres of manicured lawns. A lone security guard waved back.

"Andy, want to take the tiller? Show those landlubbers how brave you are?" asked Travis of his son sitting on the stern seat, his small hands clutching the yellow life jacket.

Andy leaned to the portside rail to get a better view of his twin brother on the bow. Freddy was as far forward as he could get while jumping up and down. He waved both hands at a second security guard stepping out from a stand of poplar trees. "I think Freddy would like to show off in front of everyone. Let *him* steer the boat."

His twin sons may look alike, but that was as far as the resemblance went. Fredrick Angus Tanner, the older of the two by three minutes, arrived in the world kicking and screaming, while Andrew Angus Tanner came quietly. Freddy couldn't learn to do things fast enough. Olivia said he was like a newborn foal, ready to stand and run minutes after his feet hit the ground. Andy preferred to sit back and watch his older brother stumble and fall until he'd perfected the art of walking—crawling had been difficult enough. Nothing had changed over the past eight years.

"Hey, Freddy. Want to take the tiller?" Travis shouted.

Freddy turned, hopped over a coil of rope on the deck, and ran toward the stern.

"No running! Safety first," yelled Travis. "It's too early in the day to be fishing you out of the water!"

"The water temperature is fifty-nine degrees. Too cold," Andy added.

Travis turned and winked at Andy, reassuring him that all was good. He didn't need to compete with his brother, and his brother wasn't perfect.

Freddy climbed onto the special box Travis had made so his sons could see over the sleek cabin roof. The eight-year-old looked up to the top of the mast to the wind vane checking the direction of the wind. Then he studied the movement of the Tell Tales, light strips of material attached to the sail to indicate whether the air against the sail was smooth or turbulent.

"Ready, Captain?" asked Travis.

"Aye!" Freddy pulled the tiller toward him. "Prepare to raise the spinnaker."

"Are you sure about that, Son?"

"Yes. The wind is perfect," Freddy said, with the confidence of an old salt.

"It will send us racing downriver," warned Travis.

"I know, but traffic is light. It'll be fun!" Freddy shouted.

The wild, impetuous side of his son was in control. Travis had fully read the river minutes after leaving the shoreline of Hopewell, Virginia. They would have an exhilarating, yet safe, sail. He moved forward to lower the mainsail and hoist the colorful spinnaker.

A rainbow of colors billowed out in front of them, pulling the small daysailer toward the Chesapeake Bay. Travis settled in the corner of the aft starboard settee, where he had a clear view of both his sons and the river traffic. Freddy had inherited more than a few of Travis's genes. He thought back to his own child-hood growing up on the Marblehead peninsula. He'd had all of the Lake Erie Islands as his playground. He'd learned to read the unpredictable waters before he learned to read a book. He'd been racing boats long before he was old enough to get a driver's license. He'd owned three boats before his first car.

Travis turned toward Andy. "Okay, Son?"

Andy nodded, mumbling something into the laces on his life vest. He held the front of the jacket with one hand and a tight grip on the boat's stern rail with the other. Maybe he'd never share Freddy's love of boating, but Andy's mind could sail circles around his brother's. At least he didn't get seasick.

⥤⥢

A week later, Travis sat at the long table in Fairfield's library. He'd just finished another very profitable phone call with a buyer for one of his boats. Olivia claimed he collected boats like other men collect baseball cards. Well, this little baby had cost him nothing more than a few parts and a lot of elbow grease. He'd stumbled on the 1952, eighteen-foot, mahogany Chris-Craft runabout in a field near Annapolis, two years ago. One more case of an oldie being left behind after an out-of-state inheritance. He'd put new tires on the boat's trailer, hooked it up to his Dodge Ram, and hauled it back to Virginia.

Five years ago, after being married for three to one of the wealthiest and most powerful women in the world, Travis realized he needed a life of his own. Something that was all his—something he was good at. Heck, the world still referred to her as Olivia Bentley. It didn't matter that she had legally added Tanner to the end of her name. He'd helped Daisy's daughter, who owned the estate next door to Fairfield, start up her therapeutic riding camp for disabled children. Daisy wanted to make Travis a partner in her growing operation and expand the new concept across the country. But the truth was, he really didn't like horses. He liked boats. He *loved* boats. He loved tools and machines and getting dirty. He'd been driving through the small town of Hopewell, across the river one day when he noticed a For Sale sign on an old abandoned factory. It was the perfect location for restoring and selling vintage boats. The next day he was the owner of the derelict hulk of brick and steel. He hadn't been wrong. Today it was a thriving business, and Travis was proud to have the name TANNER in large, bold letters across the front.

"Excuse me, Mr. Tanner," Sarah Harrison said from the archway leading into the library. He didn't respond, so Fairfield's housekeeper stepped into the room. "Mr. Tanner?"

Travis jumped at the sudden voice interrupting his mental journey into the past. He turned as Sarah's voice registered. "Sorry, I didn't hear you. Is it time for lunch?"

"You already had lunch," she said with amusement. "Three hours ago." She changed to her serious voice. "There's a Mr. James Whitaker III at the gate to see you. Were you expecting him?"

Whitaker? What was he doing here? Travis wondered. There couldn't be a problem with the purchase of Long Point. The funds had transferred early that morning. There was no way the family could back out of the deal now.

Travis shook his head. "I'm not expecting him, but it's okay. I know who he is. Have Higgins open the gates."

"Yes, sir," Sarah said as she turned and headed back down the hall.

Travis inhaled deeply, and then let it out in a blow of frustration. He hated this part of their life. His wife's wealth and position in McLeod and Morrison, a company in Norfolk that built ships for the military, meant she had a perpetual target on her back—so did the rest of the family. There'd been more foiled kidnapping attempts than he'd care to remember. Higgins, Olivia's chief of security, would want a rundown on James Whitaker III.

Ten minutes later, Sarah ushered James Whitaker III into the library. "Will that be all, sir?" Travis knew what the stern set of her jaw and sharp tone in her voice meant. For whatever reason, Sarah didn't like the man.

"Thank you, Sarah. That will be all."

He didn't miss the roll of Sarah's eyes as she turned to leave.

Travis moved to the front of the room. He shook the stranger's rather clammy hand. He was on the short side, his extra-large suit jacket ready to burst free of its buttons. His thinning dark-brown hair and clipped beard framed a decidedly red tone to his wide nose. It appeared the man had a healthy appetite and imbibed in more than one substance. "I'm sorry, but did we have this meeting scheduled? I don't remember the need for us to meet."

"No. Everything happened so fast. Suddenly you were the new owner of Long Point and we hadn't had time to draw up the agreement." He raised the briefcase he'd been holding at his side, as if to confirm that he was, indeed, there for a meeting.

"Mr. Whitaker," Travis said as he motioned toward a set of facing, overstuffed sofas in the middle of the large room. "Have a seat."

"Beautiful place you've got here. I must've been driving down that road of yours for two miles. Thought I was lost for a minute."

"We are a bit secluded," Travis answered as he guided the man to a sofa facing one of several bookcases. He glanced up at the hidden camera in a row of first editions and nodded, ever so slightly. For once he was glad the camera was there—Higgins would be watching, and with a flip of a switch—listening.

"Your maid said the place was built in 1733. Whew! That's really old. Doesn't look that bad, though . . . you know what I mean?"

Travis seethed with indignation. "Our housekeeper. Sarah was born here, as was her mother, and her grandmother. Fairfield has always been her home."

"Huh. Will your wife be joining us? I didn't know you were married to Olivia Bentley, or I would have held out for more money," he chortled.

Travis didn't know if he was more shocked by the question or the sheer audacity of the man. "Mrs. Tanner has nothing to do with our transaction. And you were paid far more than the property is worth." The steam was building in Travis faster than in a pressure cooker—and he was about to blow. "Look, Whitaker. You came here unannounced, with briefcase in hand. I assume you have business with me regarding my purchase of Long Point." He paused for a breath. "Let's get on with it."

"Tsk, Tsk. Mr. Tanner, I've come a long way…from Cleveland… to explain the situation. This is going to take a while." He set his briefcase on the seat next to him and opened the lid. After removing a stack of papers, he fanned them out on the coffee table between them. "We should start at the beginning . . . with the Native Americans living on the island . . . and then, General . . ."

"No! Let's *not* start at the beginning. Let's not start at all." Travis leaned forward, raking the fingers of both hands through his hair. Somewhere along the way, he'd lost control of this bizarre meeting, and the meeting had just begun. The land was his now, period. "Give me the deed, if that's what you came for, and you can return to Cleveland. I don't need a history lesson."

"But the General part is important. You have to understand—"

Travis raised his hand signaling Whitaker to stop talking. He'd heard the cart rolling down the hall before Sarah reached the door.

"Excuse me, sir. I thought you could use some refreshment." She rolled the dark-wood serving cart into the room. Its polished brass corners and heavily carved trim emphasized its age and the care taken to preserve it. "I've brought coffee, hot tea, iced tea and lemonade, and an assortment of pastries."

Mr. Whitaker rose and walked over to the cart. After viewing the array of sweets, he popped a pecan tart into his mouth, then grabbed a brownie. "Got anything stronger?"

Travis wanted to strangle the man. Instead, he swallowed his anger and prayed to God to give him patience. "Sarah, would you please take Mr. Whitaker over to the bar and fix him whatever he wants?"

"Call me Jimmy," he said to Travis. Then turned to Sarah. "Scotch. Single malt. I assume you have it."

"Yes, sir." Sarah motioned to the far side of the large Georgian fireplace. "Please follow me." She stopped before a paneled wall, which opened with a quick tap of her wrist, reveling a full wet bar.

Mr. Whitaker stood beside her, his gaze circling the room with its soft green paneled walls and large Palladian windows. "Wow. I expect George Washington to pop in at any moment," he said with a hint of sarcasm.

"Actually, Mount Vernon was built twenty-five years *after* Fairfield. And, yes, when in the area, General Washington was often a guest," Sarah said as she looked over her shoulder with raised eyebrows and a grin of satisfaction for putting this pompous ass in his place.

"You don't say," he quipped.

Sarah pulled a bottle of eighteen-year Glenlivet and was ready to pour. "No way!" Jimmy exclaimed. "You've got a bottle of Macallan thirty year, Sherry Oak, single malt?" He picked up the bottle of Scotch and examined the label. "What was the price on this baby—five grand? I'll have this one instead."

Travis shook his head. The audacity of the man had no boundaries. The Macallan had been a gift from Livy. She rarely touched the stuff preferring wine—which was in great abundance in the basement wine cellar. Her grandmother had left Olivia with some equally valuable bottles of wine from around the world.

Sarah glanced over at Travis with a questioning look as she retrieved the bottle. He gave her an approving nod and permission to pour.

While the two were occupied at the liquor cabinet, Travis rifled through the papers. There were surveyor's maps, property descriptions, old photos, blueprints, and what looked like a will.

"I see you started without me," James said as he returned to the sofa that faced the bookcase. "Nice to have your own maid." He added under his breath. "Has a bit of an attitude."

"Housekeeper," Travis hissed through clenched teeth.

"Got it. Sorry. We used to have servants." He sat down and finished off the last of the brownie. "I fucked up good." Whitaker waved his arm over the documents. "The trust was my responsibility. Every detail handed down from my grandfather. Long Point could never leave the family, never be sold." He took a long sip of Scotch. "Very smooth." Travis thought he was going to lick the rim of the glass. "Actually, *I* didn't sell it—I lost it. The *lawyers* sold it to you."

Travis could almost feel sorry for the slob who'd betrayed his family. "Why couldn't Long Point be sold? There's nothing there but that huge old monster called a *cottage*! What's the big deal?" Travis asked. Nothing made any sense. Not the trust, not Whitaker, not his visit. Nothing. But he didn't have the patience to hear the story that began with the Native Americans.

Whitaker gulped down the rest of the amber liquid in his glass. "Now it's *your* responsibility. You can never alter the structure, never tear it down, and never build on the land." He held up his glass for a refill. "What's there is there."

Travis stood, took the glass, and walked over to the bar that had been built into the hidden cabinet in the paneled wall. "So what would happen if you had died without heirs?"

"Long Point would be donated to the State to be used as a bird sanctuary. The house would be leveled, covered with a mound of dirt, and planted with native vegetation."

"That's it?" Travis asked as he handed Whitaker the tumbler—the contents worth hundreds of dollars. "The house is as big as a hotel. Couldn't it be remodeled? I'm sure it would be an asset to the islanders. With all that land, it would make a wonderful resort."

Whitaker took a sip—the sound of pure ecstasy escaping his lips. "They're wrong. Money *can* buy everything." His focus went from the expensive Scotch to Travis. "Nope. Everything stays the same."

"Why? What's it like inside?" Curiosity had Travis's wheels turning in his head. What would be so important that couldn't be changed or maybe removed? Museum-quality art or furniture? Probably not with the place being closed up for decades. Maybe some famous architect designed the interior, like Frank Lloyd Wright. Nope, before his time. Maybe, some famous people stayed there and left gifts or stuff. Not likely. Whatever was inside those thick walls had been placed there decades before he was even born. The walls! A shiver jolted his thoughts in a different direction—the ghost stories. Maybe there were bodies sealed up in the walls.

"Don't know. Never been there." James swirled the liquid against the side of the tumbler. "My grandparents would spend time there. They loved the old place and spent hours telling me stories about its history. Grandfather liked telling tales of pirates, smugglers, and ghosts—Grandmother called it foolish.

"You have to be kidding! You've never been there?" Travis wondered how anyone could own that magical place and not go there, especially after hearing the stories from his grandparents. "The place is your responsibility. And you *never* went there?" Travis felt this guy had to be the biggest loser in the world.

"Don't think my father ever went back after going away to school. Yale. Lawyers handled it all. Paid for everything out of the trust." He took one last swallow and set the glass on the coffee table. "Never really thought about the place—until now." He reached into his briefcase, then handed Travis a single sheet of paper.

Travis read it. A deep furrow etched his brow. "All it states is that I received these documents regarding Long Point and understand the stipulations." Travis waved the sheet in front of Whitaker. "This is it? You came here, unannounced, to have me sign a paper containing one sentence? A sentence that says I received all documents pertaining to Long Point on Kelleys

Island in the state of Ohio?" Travis tossed the sheet on top of the pile. He'd had enough. His anger reflected in his voice. "What's going on here, Whitaker? Why all the drama? I purchased the land fair and square."

"It's Jimmy. I came here to tell you the story—the history—*and to warn you,*" Whitaker snickered. "But you don't want to hear it." His short, pudgy fingers pulled a gold pen from his jacket pocket and waved it in front of Travis.

Travis took the pen, leaned over, and scribbled his signature on the designated line. He then handed the paper back to Whitaker, who tossed it into his briefcase.

"Can't say anything about any drama, Tanner. But I have a feeling *your* drama is just beginning."

He closed his briefcase and stood. "You needn't show me out. I'm sure your *housekeeper* is lurking just beyond the door."

Travis stood and moved to Whitaker's side. "No trouble. I wouldn't want you to lose your way."

They'd only taken a few steps when Higgins entered the room. "Excuse me, Mr. Tanner, but I'd like to see Mr. Whitaker to his vehicle."

CHAPTER TWO

Marblehead, Ohio
Travis sat at the large old desk in the library studying the blue-prints of *Bent Tree Cottage*. It had been a week since he'd received the keys and a list of notes for the house from the attorneys and two weeks since his meeting with the pompous James Whitaker III. His trip to Marblehead had been put off until Olivia returned from an unexpected trip to California. Then he'd received a fran-tic call from Emily Elfin, who acted as their estate manager for the Captain's House—the name that the town's residents called "the old stone mansion" sitting in the shadow of the Marblehead lighthouse. The call was short and to the point. Emily's mind was often so full of unrelated thoughts that she didn't go into much detail—if he came before the first of June, there wouldn't be any staff. He decided to go anyway. Hell, he'd never had staff until he married Olivia and moved to *Fairfield*—the old plantation on the James River, now broken up into leased farmland, that she'd inherited from a grandmother she never knew. Yeah, he'd sur-vive just fine on his own, and enjoy the peace and quiet while it

lasted. He'd have a whole month before the twins arrive, along with Mom and her entourage.

The doorbell rang. Then rang again and again. It took Travis a minute to remember that he didn't have a housekeeper to answer the door. It also registered that it was the bell for the side door.

"Ouch!" In his haste to stand, he knocked his knee against the elaborate carvings on the corner of old desk that had once belonged to the Captain. He limped through the large entrance hall and down the main hall that would lead to the side hall and past the coatroom to the side door. He saw Emily peeking through the etched glass. Remembering how the door used to stick during damp weather, he pulled it open with such force that the huge oak door nearly knocked him off his feet.

"Oh my. Be careful. I had that door planed down years ago," Emily said as her tiny frame brushed past him.

"I guess it's been a while since I opened doors myself," Travis said as he closed the door and followed Emily to the coatroom.

"Why didn't you use your key?" Travis asked, more than a little irritated, since he wouldn't have been startled and jumped up from the desk before pushing his chair further back if she'd let herself in.

She gave him a look that said it was a stupid question. "Because you're in residence now. Just good manners. Wouldn't want you to think you were being burgled or something."

He'd known Emily Elfin since he was a child. She had to be somewhere in her late sixties by now. Her short, round frame; curly red hair; and cherub cheeks reminded him, as a child, of Mrs. Claus. Now, her hair was more gray than red, but she still had that bubbly personality with a laugh that was always ready to spring forth.

Travis helped her off with her coat and hung it on the closest hook. "I have a pot of coffee on, or I can make you tea if you prefer."

"Coffee would be fine." Emily followed Travis down the hall toward the kitchen.

"Why are you limping? Something happened here—I can feel it. Let me get some temporary help in for you. You shouldn't be alone." She followed him for a few more steps, then stopped. "You shouldn't have come early." Her whole body shuddered. "Bad idea. Not good."

"Emily, I'm fine." Travis motioned for her to continue down the hall. "I just bumped my knee on the corner of the desk. You never worried about me before. In fact, I was the guy everyone called if they needed help." Travis pulled out a kitchen chair for her and went over to the coffeepot on the counter. "Think I've gone soft being married to Olivia?"

"No. You're almost like a normal family when you come back for the summer months." Emily let out an amused chuckle. "Except that you fly in on your own jet, with your own pilot and driver. Oh, and let's not forget Higgins and his security team, and the boys' tutor—I forgot his name—really smart." Travis handed her a mug of steaming coffee. "And you're going to live here alone? Fend for yourself?" She took a sip. "You *do* make good coffee, though."

"Reginald. Reginald Warrington. What, again, happened to the Campbells?" Travis asked while pouring coffee for himself. "They were very efficient and I thought happy here. In fact, they were like grandparents to the boys."

"Reginald. Oh right. I remember now. The boys call him Reggie. The Campbells finally had enough of Marblehead's storms. Couldn't take our blistering winters that drop snow by the foot, and nor'easters that leave us without power for days. They retired to Tampa, or some island nearby. I have it written down somewhere. I'll have replacements by the first of June. That is, if the candidates pass Higgins's background checks. The man does test my patience."

"Florida? Funny. They never mentioned anything to us about wanting to retire, much less to Tampa and all that heat and humidity." Travis took a sip. He searched his memory for something that seemed important. Something about the Campbells. No . . . about Mrs. Campbell. Then in seconds, he had it. "I just remembered something. Mrs. Campbell couldn't take the summer heat. We beefed up the air-conditioning, so it reached the third floor. We even added air to the apartment over the garage."

"Guess they changed their minds," Emily said before taking another sip.

Why Tampa of all places? Travis wondered. It just didn't make any sense. "Oh, well. Don't worry about me—I'll be fine—really."

Emily set her mug on the table. "Fine? Word around town is that you now own Long Point. Are you *crazy*?" She looked deep into his eyes. "I thought you had more sense. Why would you even want that derelict hulk of stone?"

"It was a childhood dream." He was getting tired of using the excuse, but what else could he say? That it had been love at first sight? Love of a lonely old mansion nestled on a lonely stretch of land on an island, that had been unloved and abandoned by its family? No. The simplest explanation was always the best.

Emily shook her head back and forth, like a dog shaking its favorite toy. Her eyes focused on some imaginary place just beyond his head, as if she were trying to sort out the images rushing around in her mind. She often did that when she was having one of her psychic moments, and Travis didn't like the looks of this one.

Emily's tiny body shuddered with some vision. "A nightmare—it was all a horrible nightmare—evil is out there! Blood. Lots of blood!"

Travis gulped the rest of his coffee. Her outburst put him on edge. More than on edge, it nearly stopped his heart. "Emily, stop! If you're trying to scare me . . . stop."

"I'm sorry," she mumbled, as if in some kind of trance.

Travis needed to defuse the moment and put life back on track. His life, and he wasn't about to get all paranoid over one of Emily's weird moments. He needed to focus on the facts. "I know the stipulations of the property. I'm okay with them. The original Whitakers built the mansion as an elegant showpiece where they entertained the cream of society. It's only natural that they would want it preserved, without changes, for future generations." He set his mug down with enough force that Emily jumped.

She finished the last sip and made a point of gently setting her mug in front of her. She gave Travis a hard look and stood. "Don't go out there alone." Emily paused as if she wanted to say more on the subject but changed her mind. "I'll send over someone to cook and clean until I find replacements for the Campbells."

"Please don't. I'd rather be alone," Travis voiced, with determination that left no room for argument. "I do remember how to cook, and I'm not that messy."

Emily stood, then turned and headed back to the coatroom. Neither said a word until Travis helped her into her coat.

"Thank you for checking on me. I can walk over to the diner when I get hungry," Travis said and found the mental image amusing. "I can grab a meal and get exercise at the same time." He let out a short, forced laugh, hoping to lighten the mood as he walked her to the side door and opened it, while remembering that he needn't pull too hard.

Emily glanced over her shoulder as she got to the bottom of the porch steps. "Call me if you need anything. Give Olivia my love," she said as she slid onto the front seat. She didn't wait for Travis to respond as she pulled the heavy door closed and started the engine.

Travis suddenly felt a chill that had nothing to do with the dropping temperature. He watched her red SUV drive through the tall, ornate gates. She closed them behind her with her remote control. Emily hadn't been her usual bright-eyed, jovial self—she was upset—with him—or *for* him. He knew about her psychic episodes but had never actually experienced one. Years earlier, Olivia nearly lost her life after one of those.

That evening, Travis drove the short distance to the diner. He'd been smacked in the face by the strong, cold wind Canada was sending them as soon as his feet cleared the last step from the side porch. His Hummer that he kept in the garage seemed the better means of travel.

It took him longer to get through the slow-moving gates than it took to drive the half mile to the diner. He chose the first seat at the counter so he could catch up on the local news from his aunt Mavis, who owned the Marblehead Diner.

"Travis, welcome home. I heard you were back. You're looking good. I see that Sarah is making sure you eat well." Aunt Mavis set a menu on the counter. "Heard Phillips, Olivia's pilot, retired." She pulled a notepad out of her apron pocket. "I liked him. A real gentleman."

Travis shook his head in amazement. "I've only been back a few hours and already you know about Phillips?"

"Well, old Henry over at the airport called Chief Wilson to say Olivia's plane landed, with just you onboard. Had a new pilot—young guy. Lorenzo or some such foreign name. Supposed to be a hotshot air force guy—flew fighters and some newfangled helicopters. He refueled, grabbed lunch, then took off, heading back to Virginia." Aunt Mavis pulled a pencil from behind her right ear. "Your Cousin Nick was shootin' the breeze with the police chief and got the lowdown, then called me."

"Good to know the town grapevine is as healthy as ever." Travis chuckled. "So how many folks have *you* told?"

Mavis tapped the side of her head with the pencil. "Don't really remember." She pulled a pad from her pocket. "Special is pot roast. Got your favorite apple crumb pie."

"Sounds good. I'll have both." Travis heard the door open behind him but didn't turn to look. A couple of seconds later, he felt a slap on his back.

"Hey, Travis, my man. Heard you were back. Good luck with Long Point." The gray-haired man laughed all the way to the first unoccupied booth.

Travis grabbed a copy of the local newspaper from a stack to his right. His photo sat under the headline, *Marblehead's favorite son snares Long Point and Bent Tree Cottage out from under the Whitakers.*

Mavis returned with his dinner. "I see you've found the paper. I meant to put those under the counter before you arrived."

"Does the whole town know?" Stupid question. He knew the answer. Why did he even bother asking?

"I expect most of two counties by now." She placed his silverware to the side. "Good news is it's too early in the season for Kelleys to be crawling with tourists. So the island will be quiet for a month, and I'm sure the folks over there are happy it's you that owns it now. There hasn't been a Whitaker set foot on the land as far back as I can remember." She grabbed the coffeepot from the service counter behind her, then turned back to Travis. "It's a shame. A real shame to let the place go like that."

Travis ate while reading the article, which was for the most part accurate. There was also a good deal of speculation on what he planned to do with the house that couldn't be altered and known to be haunted. Haunted? Had anyone actually seen a ghost? He'd grown up listening to the tales of the spirits of Bent Tree Cottage. Hell, he'd probably embellished a few himself. The fact is, he didn't believe in ghosts. Period. Travis finished his meal without further interruption. After paying the bill, he tucked the newspaper under his arm and headed toward the door.

"Hey, Travis," someone yelled in the last booth. "Don't forget to call Ghostbusters!" Travis could still hear the laughter as he climbed into the Hummer.

CHAPTER THREE

The next morning, at the diner, Travis finished the stack of pancakes and sausage as Mavis approached with fresh coffee. He checked his watch—eight thirty. "I have time for another cup. I want to catch the nine o'clock ferry to Kelleys."

"Going to check out your newest acquisition of property on the island?" Mavis topped off his coffee. "Maybe you should take someone with you."

"Aunt Mavis, I'm a big boy. It's not like I'm unfamiliar with old houses. Look what the Captain's House was like when Olivia bought it. She literally grabbed it out from under the wrecking ball. The whole town thought she was crazy for buying that hulk of stone, and her Virginia estate, Fairfield, was built in 1733. I'll be fine."

"Okay, but Bent Tree Cottage may have issues that you're not familiar with—maybe no one is. So, be careful. I had Jason pack a cooler for you—several bottles of water, a tuna salad sandwich, cut-up veggies, and the last piece of apple pie." Travis raised his hand in protest. It was one more demonstration that Aunt Mavis didn't think he'd have the sense to feed himself. Kelleys Island had several excellent eateries, and Travis knew all the owners. "No arguing. It's already in the back of your Hummer."

"Thank you, Aunt Mavis, and tell Jason he's the best cook in the world." He dropped a twenty on the counter, figuring it would cover breakfast and the lunch, and headed for the door. "See you for dinner."

There were only two other vehicles on the ferry for the twenty-minute ride to Kelleys. Fortunately, no one recognized him as he drove through town to the far northeast corner of the island. He wasn't ready for yet another barrage of questions regarding the validity of his sanity—or the ghost jokes.

Two large, limestone posts capped with what remained of stone-carved fish cautioned him to go no further. Signs hung from the tubular steel gate across the road declared Private Property and No Trespassing. Travis got out of his vehicle. He'd forgotten how close the left stone post sat next to the rocky outcropping along the shoreline. As a boy, he'd tried to jump the deep crevasse to get around the gate, only to fall and skin his knees. The bike ride back to his aunt Sally's house was painful, not to mention the tongue-lashing he'd received for trying to enter the Whitaker property. It was a lesson well learned that the easiest way onto the forbidden land was by boat. The gate had been well placed at the narrowest part of Long Point that wasn't much wider than the road. And now he held the key. Travis checked out the padlock. It was a common brand and fairly new. He flipped through the handful of keys he'd been given and found one that matched the manufacturer of the lock. It turned easily, and the red steel gate swung open. He remembered as a child the tall ornate gates with fish, tails raised, centered in each panel. He noted that the rusted hinges were still embedded in the stone posts, but the beautiful gates were long gone. He checked the battered mailbox; the door was held on by a thread and nearly fell off when opened. Travis pulled out an armload of junk mail. The island post office must have been holding it for years. He tossed it on the passenger seat.

Travis got back in the Hummer and continued down the road. Bent Tree Cottage loomed dark and foreboding in the distance. He pulled under the porte-cochere and shut down the engine. Minutes went by as he sat there just looking at the tall, double oak doors with beveled glass panels. As a young boy, he'd never ventured this close, not because he believed all the ghoulish stories, but because he was more scared of old man McTavish who took care of the property and lived over the garage. He willed his heart to slow to a somewhat normal level—he sure didn't want to have a heart attack. Not here where no one would find him for days and then they'd add his name to the list of ghosts occupying the mansion.

It was his house now and he had every right to enter, the jumble of keys in his hand said so. He slid off the seat and marched to the front doors. The filigree on the doorplate matched the largest key in his hand. But as hard as he tried, he couldn't get the lock to turn. By the number of cobwebs and bug carcasses impaled in them, no one had used this door in years—maybe decades.

He got back in the Hummer and followed the driveway of crushed stone around to the far side of the house. The building was larger than it looked from the front side, which faced Lake Erie. He pulled up to a three-story, five-car garage connected to the house by a covered walkway, built of rough-hewn timbers and a slate roof. "Yeah, this is a cottage!" Travis mumbled with sarcasm as he stepped onto the drive and waded through knee-deep weeds, long dead since last fall, to get to the side door. The key turned easily, and the door opened into a back hallway with a door on either side. A set of narrow stairs led upward. The door to his right was ajar. Giving it a push, he found himself in the kitchen. He walked in with his mouth touching his chin—it was the size of a gymnasium. He gasped at the sheer size of it, then went into a coughing spasm as dust filled his lungs. White tile covered the walls, and the floor was tiled in black-and-white squares of linoleum. Light flooded in through three windows set high on one wall above the sinks. To his right was a three-sided alcove with long leaded glass windows facing the driveway and garage. Travis set the briefcase he'd brought along with the rolled-up blueprints on one of the two butcher-block tables that ran down the center of the room. Above, hanging from the ceiling on chains were racks containing every type of pot, pan, and skillet the most skilled cooks could ever need.

Moving to the far outside wall, Travis spotted an old wood-burning stove. It was as big as a steam engine, complete with several ovens and overhead compartments of varying sizes. Two large porcelain sinks rested between long stainless steel counters under the three high windows. The vintage, 1950ish electric stove and refrigerators appeared to be the most recent additions.

Travis opened the oven and refrigerator doors and peeked inside. The odors of forty-some years of disuse assaulted his nostrils. A box of yellowed, Cow Brand baking soda had long since stopped swallowing the moldy smell in the fridge. The interiors were clean but not spotless, not unlike the condition of his mother and Aunt Mavis's appliances. He leaned against the oven door and surveyed the massive room. Coming from a large family that sprawled over most of the counties hugging the shoreline of Lake Erie, he'd learned early on that it was the kitchen that painted a portrait of the family that lived within. This in no way resembled the warm, cozy, welcoming room filled with relatives of all ages that he was accustomed to. Even the large kitchen at Fairfield had Sarah's stamp all over it. No, this was a workspace—pure and simple—nothing welcoming about it. He couldn't imagine members of the Whitaker family sneaking down in the middle of the night for a cup of hot chocolate or leaning over the stainless steel counter eating ice cream out of the container. Just who were those early Whitakers?

A need to explore further and, hopefully, get to know the family that called this mansion home sent Travis through a swinging door. It led to a butler's pantry. There appeared to be a window set above a large sink at the far end of the room, but it had been boarded up, keeping the room in darkness. Travis pressed a button on the wall for the overhead light. Nothing happened. He went back into the kitchen and pressed the switch. Nothing. "Great, the power's been turned off," he mumbled. Travis congratulated himself on his genius decision, that morning, to add the small flashlight to his briefcase.

Reentering, his beam of light illuminated the far end of the room. A large stainless steel sink was molded into the counter. The two long walls on either side sported glass-fronted cabinets that contained stacks of china and rows of glassware. There were cabinets below filled with serving pieces and trays, and drawers for linens and cutlery. A silver tea set sat on a counter; its patina blackened with time. But it was the end wall next to the door that caught his breath. "A vault. Are you kidding me?" Travis said out loud to no one but himself and perhaps the ghost of a long-dead butler.

Seeing that his house contained a safe big enough to walk in, he couldn't wait another minute to see more. The question of why the need for a huge safe rattled around in his brain before he exited through the opposite swinging door. "Aha! All butler's pantries connect to the dining room—how else would a butler serve?" Travis stated as the door closed behind him. The fact that he'd been speaking to himself didn't feel weird, or was it that the house didn't feel so quiet—or spooky—while he talked?

Sunlight peeked between the folds in the drapes. He went to the far wall and yanked back the heavy material covering two sets of leaded glass windows, sending clouds of dust into the room. Travis went into a coughing and sneezing fit. Perhaps he should tread lightly with the drapes. The view out over Lake Erie was magnificent. A freighter could be seen off in the distance, probably on its way to Detroit. With the room now flooded with light, he turned around. He stood for a moment as his jaw dropped and began counting the many high-backed chairs. "The table seats twenty-four?" He caught himself talking out loud again. But who's to care? No one else there, at least not alive, if the local tales of ghosts could be believed. It was his house now, and he could talk if he wanted to. After settling those thoughts, Travis focused on the room. The bright morning sun streaming in failed to bring life to the two huge crystal chandeliers positioned over the table. Their rows and rows of delicate prisms hung lifeless, shrouded in grime and cobwebs. "Don't worry. I'll have you cleaned and sparkling once again—I promise." There he was, now making promises to the house.

Excited to see more, Travis headed over to the tall, arched pocket doors. They easily slid open without a sound. He advanced into the two-story entrance hall—his mouth fell open. "Holy cow!" he exclaimed. He moved further into the room. His eyes followed the massive staircase up to a landing dominated by the tall Gothic-arched window he'd seen when he pulled up to the porte-cochere. The hall, if one could call it that, wore large square panels of oak, many with the pointed arches and carvings typical in Gothic architecture. "I can't believe this place." His attention was drawn to a large painting. "It's the bent tree—just as I remember it. This is my dream—it all came true." Travis danced around the room with his arms outstretched like Julie Andrews in the *Sound of Music*. "It's mine. It's really mine. All mine—all mine—all—"

⟫⊰⊱⟪

29

"Hey, man."

"Noooo!" Travis screamed and turned around to face his cousin, Nick. "Don't *ever* sneak up on me again!" He rested his hand over his heart. "If I'd had a gun, you'd be dead!"

"I didn't sneak," Nick said while laughing so hard he nearly choked.

"Yes, you did," Travis shouted in anger while lowering his arms to his sides.

"No, I didn't," Nick got out between laughs.

"I didn't hear you!" Travis tried to sound convincing while feeling like an idiot. He'd felt comfortable talking to the house when he knew he was alone, but now he was plain stupid.

"Because you were talking to the house!" Nick said, still laughing.

"I wasn't talking to the house!" Travis shouted back.

"Then *who* were you talking to? The ghosts? Were you dancing with them too?"

"There are no ghosts. I was talking to *me*! And I wasn't dancing." Travis waved his arms in a helpless gesture. "It's so damn quiet in here. Not even a clock ticking. And with these damn thick, stone walls, you can't even hear the gulls!"

Nick took a few steps closer. "Did you really expect to hear a clock ticking? The place has been closed up for decades," he said jokingly. "I'm sorry. But I really wasn't all that quiet." He looked down at his feet. "My work boots made a lot of noise on the floors."

Travis took a deep breath. Maybe he *was* a bit jumpy. Maybe all the talk about the place being haunted was getting to him. But he wasn't going to let Nick, or anyone else, know he'd felt scared—even for a moment.

"How did you know I was here?" Travis asked as calmly as he could. His heart was still pounding.

"I just followed the sound of your voice down the back hall," Nick answered like his cousin had gone daffy.

"No. I mean, how did you know I was out here—on Long Point?"

"Oh. Aunt Mavis called me. Said you were back in town and taking the nine o'clock to Kelleys. Said you were spending the day." Nick paused for a breath. "I caught the ten o'clock."

"Aunt Mavis. Of course," Travis said through a chuckle. "Speaking of noise—look." Travis jumped up and down. "You could drive a train across these floors, and they wouldn't give, not even a creak."

"That's because there isn't a basement. Place is built on a slab," Nick said, as if his statement should impress his cousin with something he knew and Travis didn't.

"How do you know? You haven't seen the blueprints yet." Actually, Travis hadn't done much more than skim over them himself. But he wasn't about to share that bit of information with his cousin.

"I followed the trampled weeds to the back door. When I got inside the hallway, I opened the door on my left first. It was the mechanical room. Amazing! I saw a huge oil tank, boiler for the steam heat, water heater big enough for a hotel, and a bunch of gauges and shutoff valves for the water system." He stopped talking long enough to take a breath. "I can't wait to check it all out."

Travis couldn't appreciate his cousin's excitement over a bunch of outdated machines while he was still smoldering over being made fun of. "Why didn't you just come through the kitchen? I left the door open."

"No, you didn't. Both doors were closed."

A paralyzing chill raced through Travis. "I'm sure. When I went back for the penlight in my briefcase, it was still open." He tried to remember his steps. "At least I don't remember closing the door." He took a few seconds to shake off the eerie feeling and continued. "Speaking of Aunt Mavis, she had Jason make up a lunch for me. I'm willing to share my tuna salad sandwich and a piece of apple pie if you grab the cooler out of the Hummer."

"Sure. I'll also grab the two big flashlights from my truck. I think we're going to need them."

Travis followed Nick down the servants' hall to the back door. "Huh. The kitchen door *is* closed," Travis said, scratching his head. "I'll get the table ready."

"Told you," Nick said. "Must have been one of the ghosts."

"There are *no* ghosts," Travis said as he felt a quiver of a chill.

The best way to rid oneself of a chill was work. And the dusty kitchen was at the top of list of what needed attention if they were going to eat lunch inside. He found a bucket of rags under the sink and turned on the water. He got nothing but a groan from the faucet. The old porcelain enamel table, set in the alcove, held at least a year's worth of dust. He was wondering how to wash the surface when Nick came through the door and put the cooler on the butcher-block worktable.

Travis grabbed one of the bottles of water and went back to the table. "The water must be shut off. Maybe so the pipes don't freeze," he said while twisting off the cap and sprinkling water on the table.

Nick investigated the woodstove. "You won't have water until the power is turned back on. It runs the pump for the well," Nick answered as he closed one of the oven doors.

"I thought the whole island had city water," Travis said as he used a clean rag to dry the table. "I know the houses and build-ings in town have city water. And so do my three rentals."

Nick moved to the cooler and opened the lid. "Most of the island does, but they didn't run the lines out this far." He pulled out two sandwiches. "Ham and Swiss on rye, my favorite. Jason's the best."

Travis tossed the rag in the sink and ran to the cooler. "What? I thought I was getting tuna salad." He grabbed the second sandwich from Nick's outstretched hand. "Huh. Tuna salad." He peered inside and pulled out a container of potato salad. "Nice. Jason knows guys don't want veggies. And I see a second piece of pie."

After sitting down with their meals, Travis shook his head in a frustrated gesture. "So, Aunt Mavis decided minutes after I ordered my breakfast this morning that she was sending you to babysit me."

"Not babysit. I've wanted my whole life to get inside these walls!"

"Just because she's my aunt doesn't mean she can control me. I need to have a word or two with her!" Travis had to admit that it felt good knowing she cared enough to interfere. "Well, I have to say that I'm awfully glad to have a licensed contractor at my side," Travis said as he pushed the tub of potato salad toward his cousin. Although Nick was older than Travis by almost ten years, they had grown up sharing a bond almost like brothers. He couldn't remember a time when Nick wasn't fixing something that was broken and tossed aside. There were years when Travis followed his cousin up and down neighborhood streets on trash day looking for things he could fix or repurpose. It was only natural that while still in high school he'd gotten a part-time job working with a local construction company. Then at twenty-one, he'd started his own venture—small jobs at first, then his reputation and skills grew, and so did his company. Now he did everything from home remodels to commercial construction. He and his team brought back to life the old Captain's House completely after Olivia bought it out from under the wrecking ball and made it the showplace of Marblehead.

"How does Olivia feel about all this? When will she and the kids arrive?"

Travis groaned. "She wants nothing to do with it. She thinks I've lost my mind. This is all on me. I guess they'll arrive at the Captain's House, with her entourage, around the first of June as originally planned." It was funny how their home was still referred to as "the Captain's House," even by them. Olivia had purchased the old mansion just days before it was to be demolished and just days before he had met her for the first time in the office of Marina DelRay, where she kept her boat, the *Lovely Lady*. He and his buddy had been speculating about the fool who had just bought the Captain's House when Olivia entered the office and walked up to the counter inquiring about the available dockage. She introduced herself as "Ms. Fool."

"Too bad. This is a lot to take on alone." Nick took a bite of his sandwich. "Good thing you have me. I can't wait to dig into this monster. Once the power is turned on, I'll run some tests and find out what needs to be replaced. You certainly don't want faulty electrical to burn the place down."

Twenty minutes later, Travis cleared the table, while Nick took one of the large flashlights and opened a door on the long wall butting up against the servants' hall.

"It's a pantry." Nick stepped inside. "How long has it been since the Whitakers lived here?"

"Not sure. Decades anyway. Maybe forty years." Travis grabbed the other flashlight and joined his cousin. "Holy cow! What do you suppose is in all these mason jars?"

"Who knows? Some of the labels have fallen off." Nick picked one up and aimed it at the light. "Says peaches." He pulled each of the square canisters off the shelf and pried off the lids. "Can you believe these are still filled with flour, sugar, tea, and coffee?" He set the last container back on the shelf and walked into the kitchen. "Come on, let's start in the main hall and work our way to the back."

"Good with me. All these jars are giving me the creeps," Travis said, feeling more than uneasy about the jars of preserved fruit and whatever else the shelves may contain.

After following the servants' hall and crossing the main hall, they entered the room in the corner of the house facing the driveway and porte-cochere. "Looks like they may have used this as a family room. There's a really cool old TV and a record player." Nick checked out a stack of records on a table. "My grandparents had stuff like this."

After gently pulling back the drapes to avoid a dust cloud, Travis stopped at an end table next to a large, brown leather club chair. "This is so weird." He picked up a pair of wire-rimmed eyeglasses. He held them up to the light. "Bifocals. There's an old *Life Magazine* here."

"What's the date?" Nick asked while checking out the titles on the stack of record albums.

"Picture of a very young Queen Elizabeth on the cover. Wow. June second Princess Elizabeth was crowned. Looks like 1953, although a mouse dined on the corner." Travis flipped through the pages. "Hey, there's an article about President Eisenhower's first six months in office." He set the magazine back down on the table and put the glasses back exactly where he'd found them. He sat on the edge of the chair facing Nick. "It's so weird. Like the Whitakers just got up one day and left the house, never to return."

"How do you mean?" Nick asked while poking his head up inside the fireplace.

"The pantry is full, and here are a magazine and glasses waiting to be picked up and read." He pointed at the phonograph. "Records waiting to be played. I bet we find toothpaste on the bathroom sinks upstairs."

Travis got up and headed to the next door. He opened the drapes in what looked like a game room of sorts. There was a round table with four chairs in the center and several seating areas. Near the fireplace was a chess table and two chairs—the pieces in play. They peeked in the last door at the end of the main hall. Without entering, it appeared to be a huge reception room on the back corner facing the lake, complete with a grand piano and harp. "I could host an annual summer ball," joked Travis.

"How about Halloween? Complete with resident spooks!" Nick teased.

"And you can come as a mummy, with your mouth taped shut," Travis shot back with humor.

Nick took off in a near run back toward another door opposite the stairway. "I remember seeing this really cool door when I first came in that blended into the paneling. I wonder where that leads."

"Your boots really do make a lot of noise," Travis muttered as he followed his cousin. "Looks like we're in another hall that dissects the house to the east. There must be half a dozen doors that I can see from here. Looks like it veers off to the left ahead. I should have brought the blueprints with us."

Nick opened the first door on their left. "Whew! This could use an airing out." He shined the light in a circular motion. "Except there are no windows."

Travis turned on his flashlight and stepped into the room. "This is the first room that smells really damp and musty. Like something died in here. Looks like a library or a gentleman's study."

Nick cast the beacon back and forth across an ornate, Victorian-style billiard table. "Now, that's what I'm talking about! Would you look at this baby? Man, we could play on this all day."

"Yeah." Travis shined his light on the ceiling. "Look up, Nick." His cousin focused the beam of his flashlight up. "The whole ceiling is made of stained glass. And look what's in the middle—the bent tree. Can you imagine what this looks like illuminated?"

Nick did another sweep of the walls with his flashlight. "This huge open fireplace is the reason for the damp smell. You could roast a pig in that it's so big. I'll have to check to make sure there is a screen over the chimney. Birds or small animals could have fallen down and been trapped in here."

The thought of a dead carcass or two in the room sent another shudder through Travis. "We need to spend some time in here, but not without power," he said while ushering Nick back out into the hall, leaving the door open to help air out the room. Opposite the library was an office facing the driveway on the eastern side of the porte-cochere, then a small bedroom and sitting room with a bathroom between them.

"Looks like the housekeeper's rooms. Sarah has similar rooms at Fairfield. I wonder what she'd say about this place!" Travis wondered if she'd ever get the chance to step foot on the island. Probably not if Olivia had any say in the matter. "Let's find our way back to the kitchen and a bottle of water. My throat feels as dry as the Sahara."

Back in the kitchen, both Travis and Nick grabbed a bottle of water out of the cooler and plopped down on the kitchen chairs.

"I don't know about you, man, but I'm beat," Nick said after taking a long swallow.

"Yeah, me too. Plus I need a long shower." Travis unscrewed the cap. He glanced at the blueprint they'd left on the table at lunch. Why had the Whitakers built something so big to use only during the summer months? His thoughts went back to the vault. Why? And why was the library so big and grand and yet have no windows? "By the looks of this, we haven't even seen all of the first floor!" He gulped down half the bottle. "I'm not coming back until this place has electricity." Travis looked at his watch.

"Let's pack up and catch the four-thirty ferry. I need to stop at home and make a list of stuff I need, then head over to Mutach's Market before they close. Eating at the diner every day just feeds the town grapevine."

After making sure the back door was locked securely, Travis met Nick at the vehicles. "You'd better get your Hummer over to Mike's Service Garage for a look-see. She's left an oil spot on the driveway."

Travis bent down and checked under the engine. "Huh. Hasn't done that before. But it has been sitting in the garage since I last drove it back in December over the Christmas holiday."

A gull flew over, causing both men to look up. A large square tower loomed over the rooftops. "Can't wait to explore that. I wonder what's up there!" Nick said, in a tone that sounded more like a kid ready for a new adventure.

Travis felt another ominous chill. He didn't answer but wondered what secrets the crenelated structure could hold. It didn't matter, so he wasn't about to race up there to find out. That could wait for another day . . . a much later day. They both got in their vehicles, and Travis followed Nick down the drive. He closed and locked the gate. Looking in his rearview mirror, the only thing he could see was the square tower glowing in the afternoon sun against a background of dark storm clouds.

CHAPTER FOUR

The nor'easter hit with a vengeance in the middle of the night. Even the blackout shades couldn't keep the lightning from penetrating the bedroom, and the relentless sound of waves crashing on the rocky shoreline filled the house. Over time, one got used to the roar and the rhythmic pounding of the water that followed winds from the north and east. But this was extreme, and finally, the rolling thunder jolted Travis from his bed. Growing up on the Marblehead peninsula, one develops a healthy appreciation for Mother Nature and the havoc her storms can cause. He tossed the covers back and reached for the sweats he'd left at the foot of the bed. After a quick stop in the bathroom, he padded down the back stairs to the kitchen. He filled the Mr. Coffee and flipped the switch, then entered the round morning room just off the kitchen to watch the light show being played out on Lake Erie. Travis felt safe, as if the old house wrapped her strong arms of stone around him. Olivia had saved the old Captain's House, built in 1836, which nestled majestically in the shadow of the Marblehead lighthouse. Ever since then the house seemed to take pleasure in protecting its family from the outside world.

The aroma of fresh brewed coffee drew Travis back to the kitchen. For the next couple of hours, he sat, bent over the dining room table, reviewing the ledgers he'd received from the Whitakers' attorneys. He needed a clear understanding of the operation of Bent Tree Cottage and how it was used and for how long. He needed its history. He began making notes on the pad of paper he'd taken from the library. But the list grew and only created more questions. The most puzzling was why a house of monstrous proportions was built on Long Point in the first place? No matter how he looked at it, it just didn't make any sense. James Whitaker the first and his wife Lucretia had four children, three daughters and a son. Not a large family back in those days, so why did they need ten bedrooms? Perhaps they entertained on a grand scale with multiple people staying for extended periods of time. What did those houseguests do for a month or more? The island was pretty isolated back then, besides the stone quarrying there were the vineyards. The kitchen was certainly set up to feed the guests of a small hotel. Not the meals of a family of six and staff. And according to the blueprints, the staff had their own, two-story wing—the section of the house that he and Nick hadn't explored yet. And then there was the second floor and attic over the garage for the outdoor staff that maintained the grounds and the chauffeur. Did they really need to house six cars? Too many questions and he wasn't finding the answers in the ledgers.

Travis glanced at the clock on the mantel. The hands were in the five and ten positions, and his stomach cried out for breakfast.

The winds still howled; the rain still pelted the windows with the furry of machine-gun fire. Travis placed the sixth piece of bacon on the griddle. Thanks to Emily he had bacon, and eggs, and milk, and butter, and OJ. In fact, when he'd returned the evening before to make a shopping list before going to Mutach's, he found the fridge nearly full, including a six-pack of his favorite beer—but that wasn't enough beer. After a quick scan of the pantry, he had grabbed his keys and headed to the market.

He'd taken the closest cart as he entered the store. Of course, he chose the one with the wobbly front wheel that went whomp-whomp on the wooden floor, and made a beeline for the peanut butter aisle, and then he tossed in a couple of bags of chips and two jars of salsa. Lunchmeat, hot dogs, buns, and a twelve-pack of Coors topped off his cart. He snatched a bag of Oreos off a rack as he waited in line.

"Good evening, Travis. I heard you were back," the cashier greeted him with a smile. Mary Simpson had worked at Mutach's, off and on, since they'd graduated from Danbury High School. She'd been his date for the senior prom. "Been out to Long Point yet?"

"Nick and I went out for a while earlier. We both wanted to get back before this storm hits." He reached for his wallet, hoping to keep the conversation on his order and not on a haunted house.

"Your order comes to thirty even." Mary watched Travis pat his back pockets.

He shrugged sheepishly. "I must have left my wallet in the Hummer."

"No problem," Mary casually said as she entered the purchase in a ledger she pulled out from under the counter. "I'll just add this to your wife's account. Emily Elfin was in earlier. Said you'd be baching it awhile, so she was stocking up on grocery items you'd need. I expect she'll find a replacement housekeeper soon. I can't imagine the Campbells leaving like they did. They'd become family and loved the twins like their own."

"Yeah," Travis mumbled as he picked up the two grocery bags with his left arm and held the carton of beer with his right hand. Seemed like everyone in town had a tight grip on the grapevine.

"Let me know if you need me to order a ghost zapper," she said through a full-blown laugh.

Juggling the bags, Travis pushed open the door with his hip. "Thanks, Mary. Nice to know you have my back."

Travis found himself smiling on the short drive back to the house. He didn't really mind the teasing he was taking over the Long Point ghosts. He'd been the source of their humor since he was a kid. Like the time he took his dad's skiff over to Put-in-Bay to explore the Crystal Cave on the grounds of Heineman Winery with his buddy Harold. The boys had misjudged the weather that afternoon and exited the cave with fog rolling in. Travis was adamant that he could easily find his way back to Marblehead despite the fog getting thicker by the minute. He patted himself on the back when he saw the dock emerging from the wall of white and easily pulled alongside. After tying off the line, he climbed up onto the dock and walked the short distance to shore to determine just where he was on the peninsula. To his horror and embarrassment, he'd misjudged his direction in the fog and found himself on Peele Island. In Canada. For years he heard: "Hey, Travis, don't forget your compass." Or "Going out for a sail? Hope you got your compass onboard." He must have gotten a dozen of the little instruments for Christmas that year. But it was all in fun. They cared enough to tease him, and every one of them was ready to help if need be.

⊰⊱

Thankfully, the buzzer for the front gate disrupted any more thoughts of his embarrassing visit. Mutach's Market had been providing for the locals since 1907 and still remained the best place to obtain gossip. He glanced up. Nick's rain-soaked face appeared on the small monitor mounted on the wall. "Come on in, cuz. The side doors unlocked." Travis pressed the button that would open the tall gates, then pressed another button that unlocked the door facing the driveway. It only took Nick little more than a minute to enter the house, but nearly five before he left the coatroom and appeared in the kitchen. He stood, towel-drying his hair, wearing only a green flannel shirt, wool socks, and navy boxer shorts.

Travis raised one eyebrow. "Playing in the rain?" he asked with a chuckle.

"Danny Wilson called around one." He nodded toward the window. "This one's bad. She's been gusting around seventy, pushing the lake up and over the roads in places. Danny ordered his officers to evacuate Bay Point and all the houses along the shoreline up to the lighthouse. The fire department is placing sandbags around town. I checked out what I could see of your yard as I pulled up. Sitting up this high, looks like only the lower part is under water. Power is out all over. Saw your lights on. I could use a break." He inhaled deeply. "Bacon."

"Yeah. I couldn't sleep. I've been up for hours reviewing those old ledgers. How about you make a fresh pot of coffee while I put the rest of the bacon on?"

Nick immediately went to the cupboard where the coffee was stored. Since he and his crew had done all the renovations on the house, he knew the ins and outs as well as Travis and Olivia, who now called it their summer home. After filling the water reservoir and enough coffee to make one's hair stand on end, Nick asked sheepishly, "Mind if I throw my jeans in the dryer? They're dripping all over the floor in the coatroom."

"Sure. But why aren't you wearing full rain gear? I have a spare pair of rubber pants you can borrow, but they'd be a bit short for you."

"Thanks, but I'll stop at home when I leave here. With the urgency in Danny's voice when he called, I just grabbed my slicker, jumped into my boots, and took off."

"Understand. While you're doing that, do you want eggs or pancakes? This griddle is big enough for either or both," Travis asked while waving the tongs over the still-unused portion.

"You still making those giant, fluffy flapjacks?"

"Yep."

"Real maple syrup—not that fake crap?"

"My famous pancakes it is. Now, go grab those extra, extra-large pants before they leave a pool in my coatroom."

Although he was older, Nick Tanner was more like a brother than a cousin. Growing up, Nick's sheer height and weight had given Travis a feeling of security whether dealing with the town bully or getting into scrapes where they shouldn't be getting. Nick was strong, like the mammoth stone quarry that gouged out the center of the Marblehead peninsula, or the smaller quarry on Kelleys—now filled with water. The perfect swimming hole. On seeing him for the first time, Olivia had described the man as Paul Bunyan, the fictitious giant lumberjack.

Nick emerged from the basement as Travis set the two plates on the table along with orange juice and large mugs of fresh coffee. Nick did a couple of squats before sitting down at the table. "Damn dryers always shrink jeans till you can't hardly get 'em zipped, let alone sit." He nodded toward the stove. "What happened to the old relic—Big Bertha? I thought you guys loved that thing."

"It came down to an ultimatum with Mrs. Campbell." Travis forked into his stack of pancakes. "Last Christmas she got a pot of potatoes ready to put on. I guess she turned on the gas, never did like those levers, and took too long striking the match. The flames singed her hair and nearly blew off her eyebrows. Spent Christmas in the hospital." Travis finished a bite. "She threatened, either the stove goes or she goes." He lifted his chin in the stove's direction. "Olivia replaced it with this stainless steel baby. I can grill a steak or make a grilled cheese sandwich in the center section. Has six burners, two ovens, and a warming drawer."

"So how come you're doing the cooking? Where *is* Mrs. Campbell?"

"You must be the only person in town that doesn't know. Turned in their resignation and retired to Florida last month." Travis took the last sip of orange juice. "Emily begged me not to come early. She wanted me to stay at Fairfield until June as planned. Of course, I couldn't. I needed to visit Long Point and explore Bent Tree Cottage." Travis grabbed the last piece of bacon. "Emily doesn't expect to have a replacement for another month."

"But why did they retire? They weren't *that* old. Heck, they were like family. The twins are going to be devastated. They loved the Campbells—heck, we all did."

"Don't know for sure. Emily said they were sick of our weather and moved to Tampa. Just wait till they spend the months of July and August in the Florida heat and humidity. Hope they have good air-conditioning!"

"What's the problem getting someone else? I would think Emily's buried with applicants who would want to work for someone as rich as Olivia."

"Not when they hear about Higgins and all his rules. Then there's the four months during the summer when it's the house-keeper's job to orchestrate life with Olivia and her entourage—claimed it was like running a hotel."

"Bummer." Nick finished off his first stack and pulled the platter in the center of the table closer. "So what happened to Big Bertha?"

"She's in the garage. Livy and I couldn't bear the thought of her ending up in the county dump."

Nick slathered the short stack of pancakes left on the platter with butter, then drowned them in syrup. The lights chose that moment to go out. Within seconds, the generator's motor kicked in, and the kitchen was once more flooded with light.

"Aren't you glad I insisted on adding that piece of machinery to the reno budget? I suggest you put one at the top of Bent Tree Cottage's list of improvements." He sliced through a good-sized wedge. "Speaking of lights, I noticed that yours have been on for hours. Storm kept you up?"

Travis pushed his plate aside. "Yes and no. I couldn't get our visit to the cottage out of my mind. There were so many things that don't make sense. Like why the kitchen pantry was filled with all the staples a cook would need, plus all those jars of preserves. And the reading glasses left next to the chair. It was as if the family had gone to the mainland for the day and never returned—but intended to. Why didn't they come back?" Travis watched Nick continue shoveling forkfuls of gooey dough into his mouth, like he had a deadline to meet. "I realize that everyone I know who depend on readers have a pair in every room, but those were bifocals. Why were they left behind? Anyway, I thought maybe if I started with the ledgers and finances, it would give me an idea why things happened as they did."

Nick pushed the last piece of pancake across the platter to soak up the little puddle of syrup. "So, what did you find out?"

"Nothing yet. But I'm starting at the beginning. Looks like a General Buchanan owned Long Point before the Whitakers. There's also a separate ledger for a place called The Vines and the name Seymour."

"Aunt Millie's place," Nick said as he washed down the last bite.

"Aunt Millie's a Seymour?"

"No. Her house is called The Vines. The Seymour family from upstate New York bought the land back in the 1850s. It ran from the Long Point boundary, along the shoreline, to where the airfield is now. They produced grapes for the winery."

"How do you know this?" Travis asked, amazed that his cousin would know so much about Kelleys Island history.

"Couple of years back, I rebuilt Aunt Millie's wraparound porch. I spent months listening to the island's tall tales of Indian lore, trappers from Canada, treasure, Civil War loot, and . . . *murder*. You should go out there and talk to her."

With breakfast finished, Travis took Nick into the dining room where he had blueprints and ledgers spread across the table. "I know it looks like a mess, but it's an organized mess. Like I said, I'm working on the accounts first. The floor plans will have to wait. It's all a bit overwhelming at the moment."

"Look. How about I study the prints while you handle the finances? Then we'll see if anything begins to add up," Nick said while scratching his beard. Any further ideas ended with his pager going off. He checked the number appearing on the screen on the upper edge of the small black box clipped to his belt. "It's the chief. Danny needs me at the police station. I'll stop by later. Maybe show me how you can grill steaks indoors. I'll even bring the steaks—big ones—none of those sissy little things folks seem to like nowadays!"

Travis followed his cousin to the coatroom. By the time Nick climbed back into his high rubber boots and slicker, the sun was just beginning to peek over the horizon through the continuing storm clouds.

Standing side by side on the porch, Nick surveyed the backyard. "Water's creeping up higher. Another twenty feet or so and your garage will be getting its feet wet. House isn't in any danger, though. Yard's gonna to be trashed when this mess recedes."

"I wonder how the cottage is fairing. Long Point could be under water. What happened out there hasn't interested me since I was a kid—just the loneliest part of the island."

"What little I saw on our visit, there wasn't any noticeable water damage in the house, but then I wasn't looking for that specifically. Next time we're out there, I'll take a look at the foundation." Nick studied the sky to the east. "Unfortunately, the ferry won't be leaving the dock until Mother Nature turns off the wind machine. Those waves are running eight to ten feet." His pager went off again. "Gotta go," Nick shouted as he flipped up the hood of his slicker and raced down the steps through the pelting rain to his truck.

CHAPTER FIVE

"What do you mean 'I don't have the authority to connect power to the house'? I own the property. I own several rental cottages on the island, and I've never had a problem."

His ego took a direct hit. Travis had never had a problem getting things done, at least not anywhere near Marblehead, Port Clinton, or Sandusky, Ohio. And his successful yacht sales companies in Toledo and Cleveland provided him with a more-than-comfortable income, not to mention his sizable real estate portfolio. His name alone made things happen in four counties along the Lake Erie shoreline.

"I see that, Mr. Tanner, and I also see that you always pay your accounts on time. But this particular property is in the name of the Whitaker Family Trust. They turned off the power two weeks ago but didn't close the account."

"So what needs to happen for me to turn the lights on? I need electricity," Travis said in his best authoritative voice.

"I understand, Mr. Tanner. You'll need to have someone from the law firm of Graven, Morgan, Huntley, and Devonshire fax us a signed copy of form RACdash79. I suggest they fax you one, as well. Then call me. My name is Sandra Fleming, and I'll get someone out to read the meter. It won't take long; we have someone on the island. Then I'll flip the switch, so to speak."

Travis took a deep breath and fought to remain calm. "So how long does this take? I want to get started. It's a big project." He was losing the battle on calm.

"I'm checking the line now to make sure it's clear for reactivation." She paused long enough for Travis to get a sick feeling in the pit of his stomach. "Oh my. I believe we have a problem." Sandra Fleming sounded as if she were reading something. "Mr. Tanner, it looks like there are multiple lines down on Kelleys Island. I'll have to schedule a separate service truck for your property in case there is storm damage in that area."

"Yeah! I know! When the ferry is running again," he said as he slammed the phone down. He'd totally lost his calm.

Travis forcefully placed both palms against the top of the desk and pushed himself to a standing position. Leaning over, he focused on the legal pad containing his notes for getting the utilities connected. He inhaled deeply, filling his lungs, then exhaled with enough force to ruffle the edges of paper. "Damn storm," he growled, before turning toward the door and storming down the hall to the kitchen. He pulled a Coors from the fridge. After popping the cap, he wandered over to the windows overlooking the lake. Waves crashed against the shoreline, while rain pelted the windows with a force that matched his temper. Breathing became somewhat normal again with the last swallow. He tossed the bottle in the trash can, then headed back to his desk in the library.

The next call was to Ma Bell. Travis was pretty sure that ordering a new phone install wouldn't take but a few minutes since it never had before. He wanted to get back to the mountain of papers spread across the dining room table. There were badly needed answers there—he just needed to dig deeper to find them.

"Good afternoon. My name is Patricia. How may I help you?"

"Hello. This is Travis Tanner, and I would like to schedule phone service for a property I recently purchased on Kelleys Island."

"Oh. Hi, Travis, it's me, Patty Jones. Well, it's Patty Tanner-Jones since I married Everett Jones two years ago. Everett's family live in Oak Harbor, but we live here in Sandusky now. Heard you bought Bent Tree Cottage. You sure are going to need a landline. Cell phone service out there on Long Point is the pits."

Travis didn't have time for small talk but searched his brain anyway for Cousin Patty among the many family members that he rarely came in contact with. "Oh. Yeah. Haven't seen you in years . . . maybe since Livy and I got married back in '85. I don't remember you coming to any of our Christmas parties at the Captain's House. But, then again, I wouldn't remember half of the family and friends who attend our annual open house . . . the number is usually in the hundreds." He hoped he'd remembered the right Patty, then continued. "For now, I sure hope you can help me with the phones—getting power to Long Point in my name is going to take an act of God." Sarcasm began oozing from his words.

"Yeah, it's easy to get lost in the crowd, and our family certainly knows how to party. The string quartet playing on the staircase landing is an elegant touch. Your sons are always dressed like proper little gentlemen—so cute." Her voice finally changed from casual to all business. "Give me a minute to pull up that address. I didn't think the Whitakers could ever sell that monster. Tied up in some kind of trust." Patty went silent for so long that Travis was sure another problem was on the way. "Well, now, do you want all new equipment, or can you use the phones that are there?"

"Are you kidding? The only ones I saw were older than me. I know I need a wall phone in the kitchen and a multiline desk phone in the office. I have no idea about the rest. Just put a selection on the truck, and the installer can figure it out."

Travis could hear paper shuffling in the background and Patty muttering to herself. This was taking more than a minute.

"Travis, we have a problem," Patty said in a puzzled voice. "Apparently, the law firm of—"

"Graven, Morgan, Huntley, and Devonshire. I know. Don't tell me they never closed out the account. The trust still has control. I can't get phone service."

"Yeah. How did you know? Sorry, Travis, you need to have them finish the transaction. They can do it by faxing us a letter. Shouldn't be a problem." Patty paused before continuing. "Oh no! I just got a message that there are power and phone lines down on Kelleys. We can't initiate any work orders until the ferry is running again and our large service trucks can get to the island. Travis, I hate to tell you this, but depending on the damage and the ferry running again, your job could take a week or more."

"Great!" his calm just exploded. "What else is gonna happen?" Travis waited for his blood pressure to come down a notch before continuing. "Patty, please keep an eye out for the letter from the lawyer, and schedule the work order as soon as you can. It could be another day or two before this storm slows down. Call me if you hear anything."

"Will do, Travis. See you at Christmas . . . and take care."

By late afternoon, Travis was frustrated, angry, and ready to punch something—anything. And the constant thunder of crashing waves was wearing on his nerves. He could understand the law firm forgetting to close the account of just one utility, but not all three. He hadn't gotten anywhere with the propane service either. If it hadn't been for old invoices from a propane company in Sandusky, he wouldn't have thought about the possibility that there wasn't a gas line to the point. He figured, like everything else, he'd probably need a new and larger tank. It should be easy enough to order, providing someone at Graven, Morgan, Huntley, and Devonshire didn't drag their feet on producing the letters and closing the accounts. But that was a possibility that was strongly thrashing around in his gut. What reason could they have for keeping him from working on or even exploring the inside of Bent Tree Cottage? Based on what he'd already seen, there hadn't been anyone using the place in forty years or more. He'd been given the keys so he wasn't locked out. But why prevent him from having utilities? Propane wouldn't be a problem until he needed gas. Why the phone and electricity? So he couldn't have sufficient light? Or use power tools? Or maybe— call for help? The hairs on the back of his neck bristled. This was one more set of circumstances to add to the list of mysteries at Bent Tree Cottage.

Travis settled back in the big leather desk chair. Maybe it was just a coincidence and a clerk in the attorney's office forgot to close out the accounts. Perhaps he was overreacting. A result of storm nerves being stretched to the breaking point. It happens after days of crashing waves that seemed to never end, thunder that rattles windows and lightning that slashes through rooms. But then, he remembered Higgins's rule: "There is no such thing as coincidence."

CHAPTER SIX

Mother Nature raged on for two more days before she turned off the wind machine and dropped the pelting rain to a drizzle. Travis and Nick arrived at the ferry dock hoping to get the first boat to Kelleys, only to watch as one after another of the telephone and power repair trucks waited in line and then were waved aboard. Fortunately, Nick was able to maneuver his truck alongside two Toledo Edison vehicles on the next trip.

The twenty-minute ride to the island was relatively comfortable with the boat easily cutting through the choppy waters left over from the storm. By the time the truck's tires hit firm ground, Travis and Nick had the rest of the day planned out. First on the list was to take care of any downed trees or limbs along the road from the gate to the house. Second on the list was to do a thorough walk around the house and garage to check for any damage from trees or water and check for any broken windows from flying debris. Third was to check the top floors of the house for any sign of leaks from the massive roof. Nick had come through with all the tools and machines they'd need for unmasking at least some of Bent Tree Cottage's secrets and hopefully not much storm damage. But all thoughts of the day ended with the blaring sounds of chain saws, hammering, and the drone of many generators and loud voices.

"That doesn't sound good," Nick said, in a tone indicating that their day just went to hell. He dodged tree limbs on their short drive into town, then stopped suddenly as he turned onto Division Street. The island's only fire truck and police car blocked the road with lights flashing. Beyond was a power company's truck with its bucket high in the air and the worker in reflective gear reaching toward the lines.

Travis scooted forward on the seat to get a better look. "Holy crap!"

Telephone poles had fallen like a row of dominoes and tree limbs blocked the street.

Nick whistled. "Looks like that first pole is fried." He lowered his window and poked his head out to get a better look at the ground in front of the tires. He inched the truck forward as Bobby Monroe, the island's police chief, walked toward them. Bobby was one of Travis's cousins on his mother's side of the family, and one of the few residents left who were actually born and raised on the island.

"Hey . . . Nick . . . Travis." Bobby waved his arm toward the commotion as the two big Toledo Edison bucket trucks that had shared the ferry ride over pulled up. "You're sure a welcome sight," Bobby shouted to the first truck's driver. "Pull on around the fire truck. The fire chief will direct you from there."

Bobby stepped forward, leaning his arms on the lowered window of Nick's truck. "Old Mother Nature threw us a whopper." He nodded toward the downed poles. "Lightning hit the first pole just as a mega gust of wind blew through. The rest of them came down like dominoes. Good news is—this is the worst of the real damage. The rest is your usual storm stuff."

Travis leaned over to Nick's side. "Sounds like every generator on the island is running."

"Yeah, both power and phone lines are down. I headed out early this morning and checked the nonresident properties before the heavy equipment started coming in." Bobby turned to watch that the Toledo Edison trucks made it through, then turned his attention back to Nick and Travis. "The east side of the island took a direct hit, and the majority of the damage is over there. I checked your places, Travis. Quarry Side Cottage is fine, just some yard cleanup, but it looks like Lakeside and Lakeview might have some water damage inside, and the yard is trashed. The whole East Point area is a mess." He glanced back toward the activity. "Good news is no one was badly hurt, at least not that I've heard of so far."

"We'll stop by on our way to Long Point and check out the cottages," Travis said as positively as he could muster. It was obvious from what they'd observed since landing on firm ground that the island was a mess, and Long Point had its long finger pointed right into the heart of the storm. He wanted to get to the house as quickly as possible. The entire ferry trip over had been spent planning for the day at Long Point, not sweeping out water from his rentals. How many more setbacks were going to prevent him from getting to the secrets of Bent Tree Cottage? Travis smacked the dashboard with the palm of his right hand.

Both Nick and Bobby sent questioning glances at Travis, but neither voiced a word. They didn't need to.

Bobby glanced at the items in the bed of the truck. "Looks like you're well prepared for what you'll find. Those two chain saws will come in handy." His attention was then drawn back to the scene with Chief Humphrey waving for him to return. "I gotta go. I suggest leaving Quarry Side for another today. You only have yard cleanup there. Go back to Addison, and then Woodford Road is pretty clear until you get east of Monaghan.

Everything from there on is covered in mud, sand, and everything that Erie tossed up. Just take it slow and you'll be fine. We probably won't get to the roads on the east side of the island until tomorrow at the earliest."

"Great. Just great," Travis said as he straightened and moved back into his seat. "What else is going to happen?"

Nick threw the truck in reverse and began to back up when Bobby shouted for him to stop.

"Hey, one more thing. While I was out checking properties, I swung by Long Point. I figured the place would have taken a direct hit, and there may have been damage to the house or garage. Strange thing is the key to the gate was missing off my key ring." He gave the door a slap. "That's never happened before. Don't know what you'll find out there," Bobby said, then walked away.

After leaving the disaster in town and traveling east along Woodford and stopping to help several homeowners clear fallen trees or large branches, they checked on Travis's two properties at East Point. Bobby had been almost right about the damage. Fortunately, only the enclosed porches of his two lakeside cottages still had some standing water. Unfortunately, they also found a few shingles in the yard. After a couple of hours, Travis and Nick had the wicker and rattan furniture moved into the front rooms of the houses and mopped up the porch floors. They left windows open to dry out and made mental notes to stop by later and lock up.

Nick climbed into the truck, while Travis was securing his seatbelt. "That wasn't too bad considering what could have happened with all these huge old trees so close to the cottages. I'll grab a pack of shingles and a tall ladder and come over in a few days and get the roof repaired. While I'm at it, I'll bring a couple of large heaters to keep the wood floors from further damage."

"I have a couple of smaller ones in my garage that I can bring out until you can pull the big heaters from your storage building in Port Clinton," Travis added.

"Now, on to Long Point," Nick said as he pulled out of the driveway.

Due to all the debris in the road, the drive took much longer than usual. Nick slowed as he rounded the bend on Monaghan Road. "Camp Gertrude doesn't look too bad. Some standing water in the open areas, but the cabins look dry. These flat-stone, dry-stacked walls along the road help hold back the rising waters during storms."

Travis lowered his window to get a better look. "The camp administrators and counselors should be arriving soon to get the place ready for the kids. Except for a couple of fallen trees and a lot of limbs on the ground, cleanup shouldn't be too bad. It should be ready by the first of June when the camp officially opens for the season."

Nick laughed while nodding his head. "I'll never forget the year I decided to see for myself what the kids did all summer at a church camp. Did they play games or just pray all day?" He shook his head. "One Sunday, I borrowed Uncle Clem's twelve-foot, aluminum boat and headed across North Bay. The wind was out of the south, so the lake was calm as glass, and I aimed the boat for the far side of Camp Gertrude. Just as I approached land, a rogue wave lifted the boat and tossed it up and onto the rocks. The boat began taking on water from a hole in the bottom. One of the counselors came running over and helped me to shore and secured the boat. I used the office phone to call Uncle Clem. That wasn't pretty. I got a tongue-lashing from every adult at the farm that day, and Uncle Clem never again let me borrow one of his boats. Dad ended up paying for the boat repairs and replaced the prop on Uncle Clem's brand-new Evinrude. That was the last time I ventured onto Camp Gertrude's property and tempted the wrath of Jesus."

"Yeah. I was old enough to understand that you got in a lot of trouble because God wrecked Uncle Clem's boat. Sure kept me away from that place."

It was now early afternoon when they reached the gate at Long Point. Travis got out and, after unlocking and pushing the large red gate to the side, climbed back into the truck. "You know, it's really weird about the missing gate key. All of us nonresident property owners depend on Bobby to let us know if there's a problem. The chief of police has always had keys—it's sorta part of the job. I wonder when the last time was that he used the key."

"Huh." Nick glanced around; his window was still down. "Doesn't look too bad out here." He paused a beat. "Wonder where the keys are kept when not needed. Maybe in a locked drawer? Or maybe just hanging on a hook? Strange that it was the only missing key."

They were both silent, sorting out their own thoughts, for the rest of the drive along the gravel road to the rear door of the mansion.

"I see the generator was delivered before the storm hit," Nick said with the enthusiasm of a kid opening his first Christmas present.

Travis eyed the huge wooden crate. "Must have taken a fork-lift to place it next to the back wall of the house."

Nick chuckled. "Yeah, wait till I give you the bill for the machine *and* the delivery charges to get it here!" he said as he slammed the door of the truck shut and walked toward the box. "Actually, you're leasing it until I can determine what size you'll need to run this place. The new one will be placed on a concrete pad behind the garage." He slapped Travis on the shoulder. "At least you won't be paying union wages for me to install it."

Travis stared with a puzzled look. "Nick?" he slowly drew his cousin's name out. "How did it get here?"

"Huh?" Nick said as he pulled a clear plastic envelope containing the packing slip off the crate. "Oh, on the builder's supply company's flatbed truck. It carries a small lift truck on the back end. Why?"

"How did it get through the gate?" Travis asked, still puzzled.

"Oh, I left instructions for the driver to stop by the police station, and the chief or someone would come out and unlock the gate. Then let them in and wait until they left to lock up."

Travis remained silent, causing Nick to put the packing papers into his jacket pocket while focusing his attention on his cousin. "Oh, shit. The gate key was on the ring—what—three or four days ago? But not today."

Travis felt a freezing chill race through his body. Something was very wrong. He slowly turned away from his cousin and the massive wooden crate to collect his thoughts. That's when he caught movement out of the corner of his eye. He glanced toward the garage. It was the size of one of those mini-mansions popping up in affluent suburbs across the country. His gaze stopped at the service pole off the far corner.

"Nick—?" Travis drew the name out long and questioning.

The sudden change in his cousin's voice caused Nick to move forward. "What?"

Travis nodded toward the pole. Several feet of wires hung ominously, swaying in the wind.

"What the hell?" Both men ran to the base of the pole. "Looks like you've got more than storm damage." Nick paused a beat. "Those wires were cut."

CHAPTER SEVEN

Mutach's Market was closed by the time they drove by after leaving the ferry dock. Back at home, Travis raided the pantry and decided on spaghetti. The fridge provided everything for a salad, and the freezer provided garlic bread and mini meatballs, left over from the family visit last Christmas.

Conversation had been limited during the meal, with both men deep in their own thoughts. Nick's original enthusiasm about his cousin buying the island's most mysterious property was now filled with more questions and very few answers. Bringing the monstrous structure up to code was going to take every resource he could find—then there would be Higgins and his own code. Nick had worked closely with Olivia's head of security when he was finishing the renovations on the Captain's House. Then a few years later, Higgins asked him to handle a project in Virginia to add a bedroom suite to the third floor at Fairfield for the new tutor, Reginald Warrington. Nick wasn't about to let his cousin and longtime friend down, but his head was now filled with a bunch of concerns—and that creepy feeling that was getting stronger.

Travis was having serious doubts about where his head had been when he'd thrown enough money at the Whitaker Family Trust to stop Uncle Sam from grabbing Long Point and Bent Tree Cottage. At the time, the thrill of winning the game over-shadowed any common sense, as Olivia had been so quick to point out. Watching the concern, worry, and uncertainties that washed across his cousin's face didn't help. Nick was his rock, and that rock was now showing a sizable crack.

After dinner, both men agreed to meet the next morning at seven thirty when Travis would have breakfast prepared and they could regroup and plan their next moves—including how to manage the storm cleanup at the two rental cottages and still have enough time for whatever faced them at Long Point.

Travis nestled in the corner of the comfy sectional in what had once been the music room in the Captain's House, now an updated rec room for the family. He'd built a fire in the ornate marble fireplace shortly after Nick left, then went back into the kitchen to clean up the mess left behind by the spaghetti dinner. He'd returned with an unopened bottle of beer, which he set on the glass-topped coffee table. The fireplace glowed with the bright orange flames, while the crackle and pop soothed his frayed nerves. Travis had tossed another two logs onto the fire before sitting down and now watched, mesmerized as the logs became engulfed in hot, licking fingers of fire. The day's events had been exhausting, both mentally and physically. And, once again, left him with more questions than answers.

The grandfather clock in the hall chimed eight times—time to call the twins. He reached over and grabbed the phone off the side table, then punched in the numbers for Fairfield.

"Daddy! Daddy! Is that you?" Freddy must have been waiting for the call, and by the sound of the excitement in his voice as well as Andy's, something extraordinary must have happened since he'd last talked to them the night before. Travis had called the office phone at Fairfield so Olivia could put it on speaker.

"Hello, boys—and you too, Livy. What's all the excitement about?"

He could hear the boys jumping up and down on the wooden floor. "Mr. Reggie made us a poster of your castle," Freddy shouted into the phone. "He hung it on our bedroom wall so Andy and I can see it all the time."

That was interesting. Travis wondered how Reggie managed to find a photo of Bent Tree Cottage and turn it into a poster of a castle.

"I know it's not a real castle," Andy calmly added. "But Freddy likes to pretend he's a knight and runs around the house with a rubber sword."

Oh boy. Travis could just imagine all the commotion racing through the house, building in intensity, week by week until they arrived on his doorstep, rubber swords and all. *Thanks, Reggie.*

"We want to come now and see it, but Mom says we have to wait until June when she can come too," Freddy exclaimed. "She's going to be the queen of the castle."

Travis laughed at the mental image of Olivia dressed as Elizabeth I. "I can see you're both really excited and want to come now, but the castle hasn't been lived in for a long time. It's really dirty, and I have to get the local village people to come and get it all cleaned up and ready for guests." He was starting to get into this. "The queen would not want to bring her knights and her court into such a gloomy castle."

"Cool. Are there dragons too?" Freddy asked.

"I do believe I saw a couple lurking down along the shoreline near the dock."

"You're being silly, Daddy," Andy snorted. "There never were any dragons. I've checked. They only exist in fairytales and movies. But Freddy likes to pretend. I bet your castle isn't really that—"

Freddy butted in. "They do, too! I think they live under Daddy's dock!"

This was getting out of hand. Travis wanted to put an end to the excitement, yet didn't want to spoil their fun. Fortunately, Olivia came to the rescue.

"Okay, boys. I think it's time for bed. How about you say good night to your father and run upstairs and get ready? I'll be up in a minute to tuck you in."

"Night. Night, Daddy," the twins said in unison.

"I love my boys. Sleep tight. I'll talk to you tomorrow." Travis could hear their running feet in the background. Then Olivia turned off the speaker. "Travis, I heard from Emily today. I'm worried. I'll call you back after I tuck the boys in."

"What? No bedtime story tonight?" Travis asked in an amused voice. "How about King Arthur?"

"I'm serious, Travis. We have to talk. I won't be long. Call you in a few."

"Yes, my queen. I'm at your command."

"Very funny." Olivia ended the call before he could respond.

Emily Elfin, Marblehead's favorite realtor and unofficial resident with more than a little ESP. And now Livy was worried. Like the time Emily nearly fainted while she and Olivia cruised past Kelleys Island onboard Livy's yacht, the *Lovely Lady*. Then shortly after, Olivia was nearly killed when the boat exploded off that very shoreline. And Emily knew Olivia was having twin boys before Livy even knew she was pregnant. Yeah, he needed to pay attention if Emily's words were upsetting Livy.

True to her word, Olivia called back in less than five minutes. Long enough for Travis to grab a beer from the fridge and throw another log on the fire. He'd just gotten settled on the couch when the phone rang. He set the bottle on the coffee table before reaching for the phone he'd set beside him in anticipation of her call.

"Yes, Your Majesty," Travis teased.

"Travis, *darling*. Don't start something that might bite you in the butt once you're dealing with the boys in person."

"Okay. Got it. So Emily called you. Was she complaining about my bad behavior? Maybe that I'm not following her orders? Maybe that I don't want her to install a substitute housekeeper to wash my clothes and feed me?" Travis paused to take a breath. "I'm fine, Livy. Nick is keeping me company. I'm hardly ever here."

"She's worried that there haven't been any applicants for the Campbells' replacements. And you've arrived early and won't let her bring in temporary help." Olivia stopped long enough that Travis wondered what was really bothering her. "And I still don't understand why the Campbells just up and left like that. They were family. They loved the boys. Not even a goodbye." The last words caught in her throat.

Whew! The housekeeper? Was that all Emily was worried about? What about ghosts on Long Point? What about doors that seem to open and close in the kitchen at the cottage? Or the cut power and phone lines next to the garage? So far Emily didn't know about those happenings—at least not yet. As far as the ghosts, well, everyone seemed to be focused on that. Except that there were no such things as ghosts.

"I'm doing just fine, Livy. It's not like I've never lived alone. Besides, Nick has been with me almost since I arrived. He likes my cooking. And although I love you and the boys, I'm kinda liking the quiet around here for a change."

"I heard the storm finally blew itself out. Having gone through one nor'easter during my first year in the house, I'm glad I'm not there now." Olivia paused a beat. "How did the house make out?"

"Just fine. Water didn't even reach the garage and is already receding. The old captain really understood Lake Erie storms when he built this house."

"I meant Bent Tree Cottage," Olivia said like he was daft.

Travis wondered just how much to tell her. She already considers him a fool for buying the place and after all the creepy things that have happened, perhaps it wouldn't be the best time to go into details. *Best thing to do now? Lie!*

"Just fine. Actually, this storm has pretty much shut down Kelleys, so Nick and I haven't had much time to explore. I imagine he'll want to start soon on what needs to be done to bring the house and garage up to code." Travis got a thought. "In fact, it's probably going to be a month or more before the house is ready for the boys and your inspection."

"Well, I've had some thoughts on the situation. I know we're still several weeks away from moving back for the summer. And Emily is driving me crazy with her calls. She's such a mother hen."

Travis suddenly felt uneasy about what his wife could be conjuring up. It was that gut feeling that said nothing good was coming.

"I'm going to send Sarah and Benjamin up to get the house ready for us and take care of you until replacements can be found. Then they can train the new people. Sarah and Aunt Mavis will have a fun time trading recipes. They haven't seen each other since Christmas."

Travis was quick to stop her idea from going any further. "I'm fine, Livy. Really. I can handle getting the new couple settled in and have the place running like clockwork before you and the kids get here." *Well, that's just a little bit of a lie. Might need some help with that.*

"Another thing I just now thought of. I'll send Higgins ahead with Sarah and Benjamin." The enthusiasm was building in Olivia's voice. "He can work with Nick on what will be needed for security on Long Point. Might as well plan for it right from the start."

He didn't want to kill her excitement. Hell, when he'd left Virginia, she wouldn't even discuss the fact that he now owned the place. She obviously wasn't listening to him. "Livy, I don't even know what I'm going to do with the property. It's huge. Maybe I'll do something like a small boutique hotel. The island could use one. And besides, you never go anywhere without Higgins."

"Doesn't matter. Even a first-class mini hotel needs first-class security. Higgins has added a couple more guys he stole from one government agency or another. He assures me that I'll be well protected. This was actually his idea once he saw the poster Reggie made. I saw him teaching the boys sword fighting this morning. He even asked if there were any foils in the attic. I'm afraid fencing may be added to the curriculum soon. I wonder if they come in mini sizes!"

"Livy, I—"

"It will only be for a few weeks. The twins will stay here with me until everything up there is ready for us. Then we'll all be together again."

"But, Livy, I—"

"Sweetheart, I've had an exhausting day, and I need to head to the yard for an early-morning meeting. We'll talk again tomorrow." Olivia yawned. "I love you, Travis. Good night."

Travis heaved a sigh of relief that the discussion was over—at least for tonight. "I love you, too, Livy. Good night." He placed the receiver on the cradle and tossed the phone to the other side of the sectional.

Crap! Reggie and that damn poster! That just topped off my already bad day. Travis grabbed the unopened bottle of beer off the coffee table and headed to the kitchen. After placing the bottle back in the fridge, he turned and pushed through the swinging door to the butler's pantry and the liquor cabinet. He poured three fingers of Jack Daniel's into a glass and topped it off with ice. Then he headed back to the comfy couch and warm fire.

Travis rested the cold glass against his throbbing forehead and thought about the phone call. What had gotten into Livy all of a sudden? Why the sudden need to take control of his life on Marblehead? Had Emily expressed more than a simple amount of concern over him living in the Captain's House without a housekeeper? Okay, maybe Reggie had inadvertently created a monster with the poster he'd made, but why had Olivia jumped on that bandwagon? He took a sip and let the fiery liquid trickle down his throat. He was really liking the quietness of the house, the daily schedule on his terms, just hanging with his cousin, eating what he wants when he wants, and not having a heard of people around as part of the household.

Travis finished off the rest of the Scotch in one swallow. The warmth of the amber liquid and the kick that followed put life back in perspective.

To hell with everyone! Long Point and Bent Tree Cottage are mine, and I will make the decisions. Period.

CHAPTER EIGHT

The next morning, Travis prepared a hearty breakfast of scrambled eggs, sausage patties, hash browns, and toast. Nick had arrived at seven thirty as planned and poured glasses of orange juice and mugs of coffee, while his cousin filled their plates.

Even early in the morning, Nick was his happy, jovial self and seemed ready to attack the day with the energy of a teenager. "I know we were going to plan our next moves at the cottage, but, unfortunately, I've got to bow out for a few days. I'm up to my ears with calls from family on repairs needed from storm damage, and the town service department has their own list for me. I'm going to hire on more help just to handle the emergencies."

Travis watched his cousin smother his potatoes in ketchup. "Not a problem. We can't do much until power is restored to the island and the transfer of ownership is sent to the utilities so the work orders can be submitted. Who knows how long that is going to take." Travis pushed his plate aside with a troubled sigh.

"What's wrong? There's more troubling you than downed power lines."

Travis tried to keep his personal life with Olivia private, since everything she did seemed to involve a national security clearance. According to Higgins, Olivia and the twins lived with a perpetual target on their backs. *Forbes* claimed she was the wealthiest woman in the world, mostly due to her being the heiress of Angus McLeod. His ancestors were shipbuilders in Scotland and due to a family feud back in the 1700s; McLeod Ship Building was founded in Norfolk, Virginia. After the Civil War and during the industrial revolution, McLeod Ship Building merged with Morrison Steel out of Pennsylvania. Their newly designed battleships, and later aircraft carriers, received government contracts right from the start. Now, Olivia and William Morrison, her mother's one-time fiancé, stood together at the helm of one of the United States' largest corporations. For some reason or other, a security team didn't seem to apply to Travis. He considered himself lucky that he could live a relatively normal life. Olivia's normal included a security team and a bulletproof vehicle that once protected a president.

"I had a troubling conversation with Livy and the boys last night." Troubling was putting it mildly. The previous night's call and all of its ramifications, both from needing a housekeeper and Livy's plans for Long Point, had kept him up for most of the night.

"Oh?" Nick held his fork in the air ready to spear something in the center of the table. "Are you going to finish your sausage?"

Travis pushed his plate toward Nick. "Take what you want. I've lost my appetite."

"Where's she off to now? It doesn't matter—shouldn't affect you—us."

"Reggie, the boys' tutor, made a poster of the cottage and hung it on the twins' wall."

"Nice." The sausage was devoured in seconds.

"They think I bought a castle. Reggie got them rubber swords, and Higgins is teaching them fencing. Apparently, they are careening around the house like two swashbucklers. They are pretending to be knights and want to bring the queen with them to the castle—like now." Travis finished the last of his coffee. "I explained how the castle is too dirty for the queen and there is no power. Then Livy decided I can't survive on my own, so she wants to send Sarah and Benjamin Harrison to manage the house, while Higgins helps us with the renovation plans for the cottage."

"Wonderful!" Nick exclaimed like he'd just won the lottery. "Well, only the Higgins part—although I do love Sarah's cooking. Higgins sees things that never occur to me or are totally off my radar." Nick washed the sausage down with the last of his orange juice. "Travis, you've got to get Higgins! He can be part of our team!"

"Our team? We have a team now? I thought it was just you and me," Travis sounded doubtful.

"Look. Everything will go so much smoother with Higgins's eyes on the project right from the get-go. You have to admit you're pretty vulnerable out there surrounded by water except for the narrow strip between the gate and Camp Gertrude."

Travis wasn't in the mood to enter into a verbal battle with his cousin over Higgins. He'd had the whole project laid out, at least in his mind, then Mother Nature threw the first blow and then last night Livy threw the second. It was like a giant piñata that had burst open with its contents flying everywhere.

"You're right about Higgins. I should have been the one to realize the need for him now. But I don't want him turning Long Point into an armed fortress. I'll see what I can do about holding off Sarah and Benjamin," Travis said with more than a little doubt in his voice. "Today I need to make some calls and see if I can hurry things along with the utilities. I also want to call Whitaker or the lawyers, and have someone come and clear out their personal belongings."

Nick glanced at his watch. "Nine o'clock. I've got to run. How about I stop by Mutach's later and pick up a couple of porterhouse? We can hash over the day then."

"Okay with me. As long as I don't have to do anything but cook."

Both men stood and walked to the coatroom. While Nick zipped his jacket, Travis reached up to a shelf high above the hooks that lined the walls. He removed something and handed it to his cousin.

"What's this?" asked Nick.

"A remote for the front gates. With all your comings and goings, you're going to need it"

"Thanks. Part of our team equipment?" Nick said with a chuckle.

"For now. Higgins will probably take it back. He's really stingy when it comes to passing these out."

Travis closed the side door behind Nick. He then walked back to the kitchen. After putting the breakfast dishes in the dishwasher, he poured himself another cup of coffee and headed to the desk in the library.

He began a list of follow-up calls he needed to make along with ways of keeping the Fairfield staff in Virginia. It wasn't as if he didn't want their help, or that he didn't realize Livy was just trying to make his life easier. But owning Bent Tree Cottage had always been a dream and now that his dream had become a reality, he wanted some time alone with her like in a new marriage.

The fax machine came to life, spitting out three sheets of paper. Travis was pleased to see the letterhead of the offices of Graven, Morgan, Huntley, and Devonshire. The letters were addressed to the three utility companies notifying them that the Whitaker Family Trust had sold Bent Tree Cottage, located on Kelleys Island, Ohio, to Mr. Travis Tanner residing at Fairfield, Charles City, Virginia. The letters were lengthy and filled with a lot of legal jargon, but that was the gist of it. *Wonderful. Now we can get this ball rolling.*

An hour later, his mood had drastically improved knowing that the work orders for the utilities were being processed. He would have both power and telephone services as soon as the crews working on Kelleys could fit him in. Even the weather was cooperating with clear blue skies, giving Travis the motivation to address the water damage to his two rentals—and swing by the cottage.

By eleven thirty, he'd changed into a pair of old jeans and a gray sweatshirt with oil stains on the front and frayed cuffs. He quickly made a ham and cheese sandwich and washed it down with a glass of milk, then went to the coatroom for a navy-blue windbreaker. It only took a few minutes to pull the Hummer out of the garage and head back in for the two portable heaters that he'd take to the soggy rentals. After loading both machines into the back of the Hummer, Travis turned to scan the space in the garage where he parked his vehicle. Something wasn't right—he was getting that creepy feeling again. Like at the cottage when the door he'd left open was suddenly closed. Or when he'd seen the deliberately cut wires. Yet, he couldn't see anything that was wrong, or out of place, or missing. He decided he must be getting paranoid and climbed into the front seat and turned over the engine. Hitting the remote button, he watched the garage door come down.

Travis nearly missed the noon ferry. The boat was full to capacity with tradesmen heading to the island to begin the cleanup and repairs from the storm. He was happy to see that power had been restored, and for the next three hours, he picked up debris from the yards of his two rental houses and hooked up the heaters in the porches. Perhaps when he came back later to shut down the heaters, he should take the time to remove the storm windows and put in the screens. It would be one thing that he wouldn't need to do next month—one thing that wouldn't take precious time away from *Bent Tree Cottage*. The boat dock that was shared by the two properties was missing half of its boards, but otherwise looked sturdy. He'd have Nick fit the repairs into his schedule in the next month before his first summer vacation family arrived.

He'd bought the three-bedroom bungalows twelve years ago from the Simpson sisters. They had vacationed on the island as children and then when the property on East Point became available, the two families pooled their money and built identical houses. The sisters, who were both teachers and had their summers off, became valuable seasonal residents. After the younger of the two died of cancer, the older sister lost interest in the summer cottage life and sold both properties to Travis, whom they had known most of his life.

After loading his tools into the back of the Hummer, Travis checked his watch—three o'clock. He still had an hour or so before he'd need to return home and begin dinner, remembering that Nick was going to bring steaks.

The gate at the narrowest point of Long Point was open. Hopefully that meant one of the utility companies had been by to at least check on the lines even if the work orders hadn't been received yet. There were only traces of standing water on either side of the road leading to the cottage. At least that part of the property drained well after major storms.

Travis parked in front of the garage. He lowered the windows and inhaled deeply. If felt good to be back even though his to-do list was getting longer by the day. He opened the door, then reached over to the passenger seat and retrieved a copy of the blueprints that he'd had made in Port Clinton, and a legal pad and pencil. After stepping out and closing the door, he looked up at the pole next to the garage. The cut wires were still hanging.

He took note of the grounds in the immediate area and was pleased that there was no standing water, although the tall grasses and weeds had been flattened by the high winds and rain. After entering the back door into the servants' hall, he was happy to see that the kitchen door was still closed as he'd left it. Remembering the creepy feelings he'd had on his last visit, Travis hesitated before slowly opening the door. Any fear he might have had disappeared when he saw the room flooded with the bright afternoon sunlight.

"Good afternoon, house," Travis said as he placed the rolled-up blueprints and legal pad on the butcher-block worktable in the center of the room. He walked through the butler's pantry into the dining room, remembering how he'd been covered in dust when he pulled back the drapes. "Next trip I'm bringing a ladder and removing all these heavy old drapes. Poor house, I feel like you're being smothered in darkness."

He wandered into the grand hall admiring the Gothic-style paneling. His hand felt decades of grime, and cobwebs filled the intricate carvings. "What a shame. You're too grand to have suffered this horrible neglect. I'll get a cleaning crew in here and have all your wonderful oak restored to its original luster."

Travis found his way to the corner room with the comfortable furniture. He settled into the large leather club chair. Everything was covered in a hazy bloom of gloom. It broke his heart to see the house he once loved as a boy just left, all locked up, as if it were dying a slow death. "I'll take care of you. You'll be magnificent again. I promise. I promise." The house seemed to give a contented sigh of relief. Or was it happiness?

Travis suddenly felt tired—sleepy. Without Nick's help, he'd spent hours of backbreaking work at the two cottages. Maybe he just needed to close his eyes for a minute—just a minute.

The dream came quickly and was so real. He felt old, his body stiff with arthritis, and his back sore under the weight of heavy and rough-to-the-touch clothes. He was in a bedroom. The furniture was big and strong, in dark woods. He stood at a window covered in white lace curtains. The view beyond was of the lawn, sloping down to the water's edge. A small skiff was tied to the long dock. A young boy sat against the old bent tree, a long-ago trail marker for the Indians who once inhabited the island. The lad gazed lovingly up at the mansion. "Poor old house. No one cares about you anymore. One day when I'm grown up, I'm going to buy you. And you won't be lonely anymore. I promise. I promise."

The dream had been so intense that Travis didn't know where he was when he suddenly woke to find himself sitting in the leather chair. Then it all came back to him. He'd fallen asleep while inspecting the house.

Oh hell. How long have I been out? I have to catch the four-thirty ferry. Nick. Nick is bringing steaks. I need to get home.

Travis jumped out of the chair and headed for the hall. There was still plenty of light in the room, so it couldn't be too late. He glanced at his watch, then stopped dead in his tracks. Three forty-five. It couldn't be. He'd entered the house around three fifteen, looked around for a while before sitting in the chair. The dream had been so real. How could it have lasted little more than a minute or two?

Don't need to rush after all. But what the hell just happened? He didn't have time to put rational thoughts together. He needed to get out of there.

Travis hurried through the kitchen on his way to the back door. He'd leave the blueprints and legal pad where they were on the table. He didn't want a cleaning crew invading the house just yet. Not until he and Nick knew what they were dealing with and the Whitakers had removed all their stuff. He'd bring what he needed for a quick once-over, including an industrial-size box of black garbage bags.

Double-checking that the back door was locked, he walked across the now crushed weeds to the Hummer. *I need to bring a string-trimmer and clean up that walkway before someone trips.*

He was halfway to the garage when the hairs on the back of his neck bristled and a chill shot through his body. Looking down he noticed the oil stain that had seeped into the gravel drive. Travis remembered Nick's remarks about the Hummer leaking oil and that he needed to have it checked out. That's what had been troubling him that morning after loading the two heaters from the garage.

There was no oil leak on the concrete floor.

CHAPTER NINE

The baked potatoes had been in the oven for almost an hour. A bag of frozen green beans rested in the microwave ready for Travis to hit the start button. He tossed the lettuce after dropping in a handful of cherry tomatoes and sliced cucumber, along with three hard-cooked eggs that he'd cut up. The croutons would wait until Nick arrived. He'd already set the table and placed a bottle of Italian dressing in the center along with butter and sour cream for the potatoes. He realized it wasn't the dinner he and Nick would be sitting down to if Mrs. Campbell were there, or Sarah who would add a Southern touch to the meal. Neither woman would consider serving frozen veggies from the microwave or garlic bread from a box. They both would be horrified at seeing a bottle of store-bought dressing sitting on the table. But hell, it was just him and Nick, and almost any meal was good enough for them.

Travis glanced up at the wall clock. It was past five. When had he ever known his cousin to be late for a meal? Mutach's must be extra busy, or the butcher didn't have a steak already cut, and in the case, that was big enough for Nick.

The gate alarm sounded, then was followed a few minutes later by the beeping from the side door alarm. Nick and the steaks had arrived.

Nick's work boots thundered down the hall to the kitchen. He handed Travis a bag that had to weigh at least five pounds. "Sorry, I'm late. I had the steaks cut special. I hope that new-fangled stove of yours works fast. I'm starved."

Travis added the baked potatoes to the warming drawer that already contained the heated garlic bread, then unwrapped the meat. After sprinkling on a generous amount of salt and pepper, he added a touch of Sarah's special blend of spices to give it that Southern flavor he loved. Of course, she never divulged what the secret ingredients were—that recipe would die with her.

"I've had a rough day, and I'm covered in grime. I need to wash up before dinner. Mind if I use your bathroom? I don't want to mess up that pretty little one down the hall."

Something in the tone of Nick's voice caused Travis to look up. "Everything okay?"

"Yeah. Sure. Just the usual problems getting the town put back together after a major storm. Everyone's nerves are fried. I'll be right back."

Something was eating at him. Knowing Nick, it would surely spill out over dinner. Travis had his own troubling thoughts of what occurred that day, but he didn't think it wise to discuss his mystery dream with his cousin—at least not yet.

Travis arranged the baked potatoes and green beans next to the giant steaks on each plate and set them on the kitchen table. He heard Nick's work boots echoing down the hall as he pulled the garlic bread from the warming drawer and placed the slices in a basket he'd lined with a cloth napkin.

"I see I'm just in time," Nick said as he settled onto the chair.

Travis removed the salad and two Coors from the fridge. He added the croutons to the bowl before placing it in the center of the table and handed Nick a beer. He sat down and eyed the table. He hadn't forgotten anything. And he was tired, more mental than physical. If his cousin hadn't come with the meat, he just might have skipped dinner altogether.

Nick raised his beer in a toast. "To the great ending of a really *bad* day." They tipped bottles and dove into their perfectly cooked steaks.

Travis noticed the emphasis that had been put on the word "bad" and wondered if something other than storm damage had happened. He sliced open his potato, then sprinkled on salt and pepper. He glanced up at his cousin while adding butter and a good amount of sour cream. "Want to talk about your day?"

Nick took his time chewing as if he were deciding how to answer. "Mmm. You got this steak perfect. It's not easy getting rare right. It's either too done or bleeding all over the plate and messing everything else up. I hate bloody potatoes." He speared several green beans. "What about your day?"

Travis swallowed his first bite of steak. He didn't want to go into detail about his day either. "It was rough. I spent way too much time on my rentals. A few of the dock boards are missing. I'll need you to make sure it's sturdy before my renters get here. I pulled out the storm windows and put the screens in. That should help dry out the place."

Nick finished the last of his steak and had his knife ready to do some major damage to the potato. "Get out to the house? Did they get anything hooked up yet? I know you're itching to get back there. Sorry, I couldn't help."

Fortunately, for Travis, the barrage of questions stopped coming out of Nick's mouth as a huge amount of potato, dripping in butter and sour cream, went in. He nearly choked when he tried to inch out one more question.

Travis pushed his plate aside with nearly half of his dinner uneaten. The remnants of the bizarre dream still haunted him, and Nick's nonstop questions had finished off his appetite. And why hadn't he talked about his day if it had been so bad? And why was he shoveling in his food as if it were his last meal? Nick loved to talk about his accomplishments and all the local gossip he could find. His head had to be filled to exploding with stories after the mega storm that had wreaked havoc on nearly everyone's lives. His cousin was holding back. What?

Nick finally leaned back in his chair and patted his stomach. "That was an amazing meal. Thank you." He eyed the other plate. "Not hungry? It's not a good sign when the cook doesn't eat. What's eating you?" He laughed at the pun hoping to get a response from Travis. But he didn't get a sound, not a chuckle, not a grunt, not even the finger.

"I'm glad you enjoyed it. I guess I'm just too tired to eat. They will be tomorrow's leftovers. Now, how about telling me about your day?"

Nick sat upright. "They found a body near the lighthouse."

CHAPTER TEN

"What?" Travis was sure he hadn't heard Nick correctly. "Did you say a body?"

"Yep. It was during the cleanup from the storm. A bunch of tree trunks and limbs and stuff, including some kind of metal toolshed, washed up on the shore down past the lighthouse. By the Stevensons' place. I'm surprised you didn't hear about it."

"Who found it? Stevensons? That's like a half mile from here." Travis felt that familiar chill that turned his blood to ice. How come someone hadn't told him about a body being found so close to their property? Their house.

"When neighbors went over to help get rid of the debris, they found his body tangled up in the mess. You didn't hear all the commotion? Or the ambulance sirens?"

"I caught the nine o'clock ferry and worked most of the day on the two cottages. Then I stopped by Long Point and checked the house. I came home straight from the ferry and started dinner."

"It happened around noon. Everyone had left the site by three or so. You wouldn't have known about it unless someone called."

"The guy was pretty messed up. Took a real battering from the storm."

"A toolshed? Really? I've seen small boats washed onshore—but a toolshed?"

Nick got up and went to the fridge for another beer. "Want one?"

"Sure. I did hear that at one point during the storm winds were gusting from eighty to ninety miles per hour. That's hurricane strength. I guess it could move a storage shed—and a lot more."

Nick brought the two bottles back to the table. "That's the main reason I was late. I spent nearly an hour at the police station getting the details."

"Who is it? Or was? Does anyone know what happened to the guy or why he was out on the lake during the worst possible weather?" Travis asked. Good thing Nick hadn't brought this up over dinner. He wouldn't have been able to eat anything at all. Especially since the body washed onshore so close to the lighthouse. And his house!

"No one seems to know who he is. His body was taken to the Lucas County Coroner's Office in Toledo for the autopsy. It's kinda weird."

"What's weird?" Travis thought the whole thing sounded weird. Nothing like this ever happens, especially in the tiny little town of Marblehead.

"The guy's clothes for one thing. They're old. I mean threadbare old. He had on jeans, a flannel shirt with the elbows worn out, a wool sweater, and a tattered leather jacket. There was no identification of any kind, no keys, no money, no jewelry, no nothing. Like he was homeless." Nick took a long draw of beer. "What's really weird is that his nails were clean and well-trimmed, his hair professionally cut, and his face clean-shaven. He also had a tan line where a watch had been."

"So where did he get a tan at this time of year?" Travis did a questioning nod. "Yep. Really weird."

"It's like a well-to-do guy trying to look homeless. Or a city dude trying to fit in to what . . . islanders during a storm?"

Travis thought about that. "Maybe he was on a boat heading to Sandusky. Or Toledo. Or Detroit. Or, maybe, to Canada. His boat capsized in the storm, and he drowned with his body washing up near the lighthouse." Travis understood boats, and it would have been a pretty large boat for even the most experienced boater to attempt a crossing in a raging nor'easter. Or maybe he went overboard *before* the winds picked up.

"Well, a whole lot of people are talking maybes. No one has any answers. I'll stop by the station tomorrow morning and see if there's any more information from the coroner." Nick finished his beer and stood. "Look. I'm beat. Okay, if I leave you with the dishes and head home?"

Travis pushed back his chair and got to his feet. "No problem. That's what dishwashers are for. Call me if you hear anything."

Both men walked to the coatroom in silence, their heads filled with thoughts of the day. But in the end, they both wondered the same thing.

Why Marblehead?

CHAPTER ELEVEN

The next morning, Travis sat at the kitchen table with a bowl of cornflakes, two pieces of toast smothered in orange marmalade, and his third mug of coffee. It was seven o'clock, and he'd been up since five. What little sleep he'd gotten was peppered with dreams of angry black clouds, mountain-size waves that hurled boats and bodies around like paper airplanes in a wind tunnel. Rather than fight it, he headed downstairs to stoke up the coffee machine.

His first cup of Columbian's finest was in the dining room as Travis hunched over the blueprints while studying the second floor of Bent Tree Cottage. He hoped to rid himself of the nightmares that had kept him from sleep. But looking at the bedroom layouts just brought to mind the weird dream he'd had the day before while sitting in the leather chair. The image of him looking out the window and seeing himself as a little boy sitting next to the bent tree was too much for his mind to delve into. He needed to put his brain on another track. He got up and headed to the library.

His second cup of joe was carefully placed next to the leather-bound ledger containing the financials for every building located on Long Point. There were more than he remembered which would be understandable since he'd only ever viewed the property from the lake, and it was heavily forested. The accounts listed the main house and garage that Travis knew about. Then there was a barn and another house. There was also a notation about a few ancillary structures that weren't listed by name. This new bit of information put Travis on a new hunt for what other surprises might be found in the ledger. It was a full hour plus when his stomach began reminding him that it was time for breakfast.

Travis had just put his cereal bowl and utensils in the sink when he heard the buzzer for the gates. He saw the police chief Danny Wilson's face illuminated on the screen. He pressed the button for the intercom. "Come on in, Danny. I'll meet you at the door." Travis wondered if this unexpected visit had anything to do with yesterday's events. As far back as he could remember, a nor'easter had never left a body behind.

Travis watched from inside the doorway as Danny got out of the patrol car and stood for a minute or so looking out over the shoreline. It was too long for him to just be admiring the view. He then turned and climbed the steps to the side door. Travis was now sure that this visit wasn't meant for two old buddies to get together and shoot-the-breeze over morning coffee. No, Danny's body language was all business.

Travis held open the door. "Morning, Chief. I've got a fresh pot on."

Chief Wilson and Nick had been in the same grade at the Danbury schools and had lived just three houses apart. They did everything together and usually included Travis in their adventures, even if he was younger.

"Coffee sounds great, but I can't stay long. I have a dozen phone calls to make and the mountain of paperwork that goes along with them."

"I take it this isn't a spur-of-the-moment social call," Travis said as they walked to the kitchen.

"I take it you've heard about our bit of excitement yesterday, although I don't believe you were there."

Travis poured two mugs of coffee and handed one to Danny. "I spent most of the day on Kelleys. Nick filled me in over dinner last night." Travis nodded toward the door to the morning room. Then he followed Danny as he chose a chair facing the lake.

"I forgot what a wonderful view you have from this room. It must be amazing during storms."

The nearly round room was perched on the corner of the house facing east. It had a panoramic view of Lake Erie, the Marblehead lighthouse on the adjacent property, and the city of Sandusky. During the eighteenth and nineteenth centuries, morning rooms were often placed near the kitchen and typically used by the lady of the house to prepare for the day and to give orders to the cook and housekeeper. Now it was used as an informal dining room, meeting room, or just a quiet space to escape to with a cup of tea or a glass of wine.

"Storms can be captivating . . . except for nor'easters. Those can be frightening," Travis said, with the recent memories still too new for a response. "You didn't stop by for coffee and a view of the lake that you see every day. I don't mean this in a negative way, but you only stop by if you need me for something."

"I need your permission to have my guys do a sweep of your shoreline to look for anything that might help us identify the body that washed up."

"Of course. I'll leave the gates open. Just let me know when. Anything specific you're looking for?" Travis could read his old friend's body language like a favorite book, and something was eating at him.

Danny turned from the view beyond the curved windows to Travis. "Specifically, the guy's wallet or any kind of identification." He took a long swallow of the black coffee, then continued. "Something doesn't sit right. I've got a bad feeling about this."

"Well, yeah. I get it. From what Nick told me, the guy was pretty messed up and had nothing on him. That would cause all kinds of questions. Any missing persons reports?"

"There has been no chatter about anyone missing that fits his general description. All we have is a male, Caucasian, maybe late thirties or early forties, athletic build, dark hair, and blue eyes. His face is pretty much unrecognizable. The waves must have thrown him against the rocky shore like a rag doll." Danny took another sip of coffee and seemed to be sorting through his thoughts. "I hope the coroner can shed some light and give me a direction to follow. Right now, I've got nothing."

"Nick said his clothes were old. Was he wearing a life jacket?"

"Yeah, but it wasn't on tight enough. Like he was in a rush when he put it on," Danny added like it was a new thought. Something he hadn't noticed yesterday.

"Okay. So, he must have been on a larger boat. People get careless about jackets when on bigger boats." Travis paused a beat. "He's not a seasoned boater, or he would have seen to the jacket first, especially since he was going out in a storm."

"Good point. Why? What was so important that the trip couldn't wait a day or two for the storm to pass?" Danny took another sip. "Based on his shabby clothes, we've been looking for a small skiff or ski boat. I'll have the coast guard search for a larger cabin cruiser."

Travis was still thinking about the whys. Why did he wash up where he did? Halfway between the lighthouse and Bay Point? Why didn't he have a wallet or some type of identification on him? Why didn't he have keys in a pocket? Who travels with empty pockets? Why did he wash ashore tangled in a storage shed? "Maybe he was coming from somewhere around Sandusky and the waves were just too large for him to handle and decided to try for the marina at Bay Point. Maybe he was aiming for that small cut that would take him across the peninsula to the marina on the bay side. Do you know where the shed came from?"

"No idea about the shed. I'll have a notice put in the local papers. Someone should claim the lawn equipment inside. I'm thinking he would need to be a local to know about that shortcut into Bay Point. And he ain't local." Danny took the last swallow and set the mug on the table. He scooted his chair back and stood. "Thanks for the coffee and brainstorming. I'll talk to the coast guard and call the chief over in Sandusky. Maybe he's heard something by now. The boys should be here within the hour to sweep your property."

Travis led Danny down the hall to the side door. "Let me know what you find out. Maybe the coroner will have the answers you need to identify your John Doe."

CHAPTER TWELVE

The following morning, Nick joined Travis for breakfast to discuss how to proceed with the work at Bent Tree Cottage since all the utilities had been restored and the cut power and phone lines repaired. Travis didn't need to ask his cousin what he wanted to eat. He just made Nick's favorite. They sat down to pancakes, this time with blueberries, sausage, bacon, and lots of butter and maple syrup.

Travis hadn't taken his first bite when the gate buzzer sounded, and the image of Danny Wilson appeared on the monitor. He got up from the table and pressed the button on the intercom and the switch to open the gates. "Come on up, Chief. Nick and I just sat down for breakfast. Hungry? We've got pancakes."

"Starving! I'm on my way."

Travis watched the monitor as the police car drove through with the gates automatically closing behind him. Then he went to the stove and poured four large circles of batter onto the hot griddle.

Danny arrived in the kitchen as Travis flipped the pancakes over. "Take my seat and dig in while everything is still hot," Travis said while he grabbed another plate from the cupboard and silverware from the drawer. After filling his plate and pouring another mug of coffee, he joined the other two at the table.

"Sorry to barge in like this," Danny said after swallowing his first bite of sausage. "But I saw Nick's truck." He motioned with his fork toward the center of the table. "Do you always make a mountain of bacon and sausage for breakfast?"

"I do when Nick joins me," Travis said with a chuckle. "I take it, you have news about our local corpse."

"Yeah. Decided to save time and fill you both in, since I have you together," Danny said while cutting through the stack. "Got the coroner's report, but we still don't know a hell of a lot more than when we found him."

Nick filled his now empty plate with more bacon and sausage from the platter in the center of the table. "So, what news do you have? Anything about where the shed came from? Did anyone find the guy's boat?"

After washing the pancake down with a swallow of coffee, Danny continued. "The shed broke loose from a yard about a mile east of Cedar Point. Even though the amusement park is still closed, they are getting ready for the season with grounds cleanup and ride maintenance. They suffered minor damage even though that stretch of the shoreline did get hit hard. No reports of an unidentified boat being found. The coast guard is still searching and have put out a warning for local boaters to watch out for a possible sunken craft."

Travis pushed his plate aside. He was getting that sick feeling in the pit of his stomach. Maybe he'd spent too many years with Higgins and his mind kept going back to the dead guy. The whole scenario didn't gel. "How about the coroner's report? You had to have learned *something.*"

"He confirmed what we know. Caucasian, late thirties or early forties, perfect, well-muscled, athletic body. Under normal conditions, the dude probably could have swum from here to Canada! Coroner thinks he was good-looking based on the condition of what was left of his face. But not enough to even begin a sketch. Our John Doe will stay in the cooler for a while until further fingerprint and DNA tests come back."

"That's it?" Travis asked. "Not even a scar or weird birthmark?"

"Too banged up to tell. His face is like a pound of ground meat with a nose. But there is a partial tattoo."

"Huh. Tattoo? What did it look like? Maybe a name or place?" Travis asked, thinking this could lead to a possible identification.

"The design isn't anything common, and it's only a partial. Detectives in Toledo and Cleveland are sending out photos hoping someone will recognize it." Just then Danny's radio sounded. "Hate to eat and run, but I'm needed at the station. I'll let you know if I hear anything."

Travis and Nick walked the chief to the door.

"Well, this bit of news should get the local grapevine sprouting in all directions," remarked Nick with a laugh.

With the morning free for both Travis and Nick and the threat of more rain, the two decided to stay in and work on a viable plan for getting as much done on Bent Tree Cottage as they could before Olivia and the twins arrive. Hopefully, he could keep them away for three or four more weeks. It wasn't much time in the full scope of the project—that would probably take all summer and then some, but at least they would have a good understanding of the property and know where the problems lie. He remembered how much trouble he had gotten into growing up on the islands. He didn't want to think how much two adventurous boys could get into.

By noon, both men had spent the last several hours hunched over the dining room table studying the blueprints of all three floors of the house and the map of the property. Travis pushed his chair back and stood while stretching his arms overhead. "I need a break. How about I grab a couple of beers and some chips, and we move to a more comfortable room and review our new project list?"

"Sounds good to me," Nick said as he got to his feet and headed toward the den.

After settling on the couch with beer, chips, and salsa placed strategically between them, Travis picked up the legal pad and began to scan the items.

"Okay. I feel good about this. I'll do a thorough search of the rooms and note any problems I see. You'll get your electrical team together and trace the lines. We'll also do an inventory of what needs to be done in the garage," Travis said while making additional notes.

"I'll get a company in to do an inspection of the well and mechanics. Plumbing stays at the top of the list." Nick had a chip loaded with salsa and halfway to his mouth. "We need to check out that other house on the south side that's mentioned in the financials and map."

"Yeah. The mystery house." Travis put the bottle of beer to his lips, then stopped. "While we're at it, we'd better check the shoreline for any debris that might connect to our John Doe. During the search of this property, we didn't find anything except your usual after-a-storm flotsam, bottles and cans, and a shredded blue tarp. I think Long Point is just too far north." Travis took a long swallow. "By the looks of this list, I don't have time to think about Mr. Doe. From now on, he's Chief Wilson's problem. Period!"

"You are sooooo right!" exclaimed Nick. "We have our own problems . . . like who cut your power lines."

CHAPTER THIRTEEN

A week later, Travis and Nick stood at the long butcher-block counter in the kitchen reviewing their project notes. The new phones had been installed, and Travis was happy that the house was now connected to the outside world. The recent inspection of the well showed major problems and all the equipment would need to be replaced to bring it up to code. Travis decided to apply for the permits that would bring city water to the house and other buildings. "Looks like we're right on schedule," Travis said as he flipped through the pages of the legal pad.

"Yep," Nick added. "I've got the well pump running and water flowing through the pipes. It's not fit for drinking, but it will get us through until the city water is hooked up."

"I'll pick up a couple of cases of bottled water," Travis said while checking his watch. "It's still early. How about checking out that other house on the property? There just hasn't been enough time so far this week."

"And with any kind of luck, we won't find any surprises," Nick said with a whole lot of doubt in his voice.

The gravel road, heading toward the widest part of the property, was narrow with thick underbrush along both sides and with a canopy of tall trees overhead. There was barely enough room for the truck to squeeze through as it bounced over ruts and exposed tree roots. And then, suddenly it was before them, nestled in a copse of pine trees.

Travis leaned forward to get a better view, his hand still holding tightly on the handle above the door after being jolted around in his seat. "Wow. I never knew this was here. It's like something out of a Grimms' Fairy Tales."

The road ended at the house. Nick parked and turned off the engine. "Looks like an early Craftsman bungalow. Maybe 1920s, and from what I can see, it was built with local rocks from the shoreline. What an architectural gem. I love that single, wide dormer on the second floor. The diamond-pane windows add a whimsical touch. There's a nameplate hanging over the steps . . . THE PINES."

Without another word, both men jumped down from the truck and climbed the few steps to the front porch. Travis reached in his pocket for the wad of keys that had been sent to him by the law firm of Graven, Morgan, Huntley, and Devonshire. While searching for a key that looked old enough to match the lock, Nick turned the knob. The door opened. "I guess one doesn't need to lock their doors out here," Nick said jokingly.

Travis dropped the keys into his jacket pocket and walked into the cozy front room. A large fireplace made of the same local stone took up most of the end wall of the room. Sturdy oak furniture with seats covered in dark-brown leather created a comfortable lounging area. Travis followed his cousin toward the kitchen. Nick stopped suddenly at the arched opening.

"Someone's living here!"

Travis moved around the room. "More like camping here." He opened the brown-colored fridge. "Looks to be from the 1960s. My mom had one just like it. It's empty. . . and stinks." He walked over to the counter next to the sink. "A Coleman propane camp stove."

Nick stopped in front of an electric stove of the same color. "I've got a large battery flashlight, and a kerosene lantern."

Travis walked down a short hallway and checked out a bedroom and bathroom. "I've got a sleeping bag rolled up on the bed." He then went to the closet. "Huh. A suit. A *really* nice suit." He then opened the top drawer of the dresser. "Some jeans, sweatshirts, and sweaters."

Nick took the stairs, two at a time, to the second floor. "Nothing up here except for a bedroom and attic." He then went back down to the living room and squatted in front of the fireplace. "There's been a fire in here recently."

They both ended up back in the kitchen, where they began opening the few cabinets and drawers. "Looks like this guy didn't plan on staying long. Not much on food," Nick said while shuffling cans around in the cupboard. "Canned spaghetti, beef stew, peanut butter, and bread.

Travis opened the doors under the sink and pulled out a duffel bag. "Huh," he said while unzipping it. "Maybe not a lot on food . . . but a lot on money!"

CHAPTER FOURTEEN

It was five thirty by the time Nick dropped Travis off at the house. After finding a bag full of hundred-dollar bills, they decided to stop by the police station and report the break-in.

Chief Bobby Monroe, of the Kelleys Island police department, was on his way out when Travis walked in carrying the heavy duffel bag. "Bobby. You're just the person we wanted to see. Nick and I chose today to explore 'The Pines.'"

"The Pines? Where's that?"

"You know. That little stone bungalow hiding among the pine trees on Long Point." Travis held up the bag. "I think we should talk in your office. We have a bit of a situation."

It was a full hour before Nick stopped in front of the Village Pump and Travis jumped down to run into their favorite restaurant and bar for the to-go order of burgers, fries, and coke. Nick had called in the order while he and Travis filled Chief Monroe in on everything they'd found at The Pines. They ate in silence while sitting in the truck during the twenty-minute ferry ride to Marblehead. They'd both given Bobby Monroe every detail they could remember and left the bag of money in his safekeeping. The chief assured them that he would do a thorough search of the place and let Travis know what they find.

"What about tomorrow? Know what you want to do?" Nick asked Travis when he parked in the driveway at the Captain's House.

"I don't know." Travis opened the passenger door and jumped down. "Long Point is just full of surprises," he answered, as if deep in thought. Then he slowly closed the door and walked toward the side steps.

A few minutes later, Travis pulled a beer from the fridge and flopped down on the couch in the old music room, now turned into a comfy family room. After finishing off half the bottle, he closed his eyes and thought about nothing. He was asleep almost immediately.

He was awoken by the ringing of the phone. The room was dark. He fumbled for the switch on the lamp next to the couch and then picked up the receiver. "Hello?"

"Travis, honey. Are you all right? I was about to hang up."

"Yeah. I fell asleep," Travis said while running his fingers through his rumpled sandy colored hair. "Just a little groggy. What time is it?"

"Nearly nine o'clock. The boys waited for your evening call but then got sleepy and went to bed. I suppose I should have called you earlier, but I figured you were out somewhere or busy."

"Sorry. I can't believe the time got away from me like that."

"Travis, are you really all right? You sound weird," Olivia asked. She sounded concerned. "I know you. Something happened. What is it?"

Travis wondered how much he should tell his wife about today's events. It had taken her days to get over being anxious about Marblehead's John Doe. She'd been sure Travis was in danger, although she couldn't come up with any viable reasons. How would she deal with a squatter on Long Point? It wasn't as if another body had turned up.

He inhaled deeply and blew it out. "Well . . . Nick and I decided to check out the house that I noticed marked on the map for Long Point. It turned out to be this cute little stone bungalow nestled in a grove of pine trees. It's called 'The Pines.' You're going to love it. You can't even see it from the road or the lake. Probably built sometime in the 1920s."

"Sounds charming. Now what happened? Spill it, Travis."

"Okay . . . We found a squatter. Well, we didn't *actually* see him. We found his stuff. Then we took his duffel bag to the police station."

"You might as well tell me the whole story. What was so important that you took it to the police?"

Livy was right. She needed to know everything. "Fifty thousand dollars in hundreds stashed in a duffel bag under the kitchen sink. There was also a passport and a box of ammunition . . . 9mm. No gun."

His wife was too quiet. She should be exploding with accusations about why this was one more reason he was stupid for buying Long Point and putting himself in danger. "Livy? Are you still there?"

"I'm waiting for my blood pressure to drop enough for me to think. I want to order you to come back home where you're safe. Where there are no bodies washing up from the James River, or bags of money stashed in the old icehouse." She paused long enough to redirect her thoughts. "But I know that won't happen. You and that cousin of yours will jump into the thick of things."

"I love you, Livy. I knew you would understand." Phew. He'd dodged that bullet. Now to change the subject and ask about the twins.

"Travis, I don't understand. Who is this guy? What did you find out?" Olivia paused a beat. "I want to know what you've gotten yourself into. What did you find out from the passport?"

"His name is Steven Anderson. He's Canadian. From Hamilton, Ontario. We're thinking he's into some type of smuggling. With Long Point being unoccupied for so many years, The Pines could be a perfect layover spot for someone wanting to avoid customs at the Windsor/Detroit bridge. He could come across the lake, which is narrow at that point and land here. This location would give smugglers easy access to Sandusky, Port Clinton, Toledo, and Detroit."

"Smuggling from Canada to Long Point? They'd have to find a way off the island first." Olivia went silent for a moment. "Could he be your John Doe? Maybe he got caught up in that storm and his boat capsized near the lighthouse."

"No. Our corpse is somewhere in his late thirties or early forties. Dark hair with an athletic build. By the looks of Steven Anderson's passport photo, he's in his late fifties with a full head of gray hair with a beard and mustache. He has a ruddy complexion and wears black-framed glasses. Definitely not our Mr. Doe."

"I hope this gets settled before the boys and I get there next month. I don't want them running around an island with dangerous criminals."

"Don't worry, Livy. The police chief sent out officers to search the grounds and house."

Olivia let out a groan. "Kelleys Island police officers? How many is that? Two? Really, Travis, that doesn't make me feel any better."

"Bobby Monroe called the FBI. They will arrive tomorrow morning. They'll get this guy when he returns for the money.

It won't take long. Nick and I are catching an early ferry and plan to spend the day working on the house. We'll see what the FBI finds." Travis wondered how much he really would find out. The FBI tended to be tight-lipped when it came to their investigations, especially international ones. "I'll fill you in tomorrow evening."

"Travis, honey, I'll have to call you. I'll be staying in Norfolk for the next couple of days. William and I are watching the latest tests for that new guidance and tracking system we're developing. It's really looking good." She went silent for a few seconds. "I'd feel better if Higgins was there. I won't need him while I'm at the yard. McLeod and Morrison have their own top-notch security force. I'll mention it to him."

Travis was near a sudden panic attack. "No! Please! Don't mention anything to Higgins." Thoughts of Olivia's head of security taking control over the Long Point land was frightening, not to mention what he would demand with the renovations of Bent Tree Cottage. Travis shuddered at the mere thought of Higgins in the house. "The FBI will be swarming the property. They won't want him butting into their investigation. Please. Let me handle this."

"Okay. I don't like it, but I don't have time to argue with you. I need to focus on these tests tomorrow. We have a presentation scheduled for a week from now at the Pentagon. Sorry, I can't go into details."

"I know—top secret. I love you, Livy. Good luck with your tests."

"Love you too. I'll call when I can," Olivia said. Then the line went dead.

CHAPTER FIFTEEN

Olivia Bentley Tanner hated keeping her husband in the dark about important projects that kept her tied to the shipyard for days. With Fairfield, her estate in Charles City, Virginia, being an hour-and-a-half drive to the McLeod and Morrison shipyard, in Norfolk. It was easier for Olivia to stay at her house located a few miles away on Freemason Street. This wasn't a life she had created or even fantasized for herself. It was a life she'd inherited from her grandmother. It was the life her mother had turned her back on when she married Frederick Thompson and escaped to Ohio. Now, it was Olivia's life, and therefore, Travis and her sons' lives by marriage and birth.

She hated the thought of her husband and the people of Marblehead and Kelleys Island having to deal with dead bodies and smugglers. The population swelled around the Lake Erie Islands during the summer with cottage people and tourists. Crime on this level didn't happen . . . at least not that she could remember. Not since her best friend tried to kill her in the parlor of the Captain's House.

Olivia debated whether she should get Higgins involved. Once he got wind of what Travis was dealing with, he'd jump in with both feet using every government agency to get the answers needed and then secure the area. The safety of Travis and his cousin, Nick, was important, but so was her schedule for the next couple of weeks.

Early tomorrow morning, Higgins would drive her to the shipyard, where they would board a helicopter to take them to a waiting aircraft carrier anchored in the Atlantic. The first open water testing of the new surveillance and tracking device, named HELIOSmm-88, would commence promptly at ten o'clock. If all goes well, the next day would be spent putting together the presentation for the Chief of Naval Operations, Secretary of the Navy, and the President. Once all the legal eagles have reviewed the contracts and any changes are approved and made, they can be signed, and Olivia and the twins can pack up and head to Marblehead for the summer.

CHAPTER SIXTEEN

The next morning, Travis and Nick caught the eight o'clock ferry to Kelleys. The gate to Long Point was wide open.

"This is downright careless. This gate is all that protects your property. It needs to be kept closed," Nick said as he drove his truck past and headed toward the cottage.

A sadness had replaced the excitement Travis had been feeling since he opened the envelope, sent from the law firm, containing the fistful of keys. "It doesn't matter. Apparently, the locked gate hadn't stopped our smuggler or who knows how many other people. For all I care, it can stay open until I get proper electronic gates made and security installed. I guess I do need Higgins, after all."

It didn't take them long to stash the cooler containing their lunch on the kitchen counter, then head to opposite ends of the house. Nick was checking bathrooms for any leaks that may have sprung after he'd turned on the water. Travis went to see what may have been left behind in the housekeeper's rooms and to get an idea of how the call bell system worked. Considering how large the "cottage" was, it may be something that should be kept.

He had just begun opening desk drawers when the doorbell chimed. "Really? The doorbell? Which door?" Travis said out loud as he got up from the chair and headed toward the front hallway. He didn't see anyone through the glass at the front door but noticed a black SUV parked behind the truck. He then turned and ran toward the door to the servants' hall.

"I've got it!" shouted Nick from the direction of the back door.

Travis arrived at the kitchen as Nick was ushering a man wearing a dark suit into the room. He was of average height, slim build with light-brown hair and blue eyes. Travis wondered who he was and why he'd been at his door. He was certainly too young to be part of the FBI team.

Before Nick or Travis could introduce themselves, the stranger reached into his inside jacket pocket and pulled out an identification badge. "Agent Jason Fisk. FBI. I'm in charge of the investigation at the house called 'The Pines' on your property."

Travis was speechless. He couldn't imagine how someone so young could oversee anything, let alone an FBI investigation. Squatters with a ton of cash must be extremely low on the agency's important case list.

"Which one of you is Travis Tanner?" asked Agent Fisk.

Travis reached his hand forward. "I am. This is my cousin, Nick Tanner."

After shaking hands, Agent Fisk continued. "Your local police chief, Bobby Monroe, suggested that I stop by and fill you in on what we know so far." Agent Fisk motioned in the direction of the driveway. "I saw your truck and thought this might be a good time and place to meet. We're treating the area around The Pines as a crime scene. It's best if you don't add any more tire tracks by driving over there."

"Understand. Does that mean you've found other tread marks besides Nick's? I assume you've already checked his for a match." Travis wondered what else they found, or whether this kid would even tell them.

"It appears that your intruder was driving a late-model sedan—possibly a Toyota. We've also found drag marks on the shoreline among some heavy underbrush. But we can't tell how long ago they were made. We've cleared the contents from the house and will take them to our lab for possible identification."

"Steven Anderson, of Hamilton, Ontario," Travis added. "Have you checked with the Hamilton police? Are you checking with locals here on Kelleys or Marblehead? Maybe someone recognized him. He had to buy the supplies we found *somewhere*."

"Have you removed anything from the house besides the duffel bag?" asked Agent Fisk in a tone that made Travis feel like he was suspected of being in cahoots with the squatter.

"No! Nothing. We went straight to the police and handed the bag over. We didn't even know there was anything but money in the duffel until Bobby emptied it onto his desk." Travis thought he should explain why he didn't know about the house and the squatter until now. After all, enough time had gone by that he should have inspected every square foot of Long Point. But his focus had been solely on Bent Tree Cottage. "I recently bought Long Point. Yesterday was the first time we'd seen the bungalow."

"Chief Monroe did mention that. He said you would leave the gate at the entrance to Long Point open until we are finished. Is it normally locked? I'm wondering how easily it would be for someone to have access by car."

"Yes. It is normally locked. Our police department has keys to all the properties on the island that are owned by out-of-towners in case of emergencies or deliveries." Travis remembered his missing key that mysteriously turned back up on the ring at the police station. "Mine was missing for a while. Bobby Monroe has the details. You should ask him."

Agent Fisk reached out and shook hands with Travis and Nick. "Thank you for the information. I'll be in touch once I know more."

"Before you leave, could this have anything to do with Marblehead's John Doe?" Travis asked.

"You did say you found tracks near the water. I assume they were made while pulling a small boat up onto the shore. And apparently, hiding it in the underbrush?" Nick asked with a furrowed brow. He appeared to be trying to connect a few missing dots. "Our Mr. Doe was most likely in a small boat when the storm overtook him. I don't believe the coast guard has found the boat yet. And what about the ammunition we found in the duffel bag?"

"I know you're anxious to have answers to all your questions. Rest assured we are looking into every angle. As for the John Doe—there is no physical resemblance to what we know of Steven Anderson." Agent Fisk walked toward the door. "Now, I must leave. My team is waiting to finish sweeping the area."

Travis and Nick walked him to the back door and watched as he got into his vehicle and drove toward the road leading to The Pines.

"Well. Are you reassured?" Nick asked.

"No! Hell no! I wish I could call Higgins . . . but I won't," Travis answered and walked back into the kitchen.

CHAPTER SEVENTEEN

At eight o'clock that night, Travis was still fuming over the day's events. Long Point had been swarming with the FBI, and Agent Fisk had officially declared it a *crime scene*. The locals were being interrogated like they were all part of a major smuggling ring, and Travis and Nick were considered, by the locals, at the root of the islanders' world being turned upside-down and inside-out. He and Nick had been flagged down four times by friends wanting details before they reached the ferry dock. He'd come home to the answering machine flashing with a dozen messages, all relating to Long Point being a crime scene and what was he doing about it. He turned the machine off, went straight to the kitchen, and grabbed a beer.

Nick had dropped Travis off saying he'd had enough of everything at Long Point and just wanted to go home, unplug the phone, and watch a movie on HBO. Travis couldn't remember another time when Nick passed up an opportunity to invite himself for a meal. Without Nick to cook for, Travis tossed a frozen pizza in the oven, then made sure he had the shades and drapes pulled in each of the rooms facing the street. He didn't want to give anyone the impression that he was home and willing to discuss the events of the day.

His nightly call to the twins went as usual, with each of them begging to come early for the summer and Travis explaining why they couldn't. He loved and missed the twins, but they needed to remain in the safety of Fairfield, not playing in the middle of a crime scene. Besides, Higgins wouldn't allow it.

Travis finished the last slice of pizza and went to the fridge for another beer. After stretching out on the couch, he thought about how he should handle Olivia's call. She'd been worried enough about the body washing up just a stone's throw from their home, then the squatter and possible smuggling going on at Long Point. Now his property was labeled a crime scene. At this rate, she wouldn't allow the boys anywhere near Marblehead, let alone step foot on Kelleys. Livy was under enough pressure with her top-secret testing. He wasn't going to unload on her tonight.

Travis was convinced that he was off the hook and Olivia wasn't going to call when the phone rang.

"Hello, Livy?"

"Travis, honey. Sorry I'm so late calling, but I came to Washington a day early. I'm staying with William and his wife in Georgetown."

She sounded tired. "How did the trials go on the carrier today? I assume all went well since you're in DC now."

"Amazing! The maneuvers couldn't have gone better." Excitement crept into her voice. "The admiral and the other powers-that-be were impressed enough that a meeting at the Pentagon is schedule for day after tomorrow. William and I will finalize our presentation and, if all goes well, our Navy will have a new toy by the end of the year."

"That's wonderful news. It's been five long years that you've been struggling with this project." Travis gave a sigh of relief that he was getting his wife back and would not have to live with the rules surrounding top-secret conversations. "I'm happy that your troubles are over, and we can get back to a normal life."

She didn't respond. Something was wrong. "Livy?" He wondered if the line had gone dead. "Livy? Are you still there?"

"Our house on Freemason Street was broken into today."

"*What?* Higgins has that building sealed up tighter than Fort Knox. Flies can't get past the security."

"They got in through an old slave tunnel." The tiredness was back in Olivia's voice.

"What slave tunnel? I don't know anything about slaves. When? How come this is the first time I'm hearing this?" Travis totally forgot about his own problems as his blood ran cold with thoughts about Livy's safety in the house. All these years she could have been in danger. They all could have been. "What did they take? Is the house trashed? Does Higgins know about a tunnel? You're not safe there."

"Travis, honey, I'm safe now. It happened while we were at sea during the test run. Nathaniel was at a doctor appointment and then grocery shopping. He discovered the break-in when he got back. He'd been gone about three hours."

"What damage did they do?" His thoughts were still spinning like a caged hamster on its wheel.

"They emptied the safe in my office. Opened drawers. Funny thing is, all the safe contained are the financials for my charities. Who would want those?"

"What about your laptop? Did they get that?" Travis asked while trying to make sense of the reason behind the burglary.

"No. I have it with me. William and I are still working on our presentation to the Chief of Naval Operations and the Secretary of the Navy at the Pentagon. This is all classified—but the outcome goes all the way to the White House."

Travis had a gazillion more questions, but he could hear the fatigue in Olivia's voice.

"Travis, honey, I really can't go on. I can't talk about the project, and the break-in at the house is just speculations at this point." She paused for a yawn. "I promise to fill you in when I have the facts. But that might not be for a few days. Not until I get back to Norfolk. For now, Higgins is looking into the story behind the slave tunnel and why only the burglars seemed to know about it."

"Okay, sweetheart. Get some sleep and don't worry about me." He heard Olivia yawn again.

"Sleep could be a problem. I had one of those horrible dreams last night. It's been many years since I've had one, and it was so vivid. I woke up in a sweat. If I have another one tonight, then something bad is going to happen."

"I think it's just nerves. Subconsciously, you fear that the presentation won't go well."

"Maybe you're right. This project is critical to the future of our Navy, and it goes without saying, to McLeod and Morrison." Olivia paused to think about what he'd said. "Yeah. I'm conjuring up the dream to remind myself to go into this meeting like my life depends on the outcome."

"Exactly." Travis sounded positive even though his gut had doubts.

"Thanks, honey. I can always count on you to figure things out. Now, I do need to get to bed."

"Good night, Livy. I love you."

"I love you too, Travis."

Then the line went dead.

CHAPTER EIGHTEEN

Travis gently set the phone on the coffee table and leaned forward, resting his forearms on his knees, his hands clasped tightly together.

His thoughts went back nine years when he and Olivia began exploring the house she'd inherited from her grandmother located in Norfolk. During that first year, he'd spent many days engrossed in Norfolk's and the surrounding areas of Hampton Roads' rich history. He'd wandered the halls of the Mariners' Museum located in Newport News for a whole day and taken his sons there three times. The first time in their stroller. He'd been to the Hampton Roads Naval Museum and toured the Battleship Wisconsin. He'd immersed himself in all things nautical, and with that, Norfolk's role in both the Revolutionary and Civil Wars.

Travis got up and began pacing around the room. A slave tunnel? he wondered. How was that possible? How come he and Olivia didn't know about it? How come no one seemed to know about it? Not even Nathaniel. Angus McLeod, Olivia's grandfather, had hired the young man who'd graduated from culinary school in New York and studied in France to run his house in Norfolk. Nathaniel, now much older with a full head of silver hair, continued in his many roles, including those of major-domo, chef, and historian for the house.

Travis thought back to those first days, after Olivia had inherited the house. With Nathaniel's help, they'd searched through Olivia's grandfather's documents, many of which had been hidden in secret cupboards in his bedroom walls. There had been no mention about a tunnel. Nothing about helping slaves reach freedom. Surely, they would have found records among her great-grandfather's papers referring to what his father had done to help runaway slaves. Travis was way too upset to even think about going to bed. The house on Freemason Street had a secret.

Travis headed to the kitchen. He needed coffee.

Fifteen minutes later, he sat at his desk with a pencil and fresh legal pad. His mind always worked better if he could take notes or sketch what he saw or was thinking. He'd kept a notebook during those first few months in Virginia, both at Fairfield and in Norfolk. He never went anywhere without his well-worn, leather satchel slung across his shoulder, like a history professor on a quest. But that had long ago been tucked away in a closet at Fairfield—like a child's favorite childhood teddy bear.

With his maps, brochure, and notes unavailable, Travis jotted down what he remembered about the extensive role that Norfolk played in the Underground Railroad primarily between the 1830s and late 1860s. Being a major shipping port for the South, the surrounding area became a well-oiled machine, thanks to the efforts of free blacks and whites. It was black slaves who did much of the work along the Chesapeake Bay area. All-black crews manned the various ferries, sloops, and ships that used the waterways throughout the Hampton Roads. African American laborers filled the shipyards and docks. That made it possible for agents to move runaways from their safe locations, many of which were located in what is now known as the Freemason Historic District, to the ship captains who were sympathetic to runaways.

Although Travis had visited the various museums and historic houses and gone on walking tours, he'd never seen any reference to their house on Freemason Street, or even any of the houses near them. Maybe the tunnel wasn't used by runaways; maybe it just connected the house to another location.

One thing was for certain. He wasn't going to find any answers sitting in the old Captain's House in Marblehead, Ohio. What he could find was sleep.

After a restless night, Travis was up at five and took a long hot shower hoping to wash away disturbing thoughts of Olivia's upcoming presentation at the Pentagon and the break-in at the house. But it didn't help—it only created a cloud of steam in the bathroom. After a quick breakfast of cereal and toast, he phoned Higgins hoping to get a positive report. Olivia's chief of security sounded tired when he'd answered the phone. Like he had spent the night anywhere but in bed. The only information Travis got from the call was that Higgins had no information—but he was working on it.

Now, frustrated beyond control, Travis knew that in order to hold on to his sanity, he needed to focus on what was actually within his realm of control. That would be Long Point. He picked up the phone and called the diner to place a hearty lunch order for two.

CHAPTER NINETEEN

Nick's truck was already parked in front of the garage when Travis arrived at Bent Tree Cottage just before eight thirty. Earlier, Travis had watched his aunt Mavis pack his cooler with the leftover pot roast from the dinner menu the night before, along with half a pan of corn bread and two slices of cherry pie. She also loaned him a small microwave oven she kept on the pantry shelf for emergencies. He then caught the eight o'clock ferry to Kelleys. Regardless of how the morning went, he and Nick would at least eat well.

After setting the cooler on the floor and plugging in the microwave he'd set on the counter, Travis looked up to see his cousin enter the kitchen from the servants' hall. "Good morning," Travis said, in a voice indicating that it really wasn't.

"You look like hell." Nick paused to study his cousin. "Didn't get much sleep? Or is it more than that? Olivia. Is she okay?"

Travis knew he would have to tell Nick the whole story. But he would ask a gazillion questions, most of which had no answers—yet. At least once a year, Nick would visit them in Virginia. One particular visit, Travis had taken his cousin and the twins to all of the typical tourist destinations in Norfolk. They had spent two nights at the house on Freemason Street—and Nathaniel had given him the full, unabridged tour. No. Travis wasn't ready; nor did he have the time to fill Nick in on the break-in.

"Oh no! Something happened to one of the boys?" Nick rushed across the room. "What is it?"

Travis couldn't wait any longer to reply. "Livy's staying at William's house in DC. She sounded exhausted last night during our call. The test at sea went off without a hitch. She and William are putting the final touches on a very important meeting tomorrow." Nick didn't seem satisfied with the answer so far. He had to give him more.

"It's all top secret, and I'm worried about it somehow failing to impress the bigwigs." Travis paused a beat. "I couldn't sleep—no big deal."

"Sorry, man. I overreacted."

Travis turned his attention to the window overlooking the drive. "A large truck and a van just parked close to the back door. Are you expecting them?"

"Yeah. I scheduled a commercial cleaning crew out of Sandusky. Charles Dempsey, owner of All Pro Cleaning. I figured it would be better if we used a company from out of town. Less chance of workers feeding the local grapevine with ghost stories," Nick said as he headed for the back door to greet the crew.

By noon, the kitchen and butler's pantry had been scrubbed and sanitized from floor to ceiling, and all appliances were ready for use. The housekeeper's rooms, including the office, bedroom, bath, and sitting room, were well underway. During lunch, Travis and Nick watched as two men carried the mattress to the trash. By the time they'd finished the cherry pie, four large, black garbage bags had followed the mattress.

"I remember Mrs. Campbell buying things out of a JCPenney catalog," Travis said, more to himself, than an important comment. "Might be a good idea to bring it along tomorrow."

At three o'clock, Travis was sitting at the housekeeper's desk making notes on what needed to be done before Livy and the boys arrived. It was his desk now and his office. It felt good. It felt right, and he was smiling when the owner of the cleaning company stopped at the door.

"Excuse me, Mr. Tanner." He paused until Travis looked up. "We've finished the first floor, and we will be back tomorrow to do the second and third floors. I'd like to catch the four o'clock ferry."

"Thank you, Mr. Dempsey, for getting so much done today. Everything your people have done so far looks wonderful. This place has been closed up for decades, and I realize it's much worse than your usual jobs," Travis said with sincerity.

"Call me Chuck. I'm glad you're satisfied. Before we go, I'd like to discuss a couple of things with you in the library."

"Sure." Travis stood and followed him down the hall. "I know the room is a challenge, and the pipe smell still seems to linger after all these years," Travis said as both men entered the room.

"I don't smell tobacco, but the soot and damp from the fireplace is pretty strong," said Charles. "This room is exquisite. I've seen rooms that aren't this nice in museums." He swept his right arm out in front of him, motioning toward the floor. "The oriental rug is very old. We rolled it up and will take it to a company in Cleveland that specializes in cleaning and restoring old rugs." He stepped over to the fireplace and ran his hand over the paneling. "The wood is dry. Both this room and the walls in the main hall are magnificent and need to be professionally cleaned and treated to bring back the luster of the grain and finish. Especially the Gothic detailing in the center hall and staircase."

Travis nodded. "I'll see to it at once."

"I think that will help with the smell along with having the chimney cleaned."

"Nick has already scheduled the four chimneys to be inspected and cleaned."

Charles motioned toward a tall ladder on the far side of the room. Then he looked up. "I've only seen ceilings like this in old hotels and museums. I've done a light cleaning of the stained glass ceiling panel. It's made unusually sturdy for being installed inside. This could easily be the window in a church or old Victorian mansion."

"Really? That seems odd," commented Travis.

"What's really odd is that the coffered ceiling is solid. I tried lifting the center panels in each of the squares surrounding the glass in order to replace the light bulbs. Nothing moved. There has to be a way to access the lights from above."

Travis thought about that for a minute. "I don't remember seeing anything unusual located above this room in the blue-prints. Or even noted in maintenance records." He shook his head in frustration. "Just one more unexpected issue for me and Nick to investigate. At least we have working bulbs for now."

Charles checked his watch. "We need to leave if we're to catch the next ferry to Marblehead."

Charles followed Travis to the kitchen where they found Nick sprawled on the floor under the sink with his hand gripping a pipe wrench.

"Hey, Nick. Charles and his crew are about to leave for the day."

Both men watched as the would-be plumber scooted out from under the sink and slowly pushed himself to his feet.

Nick shrugged with a sheepish look. "Sorry, my knees aren't what they used to be."

Chuck shook both men's hands, said his goodbyes, then left by the back door.

Travis and Nick stood at the bay window and watched as the large box truck and van, with the name ALL PRO CLEANING in large letters, turn around and head down the driveway.

Travis thought about Mr. Dempsey's comments about the library ceiling not giving access to the bulbs above. So, what was above that room that wasn't noted on the prints? He inhaled deeply and slowly let it out.

"Cuz . . . we have another mystery on our hands." He paused for affect. "Bent Tree Cottage has a secret."

CHAPTER TWENTY

Travis waited for a response from his cousin. Nick should have been jumping for an explanation of another secret. Okay, maybe it was just a little secret, and maybe it would turn out to be no secret at all—but hey, it should warrant some kind of response. Even a little one.

"Earth to Nicklaus Tanner."

"Okay, Travis. Now what? You said a secret."

"Chuck Dempsey mentioned it while he was going over stuff in the library. It's probably nothing. I'll check it out tomorrow."

"Check what out?"

"Like I said. It's probably nothing. I'm going to take the blueprints home and study the second floor."

"For what? We know what's up there." Nick was sounding frustrated. "What's this mystery about?"

"Light bulbs."

"*Light bulbs?*" Nick hurried over to the sink and picked up the pipe wrench and waved it at Travis. "I'm tired. I'm going to fix this stupid dripping feed line and head home." He got down on the floor and scooted under the sink. "You go look for light bulbs. I'm done!"

Travis knew when to leave matters with his cousin alone. The one thing Nick had no patience for was plumbing problems. The best thing he could do now was to get out of the kitchen before the stubborn fitting let loose and Nick had a gusher on his hands.

Back in his office, Travis went to a table, set against a wall, where he'd laid out the blueprints. He flipped to the page containing the second-floor layout. Nothing jumped out at him. He leaned over to get a closer look at the area above where the library should be. He noted the chimney and the areas around it. What he hadn't realized on their previous inspections of the second floor was that the wide hallway circled the chimney—or did it? The plans showed a square room next to the chimney. No, that wasn't right. The hallway, accessed by both the main staircase and the servants' stairs, circled the room.

Travis stood up. A deep frown etched his forehead. That square room sat above the library. Why hadn't he noticed that before?

"Hey, man," Nick said from the doorway. "Whatever it is, it looks serious."

Travis motioned to his cousin. "Come in here. Look at this."

Nick moved to the table.

Travis pointed to the room in question. "Do you remember this room?"

Nick bent down to get a better look. "Yeah. It's a closet. More like a room without windows. I think it was something like the maid's workroom." He stood, still looking down. "You remember. It was lined with shelves on one wall and built-in cabinets on the other three. There was a large worktable in the center of the room with an iron sitting on top. The cabinets were full of sheets and blankets and pillows. There were stacks of towels. And cleaning supplies on the shelves." Nick chuckled. "You gotta remember. It was super creepy."

Travis shuddered. "Oh. Yeah. Now I remember. Lots of weird vibes in that room. I couldn't get out of there fast enough."

"Look. I'm sorry about how I acted." He paused, as if searching for the right words. "The place had been crawling all day with enough staff to clean a hotel, and all of them had questions. Then the dripping pipe right when I thought the kitchen was finally buttoned up tight."

"Not a problem. We're both tired."

"Yeah. But I shouldn't have taken it out on you." He broke out into one of his infectious smiles. "How about we blow this pop stand and I buy you dinner at the diner?"

"You're on! I'll just close up here and meet you in the kitchen," Travis said as he slapped his cousin on the back.

Ten minutes later, both men stood at the counter where Travis had left his cooler. They each glanced around the room with smiles from ear to ear, nodding their approval.

"Looks great," said Nick.

"And smells clean," Travis added as he picked up the cooler and headed toward the back door. "I think we can just make the five o'clock ferry."

The next morning, Travis caught the seven o'clock ferry hoping to be the first one to arrive. But once again, he parked next to his cousin's truck in front of the garage.

Nick appeared just as Travis opened his door. "I saw you pull in. The cleaning crew is scheduled to arrive around nine. We'll have some time before they get here to look for your missing light bulbs."

Travis jumped down from his Hummer and opened the rear door. "Here, help me unload this stuff." After their dinner the evening before and the discussions of how great the first floor of the cottage looked, Travis drove into Port Clinton for a quick shopping trip. "I picked up a few things last night to make our days here a little easier." It took two trips to get everything unloaded.

Travis filled his lungs as he set the last grocery bag on the counter. "Smells like pine . . . and bleach. Nothing like a clean kitchen."

"Are you moving in?" Nick asked jokingly.

Travis pulled condiments out of the first bag. "Ha ha! You jest. But you're going to thank me later when your stomach is grumbling."

Nick opened the cooler lid. "Wow. I hit the jackpot. I see milk, OJ, lunch meat, a tub of potato salad, cheese . . ."

Travis grabbed a bag in each arm and headed into the pantry. "Clean as a whistle and ready for the best stuff." He filled a shelf with bread, buns, three kinds of chips, four jars of dip, canned spaghetti, beef stew, and a large can of Folgers.

"Cooler's empty," said Nick as Travis entered the room with the empty bags. "I've started on the Walmart bags." He nodded toward the counter to the left of the sink. "You're my hero! You bought us a Mr. Coffee!"

"Had to. Your body runs on caffeine. I need to keep your engine fully supplied with fuel," Travis said as he pulled a medium-sized pot with a lid from the last bag, along with a set of utensils, cutlery, a small cutting board, and a package of paper plates. "This should keep us going for a while. At least until the twins arrive." He placed a bottle of dish detergent on the sink. "That shouldn't be for another couple of weeks."

Nick walked over to the window. "The crew is here. I'll get them started on the second floor."

"Not the maid's room," warned Travis. "I'm going to head up there after I finish in here."

"How about getting a pot of coffee going?" Nick shouted as he exited through the back door.

Half an hour later, Travis unrolled the blueprints across the maid's worktable and flipped to the page showing the second floor. He studied the plans for the area over the library and the chimney. Then he looked around the room, gauging the space. Something didn't add up. The room should be larger.

"Solve your mystery?" Nick asked from the doorway. His right hand held a coffee mug that read "I LOVE WORK."

Travis held up his mug that read "I LOVE BOATING." "I thought they were cute." He then pointed to the blueprint. "Take a look at this."

Nick walked over to the table and looked down. "Yeah. We've both studied this. A square, windowless room above a square, windowless library."

"That's what the prints show. We should be standing over the stained glass window. There should be some kind of access panel in the floor to reach the light bulbs. But look at this room—it isn't square. And unless there's a panel under this table . . ." Both men bent down to floor level and looked under the table. "There isn't one." Travis stood and looked directly into his cousin's eyes. "So how does one change the bulbs that illuminate the room below?"

Nick glanced at the far wall. "Those built-in cabinets are deep. That would account for the room not being square."

"Okay. Makes sense." Travis walked over to the cabinet and opened the center set of doors. "There should be a panel on the floor." He got down on his knees and ran his hands across the floor. "I'm not feeling anything. It's just not here." He got to his feet. "Do you have your tape measure handy?"

"Always." Nick reached to his side and unclipped the tape and handed it to Travis.

"We need to get accurate measurements of the room from inside the cabinets."

When they were convinced of the size, Travis noted it on the print. "Follow me," he said and grabbed the document off the table and headed into the hallway.

"What do you see?" Nick asked as they reached the door leading to the servants' stairs.

"What I see is that this door is deceiving. The stairway doesn't line up with that on the drawing. And the hallway up here is much narrower than noted on the prints." Travis measured the width of the hall. "Short by two feet."

"So that means, two feet all the way around." Nick did the calculations in his head. "That adds up to eight feet. Plus, the offset staircase. That's a lot of square footage."

"So where is it?" Travis asked as he headed back to the maid's room.

Both men stood at the worktable studying the back wall and the three sets of cabinets. The noise from the cleaning crew was getting louder.

"Close the door," Travis said. "And lock it. We don't need any inquisitive eyes looking on."

Nick went to the door. He checked that there wasn't anyone in the hall, then shut the door and locked it.

"What are you thinking?" Nick asked when he returned to the table.

"I'm thinking about the tunnels that we have in Virginia—at Fairfield and apparently at the house on Freemason Street."

"But those were built for escaping from Indian attacks and raids back in the 1700s at Fairfield, and possibly for hiding from Yankee soldiers during the Civil War." Nick shook his head as if his cousin was losing it. "Besides, we're on the second floor. No tunnels here."

"Same principle. It's all about access," Travis said with excitement as he opened all three sets of closet doors, then stepped back.

"Look. The center cabinet isn't as deep as the other two." He ran over and stepped inside. "This back panel must open somehow."

Nick followed, and both men ran their hands over the inside of the cabinet.

"Nothing," Travis said in defeat. "I thought for sure there would be a door. There *has* to be one. It's the only answer. There *is* a door leading to the other side of that wall. We just have to find it."

Nick stepped back to study the three units as a whole. "Each of these cabinets has a lock. Do you have the keys?"

"Yeah. In my desk downstairs. Why?"

"Look at the cabinet to the right. At the back left corner of the center shelf is a small compartment with a door. It has a lock."

Travis went over to the shelf. "You're right. I didn't notice it before. Maybe it's something like a mini safe. I'll run downstairs and get the ring of keys."

Nick began to worry when Travis didn't return right away. What if he couldn't find the keys? How would they open the lock?

"Sorry, it took me so long," Travis said, a bit out of breath. "Chuck Dempsey caught me with a dozen questions."

"Got the keys?"

"Yeah. Cross your fingers that the right one is in this mess."

Travis fanned out the ring of keys in the palm of his left hand. "The lock is unusually small. The key would look like one for a tiny chest or jewelry box." He fingered through the pile. Only one was small enough.

"Here we go," Travis said as he reached for the lock.

Nick squeezed his head alongside his cousin's to get a better look at what they would find inside.

The door swung open.

"A small lever," Travis whispered. "Should I pull it?"

"Why are you whispering? And yes, you should pull it—or I will."

"Seemed right at the moment," Travis stated and then pulled.

Both Travis and Nick jumped back at the sound of wood rubbing against wood.

They silently watched as the center cabinet swung open. A cloud of damp, musty, stale air drifted into the room.

Nick rested his hand on Travis's shoulder. "How about if I follow you in?"

Travis moved to the side and peered inside. "How about we get a flashlight first?"

Nick nearly ran across the room. "Be back in a flash. Get it? Flash? Flashlight?"

"Yeah. I got it. Just go!" Travis shouted.

Travis moved to the edge of the door trying to get his bearings. If this was above the stained glass, then there should be at least a little light coming from below. Unless the library door was closed. It probably was, since the cleaners had finished the first floor, and he and Chuck had discussed what needed to be done next with the paneling. He wondered how big the space would be. Probably just enough to give access for bulb changing and maybe cleaning the glass. It sure did smell bad.

He nearly jumped out of his skin when Nick shoved the flashlight at him. "You nearly scared the crap out of me! You could have let me know you were back!"

"I did when I shut the door and locked it."

"You didn't."

"I did. You—"

"Shut up!" Travis snarled as he focused the light on the space beyond. "Looks big enough for both of us from what I can see."

Nick followed as Travis stepped through the door, then stopped suddenly just a few steps inside. "The room looks pretty big, but there's some kind of metal railing in front of me. Hold on, I need to find a light switch or something." Travis trained the light along the inner doorframe, lots of cobwebs, then found a round switch. The cavernous space was flooded with light.

"Holy shit. . . it's huge!" Nick exclaimed. "I think I just stepped into an Indiana Jones movie."

"I sure wasn't expecting anything like this." Travis held on to the railing. "This is a whole lot more than lighting a stained glass ceiling."

Nick whistled. "I'm finding this whole area hard to put together in my mind. Its size is enormous. And completely hidden within these stone walls and ceiling."

"Besides feeling like we just stepped into the rabbit hole, what is this place?"

The large square space was at least a story high, maybe more with a stone shaft rising upward from the center. A narrow catwalk circled the area containing the glass ceiling, nestled in what appeared to be a roof with wooden shingles.

"Okay. I'm lost. Nothing remotely like this is shown in the blueprints. It doesn't make sense. This was a major engineering feat. Why?" Travis said, amazement filling his voice. "Why wasn't this recorded—anywhere?"

Nick took the flashlight and focused the beam on the sides and ceiling of the space. "The light bulbs continue around the room, therefore needing the catwalk. But, by the looks of them, they must have been installed about the time Thomas Edison was doing his thing. I've only seen this style of bulb in museums. I'm amazed so many of them still work."

"Where do you suppose that shaft goes to?"

"My guess, it opened to the roof to let natural light in. There must have been a skylight. Although it seems to be covered over now. I wish I had a way of seeing up there. Do you remember seeing any square patch of roof toward the center of the house?"

"No. But that doesn't mean it isn't there. If it isn't on the blueprints, how are we going to find it?" Travis asked.

"The tower. I haven't spent much time up there except to look around. But you can see most of the roof from there. The panel covering the shaft is there—somewhere. I'll find it."

Both men turned at the sound of someone knocking on the hallway door.

"We need to get out of here," Nick said as he moved through the doorway and into the maid's room.

Travis turned out the lights and followed him, then pushed the cabinet back into place just as there was another knock on the door.

"Coming," Nick shouted as he reached for the knob and swung open the door.

Chuck Dempsey stood on the other side. "I was just about to give up. Thought maybe you'd gone back downstairs." He stepped into the room. "Whew! It smells terrible in here." He glanced around. "All those built-in cabinets must be full of mold. I'll get a couple of people in here first thing in the morning and disinfect and sanitize the whole room."

"Oh. No need. I found the culprits. A couple of dead mice. I've already disposed of them," Nick explained.

"I insist." He took a whiff. "This isn't healthy. And if this room is like the rest of the house, those cabinets are full of old stuff."

Travis stepped forward and began rolling up the blueprints. "That's a great idea. Tomorrow will be fine." Best not to make the room seem off-limits for some reason, especially since the crew had had free run of the house for two days.

Nick reached out to shake Chuck's hand. "Thank you. Your crew have done a wonderful job. I know it has been tough."

"I have to admit, this job is one we will all remember . . . for a long time," Chuck laughingly said.

"Yep. Every day is a new challenge," Nick stated as he ushered Mr. Dempsey into the hallway, then watched until he disappeared through the servants' doorway.

"That was close," Travis said as he joined Nick in the hall. "Do you realize it's after three? We totally missed lunch."

Nick checked his watch. "I guess we did. I was too excited over our discovery to notice."

"How about I make us a couple of sandwiches to tide us over until dinner and I lock myself in my office and search the blueprints for the missing shaft cover?"

"Works for me." Nick scratched his head. "You were right. Bent Tree Cottage *does* have a secret—a big one."

CHAPTER TWENTY-ONE

An hour later, Travis headed out to the Hummer for the binoculars he kept in the glove compartment. Nick came around the corner of the garage in the golf cart.

"Hey! I see you got that thing running. Good vehicle to have around here," Travis said as he jumped onto the passenger side of his vehicle.

"Yep. Just needed a good cleaning, a new battery, and four new tires. Thought I'd run over to The Pines and see if the FBI has cleared out. Want to come along?"

"You go." Travis waved the binoculars. "I want to check out the tower and see if I can get a glimpse of that cover over the skylight."

Nick shut down the golf cart and jumped out. "No way! The Pines can wait until tomorrow. I'm going with you."

Travis and Nick literally ran through the house, up the servants' stairs to the third floor, then up another set of stairs to the attic. There, near the lakeside of the house, they came to a steel door that led to an iron circular staircase. At the top was yet another steel door with a large latch. Nick pulled the lever and pushed open the door. Travis followed him through to the most beautiful view of Lake Erie and the beginnings of what was sure to be a magnificent sunset.

Nick climbed up and stood on the crenelated wall. He reached his arm down toward Travis. "Hand me the binoculars. I have a good view of the large center chimney. The shaft cover should be within a few feet of that."

Travis handed them up, then looked around at the ornateness of the other four chimneys. They each consisted of two twisted stone columns joined together in a Gothic style. The large one in the center that Nick was focusing on was square and without embellishment.

"I see it!" Nick exclaimed. "It's not a cover. There is a patch of slate that doesn't exactly match the others. Like it was added later—much later by the look of it." He scanned the rest of the roof. "Everything looks amazingly in good shape. The slates are thick and were obviously laid by skilled craftsmen."

"This spot is magical. I wish it had an elevator instead of all those steps," commented Travis.

Nick laughed as he jumped down. "You're the owner. You can have anything you want. If you want an elevator, I'll get you an elevator!"

"Thanks. But my first priority is getting this place livable."

"Agree. For now, how about closing up for the day and we head over to the diner for a real meal?"

"Locking up is good. But today was Livy's big day at the Pentagon, and I'd like to be home when she calls."

"Oh. Hell. I totally forgot about that. Yeah, you need to get home. Like now!" Nick opened the steel door, then after going through, he slid the bolt in place, and they both headed down the stairs.

CHAPTER TWENTY-TWO

O livia and William Morrison waited outside the entrance of the Pentagon while Higgins went for the car. Their presentation of McLeod and Morrison's prototype tracking and surveillance device known as HELIOSmm-88 went well. Or so they were told by both the United States Secretary of the Navy and the Chief of Naval Operations who had been present on the aircraft carrier for the maneuvers. But were their endorsements enough to get the President's signature? He wasn't a personal friend. Olivia's mind played back every question, every answer she had given, every answer William had given during the grueling four-hour meeting. The Department of the Navy was sold on the device that would give every captain of our fleet the ability to identify, track, monitor, and literally "see inside" our enemies' ships. The endless questions, concerns, and doubts sat at the feet of the politicians who had their own agenda.

William put his arm around her shoulder. "It's going to be okay, Livy. This was just the dog and pony show that had to be played out. You understand politics as well as anyone. We have a device that both Russia and China know about. Our Navy knows that the clock is ticking." Olivia briefly rested her head against his chest. Like a daughter taking comfort from her father. "I'm the attorney in this operation. Let me do the worrying."

Olivia lifted her head as an older, dark-green sedan drove by as Higgins pulled up.

William opened the rear door of the black Cadillac and began helping Olivia in. "I've got this, Higgins. You don't need to get out."

"Thank you, Mr. Morrison," Higgins said while he continued looking forward.

After closing the door, William went around to the other door and got in.

Higgins turned in his seat. "Traffic is light. I'll have you back in Georgetown in no time."

Olivia leaned forward. "Higgins, can you swing over to East Point Park first? I just need a few minutes of fresh air."

"I don't think that is good idea. It's too open. Too many people around. It's a popular place for tourists this time of year."

"Please, Higgins. I've been locked up in that room for four hours with hostile politicians firing unbelievably stupid questions at me. My nerves are fried. I just need fresh air and green grass."

William took her hand in his. "It will be okay, Higgins. Just a few minutes."

"I don't like it," Higgins mumbled as he drove from the parking lot.

The park was close, practically on their way to Georgetown. It seemed like only a few minutes before Higgins had negotiated traffic, crossed the Potomac River, and pulled into the park.

"I wish the cherry trees were still in bloom," Olivia said as she lowered her window.

"Higgins, can you please pull over so I can get out and walk?"

"It isn't safe."

"Higgins, no one knows who I am here. I'm just a lady sitting with a man in the back seat of a car."

"I can't protect you out here in the open."

"Higgins, this is not a request any longer," Olivia raised her voice. "This is an order!"

William leaned forward. "Pull over to the side and park. We'll both be with her."

Olivia let out a sigh of relief. This feeling of unnecessary panic was so unusual. Especially since all the work and preparations for the presentation were over and it had been a resounding success. And if she were honest, the questions hadn't been all that bad. She just needed some fresh air and a little walk to clear her of the jitters she'd been having after those horrible dreams. Nothing had happened. HELIOS was a success.

Olivia grabbed her purse and briefcase as William helped her out of the car. "Higgins, my things might be safer in the trunk. She raised her arm to hand them to him as he popped the trunk lid. Just then, a car approached, going much too fast on the narrow roadway. Olivia screamed. Higgins leaped forward, knocking her and William against the Cadillac. Her handbag and briefcase went flying as the car came to an abrupt stop.

Olivia was dazed and shaking when a little old lady got out of the car and rushed toward them. She was shorter than average, with curly silver hair that seemed to glisten in the sunlight. The rather round woman wore a tan raincoat over a blue dress that fell well below her knees. Support hose-covered stovepipe legs were stuffed into well-worn Nikes.

"Oh my! I'm so sorry. So sorry." She bent down and picked up Olivia's handbag and began brushing dirt off the caramel-colored leather. "Oh my, I hope I didn't ruin your lovely bag." She handed it to Olivia. "My dear, are you all right? I'm so sorry. I don't know what happened." The woman looked old and feeble.

Her voice raspy. "I was feeding the birds down at Hains Point." She gestured with her arm, indicating where she'd been. "I come here often. My daughter says that I should stop driving. Can you imagine? She wants to take my keys away from me. Can you imagine?"

William steadied Olivia, then took a step away from the hood of the car.

Higgins turned to the senior and guided her away from Olivia. "You could have killed us. Maybe you should consider alternative means of transportation."

"No, I'm a good driver. I was driving real slow, and I saw you pulled over where no one ever stops. I thought maybe you had a flat tire or something. Then I saw your trunk fly open." Her arms flew up in front of her as to demonstrate the trunk opening. "So, I stepped on the brake. Maybe I stepped too hard. Then, just like that, the car went racing toward you." She put her white-gloved hands to her cheeks. "I don't know what happened. I'm so sorry."

Higgins moved to Olivia's side. "Are you hurt? I hit you pretty hard with my body."

Olivia rubbed her sore shoulder. "I'm okay. That was a close one. Thank you."

Granny started to move forward. "My dear, you're hurt."

Higgins turned toward her. "Don't come any closer. She's fine. We're all fine. Now get in your car and leave."

Olivia watched as the old woman, now slightly hunched over, shuffled to her car, then bent down. She picked up the briefcase, which had managed to land just behind the woman's rear tire. She then walked to the front of her older model sedan.

"Wait!" Olivia shouted as Higgins took off at lightning speed to retrieve the case.

Granny looked confused when Higgins reached her and grabbed for the briefcase. "Oh my. What am I doing? I'm confused. I should give this to the lady."

"Not a problem, ma'am. We all get confused." Higgins tucked the case under his arm, then opened her door and helped her inside. He then waited until she started the vehicle and pulled away.

Olivia and William had already seated themselves in the back seat by the time Higgins returned to the car. After settling himself in the driver's seat, Higgins reached his arm back and handed Olivia her briefcase. "Are you both *really* all right?"

"I assume you mean physically. Yes, I'm fine. Except for a sore arm and shoulder due to a giant of a man slamming me against a very big Cadillac." Olivia glanced out the window. "I think we'll skip the walk-in-the-park. Georgetown has about as much fresh air as I can take at the moment."

"Good to see you haven't lost you sense of humor," Higgins said as he turned back in his seat and started the powerful engine.

William took Olivia's hand. "We were lucky. We could have been killed."

"The dream. It's come the last two nights at your house. That's why I haven't been sleeping well. It's always a warning. I figured it had something to do with our presentation. Or something bad was going to happen in the building or outside. That's why I was so on edge during the meeting." Olivia shook her head. "I let my guard down as soon as we got in the car. I felt safe."

"It was just a freak accident. A little old lady lost control of her car. Look, how many times have we seen it on the news? A senior citizen steps on the accelerator instead of the brake and crashes into a building." He patted her hand. "Just a freak accident," William said as he glanced up to the rearview mirror. Higgins wasn't buying it.

CHAPTER TWENTY-THREE

Travis checked his watch. Eight thirty. Something was wrong. Livy should have called by now. Maybe the presentation hadn't gone well, and she and William were working on a new strategy. Maybe the presentation had gone great, and she was on her way home. Maybe they were out celebrating, and she lost track of time. This wasn't like Livy. She always checked in when she was away, even if it was a quick "Hi, honey, I'm fine. Can't talk. Call you when I can."

And today, of all days, he wanted to tell her what they had discovered. He couldn't wait any longer. He punched in the number for her mobile phone.

Olivia answered on the fourth ring. "Hello?" She sounded like she'd been asleep. Livy was a working machine—she didn't take naps.

"Sorry to disturb you, honey. I got worried when you didn't call. Is everything all right? How did the meeting at the Pentagon go? You're just not going to believe what happened to Nick and me today."

"What time is it?"

"Eight thirty-five."

"Oh my. It's been a busy day. I was talking to William in the library after dinner. I must have fallen asleep." She paused a moment. "Looks like he draped a blanket over me. I must have been out cold."

"Livy, you're still in DC? I thought you were going home to Fairfield after the meeting. What happened?" Travis remembered their last conversation. "Oh no! It was that dream you had. I know something happened. Tell me!"

Olivia gave Travis an account of the entire day, ending when they arrived at William's house in Georgetown.

Travis listened without saying or commenting. He knew that if he asked for details, his wife might lose her train of thought and she'd leave something important out.

"Livy, honey, it sounds like a simple accident. I'm sure that old lady had a senile moment. Her daughter is right to take her mother's car keys away. The incident sounds bizarre, but I'm sure some random, old lady didn't deliberately try to run you down."

"I know you're right. It's just that I haven't been this close to death since I searched for my grandmother's killer. It brought up old memories—and fears."

"So, what happened after you got to Georgetown that made you decided not to head home to Fairfield?"

"Higgins did one of his debriefings with William and me, like he does when he's trying to get all the facts about something. A few minutes later, he left the house, and we filled Caroline in on what happened."

Travis thought about Higgins leaving without giving a reason. Being Olivia's chief of security, he also acted as her bodyguard. Where did Higgins go that was so important?

"How long was he gone?"

Olivia thought for a moment. "I guess close to two hours. He'd called someone as soon as we had gotten to the house to check on the woman's license plate number. Higgins then went to her house in Fairfax. He said it was a modest, brick ranch, seemed to be well cared for. The old lady was there. Her name is Mabel Polanski. Her daughter was there too—Sheryl. Higgins said they were both very sorry for what happened. Sheryl promised that from now on, her mother would drive the car for emergencies only or doctor appointments."

"Did Higgins say anything else?"

"No. Only that it appears to be the case of an elderly woman hitting the gas pedal instead of the brake. We were in the wrong place at the wrong time."

Travis thought about what his wife had said.

"Travis, you're too quiet. What is it?"

"How far away is Fairfax from the park?"

"I don't know. Maybe fifteen miles. Why?"

"I was just wondering why an elderly woman, who shouldn't be driving, drives all that way, in DC traffic . . . to feed birds."

"Huh. You do have a point." Olivia paused for a moment. "Doesn't make much sense. Anyway, it's over, and Higgins is satisfied. We'll be flying back to Norfolk first thing in the morning. After a quick meeting with the R&D department, I'll head home to Fairfield."

"Okay, sweetheart. I'll call tomorrow night at our usual time. I know the twins are anxious to have you home again."

"Good night, honey . . . Oh, wait. Was there something you wanted to tell me?"

Travis thought about Bent Tree Cottage's secret room, and how excited he and Nick had been about the discovery. But the time for his story had passed.

"It can wait. Sleep well, Livy. I love you."

CHAPTER TWENTY-FOUR

The next morning, Travis entered the kitchen at Bent Tree Cottage to find Nick at the counter pouring his first cup of coffee. He raised the mug to show the words on the front. "I LOVE WORK! Really, cuz?"

"It seemed appropriate. You are a workaholic—always have been."

"I love boats too. How come you didn't get me one of those?"

"The store only had one. And I did the picking."

"Hey, did you talk to Olivia last night? How did her meeting go at the Pentagon? Is McLeod and Morrison going to get the contract for the top-secret thing? Was she excited when you told her about our *secret* thing? Like a whole *secret room*?"

"Yeah. We talked. The meeting went fine." Travis walked over to the coffeepot and filled his I LOVE BOATING mug. "I didn't have a chance to tell her because—"

"Why not? This is big news. It's a real mystery. I can't believe you—"

"Olivia was almost killed yesterday."

"What? How? Where was Higgins?" stammered Nick.

Half an hour later, Travis finished giving his cousin the full account of what happened. And answered what questions that he could.

"Well, I certainly understand why you never got around to telling her our news. But something just doesn't sit right with me." Nick scrunched his brow and tilted his head to one side. Like he was digging in his brain for some illusive tidbit. "So, why does a little old lady, who can't seem to keep her car on the road, drive fifteen miles in DC traffic to feed birds?"

"Looks like neither of us has a logical answer for that. And if we are both wondering it, then I'm sure Higgins is wondering it too."

Both men looked up as the kitchen door opened.

"Excuse me, Nick—Travis. I wonder if I may have a word with you."

"Of course. You caught us at the perfect time," answered Nick. "Would like a coffee? I'm sure we have a mug that says 'I LOVE CLEANING,'" Nick said with a laugh.

Travis raised his eyebrows and rolled his eyes.

"No, thank you. My crew finished yesterday. I'm here to do a final walk-through. But I wanted to go over a few things with you both first."

"Of course," Travis gestured toward the kitchen table.

After the three men were seated, Chuck Dempsey continued. "As you requested, we removed all the drapes and bedding that were badly damaged or couldn't be salvaged. That includes throw rugs. The large oriental rugs will be taken to a company in Cleveland for repair and cleaning. Our insurance doesn't allow us to handle the personal items such as clothes and such. Those things were left for you to handle. Weird thing about one of the bedrooms, the big one overlooking the lake. It's almost like someone has been using it. The lace curtains show almost no wear, and even the mattress is like new. Even though it's down filled and obviously custom-made for that bed. We left that room alone."

A sudden chill caused Travis to gasp. He thought back to the day when he'd fallen asleep and had a dream that he was standing at the window in that very room looking down at himself as a young boy.

"Are you okay, Travis?" Mr. Dempsey asked.

"Oh. Yeah. I'm fine. Please continue."

"Now, for the library." Chuck took a sheet of paper out of his attaché case and placed it on the table. "Here is the name and contact information for a restoration company in New York. They have excellent credentials and will not only be able to restore all the paneling throughout the house but the stained glass as well. They are known all over the world for their fine work. This house is quite unique and, when it is finished, could rival any of the historic homes, or even boutique hotels across the globe."

"Thank you, but I haven't determined what my plans are yet," added Travis.

"Of course. You have that wonderful estate in Marblehead— the old Captain's House. I just figured that Long Point would make an amazing resort here on Kelleys."

"Winters might be a problem when Erie freezes over, and the ferry isn't running," Nick added with humor.

"That about wraps it up. I'm going to take a few minutes to nose around in the library and see if I can figure out how to access the stained glass panel to change the light bulbs. I wouldn't want you to be left in the dark when the last bulb burns out and no way to change them," Chuck said as he pushed back his chair and got to his feet.

Travis and Nick looked at each other wide-eyed. They couldn't let that happen.

Travis jumped to his feet. "Look, Mr. Dempsey, you and your people have done a wonderful job here. We really appreciate what you've accomplished."

"We sure do. And we will certainly call on you again if we need you. But, for now, I have electrical issues in the library, so I'll take care of the mystery light bulbs myself," Nick added as he got to his feet. "So, if that's all, we'll walk you out to your truck."

Mr. Dempsey shook both Travis's and Nick's hands, then turned to leave by the back door. "You can expect my invoice in a week or two."

"Great. I'll watch for it." Whew, Travis thought as he followed the two men to the door. That was a close one.

An hour later, Travis and Nick set up one of three battery-powered floodlights attached to tripods in the center of the library. "Okay, what do you see? We need to be looking at this with new eyes," said Travis.

Nick scanned the room. "At first glance, I see that this room doesn't match, in style, with the rest of the house. The paneling is simple knotty pine that doesn't match the Gothic-style oak in the other rooms. The fireplace is extra-large, and more Colonial in design, big enough to cook in. The coffered ceiling looks to be a finer hardwood like cherry or mahogany—doesn't match the walls."

"Why was a room this lovely buried in the center of the house with no windows?" asked Travis.

Nick grabbed one of the other two lamps. "Take the other one and let's head upstairs. This will be enough light to illuminate every inch of that space."

Once the floodlights were in place and turned on, Travis went back into the maid's room and grabbed the blueprints from the table.

Travis folded the large document to get a better look at the area in question. "The blueprint shows a square space exactly the same size as the library below. The notation is *storage*. The only other thing shown is electrical outlets on each of the four walls."

"Well, we know it isn't storage." Nick patted the railing. "This is made of lengths of iron pipe fastened together at intervals with uprights. It's sturdy but not made for safety—more like something to hold on to." He bent down closer to the floor. He leaned over to get a better look at the glass panel. "This is weird. I would think that the stained glass would sit flush with the surrounding wooden frame—but it doesn't." He stood. "Is there a page toward the back that shows the ceiling below? I'm looking for the structure of some kind. The stained glass sits snugly in the coffered ceiling in the library. But up here, the coffered part is covered. Maybe the last page of the prints shows the coffered design and what holds all this together."

"There isn't one," Travis insisted.

"There has to be," Nick said as he grabbed the folded blueprints from his cousin and scanned the back pages. "Nothing. Sorry. You were right."

"So how did they clean this side of the glass panel?" Travis asked.

Nick looked over the railing. "I guess they climbed down onto the wood and inched their way around. Or maybe they never did clean it. After all, this place has been closed up for decades, and it looks pretty good to me."

Travis gave a defeated sigh. "Well, we're not going to get any answers today. I'm ready to call it a day. I'd like to get home early and check in on Livy."

"Sounds good. I've got electricians and plumbers coming in tomorrow to access the job. Hopefully, they can work together."

Travis glanced at his watch. "Two thirty. We missed lunch again. I can make us a couple of sandwiches if you're hungry."

"Naw. I can wait. I had a big breakfast. Maybe I'll stop by the diner and catch an early dinner after I pick up a few things at the hardware store in Port Clinton."

"Sounds good to me. Meet back here around eight in the morning?" Travis asked as he turned out the lights and followed his cousin into the maid's room.

CHAPTER TWENTY-FIVE

Travis stopped at Mutach's Market on his way home to pick up a steak, potato, a can of green beans, and a tub of Rocky Road ice cream. He wished Emily Elfin had been in the store to see what he was having for dinner. She certainly couldn't accuse him of not eating right. He briefly thought about swinging by her office just to have her inspect his grocery bags. But the less he saw of her, the better. He didn't want to listen to her go off on another tirade about him living without a housekeeper. Especially since she was the one who couldn't seem to find one who met her expectations.

By five o'clock, he'd finished dinner, washed the dishes, and had the kitchen looking good enough for even Mrs. Campbell's approval. He hoped the couple, who had managed the house so well for so many years, were happy with their new life in Florida. He sure missed them, and her endless supply of fresh-baked cookies.

Travis couldn't wait any longer to call his wife and get an update on what had happened. He was also anxious to tell her of the new mystery on Long Point.

After grabbing a beer from the fridge, Travis settled himself against the pillows on the couch and picked up the phone and punched in the numbers for Fairfield.

"Hello, Tanner residence." It was Sarah's voice.

"Hello, Sarah. It's good to hear your voice. I sure do miss your cooking."

"Mr. Tanner, I hope everything up in Ohio is going well. The twins are counting the days before they arrive. They've finally mastered the art of sword fighting. We've only lost one eighteenth-century vase, a rather ugly ceramic duck that was given to Mr. McLeod back in the '50s, and a flowerpot on the terrace. The staircase, however, has received more nicks than those added by General George McClellan while camped here 1862."

Travis laughed, although he cringed at the thought of what damage his plastic-sword wielding sons were going to inflict on Long Point.

"Has Olivia gotten home yet?"

"Yes. She's in the library, deep in the middle of an ongoing game of Monopoly. I'll transfer you to that phone."

"Thank you, Sarah."

Only seconds went by before his wife picked up. "Hello? Travis. I'm glad you called."

At the sound of his name, his sons' excited voices could be heard in the background. "Honey, let me put you on hold while the boys and I move to my office. That way we can all talk to you."

It took about fifteen minutes before Andy and Freddy finished telling their dad everything they had done in the last twenty-four hours, since their last conversation, and what they planned to do when they arrived in Marblehead in a few weeks.

"Okay, you boys find another game that you can play together while I talk to your dad." Olivia waited until the twins had left the room and then shut and locked the door.

Travis heard the door close and the faint sound of the lock clicking into place. This wasn't a good sign. She never locked the doors unless she was in a business meeting. "Livy, is something wrong? Why are you locking the boys out? Are you okay?"

"I'm fine, except for a sore arm and shoulder. I heard from William. He's gotten nothing but positive feedback on our presentation and the sea trials his team of lawyers are working on the contracts as we speak. He thinks our only issues will be price and time frame on delivery schedules."

"That's wonderful news. Congratulations."

"I can finally slow down and relax here at Fairfield for a while. William will handle everything at the yard. So, I don't need to make any trips to Norfolk."

"What about the break-in?" Travis asked.

"Higgins has one of his contacts at the National Archives working on the history of the house. Nathaniel is still doing an inventory to make sure nothing but the contents of the safe are missing. I still can't figure out why anyone would go to that much trouble to steal financial information on my charities." Olivia paused a moment. "They are all related to children. Who would want to hurt children?"

"It will be interesting to find out more about the history of the house and maybe learn more about the surrounding area. I was impressed years ago when I did all those walking tours—a couple were right there in the neighborhood."

Olivia laughed. "I remember. You became Hampton Roads' most active and enthusiastic tourist."

"And don't forget my newfound expertise on shipbuilding and maritime history," Travis added. "I can't wait for the boys to get old enough to take them on the same tours. They already love history."

"Yes, they do. And they are going to love exploring Kelleys, and all the Lake Erie Islands. They are already talking about going back up to the top of Perry's Monument."

"Great. It will certainly be an exciting summer for them." Travis was glad that he still had a couple of weeks before the excitement began.

"Travis?"

"Livy. You sound worried. What's wrong?"

"Higgins wants to send the boys early."

Travis's heart stopped. "Early? How early?"

"Day after tomorrow."

CHAPTER TWENTY-SIX

"Holy crap!" Travis said out loud as he hung up the phone. He'd pressed his wife for more information, but she kept saying that Higgins thought it best. Higgins doesn't make spur-of-the-moment decisions like this. What did he know that he hadn't told Olivia? And why get the boys out of Virginia and not Livy?

Travis picked up the phone and punched in Higgins's private number. It would ring in his command center located in a room next to his bedroom on the second floor at Fairfield. It was like something out of NASA, or the CIA, or the FBI, or Star Wars. A row of monitors on a shelf provided images from cameras located in various areas around the house and in every building outside. The ground's cameras were sophisticated enough to pick up a stray squirrel that dared to cross its path, not to mention the ones focused on the James River and even the underside of the boat dock. Listening devices were also located at the camera sites. There were half a dozen phones, including a red one that no one but Higgins knew who would answer. From that room, he

151

could lock and unlock every outside gate, as well as the doors in the house that led outside.

"Hello, Travis. Is everything all right in Marblehead? I bet you're happy that the FBI has pulled out of Long Point."

Travis thought about that question for a moment. "How do you know about the FBI leaving? I don't remember mentioning that to Livy." He'd been leaving out a lot during their conversations lately. "Maybe I did tell her."

"I don't believe you did—I received a call."

"Of course, you did. You have eyes and ears everywhere."

"The reason for your call?" Higgins sounded like he'd been interrupted from something important.

"Livy doesn't know why you want to send the boys here early. Like this *weekend*? What's happening that you don't want her to know about?"

"I've received new information from the feelers I've got out there."

Travis wondered what feelers that might be. But he knew not to ask.

"I want to know, Higgins. I have a right to know, and I'm not going to stop hounding you until I'm satisfied."

There was a long pause, like Higgins was sorting through what he'd learned and how he should phrase it to Travis.

"You know about the events that happened after the meeting and how I later went to Mabel Polanski's house and talked to her and her daughter."

"Yes, Livy told me."

"Well, that evening, something just didn't sit right with me about the visit. My gut was telling me the two of them and the house was too perfect. They invited me in. But we never left the living room, and once they were done with their story, they all but pushed me out the door. Also, I'd forgotten to ask Mabel why she'd driven so far and dressed so nice, even wearing white gloves to feed birds. So, the next morning, before we flew back to Norfolk, I went back to the house."

Travis interrupted. "Wow. I picked up on the bird thing too."

"When I parked in front of the house and got out, everything looked the same as the day before. Mabel's older, dark-green sedan was parked in the same spot in the drive, and her daughter's car was in the garage. But no one answered the door. I walked around the yard. The garbage cans were empty, and all the drapes were pulled tight. I couldn't see inside. Before I reached the street, a neighbor stopped me. He said he'd seen me the day before and asked if I was looking for the Polanskis. I explained how I was hoping to talk to her and her daughter again. The man rubbed his head and looked at me like I was casing the place or something."

"That sounds funny. Like a guy who looks like you, wears a black suit, and drives a Cadillac would be casing a home like that one."

Higgins ignored the comment and continued.

"He said that the Polanskis only had a son, no daughter. And they were out of town for the month. I asked if she might have come back for some reason and driven her green car into DC yesterday. The guy laughed and said Mabel wouldn't be caught dead driving that old wreck. The green car was Mr. Polanski's. Mabel drove the newer white Toyota she kept in the garage."

"So that wasn't the real Mabel?" asked Travis.

"I described the Mabel from yesterday. The neighbor said it sounded like her, but she'd never wear a getup like that and especially not white gloves—and she was anything but feeble."

"Higgins? Are you saying that a woman disguised herself to look like Mabel Polanski drove Mabel's husband's car to East Point Park to run down Olivia and William, then drive back, and break into the house?"

"It does sound like a scene from a spy novel. And why does someone go to such lengths to break into a highly secure house the day before Olivia arrives in DC? I don't believe in coincidences. I'm going to find out who is behind this, and I don't want your sons here."

"But Fairfield is totally secure. Andy and Freddy will be safer there than a little town in Ohio."

"I thought the house on Freemason Street was totally secure as well."

"Point taken. I'll start preparing the house."

CHAPTER TWENTY-SEVEN

Travis jumped up from the couch and began pacing around the room. His schedule for the next couple of weeks had flown out the window with the speed of a cyclone. He needed to make calls. To whom? He needed to prepare the house for the whirlwind that would surely accompany his two energetic sons. And there would be the entourage, even without Livy. The boys lived and traveled with their tutor, Reginald Warrington, and whichever security person Higgins deemed appropriate at the time. There were rooms to prepare—that was the job of the housekeeper, which he didn't have. He needed one *now*. He needed to call Emily. Surely, by now she should have at least one viable candidate for the job. What was he supposed to do now?

He picked up the phone and punched in his cousin's number. "Hello?"

"Nick, you're not going to believe what is happening. I don't know what to do. I don't have a housekeeper. I need a house-keeper to get the house ready in two days. I have a million things to do to prepare. I love them, but this is too much. You must help me. I have to call Emily."

"Whoa there, cuz. You sound in a panic." Nick laughed. "What is it? The twins are coming early?"

"Yes, in two days!"

"Hey, man. I'm joking."

"I'm not. I talked to Higgins a few minutes ago. That little old lady was a fake."

"Okay. Slow down and tell me what happened."

Travis inhaled deeply and filled Nick in on the conversation he'd had with Higgins.

Nick whistled. "Sounds like spy stuff. If Higgins is worried about the boys' safety, then why send them here? Seems to me they'd be better off at Fairfield."

"Higgins doesn't know what the threat is about, but he is sure that it is somehow connected to the break-in in Norfolk. Also, it can't be a coincidence that Olivia and William had just left the Pentagon following that top-secret meeting. Higgins mentioned that the old lady grabbed Livy's briefcase on her way to her car. He took it away from her as she went to get inside."

Nick thought about that for a few seconds. "It sounds like those events all tie in together. My guess is that whoever is after something like documents won't stop until they get them."

"Yep. That's what I'm thinking. And I'm sure that's what Higgins is thinking. So, he figures it is best to get the boys out of Virginia and far away from whatever these guys are after. Obviously, two eight-year-olds don't have whatever is so important, nor do they know where it is."

"And I'm thinking you won't be back to Long Point until sometime next week. I'll take care of the electricians and plumbers, which you pay me to do anyway, and our mystery room can wait."

"You are so perceptive. My next call should be to Emily."

"Good luck with that one, cuz. That woman is looney. I try my best to keep clear," Nick said, ending the call.

Travis didn't know Emily's home number off the top of his head, so he headed to the library for the address book that Olivia kept in the upper desk drawer.

He flipped to the page marked *E* and found the numbers listed for Elfin—her home and office and a mobile number. The phone rang as he went to punch in the number. "Hello?"

"Travis, it's Emily."

"Of course, it is! I was ready to dial in your number. But you knew that, didn't you? It's that ESP thing you have."

"No. It isn't. Olivia just called me. Now, don't you worry about a thing. I'll have you and the house ready for my boys in no time. I can't wait to see those precious darlings. It's been too long." Emily paused long enough to catch her breath. "They must be getting so big."

Travis counted to ten in his head. "You saw them last Christmas. It's been five months. But I'm sure the little devils have grown a whole inch since then." Like his cousin, Travis didn't have a lot of patience when it came to her psychic abilities, but Olivia adored her, and after all, Emily did say she would handle everything. "I know both me and the house will be in good hands. I really appreciate your help, Emily."

"Perfect. I'll see you first thing in the morning."

The line went dead, and Travis returned the handset to the cradle.

⚒

The next morning, Travis finished a breakfast of sausage and eggs and was placing the dishes in the sink when the front-gate alarm sounded and the image of Emily, sitting in her red Bronco, flashed across the monitor. He checked his watch. Seven thirty.

She did say early morning. So, his day was about to begin. He then reached for the control panel and pressed the intercom button. "Good morning, Emily," Travis said as he flipped the switch that would open the gate. Next, he poured himself another mug of coffee and headed to the side door. Emily's tiny frame slid down from the driver's seat; her head did a little bounce as her feet hit the pavement. She looked up toward the side door and smiled—that wide, infectious smile that made her eyes crinkle. She still had a mop of short, curly, gray hair and rosy cheeks that made Travis think of Mrs. Claus. He held the door open as she waddled her way through. Her uneven gait was caused by a birth defect of her left hip. But it had never held her back in any way. It was part of the total package—her uniqueness—her psychicness.

"I have a fresh pot of coffee, if you're interested. I thought we could talk in the morning room. Have you had breakfast? If not, I'm pretty good with anything from eggs and sausage to pancakes."

"Oh my. Thank you, but no. I ate an hour ago—I'm an early riser. But I will take a cup of coffee; cream, if you have it. No sugar."

Travis pulled a carton of half-and-half from the fridge and poured a small amount into a cup he'd pulled from a cabinet in the butler's pantry. "I prefer using this to milk in scrambled eggs and my special pancake recipe. It gives a richer flavor to almost everything when cooking," he said, hoping to impress her with his culinary skills.

Emily picked up her cup and headed to the morning room. "I've always loved this room. It was one of the things that convinced Olivia to buy the house. The room gives off warm, comforting vibes. Almost like it absorbs the earth's morning energy and holds it within to be enjoyed throughout the day."

Travis didn't feel the vibes, but he'd always enjoyed the space, especially during storms. He watched as Emily pulled out a chair and casually sat down as if she did it every day. Must be those happy vibes she was feeling, he thought as he pulled out the chair across the table and sat down.

"Okay. I've got a plan for how we can make this work. I can't believe we haven't had a dozen or more applicants for your house-keeper position. But don't you fret any. I have this under control."

Travis had no doubts that Emily had worked out a campaign that would rival any of the country's top generals. He only hoped that he could follow her orders.

"I'll schedule your cleaning gals to begin the weekly schedule rather than the biweekly that you are on now. I've talked to your Aunt Mavis, and she will arrange her days so she can be here for meal preparations. And, of course, I'll help wherever I'm needed. Now, let us take a walk through the house from the cellar to that glorious room above the attic. I know that it's the boys' favorite play area. Freddy tells me they go up there to spy on the town."

There was that word again—"spy." People who weren't who they seemed—watching, listening. A cold chill raced through his body. "I think we should check the attic first where Reginald and our security people have rooms."

They did a quick inspection of the house in less than an hour, which was made easier since Emily was the real estate agent who had sold Olivia the property, and they had remained close friends ever since. After a few minutes in the basement, they headed back upstairs to the kitchen.

"Your cleaning gals are doing a great job. You don't want to lose them. I don't see anything that needs to be addressed except for a housekeeper. However, it would help us tremendously if you could find Mrs. Campbell's Bible."

"Bible?"

"Yes. You're looking for a ledger or notebook that has her household notes. Like the preferences for family members and those living in the house or guests. The entries would contain their likes and dislikes. For example, you would find things like a person's favorite brand of soap, notes on their routines, whether they have allergies to certain foods. You may also find a cook's book. That will probably be a loose-leaf binder containing favorite recipes and menus. Also, it should contain notes on the various guests and their food preferences. Notes on your entertaining habits, like for your annual Christmas open house."

"Wow. That does sound important. Especially for the new person who takes over—if we ever find one," said Travis.

"We will. For now, those two items will help Mavis and I get things moving along without a hitch."

"Thank you, Emily. I'll start looking in Mrs. Campbell's office. I'm sure it is in there."

"Wonderful. Now I must run. Apparently, I have an irate applicant meeting me in twenty minutes."

Travis escorted Emily out to her vehicle and then returned to the kitchen for a coffee refill. He thought about the last thing Emily said about an irate applicant. He was under the impression there were no candidates for the housekeeper's job. With a fresh supply of caffeine in hand, he set off to find a Bible.

CHAPTER TWENTY-EIGHT

B y ten o'clock that morning, Travis had both the Bible and cook's book spread out on the kitchen table. He flipped to the pages in the cook's book for Andy and Freddy's preferences. Except for peanut butter, the large tub, which already resided on the pantry shelf, Travis would need to do a full-blown shopping trip to Port Clinton. As an attentive father who spent as many meals as he could with his sons, Travis figured grocery shopping would be a breeze. But the loose-leaf binder took the meals and servings down to the ingredients in many cases. Then there was the dessert and baking section. At that point, Travis took a legal pad, pen, and the binder to the pantry and began running down the list of foods. Thanks to Mrs. Campbell's efficiency, and her PANTRY LIST, Travis was able to determine what items were missing.

Next came the boys' room and throwing their Star Wars sheets and bedding into the washer and adding fresh towels in their bathroom. Back when the twins were still in their cribs, it was decided that the babies would each have a room of their own with an adjoining bathroom. But that never happened. The toddlers didn't want to be separated, so they shared the larger of the two rooms, and the nanny moved into the other one. Now the bedroom had become Reginald's.

The third-floor bedrooms had been taken over by Higgins and his security team, and since there was only one security person coming, Travis quickly changed the sheets and went back down to the kitchen for a sandwich.

He had no more than taken his first bite when the phone rang. "Hello?"

"Travis, dear. It's Mavis. I just called to say that I will stop by in an hour or two and go over meal planning for next week. That way your boys will get what they like, and I can put together a shopping list."

"Thanks, Aunt Mavis. I found Mrs. Campbell's book and checked the pantry. I didn't realize how limited my eating habits have been when not eating at the diner. You are certainly welcome to stop by. But I think most of what you are going to need will be here, except maybe meats and perishables. I plan to swing by Bassett's Market in Port Clinton tomorrow and stock up."

"How about I stop by tomorrow after the afternoon rush at the diner and see what you've got? I'll also let Emily know what's happening."

"Wonderful," Travis said but didn't sound much above okay.

He hung up feeling like he had already lost the first battle with Emily and company. If those two were this deep into plans, then the whole town would know by tomorrow morning that the twins were arriving. And by Saturday morning, the whole town would know Lorenzo's flight plan and ETA at the Port Clinton airport. He was afraid the already healthy town grapevine was about to be fed a healthy dose of fertilizer.

Travis nestled into the luxurious comfort of their Lincoln Town Car. His earlier trepidation turned to excitement as soon as he had the powerful vehicle cruising along Route 163 out of Marblehead. He was ready, the house was ready, and he couldn't wait for his sons to join his world for the summer. He was surprised when he entered the airport parking lot to find Emily getting out of her Bronco. She explained that she had received a last-minute call from Olivia asking her to meet the plane. Emily wasn't sure why—she just came.

"By the way, what happened with the irate applicant that you had to meet with?"

"She sure laid into me about my lack of professionalism, and even if she didn't meet the qualifications I was looking for, I should have sent her an official rejection letter. I explained how I never received her application, but I would be happy to take a minute and review her résumé and we could discuss it in my office. She practically threw her résumé at me and said she wouldn't work for anyone who was so lax in common curtsies."

"Boy, that sounds awful. I'm sorry you had to go through that. I wonder what happened to her original letter."

"I called the postmaster about my lack of mail to my postal box. He assured me that I received all the mail that was addressed to me, or even to the box number."

"Was she a viable candidate?"

"No way! I wouldn't hire her to feed my cat and water my plants."

"Okay. That settles that," Travis said as he motioned for them to head for the terminal building.

Nearly twenty minutes later, Travis and Emily were still sitting in the small waiting room at the Port Clinton airport. Travis glanced up at the clock—noon. "They're late. I hope nothing happened."

"Olivia is usually very explicit with instructions. And she didn't explain why she wanted me here."

"Excuse me. Are you Mr. Tanner?" Travis turned to see a middle-aged man wearing an official-looking uniform approach.

"Yes, I am."

"Your wife has been trying to reach you on your mobile phone. The plane is en route, but she would like you to call her at home."

"Thank you. I left my phone in the car," Travis said as he got up from his chair.

"Do you think something has happened?" asked Emily as she too jumped to her feet.

"I don't know, but Livy is never late without letting me know in advance."

They both rushed through the small terminal and out to the parking lot. Travis had driven their Lincoln Town Car, since it was larger than his Hummer and had a lot more seating and truck space.

After grabbing the phone off the passenger seat, Travis punched in the number for the main number at Fairfield.

"Hello? Is that you, Travis?"

"Yes, Livy. Are you all right?"

"Hello, Travis? I can't hear you. Travis?"

"Damn. I can't get a strong-enough signal on this thing."

He slammed the car door and walked toward the terminal. "Livy? Livy? Can you hear me?"

"Travis. Travis. Are you there?"

"Yes. Now I can hear you. Is everything okay? The plane should have been here by now. Did something happen?" Travis sounded in a panic.

"Relax. We had a last-minute change of plans because . . ."

"Livy, I've lost you." Travis held up the phone and moved away from the building. He shook his head in Emily's direction. "Nothing but static. I hate these things!"

"Travis, you are breaking up. The plane should be there before one."

"Livy? Livy? Why—" The line went dead.

Travis turned off the unit. "It was a bad connection, but it looks like they won't be landing for about another forty-five minutes. How about grabbing a bite to eat while we wait? I'm getting hungry."

"Shouldn't we wait for them and get a proper meal in town?" asked Emily as she followed Travis back to the terminal.

"They will have already eaten on the plane. Eating is a great way to kill time."

"Why are they late? Is one of the boys sick? Did the plane have mechanical trouble?" Emily asked breathlessly as she rushed to keep up.

"I don't know. The connection was bad. I heard more static than words. We will find out when they land."

Conversation was minimal until Olivia's luxurious Gulfstream came into view.

After the plane came to a complete stop and the stairs were lowered, Travis and Emily walked out on the tarmac. Lorenzo, their pilot, waved from the doorway, while Michael, the copilot and cabin attendant, stood at the bottom to help the passengers off the rather high last step. Andy and Freddy raced down the steps, while Regional shouted for them to be careful. The boys literally leaped into their father's arms before getting to the last high step.

Travis noticed that a porter from the terminal came out with a motorized baggage cart. Then the rear compartment door opened and someone from inside the plane began handing down the luggage.

Really? Travis wondered how much gear four people could have when half of them were eight-year-olds.

He swung the boys aside to allow Reginald and another man to reach the tarmac.

"Mr. Tanner." The man was somewhere in his middle fifties. Athletic build, short light-brown hair, clean-shaven with dark-brown eyes. He wore neat jeans, pressed white shirt—open at the collar, and a dark-brown blazer. He shouted military. The man reached his hand out. "I am Lieutenant Logan Winters, Navy Seal, retired. I'm your sons' security."

"Pleased to meet you," Travis said as they shook hands. "I believe I have seen you at Fairfield recently."

"Yes, sir. About three months now." His attention turned to the baggage cart. "Excuse me, sir, while I help attend to getting the luggage unloaded."

Travis wondered just how much luggage four people could have that they needed a motorized baggage cart.

"You hoooo, Travis!"

He looked up to the top of the stairs.

"Sarah? What—"

"Benjamin?"

"Surprise!" Sarah waited before she got to the bottom step before she continued. "I just couldn't let my three favorite men live up here in Yankee country without proper help."

Travis threw his arms out wide to embrace Fairfield's house-keeper. "I don't know how you arranged this, or how Olivia and Higgins are going to manage without you, but I sure am glad to see you."

Emily stepped forward. "Sarah, Benjamin, I—we didn't expect you. Mavis and I have everything plan—"

"It was spontaneous. Literally as the car was being loaded." Sarah looked from Travis to Emily. "Why should I stay back at Fairfield when the people who need me are leaving? The house can get along perfectly well without me for a while, and the estate can manage itself without Benjamin. So, we packed up the limo, and here we are."

"Livy didn't say a thing about this change when I talked to her an hour ago."

"Remember, you didn't have much of a conversation on that mobile phone of yours," added Emily.

"Look, it's only Olivia and Higgins. And Higgins is a pretty good cook. King of the grill, in fact."

Logan joined the group. "Excuse me, Mr. Tanner, but could you and Miss Elfin bring your cars over to the security gate and we'll load up?" Although politely said, Travis understood that Logan wasn't asking for their help—he was giving an order.

Half an hour later, both vehicles were loaded, and Logan had directed Sarah, Benjamin, and Reginald to Emily's Bronco. Freddy lost out on his argument for the front seat of the Town Car as Logan claimed, "Shotgun."

The passengers in both vehicles watched as the Gulfstream climbed into the clouds on its return trip to Virginia.

CHAPTER TWENTY-NINE

"D addy, can you take us to your castle now?" asked Freddy for the fourth time.

"Not today. There's a lot to get done. We need to get everything unpacked and everyone settled in."

"Why?" Freddy asked. "The Campbells do all that. And there is always a plate of cookies on the kitchen table when we first get here. How come there are no cookies?"

"Because the Campbells don't live here anymore, and I forgot to bake some," answered their dad.

"Why don't they live here anymore?"

"Because they live in Florida now."

"They don't love us anymore and moved to Florida?"

"I'm sure they still love you, but they don't love the winters here on Marblehead."

"They could come for the summer. Mom could send Lorenzo and bring them here."

"What about me?" asked Sarah.

"Everybody knows you belong at Fairfield." Freddy thought for a moment. "Except for Christmas when you come with us."

"Okay! Enough with the Campbells. Sarah and Benjamin are here for as long as we need them! Period! End of subject! Understood?"

"Yes, Dad . . . but we liked her cookies."

"You had the cookies I made for you on the flight here," Sarah added.

"She makes them different."

Sarah rummaged in the large tote bag she'd had with her on the plane. She pulled out a tin and set it on the table, close enough for Freddy to reach. "Here are the rest of the cookies."

Freddy reached in and grabbed two, putting one in his pocket.

"Andy, would you like one?" Sarah asked.

"No, thank you. I had five on the plane."

Sarah opened the lid of the cooler they had brought with them. The first item she pulled out was a freezer bag bursting with ribs.

"Wow. Are those covered with your special, secret recipe rub?" Travis asked.

"Yes, sir. And I bet they'll be thawed out enough for the grill later. I hope you've got it ready."

"Well, it will be," Travis said as he headed for the butler's pantry for the grilling tools. "I've got a fresh bottle of propane ready to hook up."

"You Yankees, and your propane," Sarah said while shaking her head in disdain. "Can't cook *real* barbecue on propane."

"Is that true, Dad?" Andy asked.

"Of course not. It is purely a Southern thing," Travis said while giving Sarah a wink. "Come on, boys, let's get this inferior Yankee grill cleaned up!"

Sarah laughed out loud as she bent down and continued emptying the cooler of items she'd pulled from the freezer and fridge before leaving Fairfield. "It sure is good to be back."

Later that evening, after an amazing dinner of barbecued ribs smothered in Sarah's homemade sauce, potato salad, and corn bread, Travis went to the library for some quiet time. Earlier, he had set the boys up with a movie in the family room. Sarah was rearranging the kitchen pantry, and Benjamin was in the Campbells' apartment over the garage getting it ready for him and Sarah to move in.

Travis leaned back in his desk chair and stretched his legs out. His weeks alone had ended, and life was about to get hectic and probably a bit frantic, but that wouldn't be all that bad. He picked up the receiver on the multiline phone and punched in Nick's number.

His cousin answered on the fourth ring. "Hello?"

"It's me."

"Travis. How's it going with the little ruffians? Are you ready to jump ship yet?"

"No, today has gone well. The boys helped me clean the grill, and they loved their first barbecue. Even though it was cooked with propane."

"What's wrong with propane? Okay, let me guess." Nick chuckled. "Hot dogs and beans?"

"Sarah and Benjamin are here. And she brought her amazing ribs."

"What? And you didn't invite me? I'm the one who had dogs and beans for dinner!"

"Sorry, old boy. But there will be plenty of Sarah's meals. They are both staying until we find a housekeeper."

"Hopefully, that will be all summer," said Nick.

At that moment, the twins rushed into the room. "Daddy, the movie is over. Will you play a game with us?" Freddy jumped onto his dad's lap.

Travis reached over to press the speaker button on the phone. "I'm talking to Nick."

"Hi, Cousin Nick, it's me, Freddy. We are all here in Ohio. Lorenzo brought us on Mom's plane. She and Higgins couldn't come this time."

"We will be here all summer. Just like always," added Andy. "Except that Sarah and Benjamin came, too, this time."

"Cousin Nick? Do you know about Daddy's castle?" asked Freddy.

"I sure do! How about I take you there tomorrow?"

Freddy slid off his dad's lap, and both boys began jumping up and down. "Yes! Yes!" they shouted in unison.

"Please, Cousin Nick," Freddy shouted into the phone, "we want to go to the castle. We brought our swords."

"Okay then. Tomorrow it is!"

Travis took the phone off speaker. "Thanks, Nick. Did you have to do that? Tomorrow?"

The twins were still jumping around the room. "Boys! Go back to the family room and pick out a game. I'll be there in a minute." Travis watched his sons run through the room and out the door.

"Really, Nick?"

"Seemed like a good idea—at the moment. Think about it. Watching their excitement when they first see Bent Tree Cottage. The very place you loved when you were their age but were forbidden to step foot on the property. Just think about it . . . it will be fun. Trust me."

"If you say so. How about nine thirty? That way we'll be finished with breakfast, and I'll have them dressed and ready to go. And more importantly, *I'll* be ready. We can catch the ten o'clock ferry."

"How about eight and I can join you for breakfast?"

"Don't push it."

"Right. See you at nine thirty."

"Rest up. You are going to need it," Travis said before hanging up.

CHAPTER THIRTY

The gate buzzer sounded at exactly nine thirty. Nick was always punctual. "I'll get it," Sarah shouted.

Travis came down the back stairs, off the kitchen, with Freddy and Andy. All three were dressed in shorts and T-shirts. Nick was already in the kitchen. He too was in shorts and T-shirt.

Travis took a hard look at the last two adults in the room. "Sarah? Benjamin?"

"We are going too," announced Sarah.

Sarah was dressed for a day in the wilderness and holding a bucket spilling over with cleaning supplies.

"Okay. Not a problem. But Sarah, we are going to Long Point, not the outback."

"Can we ride in Cousin Nick's truck?" Andy asked.

"Yeah, we want to ride in his truck," added Freddy.

"I cleaned it out especially for you two explorers," Nick said as he squatted down, and the boys rushed into his arms. He then glanced up at Travis. "We can *all* fit in the truck."

"Yeah, it is a *really* big truck," Freddy added.

Nick stood and took a hard look at Sarah's attire and pail. "And I washed it this morning."

Travis clapped his hands. "Okay. Let's go!"

"Hey, don't forget us," Reginald said as he and Logan exited the back stairway.

"Okay. We take two vehicles. I'll go to the garage and get the Hummer." Travis turned toward the hall leading to the side door. "Sarah, leave the bucket." He then looked directly into Nick's eyes. "This has turned into an expedition," he said softly so only his cousin could hear.

Travis, Nick, and the boys got out of the vehicles and walked to the bow of the ferry for the twenty-minute ride to Kelleys Island. Sarah was a bit apprehensive and stayed in the Hummer with her husband.

"You do this twice a day when you come here?" Sarah asked as Travis drove off the ferry and onto firm ground. "What about when the lake is rough?"

"You stay in your vehicle and plan on a few more minutes. The ferry doesn't run if it is too rough or during bad storms."

"I suppose you get used to it," Sarah said, then settled back in her seat.

Travis glanced in his rearview mirror while he drove through the center of town. The twins were leaning out the windows of Nick's truck, waving at the pedestrians along the way. Many of them waving back.

Beginning Memorial weekend and running through to Labor Day, this will become a busy tourist destination, although not as crazy as Put-in-Bay on South Bass Island.

It only took the blink of an eye before they left the town behind.

"Quaint. Tiny, but quaint," commented Sarah. "What do you do for groceries?"

"We went past the market. It was on the left side."

"Huh. I missed it."

Travis continued driving north on Division Street, with both of his passengers remaining silent until Benjamin spoke. "It seems pretty desolate out here since we left the town."

"Much of Kelleys was made up of various wineries back in the mid-nineteenth century. We're coming up on the ruins of the Monarch Wine Company building." Travis pointed to the beautiful stone facade on his left. "And with much of the center part of the island having been an active stone quarry back in the day, there isn't a lot of buildable land."

Sarah remained silent until they reached the curve in Monaghan Road at the northern edge of the island. "What's that?" She pointed to a grouping of small buildings set on a large area with a lot of tall, mature trees along the road and opposite the shoreline.

"It's a nondenominational Christian children's summer camp."

"Saint Gertrude the Great Camp," Sarah said after reading the large sign. "Somehow that name rings a bell."

"She was one of the great mystics of the thirteenth century. She was appointed the patron of the West Indies and those souls in purgatory."

"Now I remember the West Indies part, but isn't that rather gruesome for a children's camp?" Sarah asked. "Lost souls? Purgatory?"

"I guess I never thought about it that way. This was originally owned by the Whitaker family as part of their estate. They donated the land to the church when they began building Bent Tree Cottage." Travis wondered about that. "I don't think I ever heard who chose the name or why."

Not far beyond, the paved road ended, turning into a narrow lane. Travis stopped at the red steel gate that was now being left open for the tradesmen. He pointed to the old stone posts. "I'm having duplicates of the large, ornate gates fabricated; they should arrive in four months." He then proceeded slowly along the overgrown road that hugged the shoreline with rocky outcroppings.

"I bet the boys are loving this," said Benjamin as he turned in his seat to get a glimpse of the twins in the truck behind. "It's going to seem like a jungle to them."

They came to a fork in the road, and Travis steered the Hummer to the left. "Not far now."

Then all at once it was before them. "Oh my Lord!" Sarah exclaimed. "It really is a castle." Travis stopped so they could get a full view of the front facade.

"I never . . ." Benjamin paused. "Just how many square feet is that monster?"

"The blueprints show twelve thousand."

Sarah sat shaking her head, while Travis drove on and parked in front of the garage. "Travis, even if you don't plan on living here, you will need a full-time, live-in staff just to maintain this place."

By now, Nick had parked next to the Hummer. The doors flew open, and the boys tumbled out of the truck.

Travis, Sarah, and Benjamin joined the exuberant eight-year-olds who were shouting, "Daddy! Daddy! It *is* a castle. It is a *real* castle. Can we go inside?"

Nick began running toward the back door. "Come on, my knights, we storm the castle."

Travis turned toward the others. "It's going to be a very *long* summer."

"Oh boy," said Reginald.

"Security might be an issue," said Logan.

"Glad it's not my problem," said Sarah.

"Maybe I'll just explore the garage," said Benjamin.

"Not a chance," answered Sarah as she grabbed his arm and pulled him along.

Travis motioned toward the back door. "Shall we?"

"What? You are not taking your very first guests through the front door for the full effect? I'm sure it's spectacular," Sarah said in mock horror.

"I would. But we can't get it open."

"Back door it is." Then Benjamin circled around his wife and Travis and followed the knights and Nick inside.

They joined the others in the kitchen.

Sarah whistled. "You could run a hotel from here." She walked around looking at everything. "What? No walk-in freezer?"

"No. But there *is* a silver safe in the butler's pantry," Travis said.

Everyone followed Travis and Nick as they toured the rooms on the first floor. The boys informed their tutor that the grand staircase was perfect for sword fighting. It was decided that the library would be kept for last.

On the second floor, the boys raced ahead, opening doors and running from one room to another. "Where is the tower, Dad?" Freddy asked.

Everyone was standing in the large square bedroom that had the most spectacular view of Lake Erie. Travis pointed toward the ceiling. "Up there."

"We still have another floor to go," Nick said. "Follow me."

They all followed Nick back to the grand staircase and up another set of steps. Once again, the boys ran ahead opening doors until they got to the large square room. "Wow!" shouted Freddy. "Look at these windows." The boys jumped up and down to see out, but they were too short.

Travis walked over and picked up Andy, while Nick boosted Freddy up onto his shoulder. "See how long and very narrow the windows are? Well, the knights would stand at the openings, that back then didn't have glass in them, and shoot arrows down on the invaders."

"Just like in the movies," stated Andy. "But now, we have glass windows, so the bugs and birds don't get in."

"That's right, Son. Very good."

"But where is the tower? The outside part," asked Freddy.

Once again, Travis pointed up.

"There's a secret staircase," whispered Nick. "Let's go!"

Travis looked at the others and rolled his eyes. "On to the tower."

Sarah, Benjamin, Reginald, and Logan trailed behind Travis as he made his way back out into the hall and to yet another set of servants' stairs, which led to the attics. A few feet beyond, they came to a steel door that had been left open. Inside was an iron circular staircase. Squeals of excitement could be heard from above. At the top was a large metal door. It too had been left open.

"Wow!" everyone said as each stepped through the door and onto the parapet with the crenelated walls.

"Being up this high, you can see for miles in all directions," Nick said while pointing in a circle.

Travis followed Logan as he walked to the opposite side overlooking the front of the house. He pointed to a clearing and a house. "Is that the—"

"The Pines? Yes. I take it, you already know about it."

"Higgins briefed me on it before we left. The FBI is finished with the site. You can take down the yellow crime tape."

"Thanks. I'll tell Nick."

"Look! I can see Perry's Monument at Put-in-Bay!" exclaimed Freddy. "Dad takes us there every year." He grabbed Sarah's hand and pulled her to the wall. "A whole bunch of guys are buried under there, and if you go all the way to the top, you can see Canada."

"Very impressive. I'll be sure and study up on it while we're here," Sarah promised.

Andy moved to the wall next to his brother and took the stance of a tour guide. "Actually, the Doric column stands three hundred and fifty-two feet and was built in 1915. It commemorates the Battle of Lake Erie that was fought right out there, on September tenth, 1813." Andy pointed to the waters just beyond. "Commodore Oliver Hazard Perry's fleet won the battle against the British. That's why it's called Perry's Monument."

"Son, I'm very impressed that you remembered all that."

"He's been studying," Freddy added, as if their dad didn't need to be so impressed.

"We have spent many hours at the Charles City library the last few weeks," Reginald added.

"Guess what I know, Sarah? You'll never guess," Freddy said excitedly. "General William Henry Harrison was in that war. The war of 1812. He was born at Berkeley Plantation, right down the road from us at Fairfield. He was a president too and has the same last name as you and Benjamin."

"This part I know," Sarah said. "And did *you* know that Benjamin's ancestors were born at Berkeley? After they became free, they took the last name of Harrison."

"Wow! That is really special. Maybe when we get back home, we can go there and tell them about Benjamin," added Andy.

Freddy ran over to the opposite side of the parapet. "Look, everybody." He pointed out over the lake to the south. "There is the lighthouse! And I can see the room at the top of our house."

"You sure can," Logan said. "From up here, you can see just about everything." He looked over at Travis. "Interesting."

"Hey, Dad!" Freddy shouted. "Can you call Mom and ask her to buy us a cannon? We can put it right up here and pretend to shoot at the British ships."

"Let's not get ahead of ourselves yet, Son. You can pretend without a real cannon."

Andy walked over to the door, pointing at the opening. "Think about this, Freddy. Remember how big cannons are? They are *huge*. So how do we get something that big up those windy steps? It's impossible!"

Freddy thought about that, then looked up and smiled. "How about a helicopter and—"

"Okay, everyone. It's noon. How about I go down to the kitchen and make lunch with some of that food I saw in the fridge?"

Travis turned to Sarah and mouthed, "Thank you."

After a lunch of sandwiches, potato salad, and Oreo cookies served in the dining room, on paper plates, Nick took Benjamin and the rest of the crew outside to explore the garage.

Travis helped Sarah clean up the kitchen. Then she motioned for them to sit at the table. She spread her arms out and clasped her hands. "I know Olivia has her concerns about this place, and she hasn't even seen it. Now that I've been here, I must be honest with you. This house is amazing. You only see houses like this in movies. People don't own houses like this anymore. They are turned into hotels, museums, clubs, or resorts. They don't live in them. And besides, you're out here in the middle of nowhere nearly surrounded by water."

"Sarah, I have loved this house nearly my whole life. It has been closed up and dying for decades. I had to save it. It's wonderful. It's amazing. You have to see that."

"I do understand and appreciate everything you have said. But I'm trying to be realistic. I can see this place swallowing you up, consuming you—all to fulfill a childhood dream. I just want you to keep your eyes and your mind open. Look at this house and property realistically and understand its potential. It's not a puppy that you've saved."

"Thank you, Sarah. I do value your opinion, and I know that you only want the best for me. But I assure you that I am keeping an open mind. I don't know what the end result will be, or what Long Point's future will be, but I'm having a wonderful time getting there."

Travis got up and went around and kissed the top of Sarah's head. "I see the gang is returning from the exploration of the garage."

His sons exploded through the kitchen door. "Sarah, Sarah," the boys said in unison, "you are not going to believe what we saw."

Freddy continued. "The garage is huge, and it is filled with lots of neat stuff. There is a golf cart that works, and Nick said he will take us for a ride the next time we come."

"Wonderful. And something for you to look forward to."

The rest of the adventurers entered the kitchen.

"We should probably think about heading back to Marblehead," said Travis. "But there is one more special room that I want you to see."

Travis and Nick led the way to the library. Travis had everyone wait in the hallway until he opened the door. He then reached inside and flipped the switch, flooding the room with light from the stained glass panel above.

The twins rushed in first. "Wow!" they both said while looking up at the ceiling.

Wows were said by everyone else as they filed into the room.

"It's the bent tree!" Sarah exclaimed. "Look, boys, that's how the house got its name."

"Who is that?" Andy asked as he walked over to the fireplace and looked up at the large portrait of a man with a full beard and smoking a pipe.

"That would be General Horatio Buchanan. He lived in a cabin on the property for many years," explained Nick.

Andy raised his head and sniffed. "I smell his pipe."

"I don't smell pipe," said Sarah. "But I do smell damp soot from the chimney."

"You need to get this cleaned," remarked Benjamin.

Nick slapped Benjamin on the shoulder. "Already scheduled, Ben."

Travis looked over at Sarah and mouthed, "Ben?" Sarah just shrugged her shoulders and shook her head.

"Okay," Travis said and clapped his hands. "This officially ends the tour of Bent Tree Cottage. How about we head back to the ferry dock?"

CHAPTER THIRTY-ONE

Monday morning, Travis and Nick were sitting on the ferry to Kelleys in Nick's truck. "You need to get a minivan," said Nick.

"No way. Even when the twins were babies, we didn't have a minivan. We managed just fine with the Lincoln. I wouldn't be caught dead driving one of those kid mobiles."

"My sister, Gloria, has a minivan, and it holds a lot."

"Your sister has a pack of kids."

"I hate to inform you, cuz, but *you* have a pack of *people* now."

"No, I don't."

"So why did I have to swing by and pick you up this morning?"

"Because I gave the keys to the Hummer to Logan so he could drive Reginald and the boys to Port Clinton to catch the passenger ferry to Put-in-Bay for the day. That leaves the Lincoln for the Harrisons in case they need to run out for supplies or something."

Nick glanced over at his cousin with a look that said *I told you so.*

"No, we're fine. I don't need a kid-hauler—period."

"For today, you don't," Nick got in the last word.

"We have the plumbing crew starting late this morning after they finish up a job in Oak Harbor. The electricians should be there in an hour. Hopefully, it won't be much more than replacing the old wiring," Travis said as the ferry's ramp dropped into place and the vehicles in front of them began driving off.

Logan, Reginald, Andy, and Freddy stepped off the Jet Express at Put-in-Bay at ten o'clock—each wearing a backpack containing a couple of bottles of water, and everything else little boys deem necessary. Logan's contained water and everything *he* felt he might need.

"That was really a cool ride," Freddy said as they walked toward Perry's Monument. "Dad brings us every year. Reggie too. Now this year you are bringing us."

"After we show you the monument, we can rent a golf cart. They have maps of the whole island," said Andy. "There used to be a really big and famous hotel on the other side of the island called the Victory Hotel. It had a fire a really long time ago and burned right to the ground. Freddy and me like to climb around on the ruins. It is so neat. You can drive us there."

"And I want to go see the cave again," said Freddy. "They have tours and everything. They have wine too, but we are too young to drink it, but you can. It will be on the map; there is a picture too."

The boys picked up the pace, moving ahead. Logan glanced around, noting the surroundings and every pedestrian who came close. "This is going to be a security challenge," he said to Reginald.

"It always is. Higgins gets pretty uptight. But we've never had a problem on our past trips. This time should be even easier since we came earlier this year. After Memorial Day, Put-in-Bay becomes a zoo. And I do mean a zoo. It's like ninety-nine percent tourists, and half of them have been drinking since breakfast."

"Thanks. I needed to hear that," Logan said sarcastically. "Andy, Freddy, slow down!" he shouted.

An hour and a half later, they were all heading down the steps of the monument. Reginald was ready for a brain chill, and Logan was ready for any kind of stress relief.

"How about that golf cart?" Logan suggested as he began walking toward the stand.

The twins charged ahead and eagerly stood before the gentleman who would provide them with their favorite mode of transportation.

"We would like a golf cart, sir," Freddy announced. "The biggest one you have."

"We need a big one because there are four of us," added Andy.

The man studied the youngsters. "You wouldn't be twins, now, would you?"

"We sure are," said Freddy excitedly.

"Identical," said Andy.

"You don't say? Well, I bet I've got the perfect one for your dad."

"Oh, he isn't our dad. He's our—"

"Uncle. I'm their uncle," Logan said as he produced his driver's license and handed it to the man.

After writing down the number in his logbook along with the number of a cart, he handed Logan his license. "I see you're from Virginia. Is this your first time here on the island?"

"Only him. Reggie is our—" Freddy started to say.

"Cousin," Logan said. "The whole family is here for the summer. We are staying in Marblehead. This is my first visit, and I'm excited to get on with our tour of the island."

The man handed Logan a map. He frowned while studying the twins. Like he'd seen them somewhere.

"Which cart?" Logan asked.

"Oh, number thirteen, at the end."

"Our lucky number," Logan said as he ushered his three charges to the large, canopied cart.

"I want to sit in front," shouted Freddy.

Logan looked at Andy. "Is that okay with you? How about the next time we get in, you can sit in front?" Andy nodded his approval. "Then you and your brother will switch each time we get in."

After everyone was safely secured in their seats, Logan turned the key.

"I'm hungry," the twins said in unison as Logan steered the cart around DeRivera Park. "Can we go sit on the canons?"

"After lunch," said Logan as they passed the Round House Bar with loud music spilling out the doors. "Is there somewhere that is less noisy and less drinking?"

Reginald leaned forward. "How about pizza?" He pointed to Frosty's. "It's been here forever, and I remember that the food was good. You can park here. Then the boys can climb on the canons after."

After pulling into the space in front of DeRivera Park and shutting off the motor, Logan turned to face his passengers. "You boys need to think before you speak. That was a close one back at the cart stand. Kids don't go around with a tutor and bodyguard. It raises issues. Your parents want you to have a normal life as much as possible. And in order to do that, we have to remember the rules when you are out in public places."

"We understand," said Andy. "Freddy and I got excited, and we almost blew it. It won't happen again. We promise."

"Okay. Now let's go get some pizza!"

CHAPTER THIRTY-TWO

The following morning, Sarah had a breakfast of scrambled eggs, bacon, sausage, buttermilk biscuits, and grits set out on the sideboard in the morning room.

Travis was the first one to come downstairs. "Wow, Sarah, it sure is good to have you here in Marblehead. If you keep putting out spreads like this every morning, we are going to need to put out an invitation to Nick just so we can finish all this food."

"Mr. Nick is always welcome. He's a good man. I wish he had a woman to take care of him."

"Now, Sarah, don't go getting any ideas. Nick is a happy, confirmed bachelor."

Logan entered and immediately went to the sideboard. "Nothing like a bowl of your grits to set the morning right, Miss Sarah."

Sarah believed that a man needed a hearty breakfast to prepare him for the day's work ahead. With the increased security team that Higgins had put together and housed in a separate building at Fairfield, Sarah had begun setting up a breakfast buffet in the basement, which could easily be entered from the outside stairs on the kitchen side of the house.

Reginald and the boys were the last to arrive.

"Sarah, have you and Benjamin eaten yet?" asked Travis.

"No, sir, we'll wait until y'all are finished."

"Nonsense. How many times have I sat at your table in Fairfield's kitchen? You are family here. Grab your plates and join us. We have plenty of room at the table."

Everyone scooted closer together around the antique oak pedestal table to make room. Then the Harrisons happily joined the group.

After what seemed like hours of silence, Sarah put down her fork. "What is everyone doing today—so I know how to plan for lunch and dinner?"

"Well, I'll be at Long Point with Nick. We have teams of both electricians and plumbers arriving, and they will literally be crawling around the house. Hopefully, not on top of each other. Water and electricity don't work well together," joked Travis.

"What about us?" asked Freddy.

Travis glanced at Reginald with raised eyebrows. "Well?"

"I have no plans, Mr. Tanner."

"Then how about if Logan takes the three of you to Cedar Point for the day?"

"Yea!" shouted the twins. "We want to go! Please, Dad!" added Freddy.

"What and where is Cedar Point, sir?" asked Logan.

"Remember when we were on the plane? Just before we landed and Andy and me showed you the amusement park?"

"The extremely big one," Reginald added.

"Last night, before I turned in, I noticed a lot of bright lights across the lake to the south," Logan said, while hoping that wasn't Cedar Point.

"Yep, that would be it," confirmed Reginald. "It's another day-long excursion."

"Sir, I don't believe that would be in the best interest of your sons. It appears to be awfully spread out and, I'm sure, highly populated."

"Dad, Mr. Logan is trying to say that it isn't secure, and we wouldn't be safe there," explained Andy.

"We learned a lot about being safe yesterday when in public places," added Freddy. "I don't think it would be so much fun there today if we have to be safe."

Travis glanced over at Benjamin, who was having a very difficult time controlling his laughter.

"Well, then. How about if *Benjamin* searches the garage for the croquet set and whatever else he can find, and you all play games on the lawn? Maybe Sarah can make you a picnic lunch down on the beach."

"Sir, I haven't secured the property yet. Yesterday, I heard a lot of what sounded like teenagers hanging out around the water near the lighthouse. I need to make myself aware of the property lines, sir. I realize it is all fenced and has high stone walls, and Higgins briefed me on his routines. But I'm not comfortable having the boys playing outside until I have walked the property. I did briefly last evening, but only down by the water."

"Okay, does anyone else have any ideas?" asked Travis.

"I suppose I could keep Freddy and Andy indoors today. We can work some more on the history of the area. I picked up several books and maps while we browsed the gift shops on Put-in-Bay yesterday," said Reginald.

"May I make a suggestion, sir?"

"Of course. At this point, I'm willing to consider almost anything."

"While we were at Long Point on Sunday, I noted how isolated the property is being surrounded by water on three sides.

I see it as a very secure place for your sons. I realize the house is under active renovations, but the grounds are perfect. I noticed that the grass has been recently mowed, which is perfect for the lawn games you mentioned. Plus, I can use the golf cart for a tour of the property, and perhaps check out 'The Pines.'"

Travis remained silent while he considered all aspects of what Logan had voiced.

"Please, Dad. That's what we want to do today. Please, Dad," Freddy pleaded.

"Okay. That settles it. We are all going to Long Point!"

"Us too?" Sarah asked. "I'll handle lunch, and work on the kitchen and butler's pantry. And Benjamin can help wherever he's needed."

"I noticed some tools in the garage that need tending too, and I'd like to check out that barn out back."

Travis looked around the table at all the eager faces. Six eager faces. "We have to take both vehicles. Benjamin, you load the games into the trunk of the Lincoln. Along with anything else you think you may need. Logan, you're with me and the boys in the Hummer. Reginald, you ride with the Harrisons. Sarah, pack up anything you need for lunch and put it in the Lincoln."

"Everyone, put your dirty plates and silverware in the kitchen sink and meet outside when you are ready to go," announced Travis as he rose from the table.

"Sarah, I'll help you clean up and put away the leftovers."

Travis then turned to Logan. "Take what you need. Put it in the back of the Hummer and cover it with the blanket—understand?"

"Yes, sir."

Sarah glanced over at Travis and nodded her head in agreement.

CHAPTER THIRTY-THREE

Travis kept his speed agonizingly slow after leaving the ferry dock so he wouldn't lose Benjamin. After turning onto Division Street, Benjamin honked the horn and motioned for Travis to pull over. He immediately thought that something had gone wrong on the Lincoln that accounted for the slower speed.

After pulling over next to the curb, Travis glanced in his side mirror and saw Sarah approaching.

"Is everything okay? Has something gone wrong with the car?" Travis asked, sounding concerned.

"No. No. I want to run into the market and pick up a gallon of milk and some ice cream and popsicles."

At those magic words, the boys began jumping up and down on the seat. "Yea! Yea! Can we come too and pick out the ice cream?" asked Freddy.

Travis turned in his seat to look at the twins in the back seat. "No. Stay right where you are!" He then turned back to Sarah. "Do you and Benjamin remember how to get to Long Point from here?"

She thought for a second or two. "I don't, maybe he does." Sarah nodded toward the Lincoln.

"Never mind. I'll wait here until you are finished shopping and get back in the car."

"I'll just be a minute." She hurried across the street.

For the next fifteen minutes, Andy and Freddy had an excited debate about what flavor ice cream Sarah would choose. Travis wondered how a minute could turn into fifteen—the store wasn't that big. Logan sat quietly while observing the people on the sidewalk, the cars driving by and the sounds of the harbor. Boat motors seemed to prevail.

Sarah finally exited the store with two grocery bags in one hand and a gallon of milk in the other. With little traffic at that time of day, Sarah quickly made it across the street and into the front seat of the Lincoln.

Travis fired up the Hummer and headed north on Division until he made the right turn onto Ward. He hoped that driving so slow, the Harrisons would take note of the surrounds for future trips. He would also pick up a couple of maps of the island at the ferry dock.

It was almost noon when Travis finally reached Bent Tree Cottage. The driveway was clogged with trucks forcing him to park over to the far side of the garage. Everyone piled out of the two vehicles, excited to be back.

"Okay, everybody," Travis shouted. "We all help unload the Lincoln. Food goes to the kitchen, and toys and whatever else is in the trunk goes to the grassy area between the garage and the house."

"Sir?" Logan moved over to Travis. He nodded toward the rear of the Hummer, as if asking what he should do with its contents.

Travis looked around at the scene before him and thought for a moment. "Lieutenant, treat this as you would if going into what could explode in chaos at any moment. I'm not suggesting a battle but—"

"I understand, sir. Everything will be kept secure but accessible."

Travis tossed Logan the keys.

At that moment, Nick sauntered over, hands in the pockets of his jeans, taking in the hectic scene of the unloading of the Lincoln. "I expected you hours ago. I figured you took the day off and forgot to tell me." He watched as Benjamin and Reginald pulled a big red cooler from the depths of the trunk. "The twins raced past me with two bags yelling 'ice cream.' I bet if you tried hard, you could have gotten at least one more item in that trunk."

Travis gave his cousin a look that said *Don't say another word. Don't ask. Don't lecture.* And most of all, *Don't say I told you so.*

Nick shook his head and chuckled. Then he walked over to the red cooler. "Here, Ben, let me take that," Nick said, then bent down, grabbed the two handles, and carried it to the kitchen.

An hour later, after lunch, everyone scattered in different directions. Travis went with the electrical crew, and Nick took the plumbers. Benjamin, Reginald, and the twins headed to the front yard with the croquet set, and Logan was seen in the golf cart heading in the direction of The Pines. Sarah stayed in the kitchen making a wish list.

By two o'clock, croquet had been replaced by hide-and-seek. Logan had returned and was asking for Travis, whom he found with the electricians on the second floor.

"Mr. Tanner, sir, I've just returned from a thorough inspection of the area around The Pines. And I removed the yellow crime tape. It looks to me like your squatter is the only one who has used that house in a very long time. The road leading to it is overgrown, and so are the weeds and underbrush going right up to the house. Although those have been trampled down, I assume, by the local police and the FBI."

"Thank you, Logan. Does it look like the boys are getting bored yet?"

"Far from it, sir. They have asked if I would take them for a ride. I would like to continue my exploration of the property, especially going further east to the point. I could take Andy and Freddy and give Reginald and Benjamin a break, unless Reginald would like to go too."

"Great idea. Nick and I haven't had a chance to check that area out yet. Do you have your mobile phone with you?"

"Yes, but I don't know how good the signal is out here. Higgins has asked that I take as many photos of the property as I can. I have a camera in the cart." He patted his right hip. "I am prepared, sir. You don't need to worry."

"Higgins said you were the best. That is good enough for me."

"Thank you, sir. We'll leave as soon as I round up my passengers."

"And, Logan, enjoy the adventure. It's not all work out here."

"I will, sir," Logan said as he walked away.

═╬═

Later, Nick stepped into the old housekeeper's office, which had been taken over by Travis and shared with Nick. Travis quickly hung up the phone. "Who were you talking to? You've been on that call for over an hour. Did something happen to Olivia?"

"Relax, Livy is fine. At least our calls the last couple of nights have been good. The boys love talking to her. We make it a family event in the library, on speaker."

"So, who was the important caller?" asked Nick.

"I called the Chrysler dealer in Sandusky—I bought a minivan."

"What? You must be kidding! The 'I wouldn't be caught dead driving one of those kid mobiles.'"

"After everything that happened this morning, it finally came down to a minivan or my sanity!"

"That bad, huh? Want to talk about it? You looked ready to explode. I thought for sure someone was going to die. And you had the means in the back of the Hummer."

"You knew about that?"

"I guessed."

"Security is definitely going to be a major consideration. I wish Higgins were here."

"Agree. Now tell me about your new ride."

A Chrysler Town & Country. It is fully loaded, with all-wheel drive. I talked to the owner of the dealership. It came in yesterday. He has it on the showroom floor and described it as the most luxurious minivan he has ever seen. His wife is begging him to bring it home."

"You bought it? It's a done deal?"

"Yep. Bought and paid for. They can deliver it tomorrow to the house; problem is, I would need to be there to sign the papers."

"How about faxing the paperwork to the house?"

"I still have to be there to sign the documents and send them back."

"So, what are you going to do?"

"The dealership stays open late tonight. I could have Reginald drive with me in the Hummer to Sandusky, and then I can drive the minivan home and test out all that special features and enjoy the luxury."

"The electricians and plumbers have left for the day. How about we pack up and get everyone home to Marblehead, and then *I* drive you to Sandusky?"

"Perfect," said Travis. "And on the way, I would like to stop by that big hardware store—the one that has all the camping gear."

"You want to take everyone camping?"

"No. I want to buy the biggest charcoal grill they have—for Sarah."

"Because she doesn't like propane. I get it."

"That too, but I want you to take it to Long Point tomorrow in your truck."

"A surprise." Nick thought about lunch earlier and how Sarah complained about how she had to make all those hot dogs in a pot of boiling water and the burgers in a frying pan. "Yep. Great idea. Sarah will be so happy."

"So will we when all of Long Point smells of Sarah's fabulous Southern barbecue."

"Maybe you should buy two. She hates your propane grill."

CHAPTER THIRTY-FOUR

That night, Travis and his sons anxiously waited for eight o'clock, the time for the nightly call to Olivia. Andy and Freddy were overflowing with excitement about their day at Long Point and couldn't wait to tell their mother. Travis had been amazed at how luxurious the minivan was and couldn't believe that it handled much like the Lincoln.

After dialing Fairfield's house line, Olivia picked up on the first ring.

"Hello? Is that my favorite sons, Andy and Freddy?" Olivia said with excitement in her voice.

"Mom! Mom! We had so much fun today at the castle. And Logan took us on a really long ride in the golf cart. And, Mom, Lake Erie is all around us there. Well, except for the road that is kinda scarry, like you could drive off the road right into the water. Mom, could you buy us a canon? Maybe bring it in a helicopter? Mom—"

"Slow down, boys. You are talking over each other, and I hardly know which one of you is talking.

"It's me talking this time, Mom," Andy said. "Dad bought a minivan for us, and it is as big as your limo."

"What? I don't believe it. A minivan? Your father wouldn't be caught dead driving one of those kid mobiles."

"I need it to preserve my sanity," Travis said in defense.

"As big as my limo, huh? Are we playing for size here, or function?" she said jokingly.

"What does that mean, Mom?" asked Andy.

"Never mind. Now, I want you both to run upstairs and get ready for bed. I need to talk to your dad for a few minutes."

"Okay," they said in unison. "Love you, Mom."

"Love you more. I'll talk to you again tomorrow evening. Pleasant dreams."

Travis watched as his sons hurried across the room and out the door.

"Okay, Livy. Now you are scaring me. What's up that you can't talk about in front of the boys?"

"Higgins heard back from his contact at the National Archives."

"About the break-in, you mean?"

"Yes. She had to dig really deep to find information on the house and my great-great-grandfather." Olivia paused to collect her thoughts. "It is almost as though documents were changed or deleted during the Civil War era."

"How so?"

"We already know that my great-great bought the house on Freemason Street in 1850 from a fellow Scotsman, named Alexander Frazier. He was a wealthy merchant who owned a dry goods store, Frazier and Son. Although, apparently, there never was a son, he also owned two warehouses down near the docks. He owned quite a few slaves, who worked in both the store and the warehouses, and I would assume his house."

"So, he wasn't sympathetic to the organized network to help slaves escape to freedom," said Travis.

"No. And he made that well known. Alexander Frazier was all about making money. By 1850, the city of St. Louis was the largest city west of Pittsburgh, and the second largest port, New York City, being the largest. So, he sold everything and took his money and his slaves with him to St. Louis, where he literally made a fortune selling goods to those pioneers and prospectors heading to the frontier."

"So, where does your great-great-grandfather come into the story?"

"That is the amazing part of the story. And it would still be a secret today if it weren't for computers. The woman at the National Archives did search on the name McLeod and everything relating to him, Norfolk, shipping, and Freemason Street, and found nothing. She was ready to call it quits when a letter written in 1870 by a Virginia slave who made it to Canada popped up. The man had become a blacksmith in Halifax, gone to school, and later had his own business making wrought iron fences and decorative hardware. He became quite wealthy. Jerimiah Franklin wrote a letter to a black-owned newspaper in Toronto telling of how a generous man named Angus risked his life and reputation to begin helping runaways. He told of how he and a group of four other men were nearly caught while seeking shelter at a house on Freemason Street. They hid in the hayloft of a barn until they could move on. When the owner of the barn accidently found them and heard their story, he promised to help them reach freedom and all others who followed. Jerimiah told of the many months that the five men dug a deep tunnel from under the barn to a storage room under the old kitchen house. He mentioned how Mr. Angus knew the ship captains who were sympathetic to the runaways and would take them on their ships to safe ports."

"How is it that there is no mention anywhere of the role the house had back then? I've been to the museums and toured the sites."

"Remember that Alexander Frazier had slaves. I remember Nathaniel mentioning that the small-frame, two-story addition at the rear of the house was the old kitchen. He's renovated it into an office and apartment for himself. The basement is used for storage." Olivia paused. "Don't you see? The house was known to have slaves. Why would it have ever been suspected of harboring them? It was perfect. And to keep the secret, Angus made sure there was never any written references to either himself or the house."

"But someone *did* figure it out. Someone who had access to our government's database. The same database that the National Archives is locked into."

"It appears so."

"And Higgins thinks?" asked Travis.

"He is connecting the break-in with the stolen diagrams for the prototype of HELIOSmm-88. The *first* prototype that failed miserably."

"Livy? You are talking corporate espionage."

"Yeah."

"That's why Higgins is keeping you at Fairfield. What about William? Is he safe?"

"I believe we are all okay. The contracts have been signed, and the plans and documents pertaining to HELIOS are safely locked away at McLeod and Morrison. I never *did* have a copy. Whoever planned this elaborate scheme now has egg on their face."

"And which government do you think is washing their face at the moment?"

"The Chinese or Russians."

"What about Mabel Polanski? Is she in on it too? She did try to snatch your briefcase."

"According to Higgins, she is—and her daughter. And both have dropped off the face of the earth."

"So, does that mean you and Higgins will be joining our merry little band of adventurers?"

"Maybe next week. Higgins wants to make sure we don't bring any of this with us. No loose ends."

"Livy, I have to go. I hear the boys yelling. I'm late for story time."

"I love you, Travis. Talk to you tomorrow."

"Love you too. Sleep well."

Travis hung up the phone and headed upstairs. He thought about how complicated life had gotten. The Campbells, whom they depended on, just up and left, leaving them without a house-keeper—like a sailboat without a rudder. Olivia was dealing with what—espionage?

CHAPTER THIRTY-FIVE

Wednesday morning, Travis crawled out of bed at five o'clock feeling like he had spent the night before drinking cheap wine with shots of bourbon. He had tossed and turned for most of the night worrying about the safety of his wife. Although she hadn't said it in so many words, Livy's life had been in danger. Why couldn't McLeod and Morrison stick to building ships and not get into this high-tech stuff? He remembered that time, three years ago, when Olivia was told that McLeod and Morrison had been infiltrated by a foreign operative who had gotten away with the plans for the new electronic device called HELIOSmm-88. At no time had Livy's life been in danger, the bad guys just grabbed the floppy disk and ran.

After a long hot shower, Travis pulled on a pair of jeans and a blue-plaid, short-sleeved shirt. He decided he needed caffeine, so he padded downstairs to the kitchen to make the day's first pot of coffee. He was surprised to see Sarah already sitting at the kitchen table, wearing a yellow robe and fuzzy slippers.

"You are up early, Sarah. Couldn't sleep, or preparing for one of your ginormous breakfasts?"

Sarah set her mug down and crossed her arms in front of her. "Something is wrong. I feel it in my bones."

"Did you talk to Livy yesterday?"

"In the morning. Why?"

"We talked last night. She told me an incredible story." Travis filled Sarah in on what Olivia had told him during their phone conversation. After he had finished, Travis got up and went over to the counter and grabbed the pot of coffee and returned to refill their mugs. "Maybe that is what you are feeling. You are picking up on Livy's vibes."

Sarah took a minute to digest the new information. "You have no idea how much knowing this means to me. As you know, I was born at Fairfield as was my mother, Miranda. Olivia's great-great-grandfather freed his slaves even before President Lincoln signed the Emancipation Proclamation on January 1, 1863, which freed all slaves living in the United States. I never knew why he had freed them. I now know it was because he was help-ing to free other slaves. He treated his workers very well, and his wife, Alexandra, who came from Saratoga, New York, made sure that everyone who lived on Fairfield property was well cared for. Miranda's mother, Belle, was a beautiful woman, a mulatto, as was her mother. Alexandra, having come from New York and unfamiliar with the south and southern ways, depended on Belle. One of the first things she did to show her appreciation and upgrade the plantation was to build a new, two-story kitchen closer to the main house and ordered a big new stove and had it shipped all the way from New York. After Miranda was born, she built a schoolroom and hired a teacher so that all children born at Fairfield would know how to read and write. Olivia's grand-mother wanted to help Miranda's daughter make something of herself other than a housemaid. So, I was sent to live with a family in Syracuse. Her grandmother even paid for my college education. I was studying finance and law. It was after Mr. Angus passed that I came back to help my mother."

Sarah shook her head. "No. What I'm feeling isn't about the past. Something else. Something isn't right."

The two sat in silence, each absorbed in their thoughts until the grandfather clock in the front hall chimed six times.

It was just after nine that morning when Travis and Benjamin began loading the minivan for the day at Long Point, when Emily Elfin called. Her excitement carried on the backs of her every word. "Travis, you are not going to believe our good fortune. I thought I would swing by the post office this morning, just in case, by chance, we got another application." Emily paused for effect. "We have a viable candidate for housekeeper." She paused again. "A husband and wife sounds too good to be true on paper, but I'm meeting them later this morning. If I believe they may work out, then I'd like to bring them to the house to meet you and the family, say one o'clock?"

Travis had a full day planned at Long Point, but if this couple worked out, then it was worth a change in plans.

"Okay, one o'clock it is. I would like Sarah and Benjamin in on the meeting with me, and if we like them, then we will bring in the others. The Harrisons understand all aspects of the job and will initially train them."

"Works for me. I'll give you a call before we come."

Travis had Sarah round everyone up and meet in the library. Logan was the last to arrive.

"I know you all were planning on another full day at Long Point, but something has come up, and we need to have a change in plans."

"Is Mom and Higgins coming today?" asked Freddy.

"Sorry, no. Probably another week."

"Good news is, Emily thinks she may have a couple to take over the Campbells' job."

"Does that mean that Sarah and Benjamin will go back to Fairfield?" Andy asked. "We like them here."

"Yeah, we don't want them to leave," said Freddy.

"We are not going anywhere, at least until we have the new people trained and we are satisfied that they can take over and run this place as well as the Campbells did," Sarah said as she put her arms around the twins.

"Does that mean you would stay all summer with us?" asked Andy.

"That is up to your dad, but we will be here for as long as we are needed."

"Emily will bring them here around one. That means we hang around here until then. If it's still early enough, we'll head to Kelleys," Travis stated.

"Y'all find something to do till lunchtime." Sarah looked over at her husband. "How about you and I clean out the Campbells' apartment over the garage, since it may have new occupants?"

Travis watched everyone file out the door and scatter in different directions. He wrestled with feelings of hope that this new couple would work out, yet he wanted the Campbells back. But that seemed less and less likely, since they hadn't heard from them since they had left for Florida—not even a "We Miss You" card for the boys.

CHAPTER THIRTY-SIX

The front-gate buzzer went off at precisely one o'clock that afternoon. Travis pressed the button and watched the monitor as Emily drove through. Then he and the Harrisons went to the side door to greet them. Introductions were made as Emily introduced Emma and Stanley Burnside. The couple looked to be in their early fifties. The woman was of average height, with a slight build. She wore a navy-blue pantsuit with a crisp white blouse that was open at the neck, showing off a string of pearls. Low-heeled black pumps completed the ensemble. Her dark-brown hair was pulled back in a chignon that rested just above her neck. Overall, her look was that of a professional businesswoman.

Stanley was tall, over six feet, with an athletic build that was evident even through his black trousers, black turtleneck, and casual-styled jacket. Thick dark wavy hair, slightly grayed at the temples, gave him a distinguished look.

"It is a pleasure to meet both of you. Sarah has set up refreshments in the morning room," Travis said as he guided the group down the hall.

After everyone was seated, Emily passed out copies of the Burnsides' résumé for review. While Travis, Sarah, and Benjamin read, Emily invited the Burnsides to the sideboard to help themselves to drinks and pastries.

Travis nodded his head in approval several times while reading. Sarah raised her eyebrows during parts of her read. The whole thing seemed to go over Benjamin's head.

"This is very impressive. Are you sure you would be happy working and living here in Marblehead? You have to drive for an hour to reach a major city, and that would be either Cleveland or Toledo."

"This suits us just fine," said Stanley.

"You were last employed, for five years, by the Embassy of Luxembourg in Washington, DC. Emma, can you tell us a bit about your responsibilities?" asked Travis.

"I was responsible for the household staff, both those who lived in and those who came in for specific jobs like cleaning and catering. I managed the day-to-day scheduling, worked with the cook on meal planning, organized special events, and saw to the needs of visiting dignitaries."

"Impressive." Travis turned to Stanley. "What were your duties?"

"The embassy was small compared to those of other countries. So, I wore a lot of hats, so to speak. I was the chauffeur, auto mechanic, butler, manservant to visiting dignitaries when needed, server at meals, and gardener."

"Also, very impressive."

"Emma, you would have a limited staff here, and do the cooking unless we are entertaining. A cleaning crew comes in weekly, but anything that needs attention between times would be your responsibility. Also, the Tanners have two eight-year-old twin sons whom you will be responsible for. Would any of that be a problem for you?" asked Sarah.

"No, ma'am. Growing up, I came from a poor family. I was the oldest of five children, and our mother held down three jobs to support us. It was my responsibility to take care of my siblings and do the cooking and cleaning."

"Why did you leave? It sounds like it was an ideal job."

"A scandal, sir." Emma paused, as if carefully choosing her words. "The ambassador was relieved of his position. The Luxembourg government let the entire staff go and replaced them with people from that country. Because of the very negative public press, it was difficult trying to get work in other embassies."

"I understand. Before the embassy, you worked for Constance and Peter Worthington in Boston for eight years. Tell us about that period," asked Travis.

"They were a wealthy family who had three teenage children. Two girls and a boy. Mr. Worthington had an import-and-export business, which meant for a lot of traveling. Stanley and I maintained the residence in Boston as well as their summer house in Nantucket."

Travis and Sarah and, at times, Emily filled the Burnsides in on the family dynamics and how important security was.

"Why do you think that you and your husband would be an asset to this family?" asked Sarah.

"For one, we are used to dealing with and managing the homes of the wealthy and the demands of that lifestyle and responsibilities. Stanley and I are both familiar with New York City and can also manage Mrs. Tanner's residence at the Waldorf and the entertaining she does there for her many charities. At the embassy, security was the highest order of business, so that comes second nature to Stanley and me."

Travis silently thanked God for sending the perfect couple to step into the Campbells' shoes. Actually, the Burnsides were in a totally different class than the sweet old couple who had retired to Florida. "Well, I'm satisfied. What about the two of you?"

"I'm good," said both Sarah and Benjamin.

"I think we bring in the rest of the gang," said Emily.

Emily went upstairs and let everyone know to go down to the morning room. On entering the kitchen, she overheard Emma. "This house is older and smaller than what we are used to, but that will be a nice change."

Reginald and the boys were the first to arrive and then Logan.

Travis introduced his sons, Andrew and Frederick first; then Reginald, their tutor. He introduced Logan as the family's security detail until Olivia and Higgins arrive in a week or so.

Travis expected to have the boys ask a million questions, especially Andy, but both remained quiet.

"Benjamin and I will remain here and work with you until you and the family are comfortable with us going back to Fairfield," said Sarah.

Emily looked elated as she turned to usher everyone out into the hallway. "I'm so happy that this is working out."

"When would you be able to start?" Travis asked Emma.

"We'll head back to Cleveland now and pack our things. We don't have much, only clothes and a few personal items. I would think we could start tomorrow," said Emma.

Travis couldn't believe his good luck. They had gone from no applicants to winning the housekeeper lottery.

CHAPTER THIRTY-SEVEN

"You did what?" Olivia nearly shouted into the phone. "In one day, Emily gets her first application, and hours later, they are hired. Travis, what were you thinking? You know Higgins must interview them and then do a thorough background check. Especially now with everything that is going on."

"Actually, they were the second applicant. The first one was a raving bitch. Emily wouldn't have hired her to watch her cat." Travis took a long breath. "Livy, honey, the Burnsides are perfect. Along with the Captain's House, they can manage your apartment in the Waldorf and handle all the entertaining you do. Emma and Stanley practically single-handedly ran the Luxembourg Embassy in Washington."

"Luxembourg? I don't think I know that embassy."

"It is on Massachusetts Avenue, near Dupont Circle."

"Usually, Travis, when things are too good to be true, they are. Now, give me their names, past employers, and any other information Higgins can use to do a background check." Olivia paused a beat. "Then put the boys on the line."

Travis eagerly gave her all the names and dates that were listed on the Burnsides' résumé, then called to the boys, who were having cookies and milk in the kitchen with Sarah.

"And, Travis, keep your mobile phone with you tomorrow. I'm sure Higgins will be calling you for more information. When do the Burnsides start?"

"Tomorrow."

"Wonderful," Olivia said sarcastically. "Now put the boys on—and not on speaker."

Olivia talked to Andy first and then Freddy. It was obvious from the boys' answers to their mom's questions that they were being grilled about the Burnsides and whether the boys liked the couple. Interestingly enough, they didn't seem to have a strong opinion one way or the other.

"Freddy, why did you hang up the phone? I wasn't finished yet."

"Mom said she would talk to us tomorrow night. She didn't say she wanted to talk to you. She hung up first."

Travis tried to remember a time when Livy hung up on him, or, in this case, didn't want to wish him a good night. There wasn't one, at least not in recent history.

"Is Mom mad at you?" Andy asked.

"No. At least I hope not. Now you two run along upstairs."

Travis was thinking Livy was mad that he'd jumped the gun and not made her part of the conversation with the Burnsides. Everyone could have met in the library where there was a multiline phone with speaker. But instead, they used the morning room. Perhaps he had unconsciously kept her and Higgins out of the decision. He was still wondering if that was the case when he entered the kitchen to find Sarah sitting at the table.

"I take it, your evening call didn't go so well."

Travis looked at his housekeeper with raised eyebrows.

"The boys came in looking for more cookies. I said no. Freddy said their mother wouldn't talk to you."

"She didn't want to talk to me *after* she had grilled her sons about the Burnsides."

"Huh," Sarah said as she stood. "How about I do bathtime tonight? You can tell them a story and tuck them in for the night after."

An hour later, Travis went downstairs to find Sarah sitting at the kitchen table with the jar of cookies in front of her.

"Looks like story time was shorter than usual," commented Sarah.

"Yeah."

"Bathtime was short too."

"Sarah, did we do the right thing?"

She didn't need to ask what he meant. She knew. She had been having the same thoughts. "I think we made the right decision about hiring Emma and Stanley Burnside. They are more than qualified. Not sure *how* we handled it was right."

"We should have included Livy and Higgins in the interview and then gotten their feedback before making the decision to hire them. Sarah, we would never have done something like this before."

"Feeling a bit of buyer's remorse?" asked Sarah.

"Maybe. Are you?"

"Maybe."

"Would Emma have done bathtime with the boys?" asked Travis as he stood and headed up the back stairs.

The next morning, during breakfast, Travis mentioned that Nick had called and was adamant that he be at Long Point today. There were issues about the plumbing that needed his decisions. "Sorry, but I won't be able to be here when Emma and Stanley arrive."

"Don't worry, Travis. Benjamin and I have this covered. We need to finish getting the apartment ready for them. You know, clean sheets and all that housekeeping stuff. I'll get the basic food items stocked for them until I can take them to Mutach's and get Emma signed onto Olivia's account. The rest is getting them familiar with the house."

"What about us?" asked Freddy.

"We want to go with you to Long Point," the twins said in unison. "Please, Dad."

"Okay. But you will need to occupy yourselves with Reginald. It sounds like Nick will be keeping me busy."

"There is plenty of food and leftovers for lunch. That is unless Nick ate it all yesterday," added Sarah.

"I'll be going with you, as well," said Logan. "I would like to continue exploring the grounds in the golf cart. We haven't checked out the barn yet."

"I would rather you wait until I can be there for the barn. Unless you were raised on a farm and know what you are looking at," said Benjamin. "I know the barn is older than the house. No tellin' what you'll find in there."

"You got it, sir. We leave the barn for another day. We can take more photos for Higgins."

"And we can go out to the very end where it is sandy and climb on the rocks," pleaded Freddy.

"Reginald, see that the boys take a change of clothes with them," Sarah said.

"Okay, it sounds like everyone has their day cut out for them. Looks like we take the minivan on its first trip to Kelleys. Everyone meets at the garage in fifteen."

Travis and Sarah were left sitting at the table in the morning room.

"Sarah, if you and Benjamin have any doubts about the Burnsides today, don't be afraid to speak up. I value your opinions and thoughts."

"I know."

"We are talking about the care and safety of our family."

Sarah nodded her head in understanding and then silently got up and began removing the dirty dishes from the table.

CHAPTER THIRTY-EIGHT

Travis was the first to enter Bent Tree Cottage's kitchen. Immediately his stress level dropped, and it felt good to be back. Andy and Freddy rushed in behind him swinging their backpacks.

"Where should we put our stuff?" Andy asked. "Logan is getting the golf cart out of the garage. We don't want to be late."

"Follow me." Travis then motioned for his sons to follow him through to the servants' hallway. He stopped at the door leading into the housekeeper's bedroom. He took the backpacks and set them on floor next to the bed frame. "How about if we make this your room when you are here on Long Point? I'll order a mattress so you can even take naps here."

"Yes! Yes! Yes! Yes!" the boys shouted as they ran back out into the hall toward the kitchen.

Travis followed, taking pleasure in his sons' excitement. Their tutor was waiting for them in the kitchen.

"Reggie! Reggie! Dad gave us our very own room here in the castle," Freddy exclaimed while jumping up and down.

Reginald gave Travis a questioning look.

"The housekeeper's bedroom. It will give them their own space when here. I'll order a mattress. Besides the bedroom, there is a fully equipped bath and sitting room. That room has a couch, chairs, tables, and even a fireplace. There is also a door that leads out to a small porch. I'll have Nick fix the door. For whatever reason, it doesn't open."

"Thank you. I've been wondering how I was going to contain them while in the *castle*. Hide-and-go-seek is going to be a challenge. Fairfield is bad enough; I might have to specify certain floors here."

"He's here. He's here," Freddy shouted. "Come on, Reggie, or you are going to get left behind."

"Hey, what's all this yelling I'm hearing?" Nick asked as he entered the kitchen in time to see the three running out to meet Logan in the golf cart.

"They are off to further explore the far east end of the property. According to the boys, they are going to play in the sand and climb on the rocks."

"Sounds like my little cousins have fallen into kid paradise. They sure seem happy here. Now if Emily can dig up a housekeeper for the Captain's House, you'll be all set."

"Yeah, about that. I screwed up royally, and Livy is royally pissed."

Travis gave Nick a detailed account of yesterday's events, including the Burnsides' impressive résumé, the interview, and then Olivia's blowup.

"Dude, what were you thinking? Sorry, but I have to side with Olivia. You two are the perfect team, you balance each other out, and you understand the need for Higgins and all his rules. Cuz, you broke the most important rule—security. You kept her out of the decision process to hire *her* housekeeper, for *her* house. Yeah. I'd be pissed too!"

"Thanks, Nick. I was feeling horrible all morning, until I walked through that door. Then all my worries vanished, and I was ready for the day." Travis stood. "Now I feel horrible again. So, show me the plumbing problem. Maybe I can at least make one thing right today."

As promised on the first trip in the golf cart, the boys would alternate who would get to sit in the front seat with Logan. This time Andy got the front, and Freddy and Reginald sat in the rear. The golf cart bumped along the narrow ruts that made up the path to the far eastern point.

After being poked and scratched by the overgrown brush and trees along the path on their last trip, Logan managed to squeeze a pair of loppers, a shovel, and chain saw into the rear compartment of the cart. Several times Logan stopped to cut back branches to make more room for the vehicle to maneuver along the rutted path.

"Why do we have to keep stopping?" Freddy asked. "We didn't stop the last time."

"Remember how you were complaining about the pricker-bushes and branches scratching you as we drove past? Well, this makes it safer for all of us."

The ride took a bit longer because Logan stopped to cut down a small tree that he had had to drive around on their first trip. Once the golf cart broke free from the dense trees and under-brush, the view before them was spectacular. The blue waters of Lake Erie glistened in the morning sun. The area down to the water had been swept clean by decades of storms that ravaged the shoreline. Large rocks and boulders dotted a sandy beach. Logan parked off to the side and watched as his passengers scrambled onto the ground and ran toward the sand. All three were wearing shorts and T-shirts. Logan was the only one in jeans, a long-sleeved white shirt, and a denim vest with large pockets.

Logan shouted for everyone to stay within his sight. He removed the backpack that he'd stuffed on the floor of the cart between his feet. After unzipping it, he pulled out a large camera and put the strap around his neck. Next, a small pair of binoculars went into his right vest pocket. He then slipped a notepad and pen into the left pocket. Before leaving the vehicle to follow the others, Logan pushed the right side of his vest aside to make sure his holster and Glock were securely in place.

After talking to Higgins earlier that morning, Logan had made a list of things to check while out on the point. Number one on the list was to further investigate the firepit that he'd noticed on their first trip. It was off to the right side of the beach, nearly hidden by large boulders. But before checking out the firepit, Logan walked over to the others who were standing around a large, rounded stone that was very unlike the darker limestone that makes up the island.

"Logan, look here. This is so cool," Freddy said. The boulder was of a pinkish color and taller than the boys.

Reginald pointed to, then ran his index finger over two marks that had been chiseled into the stone. "Looks like the letters *L* and *P*. Although they are barely visible now."

"Did the Indians make these marks?" Andy asked. "Like the ones on Inscription Rock."

"No. The Native Americans didn't use our alphabet back when they lived here," Reginald said. "These are very old, but dating them will be hard because of the natural erosion."

"I bet the *L* and *P* mean Long Point," Freddy said. "Somebody carved them so everybody going by on boats would know that this is Long Point. Like a sign."

"Looks like you boys found something important. How about you stay round here and look for more interesting rocks while

I go check out something right over there?" Logan said while pointing to the opposite side of the beach.

Reginald looked in the direction where Logan had pointed. "You noticed something?"

"I mentioned that firepit we saw to Higgins. He asked that I check out the area around it."

"You two stay around here on the beach. I'm going with Logan."

Andy and Freddy nodded in agreement as they moved closer to the water's edge.

Logan took several photos of the circle of smaller stones containing burnt branches and inches of ash. "Lots of beer cans and empty chip bags tossed around. Looks like the locals' teenage party place," Reginald said.

"Yeah." Logan continued taking photos as he moved out the parameter, then headed to a thicket of crushed brambles. He bent down to get a closer look at the ground. "I'd say the kids came by water in small boats." Logan pointed to long deep gouges in the soil. "They pulled the boats up here. Probably to secure them but also to keep them out-of-sight from the homes along the shoreline further down the island."

"Do you think this might have anything to do with the squatter at The Pines?" Reginald asked.

"My guess is no. This looks like teenagers. And not recently."

"Reggie! Logan! Look what we found!" shouted the twins.

Logan took off running with one hand on his holster. He got to the boys first who were looking down into the water.

"Look."

"What? All I see is a—"

"Road," Freddy shouted. "A road under the water."

"A road?" Reginald asked in disbelief as he reached Logan's side.

"Not a road, but a huge slab of stone just beneath the surface. Maybe six inches down," Logan said as he stood scratching his head.

Before he could get his camera aimed and the shot through the water clear, both boys were walking on the stone.

"Andy, Freddy, get out of the water; it's too cold. You are going to get hurt," Reginald shouted, but not attempting to follow them in.

"It's okay, Reggie. We have our shoes on. This is so cool. It really is like a road," Andy shouted.

"Or a dock," Logan said. "A very old dock." He tried to get a better look. "Are you sure you two are safe out there?"

"Yeah," Freddy answered while shuffling his feet.

"Okay. I want each of you to *slowly* walk out to each corner and stop." Logan watched as the boys carefully eased their way out about fifteen feet and stood about eight feet apart. "Thanks. Now I want you to move to the center and slowly come back."

"Look," Freddy shouted while waving his arms toward the pink boulder. "The rock is pointing."

Both men glanced over to the rock, then shrugged. It looked like the rounded side of a huge rock. A rock that had the initials *L P* chiseled on it. They turned their attention back to the water and watched as Andy and Freddy reached the sand. "I never want to see either of you do anything that stupid again! Never enter the water without an adult with you," Logan scolded.

"You were with us, and we have our sneakers on, and we could see the bottom. The water hardly covered our shoes," Andy explained.

"Now come and look. The rock is pointing," Freddy said as he ran across the sand to the far side of the pink boulder.

"Could be granite," Reginald said as he ran his left hand over the smooth stone. Then he followed Freddy down to the water's edge.

"You have to come back here to see it."

Everyone ran down to stand next to Freddy and look up at the right side of the boulder. "See. It is pointing at the woods."

"And I didn't notice before that the top is flat," Reginald added.

"You are right, Freddy. Good eye. The rock, marked *L P*, is definitely pointing."

Everyone ran up the beach to get a better look when they all stopped suddenly at the edge of the thicket. "Did you hear that?" Logan said. The rattle sound. "Don't move." Logan scanned the underbrush. There it was curled up, not more than four feet away. Logan pointed to a large colorful snake with a coppery head and large diamond shapes along its back. It vibrated its tail. "A copperhead," Logan said as he went for his gun.

"No, wait," Reginald said. "Copperheads shouldn't be here. This isn't their habitat. Shoot it with your camera and not your gun. It sounds dangerous with that vibrating tail, but it isn't raising its head in a menacing way. Let's back away slowly until I can check it out."

Everyone slowly backed away toward the beach.

"It sure was pretty," Andy said. "We are used to snakes in Virginia."

"I understand, but from now on, we move slowly when in the woods. I think it is time to head back to the house for lunch. The wildlife around here isn't used to seeing people," Logan said as he ushered everyone back to the golf cart.

The merry bunch of adventurers arrived back at the house to find Nick lighting the charcoal grill, and Travis in the kitchen pulling a package of hot dogs out of the fridge, along with a container of Sarah's homemade potato salad.

After a quick "Hi, Dad, you wouldn't believe what we did," Reginald hurried the twins through the kitchen and to their designated bedroom for a change of clothes. Fortunately, Reggie had had the foresight to add a pair of flip-flops to each of the boys' bags. He put their wet socks and sneakers out in the yard to dry in the sun.

Lunch evolved into an excited discussion of every action and thought describing the events from the time the four climbed into the golf cart to when they arrived back at the house and crawled out of the golf cart.

Afterward, Reginald suggested a more subdued game of croquet on the front lawn, while Nick and Travis got back to work.

"Excuse me, sir. Could I have a moment with you and Nick?" Logan said while Travis and Nick began putting the lunch things away.

"Can we talk while I finish up in here?" Travis asked.

"Sure. I just need a minute or two." Logan paused a beat. "I believe you could have some security issues according to what I saw this morning. The first is that the roadway out to the point needs to be widened. It is barely wide enough for the golf cart to squeeze through. We would never make it in an emergency. Also, this property in general has become very overgrown with lack of use."

"Nick and I have recognized that we have a major cleanup in the near future."

"The property is heavily forested, and the lanes could easily become impassible with your Hummer and truck." Logan paused for emphasis. "Last year, John Deere came out with a new all-terrain utility vehicle called a Gator. It would be perfect for getting around and has excellent hauling capacity."

"Yes!" Nick shouted. "I've seen the ads. He's right, Travis. You have to get one—maybe buy two—one for Fairfield."

CHAPTER THIRTY-NINE

At four thirty, Travis drove through the gates at the Captain's House and parked in front of the garage. Andy and Freddy grabbed their backpacks and ran for the side door. Logan slung his pack over his shoulder, while Travis loaded up his arms with the boys' dirty clothes, and together, they followed Reginald up the side steps to the porch.

"What a day," Logan said. "I sure am looking forward to Sarah's cooking."

Travis heard his sons' flip-flops smacking against the oak floor as they ran toward the kitchen followed by Reginald. Then, the sound abruptly stopped. Travis and Logan reached the other three who had stopped at the door watching the scene before them in the kitchen.

Emma Burnside stood at the stove. She wore a simply styled light-gray dress that fell just below her knees. She wore plain black flats, and her hair was pulled back in a bun. A large pot sat on the back burner over a raging flame. She was stirring something in a skillet on another burner. Sarah walked toward them with her arms loaded down with plates. "Excuse me. I need to set these on the sideboard." And without another word, she walked past and entered the morning room.

"Welcome home. I hope you all had a lovely day," Emma said as she continued to stir. "Dinner will be ready at five in the morning room."

"Sarah, you are never going to believe what we did today," Freddy shouted as he followed her into the morning room.

"Not now. I want you and your brother to go upstairs and wash up for dinner. You can tell us later."

Freddy gave Sarah a questioning look, then went back in the hall to find Andy. "Come on. We have to go upstairs and get cleaned up for dinner."

"You better come with us, Reggie. I think we are supposed to put on nice clothes," Andy said as the three of them began crossing through the kitchen to use the back stairs.

"Those are for the servants' use; you are the young men of the house." Emma glanced at Reginald. "And your tutor. It is proper for you to use the main staircase."

Travis turned to Logan. "I don't know where you fit into this new hierarchy, but I'm following them."

Travis and Logan found the other three waiting at the top of the wide staircase, at the opposite end of the mansion. "Dad, is it always going to be like this now that they are in charge of our house?" Freddy asked.

"I don't know, Son. I think we must wait until your mother arrives to set the rules. For now, we go with the flow and don't rock the boat." Travis nodded toward the landing with the large stained glass window above a window seat. "We meet down there a couple of minutes before five and walk to the morning room together."

Logan continued walking down the long hallway that would lead him back to the servants' stairs and then up to the floor above where the rooms for the security staff were located.

At five minutes to five, Travis arrived at the landing wearing beige trousers, white shirt, and navy-blue jacket. Reginald had dressed himself and the boys in casual tan slacks and short-sleeved shirts in a variety of prints. The twins were identical and chose to dress differently to reflect their individual style. No matched outfits for them. Logan wore what Travis considered his official security uniform of black trousers, white shirt, and black suit jacket. He skipped the tie.

Upon entering the morning room, Travis saw that Emma stood next to the sideboard. "Please take your seats, and I will serve." Stanley stood at attention at the far end of the sideboard.

Andy and Freddy went to the places that they usually sat at and scooted up onto the chairs. Everyone else followed suit.

Sarah entered carrying glasses of milk for the boys. "Emma has prepared a meal that was a favorite of hers when she was growing up," Sarah said as she placed the glasses in front of the twins.

Emma and Sarah served each person and then placed the bowls back on the sideboard. Caesar salad and a loaf of sliced French bread were served first. Small dishes of sweet butter were at each place setting.

Freddy and Andy both had sour faces as they chewed the Caesar salad. "This salad tastes funny," Freddy said while pushing his plate aside.

"The dressing is made with anchovies. I made it myself," Emma said.

"You mean those little hairy fish that come in a can?" Andy asked. "Freddy and I don't like those. We never order them on a pizza."

"I'll remember that in the future," Emma sounded cheerful.

The boys had two pieces of bread each, while the adults finished their salad.

Next, Sarah served the green beans.

"We love green beans," Freddy said as he watched Sarah serve the adults first. His smile turned to a frown when Sarah placed the mound of beans on his plate. "What is all this stuff mixed in?"

"This is called green beans almondine. It has sliced almonds, shallots, and garlic mixed in with a bit of olive oil and lemon juice," Sarah explained.

"It tastes pretty good," said Andy after taking a bite.

Freddy tried it, then picked out the almonds.

"I'm sure you will love this dish, Master Frederick. It's called chicken paprikash. I practically grew up on this Hungarian favorite."

The twins watched as the adults dug in and raved about the rich flavor of the sauce and tender chicken served over noodles. The boys looked at each other and shrugged before taking the first bite.

"This is pretty good," Andy said and took another bite.

"Yeah. It's pretty good," Freddy added. "Do you know how to make spaghetti and meatballs?"

"Yes, I do," Emma said between clenched teeth.

"Sarah, is there anymore barbecue ribs in the fridge?" Freddy asked.

"Okay, boys. You both are being extremely rude. What do you do when we are guests in someone's home, and you don't like what our hostess serves?"

"We eat it anyway and don't complain. Because that is good manners," Andy said.

"So, what happened to good manners tonight?" Travis asked of his sons.

"But, Dad, this is our house, and Mrs. Campbell and Sarah always cook what we like," Freddy stated.

"I prepared this meal for the adults, and I wrongly assumed that the two of you would like the dishes as well," Emma said.

"I will consult Sarah in the future." She walked over to the sideboard, while Sarah removed their plates. Emma lifted what could only be described as a culinary work of art. "I've made a lemon torte for dessert."

While everyone oohed and aahed over the delicate citrus-flavored cake, the twins ate in silence.

After the meal, everyone stood and began leaving the room, while Andy moved to Emma's side. "I just want to let you know for when you make desserts in the future, that Freddy and I like cupcakes."

"I will certainly remember that, Master Andrew."

"You can call me Andy." Then he followed his father to the family room.

Everyone was having a lively discussion of the day's events when Freddy went to the kitchen. He found the Harrisons and Burnsides eating their dinner at the kitchen table. "Sarah, how come you are eating in here and not with us? We wanted to tell you all the cool stuff we did today."

"Master Frederick, it isn't proper for the help to eat with the family."

"I know that, and at Fairfield, Sarah and Benjamin always eat in the kitchen. But here they are eating with us since the Campbells aren't here. They are like our family."

"Here you are, Freddy. I wondered where you had run off to," Travis said as he put his arm around his son.

"I was looking for Sarah and Benjamin."

"While you are here, Mr. Tanner, I would like you to, please, remove all the documents that cover the dining room table. It would be easier, since some of your staff share meals with you, that I serve at the larger table in the dining room."

"Of course. I've been living here alone until recently and the dining room wasn't used." Travis took Freddy's hand and turned to leave the room. "How about we get your brother and the two of you can help me move all that stuff into the library?"

"Freddy, I'll be up to tuck you both in after you are finished helping your dad. You can tell me all about your adventures then," Sarah said with a smile.

"Can we call Mom before we go upstairs?" Freddy asked.

"Of course, we can, and you can tell her all about your day."

Travis thought about what he was going to say during that call. He was quickly coming to the realization that he had made a terrible mistake in hiring the Burnsides. The summers in Marblehead were casual months for the family. Livy left her business life behind in Virginia and became an average citizen in a town that loved and protected her. Staff was treated as family. They didn't need a housekeeper who managed a foreign embassy and had spent a year in Paris at a culinary school. They needed the cook from Crackle Barrel.

CHAPTER FORTY

"Mom, we had the coolest day ever! You gotta come, Mom." Freddy paused long enough to take a breath. "Long Point has a beach, and it is so cool. We found a firepit full of old beer cans, and a big rock that points, and a stone road under water."

"Yeah, Mom. And Freddy and me walked out to the end. The water was real cold, but we had our sneakers on." Andy stopped talking, then remembered something. "Oh, and when we were looking at the pointing rock, we saw a really big snake. Logan pulled out his gun and was going to shoot it because it was rattling its tail, but Reggie told him to shoot it with his camera instead. Isn't that funny, Mom? Shoot it with the camera," Andy finished while laughing.

"Travis? Are you sure the boys are safe wandering around out there? On their *second* visit to the point, they were allowed to walk in the water, on an underwater road? Travis, the lake is still too cold for them to be walking in it, even with shoes on. And a big rattler?" Olivia paused. "I think Logan needs to keep the boys closer to the house. A golf cart is no protection against rattlesnakes!"

"Livy, I know all this sounds bad, but we have it under control. Logan has informed me about an all-terrain vehicle that would be perfect for Long Point. I'm going to make some calls tomorrow."

"Mom, we love it here," shouted Freddy. "When are you and Higgins coming? You don't want to miss out on the fun."

"Maybe this weekend."

Sarah stepped into the room and walked over to stand next to the twins. "Hello, Olivia. I'm ready for bathtime with the boys. I hope you and Higgins are making out all right."

"We are both fine. Higgins is almost as good as you at the grill. Speaking of food, how did Emma do with dinner? Are the Burnsides settling in without too much difficulty?"

"Her cooking is real fancy," Freddy answered. "But we like Sarah's better. Emma calls me Master Frederick."

"Okay, you two, I think you should say 'Good night' to your mother and follow me upstairs for your bath. Your dad will come up later for story time."

Travis waited until he heard the clomping of little feet on the back stairs. Was it permissible for the sons of the manor to use the servants' stairs if accompanied by a servant? Travis wasn't sure.

"Livy, honey, I'm having second thoughts about—"

"Travis, Higgins finished a background check on the Burnsides. They are exactly who they say they are. I reread their résumé, and I believe they will be the perfect couple to manage the Marblehead property. I'm very excited to meet them. Have Sarah call me when she is finished. I would like her feedback on how today went."

"You really think you'll be here this weekend?"

"Yes. Everything has been quiet here. William's people have gotten the contracts signed, and production on HELIOS will begin within the month. I can monitor the project and handle any loose ends from Marblehead."

This was a turn-of-events that Travis hadn't expected. He was sure Higgins would have found something to hold against the Burnsides—everyone had parking tickets in DC.

"Wonderful, Livy. I can't wait to show you Long Point and Bent Tree Cottage. I've missed you."

"I've missed you too. Just a few more days. Good night, and I love you."

"Love you too. We'll talk tomorrow," Travis said, then hung up the phone.

CHAPTER FORTY-ONE

The following morning, over eggs Benedict, hash browns, croissants, and cut-up fruit and fresh-squeezed orange juice, Travis announced that they would be going to Sandusky to the John Deere dealer to check out the new Gator. And stop by the JCPenney store to buy a mattress and bedding for the boys' bed at the cottage. They could run over to Kelleys in the afternoon.

Logan said he would like to find a one-hour photo shop near the mall where he could have three rolls of film developed.

Sarah said that she and Benjamin would stay and work with the Burnsides. The cleaning crew would be arriving soon, and Sarah wanted to get Emma familiar with the routine. Benjamin and Stanley would be working outside with the landscapers, who would be replacing dead shrubs, dressing the beds with mulch, and mowing.

The twins pushed aside clean plates. "Breakfast was very good, Emma. I liked that egg stuff," Andy said.

"Thank you, Master Andrew. I'm glad you liked it." Emma looked down at Freddy's plate. "It appears that you liked the meal as well, Master Frederick."

"It was good. You can call me Freddy."

"Good job with breakfast, boys. Now I want you to run upstairs, brush your teeth, and be ready to leave in ten," Travis said.

The twins slid off their chairs and ran for the door leading to the main hallway. "Yea! We are going to buy an alligator," Andy shouted.

"Sarah, could I speak with you for a minute in the library?" Travis said after the Burnsides took the dirty dishes to the kitchen.

Sarah nodded her agreement, and they both walked to the library at the other end of the house in silence.

After entering, Travis shut the door behind them. "I must tell you that I had severe doubts about the Burnsides after last night's dinner. I thought it was delicious, but the boys' likes are just as important. I was prepared to tell Olivia on the phone last night that I had made a huge mistake and the Burnsides were not going to work out. But then Livy went on about how excited to have found a housekeeper of Emma's caliber and is looking forward to meeting her and Stanley. I'm at a loss as to what to do. Andy and Freddy seemed to actually enjoy breakfast."

"I had the same thoughts last night. I actually had the feeling that Emma didn't like the boys. But this morning they seem to be two different people. We need to remember that they are coming from a very formal and highly structured environment. The two of them need time to settle into an informal family setting."

"You are right, Sarah. We all need to give them time." Travis opened the door for Sarah. "For today, I'll keep everyone away, and you can get a better feel while working with Emma. We'll return by five for dinner."

An hour later, Travis and Logan had learned everything there was to know about the capabilities of the Gator. Logan asked all the right questions about its speed and maneuverability over rough terrain, while Travis focused on the hauling capacity and safety features of the two-seater utility vehicle. Andy and Freddy complained that it only had room for two, but Travis explained that the Gator was designed to be a tough workhorse, not a kid mobile. Freddy suggested that they buy two. They all left the store happy that the Gator would be delivered to Long Point the next day.

On the way to the mall, Logan noticed a photo shop that advertised one-hour service, where he dropped off his three rolls of film.

At JCPenney's, Travis purchased a full-size mattress and box spring for the old housekeeper's bedroom at the cottage, which would be delivered to Long Point in the next couple of days. The boys picked out pillows and Batman-themed sheets and comforter set. Throw rugs and towels in navy-blue and white were purchased for their bathroom. Olivia or Sarah could pick out everything else that would make the rooms comfortable for the boys and Reginald.

It was a little after noon when the five walked out of the store with enough bags to fill the back of the minivan. Everyone agreed that they were starving, and Andy and Freddy unanimously decided on McDonalds for lunch.

The photos were ready when Logan stopped by the shop on their way back to Marblehead. He reviewed the double sets and handed the boys photos taken while up on the parapet of the tower and from Perry's Monument and their trip around South Bass Island. He gave Reginald photos taken at the beach of the snake and the pointing rock and the various trees and shrubs that Reginald hadn't been able to identify. Logan didn't share the photos he had taken at The Pines, both inside and outside the house and the matted-down brush at the water's edge. He didn't share photos of the areas at the point that he hadn't shown to the others or the ones he had taken around Bent Tree Cottage. That stack of photos was for Higgins.

⊷⊶

Travis backed up to the rear door at Bent Tree Cottage. Nick came out in time to open the back door of the minivan. "I suppose this means you have stuff to unload."

"Cousin Nick! Cousin Nick! Dad bought an alligator for Long Point," Freddy shouted as he careened around the back of the van.

"Yeah. It's coming tomorrow," Andy added as he ran into Nick's arms.

"Just what Long Point needs. I don't believe there has ever been an alligator living here."

"You are so funny, Cousin Nick." Andy laughed.

"By the looks of all these bags, you bought more than the Gator."

Travis began looking in each bag. He set the bags containing the sheets and towels aside and gave the rest to Reginald and the boys. "How about you take these to your rooms and the rest we can take home for Sarah and Emma to wash? We will bring those back tomorrow, so they are ready when the mattress arrives."

"Travis, while the boys are inside, there is something I'd like you and Logan to see."

Logan and Travis followed Nick to the front of the garage. He pointed to the ground. "I noticed this oil spot when I arrived this morning. I don't believe it was here when I left yesterday."

"Was the house broken into?" Logan asked.

"No. Everything is as I left it."

Logan looked in the direction of the garage and nodded toward the second floor. "How about the garage? Have you searched inside?"

"No. And I really wouldn't know if anything was taken. Benjamin is the only one who has spent any time in there."

"Not a problem. The two of you go in the house with the boys. I'll take photos of the oil stain and do a quick search inside." Logan moved toward the van's front seat and pulled out his backpack. After unzipping it, he pulled out the camera.

Travis and Nick headed back toward the house.

"So, do you think these oil stains are from a vehicle connected to our squatter, smuggler, or whatever the FBI is calling him?" Nick asked.

"I don't see how." Travis thought about the timeline. "Unless whatever he's smuggling was stashed in the garage. And he couldn't get back here before now. The building isn't locked, and the gate is now left wide open."

"By now, he knows his money is gone, and The Pines has been searched by both the police and the FBI."

"I'm sure glad Logan is with us, and Higgins should be here by the end of the weekend," Travis said as they entered the kitchen.

For the next hour, Nick filled Travis in on what progress had been made with both the electrical and plumbing jobs. "The electrical is a bit tricky because when this house was built, they were using oil or kerosene for lighting. When they added electricity, they ran the wires through metal pipes attached to the walls or hidden behind paneling or cabinets. It's a real challenge to trace and replace with new conduit."

They both turned when Logan entered.

"Find anything?" Travis asked.

"Yes and no. There is evidence that someone has been living or using the second-floor apartment. Not for long, but long enough to leave things behind. There are two oil lamps, one on the kitchen table and one in the bedroom. It also appears that whoever was staying there was searching for something."

"Could that person be our squatter?" Nick asked.

"I cannot speculate on who was there or when. But I'll have Higgins get a crew out here to do a thorough sweep and get fin- gerprints." He set his backpack on the table. "We'll be able to identify everyone who has been in there."

Reginald and the boys entered the kitchen. "We're done put- ting stuff away. Reggie says we can go now," Freddy announced.

Travis glanced at his watch. "You're right. We don't want to be late for Emma's dinner."

Emma and Sarah stood at the head of the dining room table as everyone entered and took their seats. Doubt crossed the faces of Andy and Freddy. Emma picked up a large bowl and moved to stand between the twins. She bent down to their level and smiled while lifting the lid to reveal a bowlful of spaghetti.

"Will this do, Master Andy, Master Freddy?"

"Yes! Yes! Yes! Thank you," the boys said in unison.

Emma heaped their plates before moving on to serve every- one else at the table. Sarah served small plates of a simple tossed salad with Italian dressing and garlic bread.

Sarah refreshed water and milk with a smile as she joined in the lively conversation about how Travis had bought an alligator for Long Point.

After everyone said that they couldn't eat another bite, Emma entered the room through the swinging door from the butler's pantry carrying a silver tray filled with chocolate cupcakes.

At that moment, Travis knew that Emma had won over his sons. Perhaps Emily Elfin had found the perfect couple to take care of his family after all.

Stanley entered through the swinging door. "Excuse me, sir. You have a call on the housephone."

Travis stood and walked across the room and out into the main hall to the library. He pressed the button with the blinking light and picked up the receiver.

"Hello?"

"Travis, it's me."

"Livy. What's wrong?"

"Your John Doe is Russian."

CHAPTER FORTY-TWO

"Russian?" Where did that come from? Travis wondered. How does some John Doe who washes up on shore after a major storm, in Marblehead, Ohio, connect to Russia? "Whoa, Livy, how do you—"

"Higgins figured it out. Remember when he said that something about that partial tattoo rang a bell? Well, with all this recent discussion about Russia and China being the obvious players behind the HELIOS attempts, Higgins remembered a case he worked on years ago involving a Russian spy."

"Okay. I'll buy that there could be similarities in a random tattoo, but the FBI is looking into our guy. I'm sure all of the FBI databases are full of Russian identifiers, and our guy's tattoo didn't come up in any of them."

"Travis, what I've told you is all I know. I believe Higgins is talking to Logan as we speak. Anyway, I'm so excited about joining you and the boys on Sunday that I've already started packing."

"Packing? You have a closet and dresser drawers full of clothes here. What could you possibly have to pack other than your purse and briefcase?"

"A girl always has new things. Besides, Higgins has been stacking boxes of stuff in the hallway all week. We may have to rent a truck to get it all to the airport in Richmond. Higgins has promised that the Gulfstream won't be too heavy to take off." Olivia laughed.

"Hey, honey, Logan just walked in. He's motioning that he needs to talk to me. Call me if anything changes. I love you."

"I don't mean to cut your conversation short, but I've just now talked to Higgins." Logan closed the door behind him, then walked over to the desk.

"Please sit down. By the grim look, this isn't going to be good. Livy told me about our Russian spy. But she doesn't know any more. I take it, you do."

"Higgins is now positive that the break-in on Freemason Street and whoever was impersonating Mabel Polanski was orchestrated by the same foreign operatives."

"What about the tattoo? Livy said that Higgins recognized it."

"Higgins remembered it because it is so unique that it isn't in any databases. The tattoo design is both a badge and identification. The design itself designates the person as a member of the organization. Then encrypted within the design is a symbol that identifies the individual, like a social security number."

"You mean an organization like the KGB?"

"Only this group is so elite that it doesn't exist, not even to the Russian government. It is literally a ghost."

"So how does Higgins know about it?"

"Back in his CIA days, he took down a Russian spy. It was a fluke; the guy wasn't even on the agency's radar. The only identification they had for him was the tattoo. The man literally didn't exist. Higgins kept a photo of the tattoo in case another one ever showed up. Your John Doe's was only partially visible, but something about it triggered a memory."

"So why would an operative at that advanced level be boating during a major storm off the coast of Marblehead, Ohio?"

"And so close to your estate? To Olivia's estate?" Logan added. "That is what Higgins is wondering. He plans on beefing up the outside cameras and motion sensors here with new state-of-the-art equipment that he is bringing with him. We touch base at least twice a day, especially regarding my findings on Long Point."

"You are saying there is a definite lack of security out there."

"I am saying there is *no* security on Long Point. Except for the thick stone walls of the house. That fortress could withstand cannon fire! Higgins is already drawing up a preliminary plan based on what information I have given him. The photos will help once he has a chance to study them after he and Olivia arrive on Sunday."

"Okay, we keep this to ourselves—at least for now. But you're sure we are safe here, on this property?"

"Absolutely," Logan said with confidence.

Everyone looked expectantly at Travis and Logan as the two of them walked back into the dining room.

"Was that Mom who called? You were talking to her for a long time," Freddy asked.

"Yes, it was. She wanted to let us know that she is busy getting ready to come here on Sunday. She is sorry, but she won't be able to call later. She wanted me to tell you both that she loves you and not to give me or Sarah a hard time at bathtime." Little white lies were sometimes necessary when being a good parent. And

Travis desperately wanted to keep everything good, especially after what he had just learned.

"Were you talking to Higgins, Logan?" asked Andy. "You always use your mobile phone to talk to Higgins."

"Yes. He called to tell me that he is bringing new security equipment for here and Long Point. Because it is important for us to keep all of you safe."

"Mom said Higgins has boxes of stuff stacked in the hallway ready to be taken to the airport and loaded into the plane on Sunday."

"Oh boy. I hope Higgins doesn't take too many boxes. The cargo compartment on the Gulfstream isn't that big, and Mom needs room for her stuff," said Andy.

"Wouldn't it be funny if Higgins filled the plane with boxes and it was too heavy to take off?"

Everyone laughed at Freddy's joke.

"I know that security is important at all times. Emily Elfin filled us in on your family. The security team at the embassy was well-trained, and there were cameras everywhere. But here, we just have you, Logan, and, of course, Higgins when he arrives." Emma sounded concerned.

"You are safe, Emma. Besides, I have Reginald for backup."

"I'm not doubting your ability, Logan," Emma said. "But how effective is a children's tutor going to be if we get attacked?"

"I know Reginald looks like he's not long out of high school," Sarah said. "However, he entered college at the age of fourteen and graduated Cum Laude. He became interested in the FBI and trained at Quantico, where he became a sharpshooter. He spent time with the Secret Service before joining the CIA, where he met Higgins."

"Higgins finds the best, hires the best—and pays the best," Logan said.

"And when you fly with Olivia, her pilot Lorenzo was also one of Higgins's *finds*," Reginald said. "You will be meeting him on Sunday."

"Well, Stanley and I are more than impressed. I can say with confidence that this household has a better security team than the Luxembourg Embassy."

"And as for cameras, they are placed all around the grounds and for those inside the house. You probably won't notice they are there."

"Dad, since we can't talk to Mom tonight, can you play a game with us and Reggie?" Andy asked.

"Sure. Which one?"

"Monopoly."

"It's going to be a long night," Travis said as he pulled out the boys' chairs and watched as they ran toward the family room.

CHAPTER FORTY-THREE

The morning sun filled Fairfield's kitchen with a golden glow. Mother Nature's way of promising a beautiful day. Olivia sipped her first cup of coffee while she watched Higgins at the stove. He'd already spooned his special recipe of hash browns onto the two plates. Not as many on Olivia's—she tended to be a light eater. He added strips of hickory smoked bacon and finally slid two eggs over easy onto her plate—four eggs for him—and a bowl of grits. Olivia had been living at Fairfield for nearly nine years, and she still hadn't acquired a taste for that staple of the South.

"Thank you, Higgins. I don't know I could survive without you. My culinary skills are limited to what I can pull out of a carton and place in the microwave."

"I grew up poor, but I loved to eat. My mother worked two jobs, plus took in ironing for extra spending money. She told me if I wanted to eat more than she had time to prepare, I'd better learn to cook. And I did."

"And I appreciate every bite. Although, I must admit, I am missing Sarah's meals."

"Me too! I sure am looking forward to her barbecue. I hope she makes ribs on Sunday. I'd better phone in my request now."

"Speaking of Sunday, do you really need whatever is in all those boxes?"

Higgins leaned forward, resting his arms on the table. He looked directly into her eyes. "I know we haven't had any incidents, but some of the equipment is eight years old. There have been amazing advancements in technology since then. It needs to be replaced—now. You and I both understand that a Russian spy could only be in Marblehead for one reason—you. We also must consider Long Point. I know how you feel about Travis purchasing the property. But from the feedback I've been getting from Logan—well, let's just say—it's amazing and has huge potential. The problem is, at the moment, it is wide open with no chance of securing anything but the house."

"And you have this new equipment?"

"Yes, during this past year, I've been purchasing and storing as much as I could get my hands on. This last purchase contains items that haven't even hit the market yet. Others are for government agencies only."

"You really believe Long Point should be a priority?"

"Logan tells me Andy and Freddy love the place. Look how excited they are during your phone calls. They can't wait to show you the castle. And if it helps any—Logan tells me it's built like a fortress. The building could probably sustain cannon fire, or, in today's world—high-powered weapons."

"Okay, I'm convinced. Will you have everything you need ready to go on Sunday?"

"I packed the last box last evening. I'm having our guys load everything into the cargo van this morning. Saturday afternoon, they will drive to Richmond and load the plane. Lorenzo will have the plane fueled, flight plan filed, and ready for takeoff early Sunday morning."

"You know that mountain of stuff you have stacked in the hallway won't fit in the cargo compartment."

"Don't worry. There will be only you and I on board. That leaves lots of room for other *stuff*."

"I trust you. Now, I want to finish packing," Olivia said as she pushed her chair back and stood.

"I thought you were finished. I've already brought your bag down."

"The only thing left to do is change over my leather purse to the new woven tote bag I picked up while we were in DC."

"While you do that, I'll clean up the kitchen and then I want to have a meeting with my security team, who will be taking care of Fairfield until the Harrisons return."

"I have a conference call with William at two o'clock that shouldn't last more than an hour. Other than that, I'll be free if you need me."

"Works for me," Higgins said as he cleared the table.

Olivia went upstairs to her bedroom. She sat in one of the floral-print wingback chairs that overlooked the lawn and the James River beyond. Her life was getting more complicated, more dangerous, more time spent away from her family. Control of her life ended the day she first stepped foot in Fairfield and into the life her mother had left behind. Olivia wondered when her world would slow down—would it *ever* slow down? She gazed up at the portrait over the mantel. Her great-grandmother, Alexandra McLeod, looked down. At that moment, Olivia felt loved and protected, as if her ancestor held her in her arms.

Olivia sat there, feeling Alexandra's presence, her strength, and her love until the grandfather clock in the downstairs hallway chimed eleven times, bringing Olivia back to her real world.

She noticed the leather handbag and tote sitting on the bed. One last task before the conference call. Olivia got up from the chair and walked over to the bed. She dumped the contents and began sifting through, putting the items she wanted to take into the new tote. After checking the inside one more time, making sure she hadn't overlooked something, she ran her hand caressingly over the smooth service. She'd purchased the designer handbag on her last trip to New York, and it was still her favorite. Olivia took the closure and tried to snap it into the corresponding lock. It wouldn't go in. She turned the handbag around to get a better angle on the fastener. It still wouldn't go in. "Darn! What's wrong with this stupid thing?" Olivia said in a raised voice. "What else is going to go wrong?"

"Hey, there. I heard you down the hall. Need help?" Higgins asked while taking in the scene of Olivia standing over the bed about ready to throw her purse.

"This clasp won't close."

"Here, let me take a look."

Higgins picked up the handbag and tried to snap it together. The clasp wouldn't go into the lock. He looked closely into the opening. "Looks like you've got a piece of something stuck inside. No problem. Do you have a pair of tweezers handy?"

Olivia went into her bathroom and returned with the tool.

Higgins maneuvered the tweezers and handbag until he pulled out the culprit. He set the piece in the palm of his hand, then walked over to the window to get a better look.

Higgins put his index finger to his lips, then mouthed, "You've got a bug."

"A bug?" Olivia whispered.

Higgins placed the tiny instrument between his thumb and index finger and squeezed to block any sound, then whispered, "A listening device."

Olivia felt a veil of ice drape over her.

Higgins rushed to her side. "You're as white as a sheet," he said as he dropped the device into a glass of water sitting on the nightstand. Then he guided her out into the hallway and closed the bedroom door.

"How? How did it get in there? Higgins, how long could that have been in my handbag?"

"Have you left it lying around somewhere, outside of the house? Maybe set it down when you were at the shipyard?"

"No. Higgins, you've practically kept me a prisoner ever since the accident. I haven't been anywhere except—"

"Except when Mabel or whoever she was picked your purse up off the ground . . ."

"Brushed it off and handed it to me."

"Whoever is listening knows everything we've said while in close proximity to your purse."

"Higgins, what are we going to do?"

"We leave for Marblehead—now!"

CHAPTER FORTY-FOUR

That morning, Emma served another award-winning break-fast, at least as far as the twins were concerned. They left no trace of the scrambled eggs, Tater Tots, sausage, or toast with the locally made strawberry preserves from Paterson's in Port Clinton.

Freddy's idea that they get to Long Point before the Gator arrived was unanimously agreed upon. Sarah and Benjamin decided to stay in Marblehead and continue getting the Burnsides familiar with the house and family routines. Sarah promised to get the boys' new bedding washed. Benjamin and Stanley were going to clean the pool and make sure all the mechanical components were in working order.

Olivia and Travis had the twins swimming in the pool at Fairfield long before they could walk. Last year the boys insisted on swimming in Lake Erie, which quickly became a problem with Higgins. The answer was to install a pool, new patio, and pergola so the boys could swim safely.

Travis had the minivan in line and ready to board the Kelleys Island ferry well before the nine o'clock departure. Freddy was convinced that they were leaving too late, and the Gator would already be sitting in front of the garage at Long Point. He wanted to watch it roll off the trailer. Travis tracked down the dock attendant and was told there hadn't been a John Deere truck board that morning. Reginald and the boys had been riding the ferry enough times that they had a routine. Once the boat cleared the dock, the twins would drag their tutor across the deck to the sides where they would wave to the passing sailboats and powerboats.

The group entered Bent Tree Cottage's kitchen to find Nick at the sink adding water to the Mr. Coffee machine.

"Good morning, Cousin Nick. We are here to see the Gator arrive."

"Well, isn't that interesting, Cousin Freddy, because that's why I'm here."

Reginald pulled the photos Logan had given him the day before. "I had a chance to study these last night. I'd like to research that pointed rock, along with some of the trees and vegetation that I'm not familiar with. Is there by chance a library on the island?"

"Don't forget the snake, Reggie. I want to know about the snake. I bet there are more of them in the woods," Andy added.

"Hey, Travis. How about Aunt Millie? Why don't you take them over to her house? It's like an unofficial history museum. Aunt Millie is an expert on everything Kelleys," Nick said. "Maybe you can go after the Gator arrives."

"Yeah, we don't want to miss the alligator. Ha ha! Ha ha! Isn't that funny, Cousin Nick?"

"Yep, Cousin Freddy. You are a million laughs."

"Dad, do we know Aunt Millie?" Andy asked.

"No. I don't believe she has ever come to one of our Christmas parties."

"But if she is our aunt, we should know her—like Aunt Mavis."

"All the islanders call her aunt. But I don't believe she is actually anyone's aunt."

"That doesn't seem right."

"Look, Andy. You know how you have always called Meg O'Brien, your aunt?"

"Of course, Dad. Everyone knows that."

"But she isn't a relative of our family. Meg is your mother's assistant."

"Oh. So, it is one of those lies, like when we call Reggie our cousin and Logan our uncle when we are in public places."

"No, it isn't like that at all," Nick added. "Your mother has known Meg since they were kids and spent their summers living next door to each other in cottages on the bay side of Marblehead. Close to Johnson's Island. Meg loves you like you are her family."

"Johnson's Island is so cool," Freddy said. "It has lots of snakes."

"Okay. Aunt Millie's it is—after the Gator arrives."

An hour later, a horn blared from the driveway.

"The Gator is here! The Gator is here!" yelled the twins as they tore out the kitchen door.

"Travis Tanner?" the driver said as he jumped down from his truck with a clipboard in his hand.

"Wow. This is quite the welcoming committee. Looks like you're all excited about taking this bad boy for a spin. And from what I saw driving up your road here, this is the perfect property for this machine."

Travis was handed the clipboard with his paperwork as the driver began unhooking the straps securing the Gator to the trailer.

The boys watched, enthralled with every task until the driver climbed onto the driver's seat, fired it up, and backed off the trailer. He pulled over to the side of his truck and began reviewing the features and operation of the Gator.

Travis and Logan felt it was pretty simple, but the boys had a million questions, as if the vehicle had been purchased as an early Christmas present for them.

"Twins, huh? Double trouble." He laughed. "Can your parents tell you apart? I bet you try switching and fooling people."

The brothers looked at each other and grinned. "Nah," they said in unison.

"Okay, Mr. Tanner. She's got a full tank and is ready to go." After signing the paperwork, Travis returned the clipboard to the driver. He then climbed into his truck and drove back down the road.

"Dad, can you take us for a ride?" Freddy pleaded.

"Yeah, please, Dad. Please!"

"Of course, we're going to check this alligator out," Travis joked. "Jump in."

Travis carefully maneuvered the Gator down the drive to Camp Gertrude. Andy and Freddy laughed and screamed as they bumped along the road. He then turned around and headed back. Travis felt like a kid again driving a fun vehicle that was giving his sons so much pleasure.

"Now I want you to run inside and get Reginald. It's time you meet Aunt Millie," Travis told the boys after parking in front of the garage. "I'll meet you in the minivan."

Andy and Freddy nearly collided with Logan at the side door. "Excuse us, we have to find Reggie. Dad is taking us to Aunt Millie's house," Andy said.

Logan waved down Travis as he was backing up the minivan.

"Higgins called," Logan said as he reached the driver's side of the van and Travis lowered the window. "He and Olivia are in the air. We must leave."

CHAPTER FORTY-FIVE

"I don't understand. Is Livy okay? Why did they have to leave so suddenly?"

"She's fine, they both are. Higgins wouldn't say what happened that suddenly changed their plans on leaving Fairfield. His instructions were explicit. He wants you and I to meet them at the airport with the minivan and the Lincoln. Reginald is to bring the Hummer for Lorenzo to drive after he's finished putting the Gulfstream to bed."

"What about the boys? Do we tell them that their mother is on her way?"

"Higgins doesn't want them to know anything until we get Olivia safely to the house. I'll come up with some excuse to leave and head back to Marblehead."

Nick, Reginald, and the twins exited the back door together.

Andy and Freddy ran to Logan's side. "Dad, Reggie says we have to leave. But you are taking us to meet Aunt Millie. Right?"

"Sorry, Freddy. Our plans have changed," Travis said while opening his door. He got out and opened the side door of the van.

"Benjamin called to say he would really like your help in getting the pool ready. Something about new pool floats and water games," Logan said as excitedly as he could.

The reasoning worked, and the boys jumped into the minivan, excited to get back home. Aunt Millie was totally forgotten. Travis did, however, point out the road to her house as they passed by on Monaghan Road.

Halfway to the ferry dock, Travis glanced over at Logan. "Any chance there actually are pool toys?" He hoped so, if not, the boys would be disappointed and feel cheated.

"Sarah and Benjamin picked up stuff at Walmart. They have it hidden in a closet. The plan was to have everything in the pool when the boys go out for their first swim."

Almost an hour after they left Bent Tree Cottage, Travis arrived at their house in Marblehead and parked at the end of the driveway. The twins spilled out and ran to the rear of the house where the Harrisons and Burnsides were waiting by the pool. The boys were greeted by a floating giraffe and Lock Ness Monster.

Happy voices echoed while Travis, Logan, and Reginald slipped silently away to the garage. Each climbed into their designated vehicle and the caravan drove through the tall, ornate gates and on down Route 163 to Port Clinton.

Fifteen minutes later Travis, Logan and Reginald arrived at the airport to see that the Gulfstream had already landed. A large, motorized cargo hauler was being loaded with stacks of boxes from both the rear cargo compartment and the main stairway.

"I guess Freddy's concerns were right about the plane being too heavy to get off the ground," Travis added with humor.

"Looks like Higgins is planning for an invasion," Logan said, then began walking toward the tarmac.

Travis followed until he saw Olivia. He ran to her and scooped her up in his arms. "I'm so glad you are okay. I can't tell you how worried I've been since I got the message that you and Higgins were already in the air." He bent down for a long kiss. "What happened?"

"Olivia had a bug in her purse," said Higgins.

"A bug? Like a fly?" Travis asked.

"Like a listening device. We are both sure it was our little old lady who tried to run over Olivia in the park. What we don't know is how much whoever was listening actually heard, considering her purse wasn't always with her. Especially after she got home to Fairfield."

"What about William's house in Georgetown? And are we safe here?" Travis asked.

"I had the Morrisons' security team do a sweep of their house, and it's clean. My team has checked Fairfield, and it's clean."

"What about here?"

"With Logan and Reginald in residence, I don't see how that would be possible, but we'll check just to be safe."

"And with all the explorations Logan has been doing on Long Point, I presume you will be looking at that too."

"Starting tomorrow. Looks like we are done loading," Higgins said, then pulled everyone together after the porter had left with the luggage carrier.

"The Marblehead house is probably fine. But until I give the word, I want everyone to speak as if the KGB is listening. Got it?"

"Got it," everyone answered.

Travis had his doubts, especially around the twins.

Andy and Freddy straddled the back of the inflated Lock Ness Monster in the middle of the back yard pretending to slay a dragon. They glanced up toward the driveway and waved as they heard the engines of the three vehicles. "But, Dad, Logan and Reggie weren't as important at the moment as riding Nessie."

Olivia stepped out of the Lincoln and walked to the edge of the driveway.

"Hello, everyone. I'm home," Olivia yelled while waving her arms above her head.

"Mom! Mom! Mom!" the boys shouted at the top of their lungs while sliding off Nessie. "Mom! Mom!" they continued shouting as they ran up the slopped lawn to the driveway.

Olivia braced herself for the impact that was sure to come when her beautiful sons reached her. She bent down and reached out to embrace them. "I'm so happy to finally hold my boys again. I have missed you so much."

"We missed you a ton. Every day," Freddy said while hugging his mother.

"We thought you were coming on Sunday. Were you our surprise? The reason we couldn't go see Aunt Millie today?" Andy asked.

Olivia glanced up at Travis with a raised eyebrow.

"Yes. Higgins called Logan while we were out testing the Gator. Your mom wanted it to be a surprise for everyone, so I didn't tell you."

Travis watched the Harrisons and the Burnsides as they walked up from the area around the pool. Benjamin looked surprised. Emma and Stanley looked more shocked than surprised—like a deer in headlights. Sarah not so much.

"Sarah? You knew."

"I called her from the plane," Higgins admitted. "She promised to keep it a secret and look surprised when we arrived."

Olivia stood and took the few steps to reach Emma and Stanley. She reached out her hand. "Emma. Stanley. I'm so happy to meet you. Your résumé is impressive, and your experience is exactly what we need. Although I'm afraid you are going to find us boring and leave."

"It is an honor to be in your employ. I find your children and this house delightful. I'm sure Stanley and I will be very happy here."

"Benjamin, Stanley, we have two vehicles filled with boxes of stuff that Higgins needs to upgrade our security. We would greatly appreciate your help in unloading and stacking everything in the garage for now."

"We want to help too. Yeah, we want to help," Andy and Freddy said while jumping up and down.

"Looks like I'm the only one without a job," Olivia said. "So, I think I'll go freshen up and meet everyone inside."

"Excuse me, ma'am, but it is such a lovely afternoon. How about after you freshen up, you come back outside to the patio? The children are having such a wonderful time playing with their new toys. I will bring out refreshments for everyone."

"That sounds wonderful, Emma. I won't be long."

"I'll come in and help," Sarah said as she started to walk toward the side door.

"That isn't necessary, Sarah. Why don't you take a break and sit on the patio? I'm sure you and Mrs. Tanner have a lot to catch up on."

"That sounds like a wonderful idea, Sarah. And I am looking forward to hearing all about your visits to Long Point."

Sarah's eyes lit up. "I must admit that monster of a house is growing on me. I would indeed like to talk to you about it. Even Benjamin is chomping at the bit to get back out there."

"What is out there that your husband is so interested in?"

"The barn. He hasn't had time to dig around in there."

"Oh yes. The boys did ask me to bring their ponies—and a canon." Olivia suddenly had a mental image of two ponies and a canon sitting on the tarmac. "I'm glad my plane is a manageable Gulfstream and not a 747!"

CHAPTER FORTY-SIX

"Look, Mom, that is Camp Gertrude. It is a summer camp for kids and starts on the holiday weekend," Andy said while pointing to the camp as Travis made the right-hand turn that would quickly take them to the beginning of Long Point.

Olivia read the large sign identifying the property as ST. GERTRUDE THE GREAT. Christian Camp. She also noted that the buildings were old but seemed to be in good shape. The grounds were crawling with cleanup crews.

"Very interesting. Thank you for pointing that out to me, Andy. I spent many years cruising these waters and never noticed a camp here."

Travis stopped the minivan at the open, red, steel-tube gate. "Well, this is it. We are now on Tanner property."

Olivia scanned the stone pillars with the partial statue of a carved fish that sat on top. It appeared to be all that remained of the original gates. "I see another one of your enormous, ornate wrought iron gates being placed here."

"Dad found the sketch of the ones that were here when the house was new. We are having some make just like the drawings," Andy said.

Travis then began the drive along the narrow road that would lead to Bent Tree Cottage.

"Look, Mom!" Freddy pointed to the left side of the road. "Look at those really cool rocks. The lake is right there, Mom. Andy and I want to climb down to the water, but Dad and Logan say it is way too dangerous."

"I would have to agree with that." Olivia watched the right side of the road. The dense trees and underbrush obscured any view of what lay beyond. "How far does the land go on this side before you get to the lake?"

"I don't know. Another part of the property yet to be explored."

The road became wider with another lane branching off to the right. "That leads to The Pines." Travis didn't want to elaborate on that subject. Instead, he turned to the left.

"Look, Mom!" Freddy pointed ahead. "Look. You can see the tower of our castle."

"Wow. That is one big tower. Sure, looks like a castle from here," said Olivia. She thought back at Sarah's description of it being a monster of a house.

Travis followed the road that took a path through less dense trees and foliage, then opened to a grassy lawn.

The huge stone, Gothic-style mansion stood bathed in brilliant sunshine against the backdrop of a vivid blue Lake Erie.

Olivia breathed deeply. It was breathtaking.

"Isn't it beautiful, Mom? Our house is really special," Andy said with pride.

"It is the most beautiful house in the whole world," Freddy said.

It didn't fall onto deaf ears as Olivia thought about how many times in the last few minutes that her sons had said the words "ours" when referring to everything Long Point.

Travis drove ahead and parked in front of the garage. As he got out, he automatically glanced down to the oil spots—there were still only two. The boys already had the side door opened and began piling out. Logan and Reginald were the last ones.

"Mom, isn't our minivan great. Dad bought it so everyone can ride together when we come here," Andy said. "We had to buy a white one because it was in the showroom, and the guy didn't have any more because this one is special. I know you buy only black cars, but we really like this one."

"I like white," Olivia said while ruffling the top of Andy's head. "I don't actually know how we end up with black ones—maybe it's a Higgins thing."

The group began walking toward the house, or, as they sometimes called it, the "cottage."

Nick came out to greet everyone. "Good morning." He stopped in front of Olivia and gave her one of his monstrous hugs. "It is so good to see you again, Olivia. And a day doesn't go by that you aren't mentioned by your sons. And Travis has kept me informed about what has been happening in Virginia. I'm so sorry about all that, but you are safe here. I have been wanting to show this place to Higgins since Travis and I first stepped foot on Long Point."

"And ever since I have been coming here, I too have been telling Higgins about it. We talked last night, and I showed him the photos. I think the wheels in his head are already spinning," Logan said.

"He will be here tomorrow. Today, he and Benjamin are sorting through the many boxes and making notes on what needs to be upgraded there."

Nick glanced around the van. "Where is Sarah? I was looking forward to her spending some time at the new grill Travis bought for her."

"Sarah stayed behind, even though Emma tried her darndest to convince her to come. But she wanted to help Higgins," Travis said. "I think, secretly, she wants to make sure dinner goes well." Everyone laughed at the joke. Except Travis wasn't joking.

Travis took his wife's hand, and together they walked through the door and into the kitchen.

Olivia's spontaneous laugh wasn't what Travis expected from his wife who doesn't cook. "This is exactly as Sarah described it to me yesterday while we chatted on the patio. She believes it has the potential to be every cook's dream kitchen. I was thoroughly surprised at how little she misses Fairfield; how little she talked about getting the Marblehead house ready for the new house-keeper and how much she talked about the cottage."

Andy and Freddy each grabbed one of their mother's hands and pulled. "Come on, Mom, we have to show you the best part," said Freddy.

Olivia glanced over her shoulder at her husband. "Is it safe? This house seems to captivate every person who enters its four walls."

"It has a lot more than four walls, Mom," Andy said.

"Yeah, like a hundred," Freddy added.

The twins led their mother, and everyone else down hallways, up the elegant main staircase, down more halls and up another staircase to yet another smaller hallway, and finally the iron circular stairs. Nick took the lead up and pulled the large lever that opened the thick metal door.

Olivia stepped over the threshold and onto the roof of the tower. "This is incredible. All of you have been telling me how wonderful it is up here." She stood in the center and turned getting a three-hundred-and-sixty-degree view. "Amazing. You can see for miles in every direction." She walked to the crenelated wall and looked down at the tops of the house roofs. Then she moved around to the next side. I see the Marblehead lighthouse and our house, Cedar Point and Sandusky."

Andy took her hand and pulled her to the opposite side. "Look, Mom. You can see Perry's Monument at Put-in-Bay and

Gibraltar Island and all the islands." He pointed out into the lake. "And that is where Commodore Perry defeated the British. If we had a cannon, we could shoot the British ships from here and win the war."

"I thought you were knights who were going to protect the castle with your swords. And if my memory serves me, I am your Queen Olivia."

"Yes! Yes! Yes! Queen Olivia," the twins shouted in unison.

⊷⊹⊶

Another hour went by as Olivia toured the rest of the house. She agreed with Sarah that the principal rooms on the first floor would make a magnificent setting for the Tanners' annual Christmas party—if only it wasn't necessary to ferry everyone to the island during the last week in December.

Andy and Freddy were already in the library when everyone else walked in. Freddy stood in front of the fireplace with the large meerschaum pipe in his mouth pretending to be the general.

"Frederick Tanner! What have got in your mouth?" Olivia voiced.

Freddy took the pipe from his mouth and showed it to his mother. "Look, Mom." He turned it so she could see the front side of the pipe. "It looks just like the general. See?" Freddy pointed to the portrait above the fireplace.

"I see the resemblance, but putting a pipe in your mouth is unsanitary and not allowed." Olivia took the pipe, which she noted was a work of art, and put it up on the mantel. "I don't ever want to catch you doing that again—or there will be conse-quences. Do you understand?"

"Yes. We understand," Freddy said sheepishly.

"Yes. Me too. Except for the tower, this is our favorite room. We play games in here. If you don't turn the big light on in the ceiling, you can't see anything. It is kinda spooky—we like the general," Andy said, then looked up at the portrait.

"He looks rather foreboding," Olivia said. "But I agree that this would be an ideal room for games. I bet your dad and Cousin Nick play a lot on the pool table."

"We are certainly looking forward to our first game, but so far there hasn't been the time," Nick said.

Olivia lazily walked around the large Victorian era table, her hand gliding over the smooth mahogany and soft red felt. "I'm not so sure you should even be playing on this—this table should be in a museum somewhere."

"Okay. I don't know about all of you, but I'm getting hungry. How about if we head to the kitchen and see what Sarah has left us?" Travis said as he waited until everyone except Olivia was out in the hallway. "And, boys, I want you to remember that the library door is to be closed—always. Understand?"

"Yes, Dad, but—"

"No buts, Freddy. Understand?" Travis scolded.

"Yes."

Olivia turned back to look up at the general. It was almost as if he was smiling. She turned out the lights and closed the door.

CHAPTER FORTY-SEVEN

After dinner, Higgins asked Travis to join him upstairs in his office for a debriefing of the day. Emma offered to clear the dining room to give the men space there. Higgins thanked her but declined, and the two of them exited and headed for the back staircase that would lead directly up to Higgins's suite of rooms. Logan and Lorenzo also had their own rooms on the third floor.

Olivia took the bottle of wine from the sideboard along with two wineglasses. "Come on, Sarah, I'm sure that Emma and Stanley can handle the kitchen. How about you and I go out to the patio and do our own debriefing?"

"I'm right behind you. I can't wait to hear how your visit to Long Point went."

Olivia reached the patio at the back of the house. She set the bottle of Cabernet Sauvignon in the center of the large wrought iron and glass table under the black-and-white striped awning. The floor made of large squares of cut stone had been there when she first bought the house but was unusable due to decades of freezing and thawing of the ground beneath. She'd had the stone slabs removed and the ground dug out and leveled. Last year Olivia and Travis had the yard beyond the patio terraced to include a pool and hot tub surrounded by a wide stone sitting area and pergola overlooking Lake Erie. A dozen chaise lounges lined one side. Colorful cushions offered comfortable seating.

Sarah poured wine into the two glasses and handed one to Olivia. She raised her glass in a toast: "To a beautiful night, much too nice to be sitting indoors."

"You are right, Sarah. It is the perfect evening to sit down there by the pool and watch those boaters who are enjoying the calm waters." Olivia grabbed the bottle and motioned for Sarah to follow. The two women walked down to the lower level and settled themselves on the lounges.

Olivia breathed deeply. "You can't imagine how good this feels. It's like being in a different world, far away from spies and the all-consuming HELIOSmm-88." Olivia took in another deep breath. "It even smells different. Not the hot humid air at Fairfield with the calm, lazy James River. This is cool, crisp air. The bit of a chop that tossed small boats earlier in the day is now flat. Jet Skis dash back and forth, while sailboats drift with the wind. Yep, it's good to be back for the summer."

"I see what you mean. I've been enjoying this weather myself. Kinda nice having to fill in for the Campbells. It just might take me all summer to train the Burnsides," Sarah said with a soft laugh. "Yep, could take all summer."

"Speaking of the Burnsides, what do you think of them? They seem pleasant enough, and I thought tonight's dinner was excellent."

"They both seemed a bit preoccupied today. She didn't put much time or effort into the meal."

"You couldn't tell by me. Although I would have loved your barbecue ribs and corn bread."

"The beef tenderloin was nothing special," Sarah said. "She just slapped on some spices and tossed it in the oven. The asparagus was simply cooked—nothing special about it. Little red-skin potatoes swimming in butter and parsley. Nothing special about the salad. The biscuits came out of a tube, and the brownies were made from a box. I've seen her culinary skills, and she misplaced them today."

"Well, it was fine by me."

"Enough about food. What did you think of Long Point?"

"Sarah, I don't know where to start. It is amazing, just like you told me. The house and the grounds need a lot of work, but I seem to be the only one who sees it as a problem. More of a time problem than a physical one. I now understand why owning Bent Tree Cottage has been a lifelong dream for Travis. The place sucks you in until Long Point is all you think about. Even the twins have taken ownership. Everything is 'ours,' the house, the grounds, the golf cart, and the Gator. Freddy was talking about *their* snake."

"So? Bottom line?" Sarah asked.

"Bottom line is I'm looking forward to going back tomorrow."

Upstairs, Higgins and Travis were sitting at the desk in his office on the third floor. Logan and Lorenzo were at the console in what was called the "War Room," like the one at Fairfield only smaller. From there they could monitor both the grounds outside and the rooms inside. This security system, in its entirety, was only used when the family was in residence, which was from June first through September, then again for Christmas. The balance of the time, it monitored the exterior only and a panic button inside in case of an emergency that was connected to the Marblehead police department. Travis had a huge family, and it had always been a Tanner tradition to be together for the holiday. So, after Travis and Olivia got married, they began a new tradition by having a lavish, catered open house the day after Christmas. It had become the event of the year for the whole town.

"I've made a list of updates for this system. Unfortunately, you only turned on the outside units when you arrived here. There has been a bit of a glitch in the system, and only the exterior cameras are working. That isn't a problem, since it was only you here until recently."

"Sorry, Higgins. I really thought I remembered how to work this stuff. I guess I missed a switch. Maybe you should give me a refresher class, so I don't screw up again."

"No need for a while. I'll be updating most of this equipment anyway."

"What about Long Point?" Travis asked.

"I have a long list of areas to check out there based on what Logan has told me. I should have enough time tomorrow to get over to the island and do a preliminary check on at least the electrical needs. I understand there have been some issues with new wiring in the house."

"There is, but you've gotten here at the perfect time. Work is in the early stages, and you can have pretty much anything you want."

"Great. I'm going to start with some testing equipment that I will bring with me."

"Just one more thing. Livy says your background check on the Burnsides was good."

"I ran it through my databases, and they are who they say they are. I also talked to someone at the embassy who gave them excellent reviews. You needn't be concerned about them. Be glad you had the good fortune to find a couple of their caliber."

CHAPTER FORTY-EIGHT

The minivan rolled off the nine-thirty ferry to Kelleys Island with six passengers on board. Travis was eager to work with Nick at the cottage, Olivia was excitedly anticipating her second visit, the twins were just plain excited, Reginald was hoping to meet Aunt Millie to continue his research, and Logan wished that Higgins could have made this trip, but he wanted to further check out the glitch in the security system. Higgins was doubting whether any place could live up to the hype of Long Point, and Logan was hoping to prove him wrong.

Nick had called at seven to review the day's schedule. Plumbing was going along as planned indoors, except running the new city waterline to the point could present a problem based on the findings from the ground geophysical surveys. Travis felt like he had been letting his cousin down since the twins arrived. His daily schedule was now dictated by how soon everyone could get ready in the morning and what time they had to leave Long Point in order to catch the four-thirty ferry that would get them to Marblehead in time for dinner. It was no longer just him and his cousin—it was Travis and his entourage.

The boys insisted on showing their mom their secret beach and the pointing rock. Logan agreed and went to the garage. It wasn't long before he brought the golf cart to the side door. "Reggie, you can sit in the front with Logan. Andy and I are going to ride in the back seat with Mom so we can show her everything along the way," Freddy said as their self-appointed tour guide.

Olivia had one arm around each boy as she held onto both of her sons as they bounced along the rutted road to the beach. "Whew, that was more like hacking our way through the jungle than a nice trip to the beach," Olivia said as she crawled from the golf cart.

"Sorry about that. Widening the road and clearing out the underbrush is already in the works," Logan said.

"You're calling that a road? More like storm runoff," Olivia said as she brushed herself off. She and Logan then followed the sound of happy voices of her sons along with Reginald's.

Once Olivia was free of the dense forest, she stopped to take in the magnificent view. White sand covered the entire point. Gentle waves lapped against the large rocks that dotted the shoreline, except for the ten feet or so directly in front of where she stood. Olivia bent down and slipped off her shoes, wiggling her toes in the cool sand and then rolled up her pant legs. There definitely was a flat surface just below the water, so she walked over to get a better look. Logan followed. The morning sun was in the perfect spot to shine directly on what the boys were calling a road.

"It doesn't look like an old road. That would have been concrete. This is stone." Olivia glanced around the beach. "Logan, can you find me a long, sturdy branch?"

"Mom! Mom! Do you see the road?" Freddy yelled while running toward her.

"I do. I don't think it is a road. But you definitely found something special."

Both boys and Reginald were at Olivia's side when Logan approached with a branch. "Found this in a pile of driftwood."

"Perfect. Looks sturdy enough," Olivia said as she took the stick and headed for the water.

"Mom, what are going to do?" Andy asked.

"I'm going to solve your mystery," she said as she put her left foot in the water. "Wow. This is cold. Here goes—" With walking stick in hand, Olivia carefully walked out to the far edge. "Huh. From here this almost looks like a dock or wharf—and I see the big pink rock. I kind of see the letters *L P.*" She then took the stick and poked around at the far corner. "There is a hole here." She then walked back toward the beach while looking down and poking with the stick. "Here's another hole." Olivia then looked toward the other side of the slab. She walked over and began poking along that edge. "Nothing here." After searching that side, she began walking back to the beach, then stopped and pointed toward shore. "I see the pointing rock. It points inland." She then continued walking to the beach.

"Mom, your feet are blue!" both boys said in unison.

"Yep. That water is *really* cold. I shouldn't have stayed in that long, but I had an idea and wanted to check it out."

"I think it was used as some kind of dock, or pier. I can see the rust stains around the holes where iron rings would have been set to tie off mooring lines. But a very long time ago when the water level was lower."

"We can add this to the list of things we want to ask Aunt Millie," Reginald suggested. "But I do have a theory based on what we know. If that stone slab was a pier, then the rock must have been some sort of marker. Like a signpost that points to Long Point, or whatever was on the peninsula at the time."

"Where's the firepit?" Olivia asked Logan.

"Over there." Logan pointed to a spot some distance away that would be protected from view of any land further down the island.

Olivia followed Logan to the spot. "Old smashed beer cans and junk food wrappers. Kids all right. They chose the perfect spot. It can't be seen from anywhere but straight out in the lake because of all this dense underbrush and trees."

"Looks like the kids come by small boats that they pull up on shore," Logan said.

"Higgins needs to see this," Olivia said and began walking back to the others. She liked the little beach. It was private, not much boat traffic, because she remembered from her many years of cruising these waters that it was shallow, and boaters stayed further out when going around the pointed finger of Kelleys Island. She also thought about what Logan had said about kids arriving by boat. Small skiffs, especially inflatables, could come in with their motors raised a bit. And unless you were up in the tower, you would never see anyone out here. Olivia was even more convinced that Higgins needed to explore the whole area—ASAP.

The trip back to the cottage was uneventful even though both Andy and Freddy scanned the passing foliage for their beautiful snake. Olivia wasn't about to let her sons loose on any part of Long Point that wasn't covered in lush grass.

Travis met the beachgoers as they pulled up to the back door. "Good timing. I called Aunt Millie, and she would love to meet us this morning. How about you boys run inside and take a bathroom break and come back out when you are finished?"

"I'd like to take a bathroom break," said Olivia.

"Follow me. We have a guest bath fit for a queen," Travis said as he put his arm around his wife and guided her to the back door.

"Aren't you going to take me through that beautiful front door to the guest bath?"

"I will. Once we get it to open."

Half an hour later, Travis drove down the long drive to Aunt Millie's. The quaint Victorian with a wraparound porch stood against the calm waters of Lake Erie. The house itself was painted white, but it was the ornate trim around the windows, porch, and roof that wore the colors of dark green and rose pink that gave the house the impression that it belonged in a fairytale. "It's called *The Vines*. The Seymour family from upstate New York bought the land back in the 1850s. It ran from the Long Point boundary, along the shoreline, to where the airfield is now. They produced grapes for the winery. The house probably dates to about the same time."

"That's about as old as our house. I mean the Captain's House in Marblehead, not our house in Virginia. Fairfield is a whole lot older than that," Freddy said.

"1733," Andy added. "Fairfield was built in 1733."

Travis stopped at the end of the gravel driveway. "I'm excited. I haven't seen Aunt Millie in many, many years. I wonder if she remembers me!"

Olivia, Andy, Freddy, and Reginald followed Travis up the wide stairs to the porch. "Beautiful view," Olivia said.

Travis pulled open the pink screen door and knocked on the tall oak door with a long oval panel of etched glass in the pattern of grapevines.

The door was opened by a tiny woman with thick silver hair, beautiful complexion for a woman who had to be in her nineties and rosy cheeks. Her blue eyes were the color of Erie on a beautiful sunny day. She wore a pink pant suit, with a pink silk blouse with a ruffled collar and cuffs. She looked like the perfect character to be living in a fairytale house.

"Welcome! I am so happy to see Travis again and meet all of you."

Travis made the introductions with his sons looking mesmerized.

"Are you really everyone's Aunt Millie?" Andy asked.

She bent down, looked him over, then tweaked his cheek. "That is what everyone has called me since your pappa was younger than you, and his pappa. And don't the two of you look just like him when he was your age?" She stood and looked at Travis. "I'm seeing double trouble if they are anything like you were as a youngster."

"I wasn't sure if you would remember me."

"Travis Tanner, I always remember the special ones. Even that troublemaker of a cousin of yours, Nicklaus Tanner. But I must admit that he has grown into a fine man. If I ever need help with fixin' something, all I have to do is give him a call and he is right here with his truck full of tools." She paused to give Olivia a studied look. "My dear Olivia, I remember hearing about all the horrible things that happened to you when you first came to Marblehead. And the wonderful things you have done since to help local families and all the charities you support. I hope you will stop by and see me from time to time while you're here for the summer." Aunt Millie paused to look at the twins. "I have made a lovely pot of lavender tea for the adults. How would you boys like chocolate milk and cookies?"

"Yes! Yes! Yes, Aunt Millie!" the boys said in unison.

Aunt Millie showed everyone to the front parlor, which overlooked the lake. "Travis, dear, would you please go to the kitchen and bring the tray that is sitting on the table?" She winked at Olivia. "I like to put strong men to work whenever I get the chance."

Olivia laughed and patted Aunt Millie's hand. "I totally agree."

After Travis brought out the tray, he set it on the round antique dining table in the center of the room.

"Please, everyone, take a seat." Aunt Millie served the tea and handed the boys their chocolate milk. "Now I know you all have reasons for coming besides paying a visit to a funny-looking old lady."

"Cousin Nick says you know everything about Kelleys Island and Long Point. Me and my brother want to learn about everything too," Andy said.

She studied Andy's face. "And which one are you?"

"I'm Andrew. You can call me Andy."

"All right, Andy. If your Cousin Nick sent you here, then he wants me to tell you about the island's tall tales of Indian lore, trappers from Canada, treasure, Civil War loot, and . . . *murder.*"

"Wow. Really? That all happened? We just know about Commodore Perry and the battle against the British," Freddy said.

"The Lake Erie Islands are rich in history. And I will be happy to share the stories with you, but that will take more time than we have today."

Olivia smiled. "Maybe we can come back again and visit Aunt Millie."

"Excuse me, but I'm looking for a library where I can do some research on a few things that I have noticed on Long Point," Reginald asked.

"Reggie studies everything. That way he can teach Freddy and me."

"What kind of things?" Aunt Millie asked.

"For one, we saw a snake out on the point by the beach. It looked and sounded like a copperhead; they aren't indigenous to this area. I'm concerned about the boys' safety."

"Well, Reggie, what you all saw was an eastern fox snake. It is common in this area and harmless. It shakes its tail when upset, and you probably are the only people it has encountered out there in a very long time. It won't hurt you, but just be aware of your surroundings."

Travis looked down at his pager, clipped to his belt. "It's Nick. Something has come up. I'm afraid we need to cut this trip short."

Aunt Millie stood. "Of course. You are all welcome to come out anytime." She ruffled the boys' heads. "I love a challenge, and by the end of the summer, I will be able to tell the two of you apart."

Reggie laughed. "Good luck with that!"

Everyone said their goodbyes on the porch. Then the group went down the stairs and piled into the minivan.

"I really like Aunt Millie," Olivia said.

"Andy and I want to hear about Indians and treasure," Freddy said while rubbing his hands together. "Maybe we can look for treasure."

CHAPTER FORTY-NINE

"Huh. The Hummer is here," Travis said as he pulled up to the garage and parked alongside Nick's truck. "I hope he managed to find his way without any trouble."

"That's what GPS is used for, Dad. Higgins showed Freddy and me how to use it."

"Yeah, you just enter the state, city, and address where you want to go and put the little box on the dashboard, and it shows you how to get there," Freddy added.

Travis had barely gotten the side door slid open, when the twins tumbled out and ran toward the back door of the cottage. "Let's find Higgins!" they shouted.

Olivia stepped out of the van and turned to Reginald. "Go ahead inside. Don't feel you need to follow the boys if you have things you want to do. I'm sure they will find Higgins and Logan."

"Yes, thank you. I look forward to meeting with Aunt Millie again, and I want to be prepared."

"Of course, *Reggie*! I believe Aunt Millie will love bestowing you with her knowledge of the area." Olivia watched him sling his satchel over his shoulder and head to the back door.

Olivia took her husband's hand and looked up at the house and tower. "You certainly did dream big as a child. I haven't changed my mind that buying this monster of a house because you made a promise to a tree was a bad idea. But it's growing on me." She breathed in deeply. "Do you smell a charcoal grill?"

"I do believe you are right. Higgins may not be as good as Sarah, but it smells like he's taking over the preparation of lunch today."

Olivia and Travis walked hand in hand through the back door and into the kitchen. Olivia dropped her husband's hand. "Sarah, I didn't know you were coming. Is Benjamin here too?"

"We came with Higgins. His first time on the ferry and the long way back here and all. We pointed out the sights along the way."

"I'm sure he appreciated your company. So why are you really here? This morning you were going to continue Emma's training."

"Benjamin wanted to ride out with Higgins so he could explore the barn. He saw a tractor when he'd poked around a bit and wanted to do a thorough inventory." Sarah shrugged one shoulder with a sheepish grin. "I like it out here and wanted to show you how special I think the house is. Besides, Travis bought me that wonderful grill, and it would be a cryin' shame not to use it."

"Travis and I did smell the hot coals when we got out of the van."

"Nothing fancy. Just burgers and brats. I had time this morning to make a batch of that potato salad you like so much and a peach pie. That will have to do us for lunch."

"So much for Emma's training," Olivia said as she gave Sarah a hug. Over the years, Sarah and Olivia's relationship had evolved from Sarah seeing Olivia as some upstart Yankee who had inherited Fairfield from a grandmother she'd never met or even knew existed, to that of a close friend and at times a much-needed mother figure.

"I believe she's planning on lamb chops for dinner. I'd be in the way, so I decided to ride along. Higgins was kind enough to load the cooler in the back of the Hummer."

Olivia glanced around the huge space that, at first glance, yesterday had seemed cold and uninviting. Today, Sarah's presence alone made the kitchen seem almost cozy. She was making it her own. And Olivia wondered if that was a good thing.

"How about you help me carry some of this food out to the grill? The view out over the lake is lovely, and there is a cool breeze from the north."

Olivia followed her out the kitchen door and around to the side of the house. Someone, probably Nick, had set the large charcoal grill up in a grassy area between the house and garage and under a stand of large trees. He had brought a picnic table and set it up by the grill, which was covered in a red-and-white checked tablecloth. Sarah motioned for Olivia to set the tray of burger patties and brats on the table.

"Nick has promised to bring out another table so there is room for everyone to eat together. Eating outside is so much a part of summers here in the north, and you have such a lovely patio at the Captain's House. It's a shame not to be able to enjoy the outdoors here considering this beautiful view."

Yep, Sarah was definitely putting her stamp on Bent Tree Cottage. She wondered if Higgins would also fall under the house's spell. Olivia hoped not. So far, it appeared that she and Higgins were the only ones left who were thinking with a clear mind.

<hr />

After lunch, Logan and Higgins took the golf cart out to The Pines. Logan gave him a tour of the bungalow, then walked him around the outside then to the shoreline, where the indents and tracks from a boat being pulled on shore could still be seen. Higgins made a full page of notes before he and Logan got back in the cart and drove to the beach on the point.

Meanwhile, after the paper plates and plastic cups had been bagged and the picnic table cleared, Sara and Olivia quickly washed the silverware and put the leftover potato salad in the fridge.

"Now for your real tour of the house," Sarah said as she grabbed a clipboard with a legal pad and pen. "We will start in the butler's pantry. I'm dying to get the combination to the safe and see what's in there. Most likely silver pieces. But who knows? Maybe we will fine gold bars!" Sarah said jokingly.

CHAPTER FIFTY

An hour into Olivia's tour, Sarah had finished the primary rooms on the first floor and was showing Olivia the copy of *Life Magazine* and the record albums that Travis and Nick had found on their first visit to Bent Tree Cottage. The sound of gravel crutching caused both women to look toward the driveway. "I see the JCPenney truck is here with the items Travis ordered."

Olivia followed Sarah to the servants' hall that would take them to the back door. "I don't know that I would ever find my way through this house without getting lost," Olivia confessed.

"I found it intimidating the first time, too. Then I studied the blueprints, and it all made sense. Primary family and guest areas run off the main entrance hall on the first floor. Same on the second floor, with family bedrooms and suites running off the main hall along with primary guest bedrooms. Doors then led into narrower hallway with twists and turns through the rest of the house and stairways leading to the third-floor rooms. Just as in your other houses, those doors and hardware will always be plain, as will the trim and bathrooms. It defines the classes, keeps the hired help aware of where their place is."

"Just like lavish main staircase and back stairs for the servants. Well, this house has a lot of both," Olivia admitted.

Sarah directed the deliverymen to the old maid's bedroom, where they placed the mattress on the bed frame. "Travis has set this room up for the twins so they can take a nap if they get tired."

"So far, I haven't even seen my sons slow down while on Long Point, let alone be tired enough for a nap," Olivia clarified with humor.

"Why don't you look around here in the housekeeper's suite of rooms? There is a lovely sitting room with an outside door and cute little patio. Reginald is—"

"Reggie," Olivia interrupted.

"What?" Sarah asked, confused about the shortened name.

"It's an Aunt Millie thing. Go on."

"Reginald, or Reggie, is arranging the room for him and the boys to use. There is also a private bath. Travis has taken over the office. The blueprints for the house are spread out on a table in the office if you want to take a look. I'm going to show these gentlemen out and return to make the bed—even if no one uses it."

Olivia found the rooms in the housekeeper's suite charming. Although the history of the house and how a house of twelve thousand square feet, perched on the far corner of Kelleys Island, would have been used, it was obvious that the woman who ran the place was well treated—but was she loved? Olivia wondered. After studying the layout of the first and second floors, she found herself opening the door into the library. The damp, musty air was softened by the sweet underlying tones of pipe tobacco. It wasn't unlike the blend that her grandfather had smoked.

She found the switch next to the door. The overhead light blanketed the room in a soft glow. "Hello, General," Olivia greeted the grim-looking man above the mantel. The oversize leather chair seemed to draw her to it, to relax, to unburden herself of the resent events that had drained her of energy and filled her with new fears. She settled into the chair and looked up at the stained glass with the bent tree prominently placed in the center. It was a comforting room despite the sour, uninviting stare from the general.

"Olivia," Sarah whispered as she gently touched her boss's shoulder.

Olivia was startled out of a sound sleep. "What? Where—Sarah?"

"I've been searching the house for you—and that ain't easy. I figured you went off exploring the upper floors." Sarah glanced down. "What are you doing holding that pipe?"

Olivia didn't remember picking up the beautiful meerschaum pipe off the small table next to the chair. "I don't know."

Olivia stood. She felt the warm, smooth surface of the beautifully carved pipe. She didn't remember picking it up, but obviously had. She then walked over to the mantel and set it on top.

"Are you ready to visit the second-floor bedrooms? A few of them are beautiful, and one, I'm assuming it is the master, is fit for a king—or queen."

"I'm surprised you didn't see me in here, especially with the overhead light on."

"You closed the door."

"I did?" Olivia didn't remember closing the door, but she also knew, firsthand, that old houses settle with time. She remembered how one of the attic doors at Fairfield always managed too slowly to close on its own.

Olivia followed Sarah down the hall to the main staircase.

Higgins and Logan returned two hours after they had left for their inspection of The Pines and the beach. They found both Travis and Nick in the mechanical room.

"Are the two of you at a point where you can take a break and meet with Logan and me up on the tower?" Higgins asked. "We would like to review our findings with you, and from up there, you can see what we are referring to."

"Sure," Travis and Nick replied in unison, while setting their tools on the floor, and followed Higgins and Logan to the tower.

"I'll start by saying that I've doubted this whole project of yours from the very beginning up until today. Not just because it is a massively big house that no one has used since the 1950s, but from a security standpoint, I deemed it impossible to secure." Higgins walked over to the south edge overlooking the grounds. "Your major problem, which Logan identified immediately, is the thick underbrush. You can see from up here that you have a limited view except for cleared areas."

"If I'm understanding you correctly, the first agenda item is clearing the thickets and underbrush and perhaps thinning out some of the trees."

"Two years ago, securing Long Point wouldn't even be a consideration. But technology has made amazing advancements. Not everything has to be hardwired, and drones have become smaller and easier to use, with more capabilities."

"What Logan is saying is, yes, not only can we secure Long Point and Bent Tree Cottage, but it has the potential to be far safer than the Captain's House on Marblehead."

"Wow! I wasn't expecting that," Nick interjected. "Our Uncle Clem owns a farm here on the northern shore of Kelleys. He understands everything ecological and would be the perfect person to oversee the removal of brush and trees. There could be things we don't want to remove for one reason or another."

"Travis, I know when you set your mind to something you go all-out. But in this case, the first thing you need to decide—and it's a big one—is what do you intend to do with everything Long Point?" Higgins emphasized. "It's the difference between securing the property and house against trespassers—and you have had some recently—and full-scale protection like at Fairfield. The major difference is that here, you are vulnerable with Lake Erie on three sides."

Travis had never had a panic attack, but what he was suddenly feeling could possibly be put into that category. He and Nick were making great headway in updating the utilities. But Higgins was asking for the endgame—and Travis didn't even have the playbook.

Higgins watched Travis and the sudden change in body language. The panic in his eyes, all color drained from his face, the slight shudder, and heavy breathing. "Look, Travis. You don't need to make any major decisions now. How about we do the basics now and think about the rest later?"

"I'll call Uncle Clem and set up a time for him to come out next week," Nick offered. "I'll oversee the whole clearing project. That is one more thing you can scratch off your growing list of things to do."

Travis felt his heart return to normal; he wiped the sweat from his brow with his sleeve. The chills began to recede. He didn't need to make decisions now. Today, he had his family to consider. This was no longer a project that affected him and Nick—it affected his whole family. He needed time—lots of time.

CHAPTER FIFTY-ONE

Logan, Sarah, and Benjamin climbed into the Hummer and headed to the ferry. Travis and everyone else piled into the minivan and caught up to the Hummer on Woodford Road and followed them to the ferry dock off Addison. They were the last two vehicles to board.

"Whew! We would be very late for dinner if we had missed this trip."

"Yeah, Dad. I bet you and Mom would be in trouble with Emma and Stanley," Freddy admonished.

"I hope Emma fixed us something good. I'm starving," Andy admitted while rubbing his hand across his stomach.

Once in the house, everyone scrambled to different bathrooms to wash their hands and meet in the dining room. The Harrisons went directly to the kitchen.

Emma and Stanley began serving after everyone was seated. Emma served Greek salad and mini baguettes, followed by lamb chops marinated in mint and served with a mint orange sauce.

Stanley served caramelized brussels sprouts with pistachios and saffron rice.

"I hope you enjoy the meal," Emma said, as if she had just presented a masterpiece.

The twins studied their plates and then glanced at their mother with questioning looks. Olivia nodded that this was one of those times when you eat and don't complain. They spread a thick layer of butter on the baguettes and picked at the salad. They liked the brussels sprouts but scraped off the pistachios, and they each managed to eat half of the lamb chops and rice. They were hoping for something chocolate for dessert.

After clearing the main course dishes, Stanley refilled water glasses. Emma came through the swinging door with a tray of lemon tarts with a swirl of fresh whipped cream on top and a sprig of mint.

After the Burnsides left the room, Andy leaned over to his mom and whispered, "Is this because Sarah and Benjamin were with us today?"

"This is a lovely meal, and Emma went to a lot of trouble to prepare it for us." Olivia hadn't exactly loved the meal either and decided it might be a good time to have a talk with Emma, or her sons would begin to lose weight. She glanced up at Travis, who was looking like he'd like to go into the kitchen and make a peanut butter and jelly sandwich.

"May we be excused?" Andy and Freddy asked.

"Yes, you may. I think we all are ready to get on with our evening," Olivia said as she rose from the table.

"How about a game or movie?" Reginald asked the boys.

"A movie," the twins yelled.

"Livy, how about you and I take a bottle of wine out to the patio? It's a beautiful evening, and we haven't had much time together. Unless you would rather spend the next couple of hours watching a movie."

"Wine on the patio sounds wonderful."

They went down to poolside and scooted into the chaise lounges. Travis poured two glasses of a Pinot Grigio and handed one to Olivia.

They tipped their glasses. "The perfect ending to an unusual day," Olivia toasted.

"Want to elaborate on the unusual part?" Travis asked while hoping it wasn't anything bad.

Olivia thought how Bent Tree Cottage was beginning to suck her in as well as everyone else who spent any time within its walls. That morning, she was thinking that she and Higgins were the only ones showing any common sense regarding the house. Now she could hardly think of anything else. And what about how she had fallen asleep while wrapped in the soft leather chair in the library and woke feeling totally refreshed?

"Well?"

"Bent Tree Cottage?" Olivia thought about what her answer should be. "It's growing on me."

"Want to go back out with me tomorrow?"

"Sure."

Travis took her hand, and together they watched the changing colors of Lake Erie as dusk turned to night.

CHAPTER FIFTY-TWO

The next morning, Travis, Higgins, and Benjamin caught the seven-thirty ferry to Kelleys. Nick had called late the night before after Travis and Olivia had gone back in the house after being attacked by mosquitoes on the patio. Uncle Clem could meet them at Long Point at eight o'clock for a couple of hours. After that, he needed to be in town to help put up the flags and banners for the Memorial Day weekend, which would be the start of the tourist season. Sarah had insulated containers of coffee and wrapped breakfast sandwiches for them to eat while on the twenty-minute trip to Kelleys.

"Boy, this holiday came up fast. I've been so engrossed in Long Point that I haven't noticed much of anything beyond the trips each day. I haven't even been to the diner since the boys arrived."

"And that isn't necessarily a bad thing. The town is buzzing with gossip about what you are doing out there," Benjamin added between mouthfuls of sausage, egg, and cheese between Sarah's homemade biscuits. "And I'd better clue you in right now, Sarah has been to the diner a couple of times—you know Sarah and your Aunt Mavis are as thick as thieves."

"Thanks; you've just made my day."

The first thing Nick did when he arrived was to put on a pot of coffee. Caffeine kept his motor running, and these last few weeks, he needed to be at the top of his game—all day.

By the time the Hummer group got into the house, Uncle Clem was in the kitchen having coffee with Nick.

"Hello! Hello! I recognize you, Higgins, and you, Benjamin, from the annual Christmas parties at the old Captain's House." He shook both their hands and gave Travis a quick hug.

"Nick here has been giving me a rundown on what you need done with the grounds. Driving in, I have to say it has grown up considerably since I was last here." Uncle Clem scratched the side of his head. "Maybe twenty years or so ago. One of the Whitaker attorneys contacted me to see if I wanted the job of caretaker of the property. Years before, old man McTavish had retired and moved off the island, to Florida, I think. Well, the off-island service they hired wasn't doing anything but rake in money and left the grounds go to seed. I came out and took a look. Do you know it's almost one hundred acres?"

"Yes, I do. And a very overgrown hundred," Travis answered.

"Well, there was no way I could take on this monster and run my own farm at the same time, so I turned them down. I don't believe they have had a live-in person since old man McTavish, but I could be wrong. Well, I'd better quit my jabbering, or I'll never get to town on time."

Nick had the golf cart sitting in the driveway, so everyone piled in. "By the way, I received the ground geophysical surveys in the mail yesterday. Everything looks good. We can run the pipeline underground along the south side of the driveway. The permits can be applied for, and we can get that project underway."

Several times Uncle Clem asked to stop while he ventured into thick areas of brush, wearing tall rubber boots. "Very interesting," he would say as he made notes on a small notebook he kept in the inside pocket of his multipocketed vest. At one point, he pointed up to the top of a tree. "Eagle's nest."

"We have two that I saw from the tower," Higgins added. "This one, and there is another one west of The Pines."

After getting back into golf cart, it was a short drive to the point and the sandy beach. Uncle Clem laughed as he walked around. "This is as I remember it as a teenager."

"You came out here? Why? The huge beach at the State Park is only a short distance to the west from the farm."

"Nick, it wasn't for swimming! We came here to party, just like the teenagers of today," he said while pointing to the firepit. "No one lives here, no one to chase us away, and we came by boat, which can easily be pulled up on shore or tied to a tree. And during the summer months, we don't have to share it with the tourists. Only us islanders know it is here."

"What I'm hearing is, security is going to be a major problem," Higgins stated.

"Maybe at first. But we are talking about islanders. And there aren't many of us anymore, and we all know what everyone else is up to."

Higgins walked over to a sandy spot in front of the stone slab that the twins were interested in. "Do you know anything about this or what it was originally used for?"

"No. It's always been there. We used to walk out to the edge and jump into the water. It's pretty deep on the left side."

Higgins noticed the sandy area beyond the slab, where the water was deeper. He noticed the marks of a flat-bottom boat, probably an inflatable. They weren't there yesterday. He kept that knowledge to himself.

Next, the group drove over to The Pines. Uncle Clem got out and studied the pine trees that circled the bungalow. "Red Cedar. Kelleys was once covered in them. But they were prized as firewood for steamboat boilers. And the Whitakers had a large yacht powered by steam. That is why the pier in front of the house is so long." They walked around the outside of the house and out to the shoreline. "I heard about your squatter and his bag of money."

"Yeah" was all Travis said.

"I'm going to check out the inside for a moment. I'll be right back out," Higgins said as he headed back to the front porch. Once inside, he went straight to the kitchen and opened the cabinet under the sink. The bag of fake money was still there that the FBI had placed, hoping that the squatter would come back for it. They had placed several cameras around the first floor in case whoever it was would come back. No one leaves fifty thousand dollars in cash and doesn't come back for it.

Travis, Nick, and Benjamin were already sitting in the golf cart when Higgins left the bungalow and jumped in the cart. Travis started the motor and headed back down the drive to Bent Tree Cottage. "Well, Uncle Clem. What do you think? How do we tame this jungle?"

"I'm afraid I can't give you a simple answer, or even a list of what needs to be done. I only have one thing to say, and it's actually a question. What do you intend to do with Long Point?"

This was the second time in two days that he was asked this question. The first time sent him into a panic attack. He didn't have an answer. "The first thing is to bring the waterline down, so we get rid of this well water." Travis continued driving, hoping he wouldn't be pressed for a real answer.

"Okay. Here's my opinion and the reason you need to make that decision before you begin to even think about clearing. You need to understand that Kelleys Island had been an isolated ecosystem. Plants and animals could only come here by flying or swimming. Then humans came and brought new insects. They brought animals such as raccoons and deer. Yes, someone back in the 1960s decided it would be nice to bring deer. Now we even have coyotes. Farmland is disappearing, as housing developments pop up for the summer people. We are losing our plants that feed the migrating birds who stop here on their way to and from Canada to the mainland and beyond. Right now, Long Point is still a haven for birds and wildlife. You saw the eagle's nest, and I saw an eastern fox snake sunning itself on a rock. Although common on Kelleys, they usually stick to the western areas around the old stone quarries. I noticed evidence of deer over by The Pines, which means they are everywhere."

"In other words, if I renovate and do nothing but come here occasionally, then the ecosystem is protected," Travis interjected.

"I wouldn't go that far. This is a beautiful piece of land, not to mention probably the most beautiful house in three counties. You could spend time here with a basic cleanup. This heavy brush is actually choking out valuable plants for the birds and creating an unhealthy environment for the trees."

"And my other options?" Travis asked.

"Many of the islanders are speculating that you will turn this into a money-making summer resort for the wealthy. Clear the land for a golf course, tennis courts, swimming pool, fine dining, even a health spa."

"People are actually thinking that?" Travis asked. "But that would virtually destroy Long Point's ecosystem and further take away from the more quiet, less touristy island we still have."

"I'm only saying what I'm hearing. Maybe folks are wondering why you are going to all the trouble and expense of bringing city water all the way out here if you aren't thinking resort or at least a seasonal hotel."

Travis pulled up to the garage feeling more angry than anything else. The islanders, people he'd know all his life, were putting him in the same category of the developers who were destroying the island of his childhood.

Everyone piled out of the cart. Travis thanked his uncle for his time and said he would get back to him after he made his decision.

Travis turned to Benjamin. "You've been rather quiet. Wasn't there something that you wanted us to look at beside the tour of the grounds?"

Benjamin thought about how excited he was about his findings in the barn, but all the air seemed to have been let out of the balloons. The party was over. "It can wait until our next trip." He looked up at the darkening sky. "Besides, it looks like it's gonna rain."

CHAPTER FIFTY-THREE

Back inside the kitchen, Higgins asked that they sit at the table and review what they had seen and consider Uncle Clem's findings. Nick put on a fresh pot of coffee.

Travis pulled out a chair next to the bay window and sat with his hands steepled on the table. "My head is spinning. I wasn't expecting Uncle Clem's comment about what the islanders are believing I will turn Long Point into." Travis shook his head in frustration. "A resort for the rich? Really?" He slammed his hand against the table.

Higgins pulled out the chair on the opposite side and slid his large frame onto the seat. "I know you are frustrated, and the only way you are going to change public opinion is to prove them wrong. But right now, we have bigger issues to tackle—that of security. Right now, without changes to the underbrush issue, our hands are tied. It's the reason we called your uncle out here."

Nick passed mugs of coffee to everyone, then sat down opposite Benjamin. "So, what do you suggest we do first—before Travis needs to inform the world what his intentions are?"

Higgins hesitated long enough to answer that both Travis and Benjamin knew he was choosing his next words carefully. "We've had a visitor since yesterday. While your uncle was talking about the stone slab and how deep the water is there, I noticed marks in the sand. Someone pulled what I think was a flat-bottom boat like an inflatable up onto the beach."

Travis started to speak, but Higgins held up his hand to stop.

"I didn't say anything at the time for two reasons. One, that I didn't want Clem to be spreading any rumors, regardless of how innocent, and two, I thought it might be our squatter returning for his money. That's why I urged us to move on to The Pines—the bag of fake money is still there."

"Who would leave fifty thousand dollars and not go back for it?" Benjamin asked.

Nick leaned forward against the edge of the table, his mug held between his hands. "Good point, Ben. I've been asking myself the same question ever since the FBI placed the bag of fakes back under the sink."

"Someone who is dead and has no accomplice, or someone who knows the money is fake."

"But that's impossible. You saw the tracks in the sand. Maybe they came by boat for the money, and we were still here, and they were scared away. You said we wouldn't see anyone with all the dense underbrush," Nick challenged Higgins's theory.

"Or they were here for another reason," Higgins speculated.

CHAPTER FIFTY-FOUR

"You three stay here." Higgins pushed his chair back and stood. "Excuse me, Benjamin. I need to run out to the Hummer for a minute. I don't know why I got myself cornered in like this. I always make a point of taking the outside seat—always." He shook his head in frustration. "I'm feeling far too comfortable here. I'm letting my guard down." He grabbed his backpack off the long butcher-block counter in the center of the room and headed out the back door.

Travis, Nick, and Benjamin watched from the window as Higgins went to the Hummer and opened the passenger door, then pulled a small device from the bag. He then used the device to scan the entire vehicle, inside and out.

"He's looking for bugs."

No one asked what Travis meant. Instead, the three men glanced around the room and then all three looked under the table. At that moment, Travis's mobile phone rang. He pulled up the antenna and pressed the answer button. "Hello, Livy? Livy?"

"Travis, can you hear me? I'm getting a lot of static."

"Yep, I hear you. What time will you guys be here? Uncle Clem left already."

"Travis, there's a—" The call dropped.

Travis dialed her number again. Olivia answered immediately.

"Livy, what were you saying?"

"There is a storm . . . stay . . . okay?"

Travis moved around the room to get a better cell connection. "Livy? Livy?"

"I hate these things. Half the time the calls drop, or you don't have a connection at all. It seems to be worse out here." He set the phone on the counter. "I'm going to use the office phone." Travis then left the room through the servants' hallway.

He returned to the kitchen a couple of minutes later. "Livy wanted to tell us that there is a storm on the way from the west. They have decided to stay at home. So, we are on our own for the rest of the day."

Higgins jogged back to the house and joined the three in the kitchen.

"Livy called to say there's a storm on its way, and they are staying put. Looks like the day is ours."

"She is right about that! The wind has picked up. I'd say we have about ten minutes before it hits. We either stay here or head out now," Higgins advised. "I've moved the golf cart back in the garage."

"You were checking the Hummer for bugs," Nick stated. "What made you do that?"

"The thought that someone has been gaining access to the property for another purpose other than retrieving money."

"Planting listening devices?" Benjamin asked.

"We already know that Marblehead's John Doe was a Russian spy. Spies, regardless of nationality, love planting bugs."

"Okay. I agree. But, at the moment, our decision is whether to stay or head back to Marblehead before this storm hits," Travis advised. "If we stay, we check the house for any nasty little bugs." At that moment, thunder could be heard in the distance.

"We stay. Do you have any more of those bug catchers?" Nick asked.

The storm hit with a vengeance fifteen minutes later. Higgins took the kitchen, butler's pantry, dining room, and library. Travis and Nick divided up the smaller rooms, while Benjamin helped move furniture and then went to the kitchen to make lunch.

By twelve thirty, the three bug hunters had finished sweeping the first floor and met back in the kitchen. Benjamin had a selection of reheated barbecue ribs, hot dogs, fried chicken, and Sarah's secret recipe of potato salad laid out on the butcher-block worktable in the center of the room.

After filling their plates, the four took seats at the table. This time Higgins chose the end chair.

"Thank you, Ben. This is a great lunch considering you didn't have much to work with," Nick said as he ripped into a chicken leg.

"My Sarah always cooks like she's feeding General Lee's troops. There are always enough leftovers for three more meals."

Higgins cut apart a section of his spareribs. "I found a device stuck to the underside of the old woodstove. Good hiding place, but not good enough."

"I found one on the backside of the boiler in the mechanical room," Nick said. "How about you, Travis?"

"Yep, got one in my office."

"Three inside the house. How is that possible?" Travis voiced. "There is such a limited number of people who even have access."

"Not really. Look at how many tradesmen have come and gone since the project began. Any one of them could have placed the devices. And look at the rooms where we found them—kitchen, mechanical, and the office." Higgins looked at Travis. "Where was the one you found?"

"Along the doorframe. So, anyone who had a question for me could simply rest his hand on the side of the door—and bang— it's there." Travis thought about his habits. He never closed the door. So even if he wasn't in the room, it could easily have been placed. He hated the thought of having to lock the door in his own house, but maybe he needed to.

Higgins glanced out the window. "It is still coming down hard. You guys up for spending a couple of hours searching the rooms on the second floor?"

"Yep," the other three confirmed.

Travis and Nick followed Higgins to the counter to grab their instruments. "Sorry, Ben, looks like you get KP duty. See you when you're finished in here."

"What's with you and the name Benjamin?" Travis asked. "You are the only person who has ever shortened it."

"Too long and formal. Doesn't fit him. He is definitely a Ben."

Everyone started on the rooms on the second floor, while Travis and Nick began sweeping the maid's workroom and the secret space above the library. So far, neither had clued Higgins into what they had found. The rain had stopped, and the sun was out, by the time everyone got up to the tower roof.

"Either of you find anything?" Higgins asked.

"No. Nothing. And we had Ben helping with the larger pieces of furniture. And it looks like nothing up here."

Higgins looked out over the tops of the trees. "Curious. What are they after?"

"Could it have anything to with Olivia's HELIOS and the bug that was planted in her purse? We know the Russians want that technology, and we have a dead Russian spy off-island."

"And don't forget the break-in at the house in Norfolk," Benjamin added.

"Maybe. But I can't connect the dots—at least not yet."

"How about our squatter and all that money? Looks like some sort of smuggling operation to me," Nick voiced his opinion. "With Long Point being unoccupied for decades, this would be the ideal stopping or transfer point—just like the migrating birds."

"Look." Higgins waved an arm in a sweeping motion over the side of the parapet wall. "It's clear from up here that we need to do some basic cleanup. Get rid of the bad underbrush and remove dead and diseased trees. I have enough new equipment with me to secure the perimeter with cameras and motion sensors. I'll use rooms on the third floor as the command center being close to the tower steps. Travis, an elevator is a must. I'm sure you can easily find the space."

"Higgins, you are talking about a lot of new technology. And as you have seen, firsthand, you can barely get cell service out here." Travis sounded doubtful of the plan.

"Old school. We go old school."

"How—"

"Nick, we'll need your electricians working on the outside. We'll run the wires underground. Do you have access to a trench digger?"

"There is a company I use for outside work, and they have a trencher. I'll call them now."

"Great. I'll bring Logan and Lorenzo out tomorrow to identify the needed rooms and begin work on the command center."

Travis didn't want to leave Livy and the boys home alone since they had been cooped all day today. "What about Livy and the boys? I know they want to be here as well."

"Sarah and I want to be here. And we are about out of food."

"Okay, everybody comes!" conceded Higgins.

CHAPTER FIFTY-FIVE

Travis pulled up to the Neuman Boat Line's ferry boat ticket booth at eight fifteen the next morning. Now that the holiday weekend was officially here, the ferry would be clogged with tourists from nine o'clock on until the Labor Day weekend. Locals knew to get to the dock early.

"Good morning, Travis." The middle-aged woman behind the window leaned forward to get a glimpse into the minivan. "Hello, Olivia, honey. I heard you were back. Glad to see you and your family. Heading over to Long Point, are you?"

"It's nice to see you again," Olivia answered as she leaned back in her seat to end the conversation.

"Travis, honey, pull around to the second row. The boys will be loading that row first."

Travis waved and began to move forward. "Thank you, and have a nice day." He checked his rearview mirror and saw the Hummer pulling up to the booth.

"Good morning, Higgins. Lorenzo, good to see you again this year. I hope you had a good flight up from Virginia.

"Yes, ma'am. Perfect weather."

The ticket lady glanced at Logan with a questioning look.

"Logan, ma'am. Logan Winters. I'm also here for the summer. I'm sure we will be seeing a lot of each other."

"Helen. I'm Helen. Higgins, follow Travis to the second row. The boys will load you first."

"Thank you, Helen. Have a nice day." Higgins followed the minivan to the second row of vehicles waiting to board the ferry. "*Helen*. I sure didn't remember her name."

"Everyone around here seems to know each other," Logan said in a jovial way.

"And that you will quickly find is both a good thing and a not-so-good thing." Higgins remained quiet until they rolled off the ferry onto Kelleys's soil.

Workers were already putting up flags. Folks were hanging banners from their porches. Travis turned right onto Addison and then right onto Woodford Road to Monaghan Road to avoid Division and the downtown area, which was still being decorated for the holiday weekend.

Logan observed all the activity. "They really go out for Memorial Day."

"This is an important holiday. There is a nice little park in the heart of downtown. In the middle is a monument to all those islanders who fought in the Spanish American War, the Civil War, and World Wars I and II. The names of those who lost their lives fighting are inscribed on the face. Each Memorial Day, many islanders will gather in the cemetery to honor those who served."

Once both vehicles were parked in front of the garage, doors opened, and everyone tumbled out. Benjamin and Logan grabbed the two coolers and carried them to the house. Travis and Lorenzo helped Higgins with the boxes he'd taken from the garage in Marblehead and stacked them in the main hallway. Sarah and Olivia, each juggling a grocery bag in each arm, headed to the kitchen. Reginald kept the boys out of everyone's way.

"It would be so much easier, Travis, if the front door would open. Easier on our backs, not to mention it is a safety hazard as long as it can't be used."

"I know it was on the top of our to-do list, but it keeps sliding down with each day that passes. Nick and I will put it back at the top—along with security issues, leaky pipes, faulty wiring, and brush removal."

"Speaking of brush removal, I think you would both be interested in what I found in the barn," Benjamin eagerly added to the discussion.

"How about we grab the guys and head out there after the last box is unloaded? Ben wanted to give us a tour yesterday, but the day got out of hand when we found nasty little bugs."

"And speaking of bugs—no word of that to Sarah or the boys. I tell Olivia, or Travis can, when we know what we are dealing with."

"One more thing. The house is clean, but we don't know about the garage or barn. So, we speak as if the bad guys are listening. Understand?"

"Yes, Higgins," everyone in the room acknowledged.

Travis, Nick, Logan, Lorenzo, and Higgins followed Benjamin out to the barn. Higgins grabbed his backpack on the way through the kitchen.

"Here, Ben, let me help you slide these doors open." With the double doors pushed all the way open, the barn was flooded with natural light. Any sun coming through the four windows set high on the side walls was choked out by decades of dirt and cobwebs.

"Wow, Travis, look at that!" Nick shouted as he ran over to a tractor. "This is like Uncle Clem's old Ford tractor—only nicer."

"Yep, it sure looks like it. If I remember correctly, it was a 1948. And look. There is a snowplow for the front. And a dump wagon, and a—what is that thing?" Travis asked. "It looks like a huge metal doghouse that sits on those rollers and that big tube."

"I bet Uncle Clem knows what it is," Nick said.

Benjamin walked over and opened a door in the corner. "There is a full workshop in here."

Nick left the tractor behind and ran past Ben and into the small room. "This is a carpenter's dream. I'll check all this out the first chance I get. I bet I'll be able to plane down the edge of that front door that is swelled shut."

Higgins took the toe of his boot and pushed aside some old sawdust. Then he followed as Benjamin led everyone to the far side of the building.

"Along this side wall are stalls for four horses." Benjamin pointed up. "That's a hayloft, and there is a ladder in the center of the isle. At the far end is a small tack room and bins for feed."

Travis noticed Higgins moving the toe of his boot in circles on the floor. "Higgins, what are you looking at?"

"Back in the toolroom, there were scuff marks in the flooring under each machine. Like someone has pushed them aside and the old rusty wheels left scrape marks. The tractor has been pushed closer to the front doors. If you look behind it, there is an open area with little dust. And in each of these stalls, the old remnants of hay have been raked aside."

"Come on, Ben, let's take a look at the floor in the tack room," Nick urged.

Everyone followed Nick to the tack room.

Higgins walked into the room first. "The feed bins have been moved out of place."

"Maybe the Whitakers thought about taking the tools and tractor when they were here, then decided it wasn't worth the trouble," Travis suggested.

"And the feed bins?" Logan questioned.

"Someone has searched the barn," Lorenzo stated the obvious.

"And recently," Higgins added as he left the tack room and headed back toward the main doors.

"I feel stupid. I was so excited when I opened those doors and saw everything in here. Well, I wasn't thinking straight."

"Don't feel bad, Ben. None of us noticed it either," Nick said while putting his hand on Ben's shoulder.

Everyone left the barn and remained silent as they walked over to the Hummer. Higgins reached into his pocket and pulled something out, then opened his hand, palm up.

"A listening device," said Logan.

"I found it stuck to the underside of the tractor seat."

CHAPTER FIFTY-SIX

Sarah walked to the edge of the driveway. "Hey, you guys. Lunch in five on the picnic tables," she shouted. "Nick, that is your cue to hop on it."

"I smell hot charcoal," Lorenzo said.

"I smell burgers," Logan said.

"And I smell my wife's cooking!"

"Tables?" Travis questioned. "As in plural?"

"We will have another table once *we* pull it off the back of my truck."

All five men scrambled over to Nick's truck and within a couple of minutes had it securely placed next to the other one.

"After lunch, the five of us stay here at the table for a debriefing. This new activity in the barn doesn't match up with our squatter." Everyone nodded their understanding as Sarah and Olivia headed their way with the platters of burgers and brats. Andy carried a large bowl of cut-up fresh fruit, Freddy followed carrying a bowl of coleslaw, and Reginald carried a hot casserole dish tightly between pot holders of baked beans right out of the oven.

"If it would be all right, Andy and Freddy would like to visit Aunt Millie this afternoon," Reginald stated while platters and bowls were being passed around the two tables.

"I would like to go as well," Olivia added. "Aunt Millie is charming, and I would like to learn more about the island."

"That sounds like a wonderful idea. I'll call her after lunch and see if she is available." Travis was happy to see his wife take an interest in the island, and perhaps, with her input, he could come closer to making a decision about what to do with Long Point and Bent Tree Cottage. The idea of a luxury resort wasn't even a consideration.

Half an hour later, the picnic tables were cleared of everything but a pitcher of lemonade and five glasses. Reginald had left in the Hummer with Olivia and the twins to visit Aunt Millie. Nick was making phone calls to his contacts for the commercial electrical and brush clearing. Uncle Clem promised to oversee the brush removal.

Higgins had remained at the table making notes on a legal pad. Once the others had returned, he began by addressing Logan and Lorenzo. "Long Point is going to present our greatest and most difficult security operation yet. Even more diversified than Fairfield. Unlike the James River, which borders only one side of the Fairfield property, Long Point has three sides open to Lake Erie. Although Fairfield is comprised of over a thousand acres, only a small portion of that is secured by high walls and is easily maintained. Long Point may only be a hundred acres, but *none* of it is easily secured—at this time."

"The Marblehead property borders Lake Erie, and our cameras and motion sensors work fine," Lorenzo pointed out.

"But again, it is a relative short distance of shoreline, and the remainder of the property is protected by high walls."

"You are right, Higgins, but I've been here enough times to know it can be done," Logan emphasized.

"I've talked to the brush people, and they can start on Tuesday. The company with the trencher is a week out," Travis announced.

Higgins placed the listening device in the center of the table. "Don't worry; it's deactivated. But this little guy isn't high-tech. It is your basic, buy-it-at-Radio Shack model."

Logan picked up the device and studied it closely. "I thought we were dealing with a Russian spy."

"Maybe we are—but not in the barn. The ones in the house—yes."

Travis raised his arms to get everyone's attention. "I'm worried. What have they already heard? What have we talked about that is *helping* these people or *hurting* us? What if we do have Russian spies? Are they after HELIOS details? Maybe we've talked about the FBI and them placing the fake money under the sink. Maybe that's why no one has come back for it. Maybe all the bad guys know we are on to them."

"HELIOS is under high security at the shipyard. There is no reason to connect it to Long Point. And the house is the only place we have found high-tech equipment—even Fairfield is quiet," Logan informed everyone at the table.

"But we are still dealing with *two* different intruders," Travis stated the obvious. "With two different agendas."

"Quite possibly *three*. Don't forget The Pines," Higgins mentioned.

"Why here?" Travis asked. "There is nothing here but a house that hasn't been used in four decades and doesn't show any signs of forced entry. A bungalow that has had recent use by a smuggler, and open, untamed land. Period!"

Higgins leaned forward and looked at each man, making sure he had their attention. "What we have is The Pines—lots of money and no bugs. In the house, we have high-tech devices—no money—no break-in. And we have an amateur searching the barn with off-the-shelf equipment. I don't see a connection—yet. Our barn guy may be the easiest to catch, or at least identify if we get cameras set up, both inside and outside."

"We haven't searched the garage," Logan added.

"Okay. Lorenzo and Benjamin, sweep the garage as soon as we're finished. Logan and Travis, you are with me unpacking the cameras and equipment. Nick, I want you to grab a tall ladder and help secure the wiring."

"What power source do I connect to?"

"Anything you can. We are going to catch this son of a bitch."

CHAPTER FIFTY-SEVEN

"Welcome! Welcome! I'm so glad you've come back to see me today. Us islanders take our Memorial Day seriously, so I will be partaking in the festivities for the whole of the weekend."

"Then our timing is perfect," Olivia said. "I'm quite interested in Saint Gertrude the Great summer camp. The place was virtually swarming with activity as we drove by."

"Oh. Yes. The camp begins its summer season tomorrow. The children will be arriving this weekend."

"I'm interested in the flora and fauna of the island, and the boys are fascinated with history," Reginald stated.

"You are the young lads' tutor, I believe—Reggie."

"Yes, ma'am. I taught at Georgetown University before being employed by Mrs. Tanner and working with Andy and Freddy."

"My! My! You hardly look old enough to have gone to college, let alone taught there. Well, you are welcome to review and study anything I might have."

"Hello, Aunt Millie. Andy and I want to hear stories."

"And I will be happy to tell them to you. But, first, I think there is a pan of peanut butter cookies that is ready to come out of the oven. Care to help me with them?"

"Yes! Yes, Aunt Millie!" the boys shouted as they followed her to the kitchen.

"Do we have our own Pied Piper?" Olivia asked Reginald.

"Not sure, but I think I'd follow her."

"Me too!" Olivia said as she walked around the room.

A few minutes later, Aunt Millie walked into the room carrying a tray of tea and cookies. Andy and Freddy followed each with a glass of chocolate milk. She set the tray on the round table and had everyone take a chair. During cookie and milk time, she talked about the importance of Memorial Day and what part the islanders played in the wars. She finished by saying that on every Memorial Day, islanders meet at the cemetery to honor our fallen heroes. "You may join us if you can. Travis has always been considered an islander, even though he lived in Marblehead."

"We have Uncle Clem," Freddy announced excitedly. "Does he count as my family too?"

"Oh my! Yes! Your Uncle Clem's a Tanner. His family have owned that farmland since the 1850s. You won't find a better man for an uncle."

Aunt Millie looked at Andy. "I would say that based on your ancestry, I pronounce both Andrew Tanner and Frederick Tanner official islanders!"

"Yeah! Yeah!" both boys shouted.

"How about your mom and I take those nice chairs over there and you three sit on the floor and I'll begin to tell you about your island—Kelleys Island?"

"Shall I begin with the glaciers?"

"No, Mom and Dad take us there every year. We know all about the glacial grooves."

"Okay, Freddy. How about we start with the Indians?"

"When we come to Kelleys, we always stop at Inscription Rock, probably because it is between the ferry dock and downtown. The markings etched in the rock are called pictographs. Kinda like the Indians' newspaper. I think they were made by the Erie Indians and date from 1200 and the 1600s. Reggie knows about them too."

"Well, Andy, you are quite the little historian. And you are absolutely correct. I should probably skip over the early settlers."

"Dad bought a castle on Long Point. Reggie has been teaching us how to fight with swords. Not real ones. The ones we use are plastic and rubber. Reggie uses a fencing sword. It has a special tip, so it can't hurt us. Freddy and I are knights who will defend the castle and our Queen Olivia."

"That would be me," Olivia confided.

"Well, if it is being brave knights, and defending the land, I have just the places for you to go. But it must be with Reggie or other adults—promise?"

"I promise. I promise," both boys said while holding up their right hands.

"Your dad owns a cottage called Quarry Side. Ask him to take you along the rim to the ledge. He'll know what I mean. At that point, it will be like you are on the rocky cliffs of Scotland and true knights."

"That is so cool. Maybe Dad will take us next week. We have to remember to bring our swords tomorrow. We need armor," Freddy said. "Mom, can you buy us some armor?"

Olivia looked over at Aunt Millie. "Earlier in the week, it was a cannon."

"I suppose armor *is* more manageable." Aunt Millie chuckled.

"What about the other place?" Freddy asked.

"If Reggie drives you to the entrance to the glacial grooves but keeps going, you will come to a small road on the left. Take it till it ends. You will be at the ruins of the old limestone crusher.

It's a wonderful place for knights to fight battles, but like at the quarry, you must be very careful and only go there with Reggie or another adult. The walls are made of stone and crumbling. With the roofs and ceiling gone, trees and vines are taking over. The two-story railroad bed where the trains carried the crushed limestone out to the boat dock. The rails are gone, but the bed can be dangerous to walk on."

She looked over at Reggie. "It really is a magical place, even for adults. Maybe take a lunch and a blanket and eat down by the water. Also, have Travis take you to all the old places, like the old dining hall that was built for the quarry workers and the old oven. A lot of the old winery ruins are on privately owned property, but Travis knows all the owners."

"Speaking of stone, we noticed a slab of rock that juts out from the far eastern point of Long Point. It looks cut," Olivia mentioned.

"Ah, that would be the general's old wharf. General Horatio Buchanan bought Long Point after the Civil War ended in 1866. I believe it was one hundred forty acres. At the time, there were two cabins on the property. One was somewhere around where the Whitakers built Bent Tree Cottage. The other one was much larger and was closer to where Camp Gertrude is now. The general built the barn about a year or two after he bought the land."

"And the wharf?" Reginald asked.

"Ah yes, I quite forgot about that. The general bought the land from a family who lived in Cleveland. They leased the land to a farmer, who only farmed the area where the camp is. They lived in the large cabin."

"How come they only farmed the front part of the land?" Olivia asked.

"The soil is better, and the land is higher, less flooding during storms. There was an old trader living in the other cabin. He'd been there trading with the Indians and Canadians.

That far point of land provided a shorter distance between the island and Canada; plus it was a direct route to Sandusky. The general figured the trader had a good thing going and decided to expand. If you notice, the eastern shoreline of Kelleys is primarily made up of large flat tables of limestone that extend out into the lake. The general wanted a wharf for boats to come in and dock. He had the one side blasted and dug out to make the lake deeper there for the ships and fast schooners to come in. There was a narrow channel, but I would imagine that has been filled in by now. I guess you could say he was in the import-export business. Not sure if anyone ever knew what the business was."

"So, the pointing rock showed the way to the general's cabin," Andy surmised.

"Exactly. There wasn't all the dense foliage back then. I would assume a roadway of some sort connected the wharf to his cabin and barn."

"What about the bent tree that Travis remembers from his childhood?" Olivia asked.

"Now that was a carryover from the Indian days. It was like a road sign from the water. The bend in the tree gave the direction of the original trail that led from Long Point to Monaghan Road and the rest of the island."

"Wow, that is so cool. I think Andy and me and Reggie should look for the old wharf road."

"Now, boys, remember to wear tall rubber boots when you go into the brushy areas. The island has a lot of snakes, and you may be allergic to some of the plants."

"Mom, can we go to Walmart today and buy rubber boots?" Freddy asked.

"At least they aren't asking for a schooner," Olivia joked.

They had been there for over an hour, and Aunt Millie was beginning to look tired. Travis hadn't mentioned a time for them to be back at the house, but Olivia didn't want to wear out their welcome.

"Aunt Millie, we should head back, even if it is just around the corner, so to speak. We'd love to come back sometime soon."

"I would love for you to see my room of pictures and artifacts that have been found or donated. Maybe next time."

Everyone said their goodbyes and headed out to the Hummer.

"Mom, what's a schooner?" Freddy asked.

CHAPTER FIFTY-EIGHT

Olivia and company pulled up to the garage to find all of the men and Sarah standing inside the garage huddled around something in the rear corner of the building. Andy and Freddy jumped out of the Hummer and ran over to join the others. Reginald looked over at Olivia. "I have no idea what they are looking at. The only thing in the garage that I've paid any attention to is the golf cart."

"What did you find?" Freddy yelled as he reached the group.

"It's a Ford woody," Nick answered. "Probably around a 1950 or '51."

"Dad, what's a woody?" Andy asked.

"A woody is a station wagon with fancy wood panels on the sides and back. It was covered with a tarp and none of us thought to look under until now."

"Why did you look under it now?" Andy asked. "What were you looking for?"

"Bugs," Nick said.

Everyone except Olivia and Sarah jerked their heads around to scowl at Nick.

"Cockroaches. If you've ever seen one, you know how nasty they can be." Nick tried to sound convincing. "Ben thought he saw one in here. That is when he pulled the tarp off and found the car."

"Nice save," Travis whispered to his cousin.

"Travis, do you mind if I take the Hummer? Aunt Millie has convinced the boys that they shouldn't be walking around in the brush without tall rubber boots on. I thought I'd try Walmart first, and if not there, then I can still make the camping store in Sandusky before it closes."

"Sure, I'll see you at home for dinner. Logan, you're driving."

Everyone watched as Olivia and the twins piled back in the Hummer with Logan at the wheel and headed down the driveway.

"Do you think it's safe for them to go off like that?" Reginald asked.

"Logan's with them and driving. I'd rather have them off-island. Any threat seems to be centered here on Long Point," Travis pointed out. "And speaking of threats, we understand now that the garage is clean, no bugs and our searcher isn't interested in the house or the garage—only the barn."

Higgins backed away from the station wagon. "We can't spend any more time on the garage. I agree that the woody is super cool, but it has sat under a tarp for decades—it can sit a little while longer. We have wire to run and cameras to place."

Olivia, Logan, and the twins were the first to arrive at the house. The boys wanted Logan to go down to the shoreline while they climb on the rocks and wade in the water wearing their new rubber boots.

"Please, Mom. We want to see if our new boots really do keep our feet dry," Freddy begged.

"Okay. Logan, twenty minutes, then they must come in and wash up."

"Understand. Twenty minutes."

Olivia walked into the side hallway to the aroma of a fine French restaurant.

"Hello, Emma," Olivia announced so as not to startle her housekeeper.

"Ah, back so soon? Are the others with you?"

"I took the boys shopping. Logan and the twins are outside, and the rest of the crew should be arriving in a half hour or so depending on how long they have to wait for the ferry."

"We understand about having to depend on ferries. We managed a house on Nantucket during the summer months."

"Yes, I do remember reading that in your résumé. I've only been to Nantucket once, and we flew in."

"Ferries out of Hyannis don't run as often as those from Oak Bluffs. And it takes about an hour each way."

"I guess we shouldn't complain about our twenty-minute trip to Kelleys."

"What smells so good?"

"We'll be serving veal Oscar with asparagus and béarnaise sauce, roasted vegetables sprinkled with herbs and olive oil, mashed potatoes, sautéed mushrooms, and we will start off with a fresh spinach salad with sliced almonds and crumbled bacon. And for dessert, I've made a fruit trifle."

"Emma, you must have spent all day preparing this meal. We should be serving this to the governor, not our little family." Olivia wondered how to explain to Emma that they weren't gourmet food enthusiasts without hurting her feelings. If she didn't, there would be a lot of midnight raids in the kitchen.

"No work at all; I love cooking."

"Emma, you have amazing culinary skills. But both Travis and I come from middle-class families. As you know, Travis grew up here in Marblehead, and I'm from a small town about an hour and a half south of here. I would be happy with pot roast or meat loaf, and Travis is a steak-and-potato kind of guy."

"I'm sorry. I only want to impress you and create meals that are worthy of your status in the world."

"I understand, and I'm happy with you and Stanley, but go easy on yourselves. We may have money, but we are just down-to-earth folks."

"Now, I'm going to go up and put on a gown for dinner," Olivia joked.

At precisely five o'clock, everyone filed into the dining room. Olivia was pleased to see that each individual had taken extra care with their appearance.

"I'm really excited about the woody. It looks to be in amazing condition for its age. I think I'll give Uncle Clem a call this weekend and see if he wants to take a look at it. My guess is he knows its history."

"Dad, Aunt Millie made us official islanders because Uncle Clem is a Tanner too. And our ancestors were islanders and so we are now islanders," Andy informed everyone.

"Did she now? Well, she is very smart and knows everything about Kelleys."

"Yeah. She told us how it is important for the islanders to visit the cemetery on Memorial Day to honor our heroes. Kelleys Island has a lot of soldiers who fought in the wars. Did you go to the ceremony, Dad?" Andy asked.

Travis thought about the question. He could have when he was a child and tagged along with other family members. "I think when I was about your age."

"Well, I think we should go. Aunt Millie says it is important, and we are islanders," Freddy added.

"She knows about General Horatio Buchanan and the wharf he made out of the stone so ships could dock at the point," Andy said.

"Yeah. He blasted it for schooners, because they are really fast boats," Freddy shouted. "Mom said so."

"No shouting at the table. Try to keep your excitement to lower decibels," Olivia admonished.

"What?"

"Softer. Inside voices."

"Okay. Sorry, Mom. Yeah. He made a road from the wharf to his barn so wagons could import stuff. And the pointing rock showed the guys on the boats how to find the barn."

Travis, Higgins, Logan, and Lorenzo all looked at each other with raised eyebrows.

"So, what you are saying is that General Buchanan built the barn, and it's a lot older than the house and garage. Did Aunt Millie say anything about who he was, or what he did on the island that he needed a wharf?" Travis asked.

"It sounded like the general was doing something like buying and selling of goods. Perhaps he was using the barn for storage," Reginald offered.

"Interesting. I'd like to learn more about our General Horatio Buchanan," Higgins mused. "It can't be a coincidence that someone is searching the only building on the property that belonged to our general."

CHAPTER FIFTY-NINE

Travis and Olivia stood hand in hand in the Kelleys Island Cemetery, on Division Street, for the Memorial Day ceremony. Andy and Freddy stood together in front of their parents. They had taken particular care in choosing what they would wear. Andy insisted they dress appropriately for a somber occasion. Olivia put her right hand on Andy's shoulder, impressed with how her sons had dressed in matching tan shorts and navy blazers. The difference was that Andy wore a light-blue shirt and Freddy chose one of bright yellow. Olivia thought they could have been waiting to board the Queen Mary. Reginald stood next to Travis, while Higgins was positioned behind Olivia.

Andy was scanning the crowd for familiar faces when he spied Aunt Millie with a group of older ladies. She wore a floral-print summer dress with a lace collar, the handle of a white handbag slipped over her left arm. White gloves and a dainty straw hat completed her demure ensemble.

Andy waved. "Hello, Aunt Millie. It's me, Andy Tanner. We came, just like you said." She waved back.

Suddenly everyone at the cemetery turned in the direction of the celebrity branch of the Tanner family. "So much for being inconspicuous," Travis whispered to his wife.

"Uncle Clem! Uncle Clem!" Freddy shouted while waving. "We're over here!"

Clemson Tanner walked over to his nephew. "Hello to you too, Freddy," he said while giving his youngest nephew a good rub on the head. "Travis, Olivia, I think this is the first time I have seen you here since . . . since you were about these guys' ages."

"Aunt Millie said since you are our uncle. That makes us official Kelleys islanders. And Memorial Day is important to us islanders. So here we are to pay our respects to our heroes," Andy explained.

"Excuse us, but Freddy and I have to go over and greet Aunt Millie." The boys took off in her direction, with Reginald trailing behind.

"Hey, Uncle Clem. Do you happen to know anything about an old woody that we uncovered in the garage?"

"No! You didn't? It's still there?" He motioned for two other men of about the same age as Clemson. "Travis, do you remember Shorty and Hank?"

Travis shook each man's hand. "Sure, Shorty owns the service garage, and Hank manages the market. And they are both part of our volunteer fire department and police force when needed."

"I sure am glad you bought Long Point. It's in good hands now, and whatever I can do to help, just let me know."

"You two aren't going to believe this, but Travis just told me that the Whitakers' old Ford woody is still there, in the garage."

"What?" Shorty exclaimed. "After old man McTavish turned up his toes, the three of us tried to buy the woody from the Whitaker Trust Fund. They wouldn't budge. We figured they had it taken to Cleveland."

"I'd love to play with it, but I don't have the time. And at the rate things are going, it will be years before I can get her running again. How about I pay you to take it to your garage and get it running again?"

"Pay us? Hell no! The three of us would pay *you* for the thrill of putting her back on the road. When can we come out?"

"Any time. Come out with Uncle Clem in case I'm not there."

Hank looked up at Higgins with a questioning look. As if Olivia's private bodyguard might have other ideas of them being on the property.

Higgins reached over and shook each man's hand. "No problem. I'll remember you. And I'm happy to know members of the fire department and police force. Never know when I might need you."

"Well, we sure know about you, Mr. Higgins. Everyone in two counties knows about you." Hank paused and looked over at Shorty and Clem. "How about if we come out in an hour or so?"

"Works for us," Travis agreed.

"While you guys talk cars, I'm going over and join our sons and Aunt Millie."

"Mom, hurry," Freddy shouted. "These nice ladies are Aunt Millie's friends. Guess what? There are Tanners buried here. Uncle Clem can show us where they are. And see that big monument over there?" He pointed to one of the obviously older monuments. "That is where our General Horatio is buried."

Olivia introduced herself to the group of older ladies. "I hope my sons haven't totally dominated the conversation and worn you all out—I know from eight years of experience."

"Oh no, my dear. They are a breath of fresh air. And it appears Reggie is quite well-versed in about everything. I've made a tentative date of Tuesday for them to come by and visit my room of memorabilia, if that is all right with you."

"Mom, can Andy and I go over and visit where the general is buried?"

"Sure." She then nodded at Reginald to follow.

"I'm sure Tuesday will be fine. I may even join them. I'm finding Long Point and Bent Tree Cottage quite interesting."

"I must say you look lovely in your fashionable peach-colored sundress. You didn't buy that at Walmart. I'm Ida, by the way. Ida Hamilton." Olivia shook the elderly woman's hand. She suddenly felt guilty for buying her dress at Bergdorf's on her last trip to New York. "I remember back in the early eighties when you first moved to Marblehead. I was selling real estate with Emily Elfin. I wasn't in the office the day Emily first showed you the old Captain's House. I have to say, we were all shocked when you bought it. Scooped it right out from under the wrecking ball, you did. Everyone loved that old pile of stone and the sisters who had lived there since they were born." A sadness washed over her wrinkled face. "I also remember your boat, the *Lovely Lady*. She was a real beaut. I also remember the day she caught fire and nearly killed you, right off Kelleys's west shore. The whole island shook when she blew."

A chill washed over Olivia. "I'd anchored off the north shore for the day. Once of Uncle Clem's grandchildren was having a birthday party on the beach. Travis was helping fix the cooler for Aunt Mavis and couldn't make it out." Olivia laughed. "I had balloons tied everywhere on the boat; the poor old gal looked ridiculous. Then that horrible storm blew in and I was stranded for the night. The next morning, I pulled anchor and headed north and around the west side of the island. It happened just after I passed the old loading docks." Olivia pressed her hand to her throat. Her breath seemed to catch in her throat. The memory was so real.

"I'm sorry, dear; it was wrong of me to bring it up."

"Not a problem. It's just that I haven't thought about it in years."

"I know that everyone in Marblehead is so happy that you have kept the house and spend your summers here. And now Kelleys have you as well."

Olivia wasn't so sure about that. Long Point was still Travis's dream—she was just a visitor.

CHAPTER SIXTY

Travis, Olivia, Higgins, Reginald, and the twins arrived at Bent Tree Cottage to find the garage and barn doors wide open. Logan was on the top step of a ladder with a camera and battery-powered screwdriver, with Lorenzo holding the ladder.

"What's going on?" Higgins asked two of his security team.

"We thought we would go ahead and continue mounting cameras, but this ladder isn't long enough to reach any further than at the corner of the buildings," Logan explained.

"What about that long ladder that's hanging on the back wall of the barn?" Travis asked.

Lorenzo nodded in the direction of the brush next to the driveway. "It's over there." He then picked up his left leg showing rips in his jeans. "A few of the rungs broke while I was climbing."

Higgins remembered Shorty and Hank's offer of help. "I happen to know where we can borrow a strong, tall ladder."

Olivia rushed to his side. "Are you hurt? Looks like you are bleeding."

"Not bad. I've already washed my leg and put an antibiotic cream on the cuts. Good thing Travis keeps a first-aid kit in the Hummer. There isn't anything but soap and towels in the bathroom."

Olivia glanced at Travis, as if to say he'd been lax in what basic supplies he stocked in the house that was crawling with workers. "I'll take care of this—tomorrow." She looked at the house, then the barn. "Where is Sarah and Benjamin?"

"After the situation with dinner last night, Sarah said she and Benjamin would be better served if they spent the day in Marblehead with the Burnsides," Logan informed Olivia.

"Probably a good idea. Reggie, how about you show the boys what a Ford woody is? Since that is going to be the hot topic around here in about an hour."

Olivia picked up the boys' blazers, which they had discarded when they got out of the minivan, brushed them off, and laid them on the seat. She glanced up at the buildings. Higgins and Travis were helping with the cameras, and she wasn't particularly interested in an old station wagon that didn't run. So, Olivia grabbed her handbag and went into the house. With no particular task in mind, she decided to check out the sitting room that Reggie and the twins were using. Entering the room, she was immediately drawn to an easel containing a large drawing of the island. Andy and Freddy were adding places they had been or knew about. So far, there was only a photo of Bent Tree Cottage, placed in its approximate location on Long Point, the photo of a snake, pointing rock, the firepit, and the wharf all tacked around the point. They marked the location of the downtown area but had no photo. They also had marked the location of their dad's three rental cottages but still no photo. Olivia remembered that there was a Polaroid camera in the desk drawer back in Marblehead. Taking pictures was something she loved to do as a child. Perhaps Andy and Freddy would like to add their own photos to the board.

Olivia left the sitting room and headed to the library. "Good afternoon, General. Or can I call you Horatio? That's a very masculine name. Perhaps commanding is also appropriate. You were a general, after all." She walked over to the bookcase that covered one wall and began studying the titles and topics. The classics rested in a small corner of the upper shelf. "I see the Civil War was a huge favorite with the Whitakers, especially the Confederacy and General Lee. Here's something on prison camps. It looks well-worn. I wonder why this particular book was read more than the others!" She pulled it out and set it on the table next to the chair. Olivia then went back and looked at the other topics of steamboats on the Great Lakes, the Battle of 1812, Canadian history during the 1700 and 1800s. And a book on financing the Civil War. There appeared to be a definite theme going on.

Olivia walked back over to the chair and settled back into the soft leather. She thought back to James Whitaker's visit to Fairfield. He didn't seem interested in the old plantation's history, especially since the Union Army camped on the grounds as well as other plantations in the area, being that they were close to Richmond. "So why was the older generation so engrossed in the Civil War and yet James didn't seem to know anything?"

"Who are you talking to? I heard you and figured you were on your mobile phone."

"Oh hello, Travis. After looking at the twins' map of Kelleys that they are working on in the sitting room, I thought I would check out the books in here. I guess I was talking to Horatio."

"Horatio? You are on a first-name basis now." Travis chuckled.

"When we get home tonight, remind me to find the Polaroid. I bet the boys will love taking photos with it."

"Sure. I think I recently noticed it in the lower desk drawer."

He walked around the pool table and took the chair opposite the one his wife was sitting in. "What have you found?"

"Oddly, a heavily used book on Civil War prisons."

"You know that there was a prison camp on Johnson's Island for Confederate prisoners."

"I do know that. My grandparents' cottage was close to the island. I spent many hours walking around the cemetery there. Lots of snakes. Hey, speaking of snakes, I saw that the boys tacked a photo of the snake they saw on the point. And today at the cemetery, Ida mentioned that she remembered when I was cruising by the old loading dock and the Lovely Lady blew up."

"I'm sorry, Ida Hamilton is quite the busybody. Mentioning that was in bad taste."

"That's not the point. I was thinking how much I loved boating in these waters. How you get a totally different perspective of the land when seen from the water."

"And?"

"And I think you should bring the Sea Ray and the inflatable out here."

Travis thought about what she had said. One does get the best view of the shoreline from the water. Kelleys has an amazingly diverse shoreline made up of rock, from huge rough rocks to small skipping stones and the flat shelves along the eastern side. Long Point seemed to represent nearly all of it. He and Nick had inspected the pier when he had first taken possession of the property, and except for sinking new cleats for tying off the boats, it should work. Plus, it would give them more to do while on the island during the summer.

"Livy, my love, that is exactly what we are going to do."

CHAPTER SIXTY-ONE

Later that day, the four-thirty ferry was already full and preparing to leave the dock when Travis and company arrived. They would have to wait in the long line along with the people who were on Kelleys for the Memorial Day weekend and were heading back to the mainland.

"I forgot about accounting for the added traffic during the summer months. It will be like this until after Labor Day. We need to plan on leaving earlier or later in the evening, although this is worse due to the holiday."

"Nick said he might spend the night, since there is a bedroom and bath set up, and thanks to Sarah, there's plenty of food."

"If you ask me, Higgins. I think he wants to watch that monitor you rigged up in the office."

"I don't know how much he's gonna see with only the cameras on the garage, barn, and the servants' corner of the house hooked up. At this point, we aren't much better off than your average home security system."

"But that is more than you had yesterday," Olivia added.

"I hope he doesn't mind sleeping on our Batman sheets." Freddy giggled.

"I'll call Emma and let her know we'll be a half hour late for dinner."

"Mom, do you think she is going to cook something weird again? I'm getting tired of pretending I like what she makes," Freddy said.

"Yeah, I'm getting tired of pretending to like what she makes. Some of it is okay, but it sure isn't like what Sarah and the Campbells make. I sure do miss them. I wish they would come back," complained Andy.

The minivan and Hummer were the second and third vehicles to board the next ferry. The twenty-minute ride plus the time to disembark and drive the short distance to the house put them walking through the side door at five thirty.

Andy and Freddy burst through the door first and stopped just in time not to run into Emma.

"Welcome back. Don't worry about rushing. Take your time washing up. Dinner can hold until you are ready."

Freddy inhaled deeply. "Something smells good."

"I'm serving pot roast and corn bread for dinner. And a peach pie made with fruit from the Paterson's stand in Port Clinton."

"Yea! I get the bathroom sink first," Freddy shouted as he ran up the main staircase.

After dinner, Travis, Logan, and Lorenzo followed Higgins to the library to discuss the day's events and plan for Monday's schedule. Andy and Freddy asked Reggie to choose a movie to watch in the family room. He picked *Batman*. Olivia grabbed the bottle of Merlot from the sideboard, along with two glasses, and asked Sarah to join her on the patio.

"So, how did the day go on Kelleys?"

"The Memorial Day celebration was nice. The boys enjoyed meeting people at the cemetery. Andy and Freddy are really taking their designation of being official islanders seriously. They have already promised Aunt Millie and her friends that they will attend next year's celebration. I think Travis liked talking to old friends."

"And you?"

"One of Aunt Millie's friends, Ida Hamilton, mentioned how she was in real estate with Emily Elfin back when I bought this house. She also brought up the day the *Lovely Lady* blew up off Kelleys west shore and I almost died. I guess comments like that are to be expected. It just took me by surprise and dredged up a lot of old feelings—and hurts."

"I'm sorry to hear that. I hope it didn't spoil the rest of your day."

"No. Actually, I spent quite a bit of time in the library looking at the Whitakers' books. They seemed very interested in the Civil War, especially the Confederacy."

"That's odd. Yankees, and the Whitakers no less, owning books on the Confederacy? Why, that James Whitaker the third didn't seem to know or care about anything to do with the south, much less the Civil War."

"I know. One more mystery of Bent Tree Cottage."

"What about you? What spell have you put on Emma? Pot roast and darn good corn bread for dinner?"

"We had a bit of a chat. I told her this isn't one of her highfalutin families, and if that is the kind of snobs she wants to work with, then she and her husband can pack up right now."

"Wow, Sarah. What happened next?"

"We went grocery shopping in Port Clinton and stopped at Paterson's on the way back."

"What about Stanley?"

"He said he wasn't feeling well and stayed in their apartment over the garage."

"To bad. Benjamin could have come with us. All the Ford woody hoopla would have been right up his alley."

"He was fine. He worked in the yard, pulling weeds, dressing and watering the flower beds, and waving to the boaters as they went by."

"Do you think it will be safe for you to leave the Burnsides for the day and spend tomorrow with us?"

"Probably. Emma has increased the cleaning crew and expanded their duties to include about everything except cooking. Not sure what Stanley does."

"Huh. Well, it sounds like you and Benjamin will be spending another fun-filled day on Long Point." Olivia chuckled.

Sarah leaned forward in the lounge. "The wind is picking up. It's getting cooler."

"Let's head back inside," Olivia said as she scooted to the edge and stood.

Sarah arched her back and stretched. "My bones are telling me we are in for some rain."

CHAPTER SIXTY-TWO

Sarah's bones were correct in forecasting the rain that moved in during the night and continued through breakfast.

"Higgins and I need to meet with Uncle Clem this morning to discuss the scheduled brush clearing that will begin tomorrow. Yesterday, Shorty and Hank determined that the woody will need to have the four tires replaced before the station wagon can be moved. He will bring those out this morning along with his tow truck. Nick called me earlier to say he had spent the night and would get the electricians working on the third-floor rooms as soon as they arrive."

"We want to come too," Freddy insisted. "We have rubber boots and will wear our rain slickers. We promise not to get in the way. Reggie will make sure. He always does."

"I would like to go as well. There is a book in the library that is calling my name. And I'll bring the Polaroid. I just have to toss it in my tote bag."

"Okay, we have Higgins, the twins, Livy, and Reggie going to Kelleys. That's six in the minivan," Travis verified.

"I'll need Logan's help," Higgins added.

"What about Benjamin and me? He can help where needed, and I would like to tackle that monstrous laundry room. We are beginning to create laundry, and our only washer and dryer is here."

"Okay, full crew to Long Point?" Travis asked.

Lorenzo raised his arms up in front of him with palms up. Being a first-generation American in his family, he tended to rely on familiar Italian hand gestures. "What about me?"

Travis looked at Higgins and shrugged.

Higgins considered whether he needed the security protection for the Burnsides. "Okay, Italy. You too—take the Hummer."

The rain had ended as Travis came to a complete stop when he broke through the trees to see that the entire driveway ahead was clogged with vehicles. Nick's truck was in front of the barn doors, the electrical and plumbing cargo vans were parked nearest the house, and Shorty's tow truck sat in front of the garage. The woody was out of the garage and was being hooked to the tow truck. Travis pulled the minivan over to the far edge of the driveway and parked with Lorenzo squeezing in behind.

Andy and Freddy ran up to Uncle Clem. "This is a woody?" Andy asked.

"Yep. And she's a real beaut. Want to jump inside before I hoist her up?"

Both boys scrambled into the front bench seat. "This doesn't look like a car inside. What are these crank things for?" Andy asked while trying to turn the big steering wheel.

"Those cranks open the windows. One for the big window, and the other opens the smaller triangle-shaped one. And in 1951, Ford made a lot of changes to the dashboard. It was state-of-the-art at the time."

"So, this station wagon is really special, even if it doesn't look like a real car inside," Freddy stated with pride.

"She sure is. Now you boys hop out and stand back while I lift her up."

A few minutes later, everyone watched as the light-blue vehicle headed down the driveway. Her slanted rear door with its split window and spare tire cover gave the station wagon a unique look.

"Dad, I heard guys at the cemetery talking about an islandfest parade in July. Can we drive our woody in the parade?" Andy wanted to know.

"If the old girl is finished in time—I guess we could."

Olivia inhaled deeply. The island was quickly taking hold of her sons.

Everyone took off in different directions. Reginald and the boys went off to take pictures of the sodden landscape along the way to the point. Nick, Logan, and Lorenzo went inside to continue working with the electricians on the third floor. Travis, Higgins, and Benjamin headed to the office to plan for the ground-clearing crew that was due to arrive the next day. Olivia and Sarah headed to the laundry room.

"Sarah, do you know why they needed a room as big as a gymnasium for laundry? Except for those huge wringer washing machines, I can't see the need."

Sarah walked over to the two round machines that stood on either side of a double-deep sink. "I remember helping my mother with one of these in the basement at Fairfield."

"My grandmother had one as well. I bet I even remember how to work it. The trick is feeding the washed clothes through the wringer on top without getting them stuck."

"Appliances were pretty basic back then. See all those hooks in the walls? They would use them to run ropes back and forth across the room and hang the wet clothes. These three woodstoves would keep the room warm enough to dry the clothes. Everything was ironed, no permanent press, so there would have been ironing boards set up next to the stoves to heat the irons."

"Wow. So, what do we do with all this space now?"

"Since we don't know what Travis will do with the place, we have to plan for the worst-case scenario, which in my mind is a bed-and-breakfast."

"Okay. So, what does a small hotel need?"

"First off, two sets of commercial-sized washer and dryers. Two large slop sinks, plenty of storage cabinets. Tables for sorting and folding and—"

"Hold on. You lost me at commercial size. How about you work out a diagram and layout with a list of supplies?"

"I'll work with Nick on the plumbing and electrical needs."

"Perfect. I'll be in the library. I want to look further into why the Whitakers were so interested the Confederacy."

The door to the library was closed as usual. Olivia walked into the room with the scent of damp air and that hint of sweet tobacco. "Good morning, General," Olivia said as she set her tote bag on the pool table, then looked up at his portrait over the mantel. The pipe was sitting where Travis had put it last. Although there were several comfortable leather chairs in the room, plus a beautiful tan leather chesterfield, Olivia immediately went to the same chair she had used the day before. As she scooted back to get comfortable, she noticed a second book on the small table. She only remembered setting the one having to do with Confederate prisons on the table. This book was also well used. The title was *Funding the Confederacy*. Olivia picked it up and began reading. An hour later, Sarah knocked on the door. "Excuse me. Lunch will be ready in five in the dining room. Although the sun is out, it is still too wet to eat outside."

"Thank you, Sarah. I'll be right there. Can I help you with anything?"

"No. I grilled the brats outside. I've already brought them inside and set everything on the sideboard."

Olivia picked up her tote bag off the pool table and left the library. She went to the bathroom to wash her hands and then found her way to the formal side of the house and the massive dining room. She was the last to arrive. Olivia looked up at the two huge crystal chandeliers, now clean and sparkling like a million diamonds. The view from the multipaned windows was of an endless horizon of Lake Erie. Even with all ten of them seated, they only took up half of the chairs at the table. Olivia made eleven.

"Welcome, Queen Olivia." Travis bowed while standing at the sideboard. "We've decided we should have changed into tuxedos before dining."

"I do agree. Remind me to bring a ball gown tomorrow," Olivia said with humor as she walked over to fill a plate with grilled brats, German potato salad, sauerkraut, coleslaw, and baked beans. A plate of chocolate cookies sat at the end of the sideboard.

"This is our castle," Freddy emphasized. "We brought our swords, and Dad says that Reggie can take us over to the stone crusher and be knights and take pictures."

"Travis? Is that place safe? Shouldn't you check it out first?"

"It's one of our less-dangerous sites on the island. They'll be fine. Besides, the rest of us will be tied up for the rest of the day."

"How did you make out last night, Nick?" Olivia asked.

"Best sleep I've had in years! This place is so quiet it's like sleeping in a bank vault. I did find one problem, though, but it's no biggie. The doorknob in the sitting room that the boys use isn't good. Anyone with a credit card can get in."

"I've been thinking about Nick staying here last. I remember in past years when storms blow in so fast, it would be hard to get off the island in time. What about if I get a few of the bedrooms upstairs made up for emergency use? I can check them out this afternoon and see what it would take," Sarah pointed out.

"I think that would be a great idea. And maybe we should get a supply of air mattresses to have on hand as well," Nick said.

"I must stop by Port Clinton Yacht Sales and pick up the cleats and supplies for the dock. In fact, I'll swing by Walmart and get the air mattresses at the same time. Maybe, if we leave early enough, we can do that on our way home."

"No need to worry about time. I told Emma before we left this morning that we wouldn't be home for dinner. I've pulled out a couple of slabs of ribs from the freezer. We're all set."

CHAPTER SIXTY-THREE

Travis entered the library to find his wife studying one book with a stack of additional ones on the table next to her. Most of them were feathered with sticky notes. "Hey, isn't it about time you give your brain a rest? Are you still on the Civil War, or have you moved on to World War I?"

"Do you have a minute, or do you need to get back outside?"

He sat in the chair opposite. "What have you found?"

"These books, as you can see, have been read many times. They are full of pages with dog-eared corners. I have read those pages and have added sticky notes because what is written on those pages is important—important to Marblehead, Kelleys Island, and even Long Point. Do you know that British money helped fund the Confederacy? Along with France and a few other countries, but mostly the British."

"I didn't know that. Why Marblehead and Kelleys?"

"Money was smuggled in, and Canada is British. Connect the dots."

"I still don't get it. Richmond, Virginia, is a long way from here, especially in the mid-1800s."

"We both know that it was Confederate officers who were held on Johnson's Island. And Kelleys Island, as well as South Bass and Middle Bass, but mostly Kelleys because it is the largest of the islands. It was known that British funding was smuggled across the great lakes and then taken south. Confederate officers knew the routes."

"So, you think British gold arrived on Kelleys and Marblehead and somehow the Confederate officers knew the times of the shipments? I found a handwritten note in this book. It lists the dates shipments arrived KI. The next column lists the dates of skirmishes or disturbances that caused Union soldiers to leave their posts to help with uprisings on Johnson's Island. Guess what? They match."

"So, there is a connection."

"Guess who the Union general was who was in charge of Ohio, Pennsylvania, and Indiana?" Olivia nodded her head in the direction of the fireplace.

"General Horatio Buchanan?"

"None other. What I'm trying to figure out now is whether the Whitaker interest was purely because they bought the general's land or something deeper."

"What's your next move?"

"Keep reading and visit Aunt Millie tomorrow."

"How about you?" Olivia asked. "Made any progress on the cameras?"

"Higgins isn't too happy, but we are trying to connect new technology to an infrastructure that is forty years old. Uncle Clem and I worked out the plan for the brush clearing that begins tomorrow. Higgins is thinking that will help give us a better perspective of the land from the viewpoint on the tower."

"What is everyone else doing?"

"Waiting for us out on the picnic tables. Reggie and the boys are back from their adventure at the stone crusher."

Travis and Olivia arrived at the tables in time to see Reginald pulling the photos that the twins had taken that day, both from the sandy point and the ruins. They each sat down on either side of their sons. Ben began lighting the charcoal so they would be hot enough when Sarah was ready to put the ribs on.

"I saw your storyboard in the sitting room. Very impressive. Are you going to add these photos to the island map?" Olivia asked the boys.

"What's a storyboard?" Freddy wanted to know.

"A board that shows the details, or story of the project you are working on. Kelleys Island and what you have done there is the story."

"Now I understand. Yes, we are going to pick the best pictures and place them in the correct position on the map. Like this one of the pointing rock, and this one of me standing with my sword in the doorway at the crusher." Andy pointed to another photo. "Here's one that Reggie took of us sword fighting on the top of the wall."

"Andrew, Frederick! Reginald, how could you let them do something that dangerous?" Olivia scolded.

"It wasn't dangerous at all, Mom. Freddy and I only look like we are on the top of the wall from below where Reggie is. There was ground next to us."

"This one is cool. It looks like we are fighting in some old castle ruins," Freddy pointed out.

"It does. What about this one?"

"Oh. I just took that one because the lake looks so pretty. And this one is our picnic with Reggie.

"Who is the man in the background?" Higgins asked.

"Huh? Oh, I think he was fishing," Andy answered.

Higgins handed Reginald the photo of the picnic. "Recognize him?"

Reggie studied the photo. "I believe Andy is right. The man was fishing down a ways from us."

"Was anyone with him? Had he caught any fish?" Higgins asked.

"No. There were no other people around. He's the only person we saw, and he didn't do anything to catch my attention until now, looking at this photo."

"Odd, that this fisherman seems to be looking at you and not the lake," Higgins mused. "Can I have this one, Andy?"

"Sure, the man kinda spoils our picnic photo. I have a better one with just us."

"Reggie, can you get our remote-control boats so we can put them in the water by our dock?" Reggie asked.

"How do you know they are here and not back at the house?"

"Because Andy and I saw you put them in the back of the minivan."

"Of course, you did. Okay, I'll get the boats and meet you at the dock."

A few minutes later, Reggie jogged down to the dock. He saw Andy and Freddy standing at the edge of the dock looking into the water.

He set the boats and remote controls on the ground and walked over to where they were standing. "What is it? What are you looking at?"

"I thought Dad said he couldn't bring the Sea Ray and the inflatable until he attached the cleats."

"That is correct. He wants to get that done tomorrow morning."

"Then why is that dock line tied to that post?" Andy pointed to coiled rope that was partially hidden under the pier.

"Freddy, run up and get your dad and Higgins."

"What should we do?"

Reggie scanned the shoreline in both directions but didn't see anything that would cause alarm.

"We stand here quietly and wait until the others get here."

Travis and Higgins came running down to the water's edge. "Freddy said he and Andy found something?"

Reginald pointed to the side of the pier. "Travis, did you tie off a line in preparation for bringing the boats?"

"No. Why?"

"There's one now."

CHAPTER SIXTY-FOUR

"I don't get it. We've walked up and down the shoreline. Between the large rocks and sections of small stony areas, we aren't going to find any prints or signs that someone was here. Just the rope. Why?"

"Travis, I wish I had the answer, but I'm as baffled as you are. The house hasn't been broken into. There's no telling how long that rope has been there. It's been weeks since you and Nick inspected the pier; would you have noticed if the rope was there then?" Higgins racked his brain for anything that would make sense.

"Yes, I definitely would have noticed the dock line."

"We know a boat was pulled on shore at The Pines, so this would be way out of the way for someone to tie up here. And we have evidence of boats being beached at the point."

"This isn't something a seasoned boater would do," Travis stated. "One line to hold a boat against a post. Number one, he couldn't step out onto the pier without losing control of the stern, unless it was a good-sized boat, and that cheap line wouldn't hold it. Plus, look at the knot. My eight-year-olds can do better than that."

"I did notice the knot," Higgins said. "So, we have an inexperienced boater and an off-the-shelf listening device, and someone searching the barn. Those are the only dots that connect."

"But we go back to my original question. Why?"

"The answer to that, Travis, is . . . what is he or they looking for in the barn?"

"Travis, Higgins's dinner is ready," Sarah shouted from the picnic tables.

"I guess we put our mystery rope on the back burner for now," Higgins stated.

"And add it to the growing list of mysteries at Long Point," Travis said.

Sarah served her special recipe ribs, along with the leftover coleslaw and baked beans from lunch. Strawberry shortcake topped off the meal.

Afterward, Benjamin helped Sarah clean up outside and put the food away. Reginald and the twins went to the sitting room to tack their newly taken photos to the storyboard. Higgins, Logan, and Lorenzo went up to the third floor to test their newly installed equipment.

Travis and Nick went to the office to review the day's progress and agree on tomorrow's schedule with the brush removal.

Olivia stopped at the office door on her way to the library. "Nick, are you planning to spend the night?"

"No. One night with Batman sheets is enough for me. I'm heading home as soon as Travis and I finish here."

"Honey, I'll be in the library. I think I left my tote bag in there."

Olivia opened the library door and flipped the overhead lights on. After getting comfy in the big leather, she opened the book titled *Funding the Confederacy* and began flipping to the dog-eared pages.

Just then Travis poked his head in. "Honey, we are about to leave. Okay, I'll be right out."

She started to put the book on the table. No, there was something important between those pages. She only needed more time to find it. Instead, she got up and walked over to the pool table and slipped the book into her tote bag. At the door, she turned back and looked up at the general.

"If only you could speak." She then turned out the lights and closed the door.

CHAPTER SIXTY-FIVE

The next morning, Emma prepared an easy breakfast of scrambled eggs, hash browns, sausage and bacon, and toast with a selection of Paterson's own preserves.

"I picked up enough cleats last evening to line both sides of the pier. With Nick's help, we should be able to bring the boats over this afternoon. I also grabbed six large fenders and enough heavy rope so we can tie them to the concrete. I'll have permanent posts installed as soon as I can make the necessary arrangements."

"Dad! You mean we can have our boats on Long Point? We can go boating any time we want?"

"Any time *adults* want to go boating. Yes, I admit I'm looking forward to getting the Sea Ray out in the open waters and letting her go." Travis looked over at Higgins. "Maybe you and I take a camera and check out the shoreline around the entire perimeter in the inflatable."

"Agree. And with the brush crew coming in today, we can direct them to any areas where we see recent activity from the water."

"More coffee, gentlemen?" Emma offered.

"No. Thank you, Emma. Breakfast was delicious. All of us will be heading out in a few minutes," Travis said as everyone pushed back their chairs and left the dining room.

"The Harrisons as well?"

Travis thought about how Sarah and Benjamin had so easily become a valuable part of the Long Point crew. Not in the roles of housekeeper and estate manager as they were at Fairfield, but as family and decision-makers. "You'll have to ask them, but I assume they both have projects they want to get back to."

━╬╬━

While Travis and Nick were securing the last cleat to the pier, Higgins finished checking the equipment in the new security center, for any recorded activity from the night before. All looked good, and not even a raccoon had passed by. With Logan and Lorenzo deciding to check on the progress of the ground crew from the tower, Higgins went back down the rear stairs to the servants' wing. Reginald and the twins were excitedly working on their storyboard. Remembering the photo of the fisherman, he decided to see what other interesting photos they may have taken.

"Hello. You keep snapping everything you see, and you're going to need another board."

"Come look, Higgins," Andy offered.

The little guy literally had a picture of everything from turtles to grass. At the rate Andy was going, Travis would have to order film packets by the case. His eyes stopped at one in particular. It was taken with the grass stuff.

"Andy? What is that? It looks like a giant rock covered in vines."

"Yeah. It's like the pointing rock. Only it's square like all the other ones we see everywhere."

"Do you remember where you took this photo?"

"Sure. It's kinda close to that house you call 'Pines,' but more in the middle."

Higgins saw from other photos Andy had taken in that same area that there were more of the short dry-stacked stone walls. He looked more closely at the vine-covered rock.

"Do you have a magnifying glass?"

"Right here," Andy said as he picked one up from the table and handed it to Higgins. "We use it to look at fossils. We have a whole bowlful now."

Higgins removed the photo from the board and held it up to the glass. "Hmmm."

"What do you see?" Reginald asked.

"Since when do rocks have wood attached to them?"

"What?" Reginald exclaimed.

"You need to take me there—now!"

On his way to get the Gator out of the garage, Higgins shouted to Travis and Nick and motioned for them to follow.

"What is it?" Travis asked while catching his breath after running up from the pier.

"The boys found something interesting. Take the golf cart and follow us to The Pines."

It took a bit longer for the golf cart to reach the clearing and park next to the Gator. "Reginald said there is a path but not wide enough for the Gator."

"What did they find?" Nick asked.

"A rock," Higgins stated.

"Well, that certainly helps. Kelleys is one big rock. Everywhere you look, there's a rock. Which one are we looking for?" Travis jested.

"Come on, guys. Follow us," Andy and Freddy shouted.

They had gone far enough that Travis wasn't sure if what lay ahead was part of The Pines, or perhaps another structure that was no longer there, since this area had the hip-high dry-stacked stone walls. It appeared to be another one of the large stones that the receding glacier left behind. Oddly, this one was covered in grapevines.

Travis and Nick joined Higgins in ripping away the vines where a panel of wood had been placed.

"Huh. This isn't a rock. It's a small stone structure of some kind," Travis said.

"Interesting that the vines have securely attached themselves to the stones over the years, but the vines on the wooden door seem to have been placed there," Higgins observed. "And recently."

"How about all of us start pulling and get all the vines off?" Travis suggested.

Within minutes, the stone structure was uncovered. "It looks like an old icehouse. Uncle Clem has one on the farm. This one is smaller, but it looks the same. Nick and I used to play in it when we were kids."

"Okay, let's pry this door open and see what's inside."

"Higgins, we don't have any tools with us," Nick admitted. Then he grabbed the edge of the door and pulled. "Wow, that was easy."

"Here, Dad. I got this flashlight out of the golf cart," Andy said.

Travis pressed the button and directed the light into the cavity. "It's larger and deeper than it looks from the outside. There's a ladder—a new ladder."

"Give me the light. I'll go in and see what we have."

"I'll go, Cousin Nick. I'm not afraid of anything," Freddy said as he headed for the opening.

Nick grabbed him by his shirt. "Oh no, you don't. This adventure belongs to me. Nick swung his leg over the edge and eased himself down. "Three boxes are stacked down here. I'll bring them up." One by one, Travis and Higgins each grabbed a carton and set them down. Nick hoisted the last one on his shoulder and headed back up. "Let's see what we have."

Travis was the first to get his box open. "Looks like some kind of ham-operator machine."

"I've got electronics," Nick voiced.

"We have the other end of our listening devices," Higgins confirmed.

CHAPTER SIXTY-SIX

Meanwhile, Olivia was visiting Aunt Millie. She had called that morning to ask if it would be all right if she could come by and talk explaining that the twins were working on projects and the afternoon was taken. But perhaps she could bring the boys by tomorrow. This visit Olivia wanted to talk about the history of Long Point, General Horatio Buchanan, and the Civil War.

"I made us a pot of tea, orange spice, very invigorating. I thought it might be nice if we sat in the history room. There's a lovely reading corner overlooking the lake."

"I hope I'm not keeping you from something."

"My dear, at my age, I welcome distractions."

"The library at Bent Tree Cottage is amazing, and I've been spending quite a bit of time looking over the collection of books. One thing that strikes me as odd is all the books on the Civil War and particularly on the Confederacy. After Travis purchased Long Point, James Whitaker the third traveled to Fairfield with some documents. He never mentioned that his family had been interested in the war, or the city of Richmond, especially since Fairfield is only a few miles from the capital of the Confederacy. What's more, General George McClellan's Union troops camped on Fairfield's land. Mr. Whitaker was literally sitting among Civil War history, and the subject never came up."

"I must agree with you. If that had been me, I would have been soaking up your history like a sponge. I would probably still be there with my nose in *your* books." She thought for a moment. "We had a connection, in these parts, with both the Union and Confederate armies. I'm sure you know about our Confederate prison on Johnson's Island."

"Yes, I spent many hours as a child exploring the cemetery. And I've only yesterday read in one of the books that General Buchanan oversaw the prisons in three states. But little else is written about him, at least that I've found."

"The general graduated from West Point, and although he was a natural leader, he also had fire in his belly, and he was ambitious. Some said he had a talent for giving orders, but not so with following them."

"How did he come to buy Long Point? Or why? From what I understand, he wasn't growing grapes for the wine industry, which was taking off about that time."

"How did he even know about Long Point? It was pretty much a waste land that still saw some Indian and trading traffic, mostly pelts from Canada. The settler who lived in the larger cabin leased the land and kept to himself." Aunt Millie pointed to the far corner of the room. "There is at least one old photo of the settler and his cabin. Name was Stanton. Joshua Stanton. His name is written on the photo."

Olivia walked over and studied the old photo, now a dark brown with age. "He looks rugged, stern expression with some animal pelt over one shoulder and a rifle over the other. Cabin looks to be in better shape than him. Here's a photo of five young men dressed in Union Army uniforms. But that doesn't connect them to our general." Olivia moved to her right and spotted a photo of the general. "Here he is standing outside the same cabin. He's not wearing his uniform. The year is 1866. The war ended on April 9, 1865." Olivia glanced over her shoulder at Aunt Millie. "You can't live near Richmond and not know that date."

"So, you are wondering how the general went from watching over prisons to owning Long Point. That nice professor who visited me quite a few times last summer also was interested in the general."

"A professor was interested in General Buchanan? Do you remember his name?"

"Sure. He was a regular visitor. A nice man but asked a lot of questions. He headed the biological sciences and research programs at Ohio State University's Stone Laboratory on Gibraltar Island. Professor William Sherman."

"Do you happen to have a photo of him?"

"No, but I think my friend Ida Hamilton might have one. The professor was camera shy, but I think Ida got him in one of the photos taken around the time of the July fourth celebrations."

"What kind of questions was he asking?"

"He said he was doing research on the stories he'd heard about British gold that was being smuggled from Canada to this area and then transported down to Richmond or other locations to fund the Confederate army."

"There could have been gold brought across Lake Erie to Kelleys? That seems rather far-fetched."

"Oh yes. In fact, back in the early days of 1861, the Kelleys Island Union Guards determined that an artillery company was needed to protect the islanders against an attack by rebels and Southern sympathizers from Canada. They even obtained a cannon that had been used on board one of Commodore Perry's ships."

"So, it was well known here on the island that Canada supported the Confederacy."

"I believe Professor Sherman got it in his head that General Buchanan knew about the gold shipments. There had been rumors that not all the gold made it to Richmond."

"Interesting. Very interesting. Aunt Millie, do you think you could get that photo of the professor from Ida?"

"Of course. I'll call her right after you leave. We play bingo at the town hall on Monday nights. She can give it to me then."

Olivia got the feeling that perhaps it was time for her to leave. She glanced down at her watch. "Oh, I had no idea it was getting close to noon. I had better head back. Travis has a crew starting today to begin clearing the underbrush and dead trees. I think some of the men are starting to clear along the road to make it easier for when digging begins for the new waterline."

"I heard about that. Why would Travis want to do that when he has the best water on the island?"

Everything Olivia knew about the well water on Long Point was that it wasn't fit to drink. Nick was having large bottles of water delivered each week to use for cooking and drinking.

"I don't understand. One of the first things Nick tested was the water in the house. He said it was horrible."

"Callum McTavish was sweet on me while he was the Whitakers' estate manager. Besides picking bouquets of wildflowers for me, his favorite gift was bottles of water from the well. Long Point has a small natural lake under it, much like Perry's Cave on South Bass Island."

"But Nick had a ground survey done, and an underground lake wasn't found."

"Did the survey cover the entire property, especially around the center?"

"No, it was for the waterline only. So, the roadway and the south side."

"I would suggest Nick and Travis test the water again before they go any further. I know that Bent Tree Cottage's well runs off that lake. I believe the entrance to the cave is somewhere around the garage or barn. The original settler certainly knew about it."

"Thank you, Aunt Millie. I will talk to my husband as soon as I get back."

"Perhaps, on a future visit, you could spend some time telling me about Fairfield and its role in the Civil War. I understand General Harrison's family lived next door to Fairfield. He was around these parts back in the War of 1812. I would have loved visiting the area back in my younger days. It is far too difficult for me to fight my way through airports. Nowadays, I don't much like the hassle of going off-island."

"I would love to have you as a guest at Fairfield. And Berkley Plantation, the former home of the Harrisons, and Shirley Plantation are both down the road from me and open to the public. I bet I could even get you a private tour. And don't worry about struggling through airports and departure times—I'll take care of all that," Olivia said with a wink.

CHAPTER SIXTY-SEVEN

"Mom! Guess what? We found an icehouse. Like the one we have at Fairfield, only smaller. Nick climbed down the ladder and carried three boxes up to Dad and Higgins. The boxes are filled with stuff," Freddy told his mom as soon as she stepped out of the Hummer. The roar of multiple chain saws and trimmers competed with her son's excited voice.

Sarah poked her head around the kitchen door. "Lunch in twenty, at the picnic tables."

"Travis, Nick, Higgins, can I speak with you?" Olivia glanced at Reginald. "How about you take the boys inside and get them cleaned up for lunch?"

Both parents watched in silence as the twins skipped their way to the house.

"How did your session go with Aunt Millie?" Travis asked as they walked toward the tables.

"Very interesting. Remember Perry's Cave on South Bass? Well, it turns out that Callum McTavish knew about a smaller one here, probably under the garage or barn."

"Impossible. We would know about it. It isn't shown on any of the blueprints, and I haven't seen any reference to an underground lake," Travis stated.

Nick's brow furrowed. "The well *is* connected to *something*. I never considered the sources. Cousin, if the well water is good and it sounds like there would be an endless supply, we would need to cancel the pipeline—now."

"Aunt Millie wants you to test the water again, since its being used now. Could it be that what water you tested, early on, was running through bad pipes?"

"Anything is possible. One more mystery on Long Point. The list is getting longer by the day," Travis said as Freddy came running toward them.

"And then there is the gold," Olivia added as she slung her tote bag over her shoulder. "I'm going in and washing my hands. I'll be right back."

Reginald was standing at the sink washing his hands when Olivia arrived at the only working bathroom in that wing of the house. She continued down the hall and into the main part of the house and entered the library. "Well, well, Horatio, did you have your hand in the cookie jar?" Olivia asked of the general as she set her bag on the pool table. "Aunt Millie was full of information this morning," Olivia voiced, then went back to wash her hands.

━━╬━━

Olivia was the last to arrive at the table and squeezed in between her husband and Freddy. "So, what were you telling me about an icehouse?"

"We found it, Mom. Andy and me. Then Higgins looked at the picture I took, and we all went to the pine house."

"Then Freddy and me and Reggie showed Dad and Cousin Nick and Higgins where to find the big rock covered in grapevines—but it wasn't a rock. It's a really old icehouse, right here on Long Point."

"Well, it sounds to me like you two boys are real adventurers."

She looked up at Travis. "I know there is more to this story. What was in the boxes Freddy mentioned?"

"Electronic equipment. The receiving end of the listening devices," Higgins explained. "We did a sweep of the surrounding brush but found nothing, except the path had been used."

"Then our squatter or smuggler wasn't smuggling but listening. To what or whom?"

"I'm guessing—us."

"Our barn searcher?" Olivia asked.

"Who's a barn searcher?" Andy asked.

Reginald shook his head, indicating that further discussion should wait until a more private time.

Olivia realized her sons' knowledge of The Pines and the icehouse was superficial. Part of their explorations. "Speaking of icehouses, isn't there a *boathouse* back in Marblehead with two boats that want to come here?"

"Yes! Yes! Dad, can we go get the boats now? Andy and I want to go for a ride."

"After lunch, your mom and I will take the two of you and Higgins, Logan, and Reginald back to Marblehead for the two boats. The Harrisons and Nick will stay here to handle the brush clearing with Uncle Clem.

"Lorenzo, continue working on the cameras and security feed. I'll bring out a few more spools of wire. I want cameras at The Pines ASAP. We need to get eyes on that area. Maybe catch who left that valuable equipment behind."

Travis thought about what Olivia had said about the well water. "Nick, taste the water and see if it's drinkable. It sure tasted bad when we first came here."

"It tastes just like water," Freddy informed them.

"What do you mean, Son? No one is supposed to drink the water. It is only used for washing."

"Sometimes I don't want to use the bottle, so I put my face under the faucet and drink. It tastes like water."

Travis shook his head and rolled his eyes. Why didn't he simply hold a debriefing session with his sons each evening? They would probably be further ahead. "Nick, Benjamin, while we're gone, check out the old well head. The water pump system in the mechanical room was added some time after the house was built. See if you can locate the older one, maybe even the original well. There is that shedlike structure behind the garage. I didn't think it was important until now."

A lake? He'd known since he and Nick were kids that there were some twenty-five to thirty caves on South Bass Island, which is smaller than Kelleys. Perry's Cave has a lake, and Crystal Cave was the largest known geode in the world. Why couldn't Long Point?

CHAPTER SIXTY-EIGHT

During the drive to the Kelleys Island ferry, Olivia talked about Professor William Sherman who headed the biological sciences and research programs at Ohio State University's Stone Laboratory on Gibraltar Island. "Aunt Millie said he spent a lot of time with her last year. He said he had heard stories about General Buchanan and was interested in doing research on him. She mentioned that he asked a lot of questions about Long Point and even the cabin that he lived in. I saw photos of him and the cabin." Olivia reached for her tote bag. "Oh darn! I must have left my bag on the pool table. I took some notes while I was there."

"I can turn around and go back for it," Travis offered.

"No, we are almost to the dock. I was only going to check my notes."

"Why does the name William Sherman sound familiar?" Travis asked.

"I'll give the office a call over on Gibraltar and see if Professor Sherman is working there this year," Higgins offered while pulling a small spiral notebook from his pocket and jotting down the information.

"Do you think we should call the Burnsides and let them know we're coming?" Olivia asked.

"I don't see why. I need to check the security room for messages and any recordings that may have been taped while I've been gone. Logan, I want you to grab a change of clothes and whatever else you need to spend the night. There are too many things going on when we aren't there. And we don't know who belongs to the electronics we found today. Travis, you and the boys can go straight to the boathouse and prepare to leave."

"Mom, can we still go see Aunt Millie tomorrow? I want to learn more about the cave with the lake," Andy asked.

"I hope she remembers to make cookies," Freddy added.

The tall gates silently opened. Travis drove through and parked the minivan at the end of the driveway. The front-seat passengers were the first ones out. Olivia saw that Travis and Higgins stood in front of the hood looking down by the pool. She slid the side door back and stepped out, then joined her husband. Emma was doing laps in the pool.

"Hello, Emma," Travis shouted to her.

Emma stopped midway in the pool and looked up. She swam to the edge, pushed her hair back from her face, and hoisted herself out of the water.

Emma's skimpy white bikini was set off by her dark tan.

"Wow! If doing laps creates a body like that, then perhaps I should start," Olivia softly said as she watched Emma reach for a white terry cover-up. She then jogged up the hill to the house while tying the belt of the wrap.

At the same time, Stanley exited the door to the couple's apartment over the garage. He wore khaki shorts and a white polo shirt with the collar open. They both reached the minivan at the same time.

"We didn't know you were coming home so early," Emma stammered.

Stanley checked his watch. "It's only one thirty." He looked at Emma with a questioning look.

"I'm sorry . . . I . . . we didn't . . . know . . ."

"No need to apologize. We decided to take the boats out to Long Point. We'll have more time for boating with the boats docked at the pier," Travis explained.

"Your free time is your own. I'm glad you are enjoying the pool," Olivia added.

Higgins and Logan excused themselves and went into the house.

"Andy and me found an icehouse this morning!" Freddy exclaimed. "And it had stuff in it."

"It sounds like you are having a real adventure," Emma said, then looked at her husband.

"Can I help you with the boats?" he offered.

"Sure. You can take care of the dock lines after we back out."

"Last one there is a rotten egg," Freddy shouted, then took off running down the hill to the boathouse. Andy followed at a slower, more careful pace. Reggie followed.

"Andy never will beat his brother. They may be identical twins but are quite different," Olivia said with pride.

"How so, although I have noticed that Andy is more articulate and has a remarkable memory for an eight-year-old."

"Andy is the brain, and Freddy is the doer. Andy is cautious and Freddy spontaneous."

"But how do you tell them apart?"

"As parents, we know instantly. But for everyone else, at first glance it's their clothes. They will never wear the same outfit. Andy will be in pastels, and Freddy the brightest shirt he can find. Andy will be neat and tidy, and Freddy looks like he just got out of bed."

"I see. Well, I should go in and change," Emma said as she walked toward their apartment.

Olivia headed down toward the boathouse at a leisurely pace. She entered to find the large overhead doors open and the Sea Ray's engine blower had been started. Travis and Stanley were examining one of the dock lines on the inflatable.

"Stanley, have you taken this out?" Travis asked.

"No, sir. Neither of us know how to operate a boat. Why?"

"The knot. This isn't the way I tie off lines. If you look at the Sea Ray, those lines have an easy quick-release knot. This rope has been twisted back and forth a half dozen times around the cleat."

"Sorry, sir. Maybe some kids got in here and took her out for a joy ride. Although I thought you have a lot of security cameras around the property."

Travis shook his head and rolled his eyes. How could a couple who spent so much time on Nantucket not be boaters?

"Livy, honey." Travis nodded toward the larger boat. "Want to take the helm? The boys are already on board."

"Sure. It will be my first time this year."

"I wonder what's keeping Higgins!" Travis said.

"Excuse me, Olivia, but I've been talking to William. There was another breach in security at the shipyard. Someone was attempting to steal HELIOS."

"What? You said attempted. HELIOS is safe?" Olivia threw the questions at Higgins. "I should leave immediately for Norfolk."

"William assured me that everything is under control. They have arrested the person responsible. She was one of the scientists working on the project. We will be given the details once William has them."

"Are you sure it is all right that I stay?"

"Absolutely. I have already sent Reginald back to the island with the minivan."

Olivia noticed Emma standing in the doorway. She was now dressed in her gray-and-white uniform. Her hair was pulled back in a bun. What a difference from the stunning, well-toned body in a bikini!

CHAPTER SIXTY-NINE

Olivia stood at the helm of the thirty-six-foot Sea Ray, Sundancer as she pulled away from the boathouse and headed further out into Lake Erie. Higgins followed in the Zodiac.

"Mom, can you turn on the radar? Andy and I want to watch the thing go around."

Olivia flipped the switch on the dashboard. The radar unit mounted to the arch above the cockpit, came to life with its arm turning in slow mesmerizing circles. She looked back at the rear seat. Her sons sat, one on each side. Freddy lounged comfortably in the starboard corner. Andy, sitting upright, held the front of his life jacket with one hand and the port-side railing with the other.

"Ready, boys? Should I let her go?"

"Yeah," Freddy shouted.

Olivia buried the throttles. The engines roared, and the *Livy VI* raced forward skimming over the light chop of Erie. The vibration beneath her feet energized her very core. She felt alive and free as the wind swept through her long black hair. She glanced over at Travis. His smile said it all. He had given her this time—time to rejuvenate. "Thank you" was all she needed to say.

Olivia left Higgins far behind in her wake. Once she'd past Kelleys, she made the wide turn that would take her to the north side of Long Point and Bent Tree Cottage. About a half mile out, she pulled back on the throttles and aimed for the pier. She slowed even further as she approached. Sarah, Benjamin, Lorenzo, and Nick all began filing onto the lawn.

"How's your depth?" Travis asked.

"We've got eight feet . . . seven . . . six."

She pulled back even further as her bow lined up with the end of the eighty-foot pier. Everyone on shore began cheering as the port side of the long, sleek boat kissed the fenders that had been attached when Travis and Nick attached the cleats.

Nick jogged down to the boat, while Olivia shut down the engines and turned off the electronics. "Beautiful docking. You haven't lost your touch."

"It felt good—it felt *real* good." She looked down at Nick, who stood about four feet lower than the deck. "I'd say we need to get a set of steps out here before we do any serious boating."

Travis jumped down from the swim platform, then grabbed each of the boys and swung them onto the pier. Logan tossed his duffel bag onto the dock, then followed Travis. Olivia was last, and then she and Travis both secured the bow and stern lines.

Sarah handed Travis a large manila envelope. "The police chief dropped this off for you." She looked out across the water. "Where's Higgins?"

"I saw him swing in toward the southern shoreline. I think he wanted to check out the areas around The Pines and the point. I know he had his camera with him," Travis informed the group as he opened the envelope and pulled out the contents. There were several photos, but it was the first line of the report that caught his attention.

"Our squatter and Marblehead's John Doe are the same man."

Twenty minutes later, Higgins docked the inflatable and jogged up to the picnic table, where everyone but the twins was sitting. "I got a lot of good photos of the shoreline. It looks like the clearing crew has about finished with everything up to the point." He looked at the group's somber faces. "Who died?"

"I hope you got some good shoreline pictures at The Pines." Travis sounded like he'd just lost his best friend as he handed the envelope to Higgins.

"Why?"

"Our squatter and John Doe are one and the same—a Russian spy. Uri Kozlov and Steven Anderson."

After reviewing the photos and reading the report, Higgins glanced around the area. Chain saws could still be heard in the background along with a woodchipper. "Where's Andy and Freddy?"

"We sent them inside to play. Andy is probably working on his storyboard." Olivia answered.

"Uri Kozlov and Steven Anderson of Hamilton, Ontario, don't resemble each other in any way. But I do remember one of the reasons these operatives are so successful is their way to change their appearance as easily as a chameleon." Higgins slid all the photos and report back into the envelope. "Nick, have the crew move toward The Pines. I want to know everything about that side of the property."

Nick got up and ran over to the Gator and jumped in. He then headed toward the road that led to the point.

"What do you think?" Travis asked.

Higgins inhaled deeply. "I think the fifty thousand dollars wasn't smuggling money but to cover operating expenses. He needed to pay cash for everything. He couldn't leave a credit card trail, and that much money would last him quite a while and easily cover boat and car rentals. We found his electronics, so he was the one who planted the sophisticated bugs. But why? What information could he get from here?"

Olivia thought about their trip out on the *Livy VI*. "I was closely monitoring my depth after leaving the boathouse. It stays fairly shallow until you get out a way. I assumed that all of Long Point reached further out into the lake from the Marblehead lighthouse than it does."

"So, what are you saying, Livy?" Travis asked.

"I'm thinking that The Pines might not be directly in line with our house if our spy was listening and watching us."

"Good point, but remember we didn't find any bugs in the house on Marblehead. Just here," Travis added.

"It doesn't matter. The equipment we found could probably follow a signal anywhere on the eastern sides of Kelleys or Marblehead. What we know is our spy is dead."

"What about Professor Sherman?" Olivia asked.

"He is still on our radar," Logan said. "And will be tonight when I'm here watching."

Higgins placed his hands on the edge of the picnic table and stood. "I'm going inside and make some phone calls. One of them is to the Ohio State University's Stone Laboratory on Gibraltar Island."

"By the way, Travis, I had a lot of vibration out of the motor on the Zodiac. You might want to check out the prop."

Travis looked at Nick. "Let's check it out. Although I replaced the propeller at the end of last year. It should be fine."

"You can find me in the library," Olivia added.

Down at the dock, Nick raised the heavy Mercury outboard motor. "Huh. The prop is bent and badly nicked," Travis observed.

Nick leaned over and looked. "How do you suppose that happened?"

"The question is, who took this out and ran it over rocks?"

⋉⋊

"Andy, Freddy. What are you doing in here?"

"We always play in here. We like the general," Andy answered.

Olivia glanced up to the portrait. "I do too," she said under her breath.

"I promise we don't get into stuff. Dad said the pool table is really special, and we can't climb on it."

Olivia noticed her tote bag was right where she had left it. How could she forget something that large? she wondered.

"This is the best room for hide-and-seek. Andy found the secret place, but since we know about it, it is the first place we look."

"I'll show you," Andy said as he ran over to the wall to the left of the fireplace. He used his shoulder to press against the panel and a door popped open. "See, it's a little closet." He then walked inside.

"I see that is special. It is a firewood box. I bet there is one on the other side."

"Yes, there is. How do you know about that?" Freddy asked.

"It is used to store wood for the fireplace. People would fill it with logs for the fire, and it would be out-of-sight."

"So, the people in here wouldn't see a pile of dirty wood," Andy surmised.

"You are exactly right, Son. But be careful that you don't get locked in."

"We know. Freddy almost couldn't get out."

Olivia pulled the book on the Confederacy from her tote bag and settled into her favorite leather chair and started reading where she had left off. Fifteen minutes went by as she tried to remain focused while her sons took turns jumping up and down in the firewood boxes.

"Okay. Enough. How about you two find another part of the house to play in?"

An hour later, upstairs in the security room, Higgins reviewed the photos he had taken with his new digital camera. The shoreline closest to The Pines was made up of small stones, creating a beach area. The brush had been matted down, but the foliage was still green. That told Higgins any activity by boat had been recent. What he remembered from the times he had explored that spot was there was definitely enough room to pull a small boat up on the stones. He thought about the photos Andy had taken of the icehouse. Higgins wondered how many more he had taken. He decided it was time to compare photos. He went downstairs and found the brothers working on the storyboard.

"Hello, boys. I was looking over the photos I took today while out in the Zodiac and thought you might like to see them. And maybe you will share some of yours with me."

"Cool." Andy reached for the camera as Higgins put the strap around Andy's neck and showed him how to operate the rather cumbersome camera. Andy then handed Higgins a stack of Polaroids.

"Andy, Freddy, you have quite a few pictures of The Pines. You were told not to go in there."

"We didn't, Higgins. Promise. You and Dad said we couldn't, but it is a neat old house. Andy only took pictures. Promise."

"May I borrow a few of these? I'll return them when I finish."

Andy returned the digital camera. "This is really cool. You can see the pictures as soon as you take them. But I still like my Polaroid better. After I take a picture, the film comes right out the front. After you wait a minute, the picture appears, and I don't have to wait and take a roll of film to the store."

"You are right about that. I think I'll go to the office and look at these."

Travis and Nick were at the desk reviewing the brush-cutting schedule for the next day when Higgins walked in. "Excuse me. I need to show the two of you something."

"Sure. I see you've been combing through Andy's pictures. I believe my son may become a photojournalist."

Higgins laughed. He set three photos on the desk in front of Travis and Nick. "What do you see in all three of these?"

"Huh. This view of The Pines shows someone looking out the window. This one was taken the day the Gator was delivered."

"Travis, look closely at the background."

"Higgins! Someone is standing at the back corner of the barn!"

"This one shows the side of the pointing rock. Andy caught it at a nice angle. The sun is reflecting off the pink tones in the rock . . . and there are tools piled up off in the brush. Looks like a shovel, long pry bar, sledgehammer, and a duffel bag," Nick exclaimed.

"The guy in the window was the same day Andy took the ice-house photo. We can time both the Gator and the pointing rock. These are recent. The pile of tools is the key—this guy is looking for something."

Travis looked up at the wall clock. "We don't have time today, but how about we take our own tools and check out The Pines tomorrow morning?"

CHAPTER SEVENTY

The next morning dawned gray with drizzle. The weather forecast was for more of the same all day. But it wasn't enough to dampen the spirits of everyone who was on their way to more adventures. Travis and Higgins were armed with the necessary tools to go looking for whatever they were looking for and would meet up with Nick when they arrived. Olivia, Andy, and Freddy, along with Reggie, were excited about their morning visit with Aunt Millie. Lorenzo had packed his duffel bag in case he too decided to spend the night in a castle. Sarah had brought more food for the freezer and pantry, along with a stack of pillows and bedding for the air mattresses. Sarah now had quite the collection of mail-order catalogs in the office and thought today might be a good time to order rain slickers for everyone. Benjamin was there for whatever job came his way.

Logan sat at the kitchen table sipping his second cup of coffee. He waited until everyone filed in, and Sarah put a kettle on the stove for tea. Andy and Freddy announced they would be working on the storyboard and left the room.

"I have good news, and I have bad news," Logan began. "The good news is the surveillance cameras and lights work, and I was alerted at eleven ten that we had an intruder. I checked the monitor to see him in the process of opening the barn doors. I immediately turned on the hall and stairway lights and ran down three flights of stairs to reach the back door. Unfortunately, by the time I got to the barn, he was gone. Knowing that he had stashed his tools at the point, I jumped in the Gator and took off down the road. I got to the beach in time to see him in a skiff heading to the east."

"How do you know it was a skiff and not an inflatable?" Higgins asked.

"The light from the moon reflected off the aluminum hull."

"I don't suppose you got a good look at him."

"I didn't, but the cameras did." Logan then slid three photos to the center of the table. He was wearing black pants and a black hoodie. None of the angles got his face straight on. But enough to catch what looked like a full red beard and light-colored eyes.

"He looks startled in this last photo. He wasn't expecting anyone to be here," Higgins noted.

Sarah fixed mugs of Earl Grey tea for Olivia and herself, then turned to Logan. "Did you sleep well? Other than your late-night adventure. I tried to stock the bathroom with towels and bath products."

"Thank you, Sarah. I had everything I could possibly need. I thought at first, I would have a hard time getting comfortable on the air mattress, but once the adrenaline wore off after chasing the bad guy, I had one of the best nights ever." He looked at Travis and Nick. "I do have one big suggestion—we need an elevator."

"Speaking of bad guys, I think it's about time we make our way to The Pines. Nick, we should take your truck. With this rain, we could get the minivan stuck, and the Hummer won't fit all of us," Travis said as he stood. "We need to transfer the tools from the minivan to the truck."

"I'll take the Hummer for our visit to Aunt Millie's. I told her we would be there in about half hour."

⟞┼┼⟝

Nick parked his truck in front of The Pines. Everyone piled out of the truck and grabbed a tool. The rain had become a light drizzle. Nick picked up the large flashlight he always kept in the back seat.

The men walked single file along the path that would lead them to the icehouse. Once at the site, Nick pulled the door open and turned on the flashlight.

"The ladder is still here. I'll go down first."

Nick aimed the light along the wall as he climbed down each rung. "This icehouse was manmade. I can see the drill marks where the dynamite was placed. It probably is older than the house."

Once on the bottom, Nick aimed the beacon of light around the walls, then the floor. "Wow! You better get down here."

"Who should go down?" Travis asked.

"All of you!"

One by one, Travis, Higgins, Logan, and Lorenzo descended into the bowels of the icehouse. And each one had the same comment—"Wow!"

"There's a cave!" Nick exclaimed as he aimed the beacon into the opening beyond.

"How far do you think it goes?" Higgins asked.

"I have no idea. We need more light—lots of light. There's something tucked up inside this crevice." Nick handed the flashlight to Higgins. "Hold this while I reach in."

"Nick, don't. There may be snakes in there," Travis warned.

375

"Got it," Nick said as he pulled a duffel bag out of the crevice and put it on the floor.

Higgins reached down and unzipped the brown bag, spreading it wide open.

"What's in there?" Logan asked.

⸻

"Hello! Hello! Welcome! Please come right in," Aunt Millie said as she held the screen door open for her visitors. After everyone was inside, she closed the door and bent down to the twins' level and pointed. "You are Freddy. And you are Andy. Am I right?"

"You are! No one ever gets it right," Freddy exclaimed.

"I must confess; your mom gave me some hints on her last visit. I went by your shirts this time. Freddy always wears bright colors."

"Did you make cookies?" Andy asked.

"Of course, I did, and they are on the table in memorabilia room."

The twins immediately moved to the display case where the model of Commodore Perry's ship, the Lawrence, could be viewed from all angles.

"Do you know what made the commodore's fleet so special?" Aunt Millie asked.

"They were fast," Freddy answered.

"The commodore didn't have enough ships, and he had to get them fast in order to fight the British. The shipyard in Presque Isle, Pennsylvania, could build them. So, his ships were built with shallow drafts; they only needed five feet of water. His ships could maneuver quickly and sail close to shore where the big, heavy, British gunboats couldn't go."

"We have been to the monument at Put-in-Bay. We know all about Commodore Perry," Andy informed Aunt Millie.

"Do you know about Perry's Cave?"

"We have been to Crystal Cave lots of times. It is the largest geode in the world," Andy answered. "Is there another cave?"

"It is one of the reasons he was able to defeat the British. Sailors got sick a lot from the lack of fresh drinking water. The cave is deep and has a freshwater lake. Commodore Perry used the cave as a place for his sailors to rest and drink the fresh water. His sailors were healthy and able to better fight the British."

"Mom, can Reggie take us to Perry's Cave? Please? Please, Mom," Freddy whined.

Olivia glanced over at Reginald with raised eyebrows. He gave an affirmative nod. Then he joined the twins as they moved to the wall and studied the pictures of the battle.

Aunt Millie removed a photo from her apron pocket and handed it to Olivia. "Here's the photo showing the professor." Aunt Millie pointed him out. "He's a good-looking man. Probably of Irish descent with his reddish hair and green eyes."

"Yes, he is."

"Did your husband find the entrance to the lake?"

"No. Not yet. They were going to check out an icehouse they found over by The Pines today."

"Yes. In the early days, there was a settler who built a cabin and thought he'd make a living selling fish to the market in town. He had one of the quarry workers blast out enough stone to build the icehouse to preserve the fish. Once the dynamite guy went down to check out the shaft, he saw that a hole had been opened into the cave. Problem was the settler didn't have good access to the lake for fishing because of the limestone shelf. You can see the entire southern shore from my dock. He eventually left. The Whitakers built that bungalow and used the cave for cold storage. They named the house 'The Pines' and lived there during the summers until they built Bent Tree Cottage."

"Interesting. I don't think Travis knows that," Olivia commented as she walked over to the wall with the photos of Long Point. "Some of these photos of the early settler are very old. Here's one taken with him and a Native American. The Native American is holding up several pelts. Here's one showing the same man and settler with a string of fish. The bent tree is in the background."

"His name was Clarence Smith—don't think that was his real name. He kept to himself mostly. I had more old photos of the cabin and barn, but they seemed to have disappeared. I'm thinking the professor might have taken them."

"Here is one showing the settler with a wagon hooked up to a horse."

"He had a regular farm going out there. Raised chickens and a couple of goats. During the winter, he had a rather crude sled. That picture is gone too."

Aunt Millie showed the boys where the photos of the wineries were hung. "Remember when I told you about the Monarch Winery? Here are pictures when it was new and now in ruins."

"Wow! Mom, you have to take us there. Please. Pretty please," Freddy whined.

"Your dad knows the owner. It's private property. You can't just go there."

"I remember you told us. Dad has been too busy. Maybe he can take us tomorrow," Andy said in a tone that said it might not happen for a while.

Aunt Millie glanced at the boys and then to Olivia. "Would it be all right if I called the owners?"

"That would be wonderful. Reggie, would you be willing to take them? Maybe take Lorenzo with you?"

"Sure. It would be a great place for Andy to take his camera. Tell me where it is, and we can drive by and check it out on our way home, so I know where I'm going. Maybe we can do that tomorrow if this rain stops."

Aunt Millie left the room and returned a few minutes later. "You have their permission. I explained who you are and that you promise to be very careful. I will also let our police chief Bobby Monroe know that you will be there. It is one of the sites on the island that the police keep an eye on. Tourists sometimes treat our island as if it were Disneyland."

"Well, boys, I think it's about time we head back. I'm sure Sarah has prepared a wonderful lunch."

"You should come to Long Point sometime. Sarah makes really good food."

"Well now, Freddy, your mother has invited me to come to Fairfield for a visit sometime. I will get to experience Sarah's excellent cooking."

"We would like that very much, Aunt Millie. And you can stay as long as you want because we have guest rooms." Andy took her hand in his. "There is a really nice room close to the kitchen. It used to be Sarah's mom's. Then Freddy and I took naps in there so Sarah could watch over us, but now we are bigger. I think you would like it the best."

"Thank you, Andy. I will certainly come. Maybe when the weather here gets cold and my bones start to ache."

"That will be fine. Just call Lorenzo, and he will bring Mom's plane and get you," Andy offered.

Olivia gave Aunt Millie a hug. "Yep, just call Lorenzo," she said with a wink.

Olivia guided her sons and Reggie to the door. "I hope you two aren't inviting everyone you meet to Fairfield, or I'm going to need a bigger plane." Once out the door, Olivia turned back to Aunt Millie. "Thank you," she mouthed.

CHAPTER SEVENTY-ONE

"Where is everyone?" Olivia asked Sarah as the Aunt Millie group entered the kitchen.

"All the excitement is in the living room. They found a cave and Steven Anderson."

"What? I thought he was Uri Kozlov."

"You'll see. Lunch in fifteen in the dining room."

Olivia, Reginald, and the twins all headed to the family room in the front corner of the house that overlooked the driveway and lawns.

"Hi, guys. Sarah says you found Steven Anderson—I thought—what's all that?"

"Hi, Livy. This pile of stuff is what turned Uri Kozlov into Steven Anderson."

Logan began holding up the various items. "Wig, beard, padded shirts and pants to make him look heavier, glasses, and a makeup kit."

"What does this mean exactly?"

"From what I've pieced together, Olivia, we have a Russian super spy who was hanging out here monitoring, with the latest electronics, what I assume was the Captain's House. He used an alias, Steven Anderson. Why he risked being out in that storm without his disguise is anyone's guess. Since he washed up on shore not far from the lighthouse, it could possibly be that he was attempting to gain access to the property by water."

"I don't understand."

"HELIOS," Higgins answered. "We are talking highly sophisticated operatives. They would cover all basses. That means any place you might be or talk to someone who could give the Russians valuable information. We know that your little old lady tried to take you out or maybe only get close enough to plant the bug."

"Why here? I wasn't due to arrive until June first."

"Travis. You talked to Travis every day."

"Excuse me, everyone. Lunch is served in the dining room," Sarah announced from the doorway.

Olivia picked up her tote bag. "I'll be right there. I want to stop and wash my hands. You too, boys."

She let her sons use the bathroom first, while she went to the library and set her bag on the pool table. "More interesting stuff, Horatio. I'm going to find your cabin."

The conversation over lunch centered around the cave. It was decided that Nick would borrow one of the large battery-powered light stands from the electricians and the guys would go back and explore the cave.

Olivia informed them of everything Aunt Millie had said about the icehouse and The Pines.

"This is all news to me. The bungalow is listed in the records but no mention that the Whitakers lived there." Travis thought about that. It didn't make any sense. "Why did the family go from living in a modest bungalow to building a twelve-thousand-square-foot house made of limestone that would stand forever?"

"Also, Aunt Millie showed me a photo of the professor. She thought he might be Irish with his red hair and green eyes. She believes that he might have walked off with some of her photos of the old cabin."

"Hold that thought. I need to run upstairs for a moment." Higgins hurried out of the dining room.

It was actually several minutes, during which time Olivia described the photos she had observed.

Higgins returned a bit out of breath. "We must put in an elevator. Here, does this look like the professor?"

Olivia studied the image. "I can't say for sure. Could be. He appears to have reddish hair and light eyes. The picture I saw showed a clean-shaven man with a neat, styled haircut. I should have asked her for it, but I knew she had borrowed it from a friend."

"I'll stop by on our way home and take a photo of it. Perhaps someone local will recognize him."

The sound of thunder was heard in the distance, and in less than a minute, the heavens opened. "Is everything buttoned up?" Travis asked.

"The drizzle all morning kept the golf cart and Gator in the garage and windows up. I believe we're okay," Benjamin added.

A loud clap of thunder sounded close by.

"I think I'll go to the library. It may be a bit quieter there, and I have plenty to read," Olivia announced.

"I'm going upstairs and see if I can reach someone on Gibraltar Island. Yesterday, I only got an answering machine," Higgins said as he stood from the table.

"I'll be in the office. Maybe I missed something in the Whitaker documents about The Pines and icehouse or cave," Travis said while he too stood and left the table.

A minute later, the room was empty, except for Sarah who was clearing the table.

Back in the library, Olivia settled back in the leather chair. She rested her head back and breathed deeply. "I do love the sweet smell of pipe tobacco in here," Olivia voiced out loud. She looked up at the stained glass ceiling with the bent tree. "Huh, the bend in the tree points north, directly at the fireplace." Who was she talking to? Olivia wondered. She thought about the photo she saw that morning with the Native American. The bend in the tree pointed *south* toward the cabin. It had been explained to her that the tree was like a road sign—pointing at the cabin. This tree pointed at the fireplace.

Olivia stood and hurried to the office. "Travis, Nick, we have to go upstairs to the secret room."

"Livy, honey, Nick and I are—"

"Now!" She turned and headed down the hall to the rear stairway. She took the stairs two at a time.

Nick locked the hallway door as Travis entered the closet and the secret door behind. "Okay, Livy. What is so important?"

She entered the space and flipped the switch. The cavernous area was flooded with light. She walked over and looked down at the stained glass window surrounded by a roof. The bend of the tree pointed to the right—*north*—to the bricks of a chimney rising along the north wall.

"What is it, Livy? What do you see?"

"General Horatio Buchanan's cabin."

CHAPTER SEVENTY-TWO

"Livy, how did you—no—it can't be."

"Look, I've been studying the photos at Aunt Millie's. The distance and position from the tree to cabin matches. The distance and position from the cabin to the barn matches. The fireplace in the photos is on the north wall of the cabin. The fireplace in the library is on the north wall." Olivia pointed to the fireplace. "North wall."

"Let's go back to why?" Nick asked. "The Whitakers buy Long Point from the general and build The Pines on the other side of the property, close to the old icehouse and cave. Then several years later, they build this monster of a house *around* his cabin—why?"

"I buy Long Point from the Whitaker estate and can't change anything—why?"

"Because the cabin is in the middle?" Olivia asked.

"Why not say the house was built around the original cabin and, for historical reasons, can't be altered? But I also can't alter the land—why?"

"Because of the caves and underground lake?" Olivia asked.

"But there is no mention of those anywhere in the documents, only by word of mouth from those who lived here, like Callum McTavish."

"I think we just found what our professor has been so determined to find. But again—why?" Olivia stated.

"It's time to let Higgins in on our little secret," Nick stated the obvious.

The three locked up the room and took the servants' stairs to the third floor and found their way to the newly thrown-together security office. "We're looking for Higgins," Travis asked Lorenzo.

"He left a minute ago for your office."

Olivia, Travis, and Nick took the stairs down to the first floor.

"We *must* install an elevator," Nick said between breaths.

"I second that," Olivia added.

They reached the office in time to see Higgins writing a note. "I've got news."

"So do we," Travis said. "But you go first."

"I finally got through to the person handling personnel at the research center on Gibraltar. There was never a Professor William Sherman working there or even at the university. I need to find this guy and find out what he's looking for."

"That's part of our news," Travis began. "We don't know the who part, but we think we know what he is looking for. You need to come with us."

Nearly an hour later, the four stood at the railing overlooking the cabin.

"I don't like the fact that you have kept your little secret room from me," Higgins admonished.

"But this has nothing to do with security. It is only part of the house," Nick explained.

"You asked me to secure the property. This is the property—no more secrets." Another clap of thunder caused everyone to look up.

"Do you hear that? It sounds like drips." Nick walked around the catwalk to get a better look at the shaft above them.

"I hear it too, but I don't see any water," Travis added.

"I've spent a lot of time on the tower. There is a patch of roofing that looks bad. I suppose it could be above us," Higgins informed the other three.

"When this place was first built, that shaft over the stained glass window would have let natural light in. I bet there is a skylight up there, and the roof is leaking onto the glass," Nick explained.

Another clap of thunder stopped the conversation.

"I suggest we leave this for another day. I'll call my roofing guy to come out and take a look," Nick suggested. "It sounds like this storm is building. Maybe we should think about heading back to the mainland."

Back downstairs, they found everyone else in the kitchen.

"I'm not liking the sound of this storm. The wind is kicking up something fierce. I may be new to island life, but I'm guessing the ferry stops running if the lake gets too rough."

"You're right, Sarah. We need to pack up now," Travis advised.

"I'm taking the Hummer and running over to Aunt Millie's. It will only take a few minutes. Then I'll be back in time to help load," Higgins said, then headed to the closet for a rain slicker.

"I brought clothes and things for the night. So, I'll stay here and watch over the place," Lorenzo informed everyone.

"What will you do if the power goes out?" Andy asked.

"No problem. We have a generator. You know how generators work. Right, Andy?" Nick mentioned.

"Yeah, but it's still scary."

"Okay. Everyone, get your stuff ready to leave and be back here so we can load up," Travis ordered.

After everyone else scattered, Nick put his hand on his cousin's shoulder. "You realize this is a bad one."

Travis grew up on Marblehead and Kelleys. He knew how fast a storm could blow in and the devastation it could leave behind—and Long Point was only a narrow finger jutting out into the lake. "I do. But stay calm. I don't want to panic the boys."

"Higgins should be back any moment. As soon as he returns, I'll pull the minivan as close to the door as possible and we get the boys loaded first."

Sarah and Benjamin returned to the kitchen. "Where is Higgins?" Sarah asked.

"He's not back yet. But don't worry; he has his mobile phone with him."

"Travis, you know it won't work in this—"

At that moment, the side door slammed shut and a drenched Higgins stumbled into the kitchen.

"We aren't going anywhere."

Benjamin helped Higgins out of the slicker and draped it over a hook by the back door. Sarah gave him a towel to dry his face.

"I was on my way back when a tree came down across the road about where the land gets real narrow. There's no way to get around it, not even with the Gator. I had to leave the Hummer parked in the road." Higgins untied his boots and left them by the back door with the slicker. "I'll be upstairs. I want to make a few calls before the phone lines go down."

"I'll call the Burnsides," Sarah said as she walked over to the wall phone.

"Mom, can Andy and I sleep on an air mattress?"

"You have a nice bed with Batman sheets."

"We'll let someone else use our bed. We want to sleep on an air mattress."

"Freddy, we will discuss this later. Right now, I'm going to help Sarah."

Reginald ushered the boys from the kitchen. Nick and Travis went to the north side of the house to check on the boats. Lorenzo and Logan followed Higgins upstairs.

At five o'clock, Sarah sent Andy and Freddy to find everyone and let them know that dinner was ready. Sarah and Olivia set bowls of spaghetti, meatballs, two loafs of garlic bread, and a tossed salad with all the fixings onto the sideboard in the dining room. The chandeliers sparkled against the darkened storm clouds.

Everyone was seated, except Higgins. Logan informed Sarah that he was working on something important but would be down shortly. The conversation revolved around the storm, and the boys wondered if the stranded Hummer would be washed away.

Midway through the meal, Higgins arrived and appeared to be excited about whatever he was about to say.

"Our Professor William Sherman is Kenneth Harlow—a treasure hunter. He's been somewhat successful in locating gold from sunken shipwrecks off the coast of Florida. For the last year or so, he's been following some stories about lost gold that was to help fund the Confederacy during the Civil War."

Olivia laughed. "William Sherman—the perfect alias."

"Why?" Logan asked.

"You want to tell them, Sarah?"

"Oh no. That's a Yankee story."

"General William Tecumseh Sherman is the Union general who attempted to destroy or burn his way through Georgia and the Carolinas. He is responsible for the burning of Atlanta," Olivia explained.

"Got it. So, he somehow believes gold coming from Canada and en route to Richmond ended up here?" Travis surmised.

"According to Aunt Millie, yes. And remember the note I found in the *Funding the Confederacy* book, here in the library? The Whitakers were studying it as well."

"I don't know what this guy believes, or what his story is, but I will find out. Because I now have pages of information on Kenneth Harlow and intend to pay him a visit—unless we catch him here first."

CHAPTER SEVENTY-THREE

The following morning dawn broke with clear skies. Travis woke to light filtering in through the leaded glass window. He turned his head to watch Livy sleep. The twins, although insisting on using their own air mattress, chose to sleep in the far corner of the suite away from the flashes of lightning. She and the boys probably wouldn't wake for another couple of hours. He gently rolled off the air mattress and got to his feet. Thoughts of the boats and how they had weathered the storm had him moving toward the large window overlooking Lake Erie and the long pier. Except for some debris in the yard, the dock lines and fenders seemed to have held. The spring line he had attached after docking yesterday did its job in preventing the boat from moving too far forward or back. Essential since the monster storm came right out of the north. Travis lifted his clothes from where he had draped them over the end of the large poster bed frame and padded down the hall to a bathroom. He hadn't wanted to use the one in the suite for fear of waking Olivia or the boys.

Ten minutes later, he followed the welcome aroma of coffee to the kitchen. Higgins, Logan, and Lorenzo were sitting at the table. Nick and the Harrisons were standing at the long butcher-block counter. He poured himself a mug of caffeine and took the empty seat at the table. "I see we are still running on the generator. I assume phone lines are down."

"But we have everything we need. How did everyone sleep?" Sarah asked. Then she walked over to the sink and started a fresh pot of coffee.

"Like a baby," Logan and Lorenzo both said.

"Yesterday morning I thought I was simply overly tired that I slept so well, but last night was the same," Logan confessed. "Maybe I'll stay again tonight. Especially since Sarah keeps the fridge stocked."

"I woke every hour or so to check the monitor, but once my head hit the pillow, I was out," Higgins added. "We had a lot of debris flying, but that is all I picked up on the screen. I'm glad you put the minivan in the garage, Travis. It was wicked out there. I'm sorry I had to abandon the Hummer. I hope it's okay."

"What about you, Nick?"

"I'm moving in until the work here is done, or Travis starts charging me board."

Everyone was laughing as Reginald entered the room wide-eyed and ready for the day. "Looks like sleeping with Batman agrees with you," Sarah said with humor. He only grinned in response.

The Mr. Coffee stopped dripping as he chose a mug from the selection on the counter. "If we start collecting more dishes, we're going to need some cabinets."

"Tell Sarah. She's in charge of designing the kitchen," Nick stated, then looked at Sarah with raised eyebrows.

"I'm on it" was all she said.

"Pull up a counter and have a lean," Travis joked. "Sarah, maybe we could use some stools."

"Already on my Walmart list," Sarah sighed. "Maybe I should post my list on the wall so everyone can add what they want," she said jokingly.

"Great idea!" Nick said.

"It would be nice if we could all sit in here for casual meals like breakfast and lunch," Travis admitted.

Sarah thought about all the furniture in the game room that wasn't being used, particularly a large oak pedestal dining table. She had found four leaves for it in the closet, which would expand the table to seat at least ten. "I think we can do that. Everyone up from the table. Move it to the end of the sink. Then follow me."

Twenty minutes later, everyone was having coffee at the large table. "Sarah, how long before breakfast?" Travis asked.

She looked at the wall clock. "An hour. I want to give Olivia and the boys more time to sleep."

"Perfect. Nick, how about you and I throw a couple of chain saws and tools in your truck and see if we can open up the road and rescue the Hummer?"

"Let's do it."

"I'm in," Logan offered. So did Benjamin and Lorenzo.

"I'm the one who left it behind, so I'm in," Higgins added.

"Then who stays behind to watch over everyone here?" Travis asked.

"I will," Reginald offered.

Forty minutes later, everyone returned but Higgins and Nick. Travis explained that while they were cutting up the tree and dragging it off the side of the road, Higgins and Nick went to check on Aunt Millie and assess storm damage in the area.

Travis looked out the window when he heard the Hummer. Higgins opened the driver's door and then went around the hood, while Nick opened the passenger-side rear door and got out. They both opened the front passenger door.

"Aunt Millie?" Travis couldn't believe his eyes. Hearing his words, everyone gathered to watch the elderly woman, flanked by strong men, walk to the back door. After she was safely inside and had been introduced to everyone, Nick went back out to the Hummer to retrieve her suitcase.

"Hello, everyone. Nick and Higgins were so kind to come and check on me. I must say I had a scary night."

"When we got to her driveway, Nick and I saw that the telephone pole had snapped off. Wires were hanging, and we had to drive down Monaghan Road a way in order to find a safe way to drive back to her house. I didn't realize how isolated she is back there on the shoreline. This is one tough old gal," Higgins said while helping her to a chair. "There she was putting a kettle on that old gas stove."

Nick set her suitcase on the floor. "It could be days before power is restored. We couldn't leave her there to fend for herself."

"The most damage we saw while driving around is the northern half of the island. Downtown was barely touched," Higgins said.

"Aunt Millie!" the twins screamed as they ran across the kitchen and buried their heads in her lap.

Olivia entered the kitchen and joined the others. "This is a welcome surprise. I admit I was worried about you as the storm continued to rage during the night, but with the tree blocking our roadway, we couldn't have gotten to you."

"Nick and Higgins came by this morning. I asked them to take me to the shelter in town, but they wouldn't hear of it. I don't want to be a bother."

"There is no way I am going to let a ninety-six-year-old friend of ours stay in a shelter. You will stay with us until it is safe for you to return home."

Olivia looked over at Sarah. "I think Aunt Millie could use a cup of tea."

"You can stay in our room, Aunt Millie. We have the only bed in the whole house!" Andy offered. "I hope you like Batman."

Sarah ended up serving breakfast in the dining room, after all. The conversation was lively and a mix of everyone explaining to Aunt Millie what they did for the household and Aunt Millie telling stories about the old days on Kelleys. No one was anxious to leave the table.

"Please excuse our rather crude living conditions." Travis glanced up at the huge crystal chandeliers and swept his arm out to include the beautiful furniture. "This may resemble a palace, but we're residing within these walls like campers."

"Yeah, we live in Marblehead and ride on the ferry to get here every day. We had to stay here because of the storm," Freddy informed Aunt Millie. "It's fun here. Andy and I like Kelleys Island. We wish we lived here all the time—well, not all the time. We live in Virginia too."

"There is a lot about Kelleys to like, my young friend."

Olivia cringed at her sons' comments. What was it about this island? With all its hardships, people still fell in love with its charm.

"I hate to break this up, but Nick and I need to check on my rentals, and Uncle Clem might need help, since his farm sits on the north shore. We'll take the truck and give help where needed," Travis said as he stood.

"Why are you doing that?" Freddy asked.

"Help people, Son? That's what islanders do. We help each other in times of need."

"Andy and I are islanders. Can we come and help?"

"How about you help by showing Aunt Millie around the house? And make her comfortable in your room." Travis stopped at the door and turned around. "Maybe just show her the first-floor rooms. You can show her the rest *after* we install an elevator."

"If anyone needs me, I'll be in the library," Olivia announced as she stood and helped Aunt Millie from the table.

"Logan and Lorenzo, take the Gator and whatever tools are still left, and check out the point and then The Pines. I'll be upstairs checking out the security feed from last night and the view from the tower," Higgins said.

"I'll protect Aunt Millie from the boys," Reggie added with humor and left the room.

Olivia stopped in the office first to make a phone call—the lines were still down. She then went to the library and pulled her mobile phone from her tote bag. She went back to the office and dialed the housephone at the Captain's House. Her phone showed no service. She walked to the main entrance hall holding her phone above her head—nothing. She tried the music room, the game room, what they were now calling the family room—nothing. She finally ended up on the tower roof and got a signal. She pressed the speed dial button for the housephone.

It took Emma a while to answer. "Hello, Emma, it's Olivia."

"Oh, hello. I hope everything is all right out there."

"We are fine, but yesterday's storm left a lot of downed power and phone lines in the area. We will need to stay here another day or two."

"The ferry is running. I can see it from the upper windows."

"It's not the ferry. Due to damaged property, we have an added guest who can't go back to her house until the power is restored."

"I understand. Should Stanley and I come over and help? We can bring food and supplies and help with the children."

"Thank you. You are very kind, but Sarah has us well-stocked, and Kelleys does have a market and general store should we need anything."

"Very good. Please let us know when you plan to arrive so we can be prepared."

Olivia pressed the END button. There was just something about Emma that Olivia didn't like. Her voice? Her attitude toward the twins? Maybe it was simply because she wasn't Helen Campbell. She could see the top of the Captain's House from where she stood. Something about what Emma said struck a bell—the ferry. What had Emma said about a ferry in her initial interview? Then she remembered—Nantucket. Emma had said she took the Oak Bluff ferry from Hyannis to Nantucket because it ran more often. But the Oak Bluff ferry runs out of Marthas Vineyard, not Hyannis. Olivia walked over to the opposite parapet wall and gazed out over the unbroken vista of Lake Erie. They had the same view from the top of the Captain's House, but this was different—it was better here. A few minutes later, she gently closed the door behind her as she descended the steel spiral steps and on down more steps to the first floor and the library—her room.

CHAPTER SEVENTY-FOUR

Power and phone lines were restored to the northeastern corner of Kelleys after two days. During those two days, Andy happily took photos of Aunt Millie in various rooms of the house, especially the kitchen and library, as well as their many trips around the property in the golf cart with Reggie driving. She acted as their tour guide, reliving the times she had visited Long Point since her early years as a young girl up until her golden years with her friend, Callum McTavish. Olivia often joined them for a history lesson. The weather was perfect for their outings around the Long Point property, and Aunt Millie always found time to talk about other places on the island that the boys should visit. After observing several battles between Sir Fredrick of Long Point and Sir Andrew of Bent Tree Castle, Aunt Millie urged that the Monarch ruins would be a much better place to sword fight than the main staircase and the ballroom.

After hearing Aunt Millie's many descriptions of the various rooms and catacombs beneath the old winery, Reggie felt he could find his way around the site in the dark. With the ground having had two days to dry out, Olivia and Travis agreed that Reggie could take the Hummer after lunch that day and let the twins have their adventure.

That morning, Olivia and Higgins packed up Aunt Millie and drove her home in the minivan. Higgins checked the property and the outside of the house for any damage that might need addressing by Nick. While he was doing that, Olivia guided Aunt Millie inside and checked each room for any water leaks that may have been the result of the storm.

"Looks like your lovely home came through with nothing more than a snapped pole out by the street. I'm sure you're glad to be back, but know that we will all miss you."

Aunt Millie motioned for Olivia to have a seat in the chair by the window overlooking the lake. The frail woman looked serious, as if she had something unpleasant to say. She sat in the opposite chair and took Olivia's hand. "I can't thank you enough for taking me in the way you did. You certainly didn't need to. I've read and everyone believes that you are the wealthiest woman in the world."

"I don't believe that. All totaled, I think Queen Elizabeth has me beat," Olivia joked.

"See, that's what I've learned about you. You don't take yourself too seriously. Sure, you may live with a security crew and a bodyguard, and by the way, I really like Higgins. Everyone in your household is family. Lorenzo doesn't brag that he is your pilot; in fact, I don't think he ever mentioned a plane. Sarah acts more like your mother than a housekeeper. And precious little Andy and Freddy are about as normal as any eight-year-olds that I've ever known. Except they have Reggie."

"Thank you, Aunt Millie. Your words mean a great deal to me. As you must know, I came from a middle-class family in mid-Ohio and lost my family when I was fifteen while spending the summer at my grandparents' cottage over near Johnson's Island.

When I lost everything but my boat, the *Lovely Lady*, it was the people of Marblehead who took me in as one of their own. I'm only a local woman who happened to fall into a pot of money."

"That you are, my dear."

Olivia stood at the sound of the screen door slamming shut. The two went into the front hall to meet Higgins.

"Everything looks fine, ma'am."

"Thank you, Higgins, for taking such good care of Olivia and her family and watching over me while I was staying there."

He smiled as the tiny woman reached up to give him a hug. "You are welcome. And if anything happens and you need help, you just call me, and I'll be here."

Olivia gave her a hug. "We must leave, but remember you are part of our family now. Me and the boys will be back for another one of our special visits. I want to study more of your old photos."

"Any time, my dear, any time."

Reginald parked the Hummer along the street in front of the Monarch Winery ruins. Each of the boys emerged wearing their tall rubber boots, as Aunt Millie had recommended, and carried their swords and shields made from decorated garbage-can lids.

"Look over there, Reggie." Freddy pointed to the cemetery across the street. "That man is in a wheelchair with an American flag stuck in the back. He's just sitting there in front of that grave with his head down. Do you think he's praying? Or very sad?"

"He looks like a veteran."

"Should we go over and see if he's okay?" Andy asked, always concerned for the welfare of others.

"I'm sure he has noticed us. If he needs help, he will let us know. Now, we have a Scottish castle to conquer."

"Yea! Yea!" the boys shouted as they ran off with shields ready and swords waving.

Following Aunt Millie's directions, Reggie led the knights through the castle to the catacombs below. "This place is really cool," Freddy said as he explored one area that was partially hidden. "This is the dungeon. Every castle has a dungeon."

"Look up there." Andy pointed to an old pail sitting on a ledge. He scrambled up the stones to reach it.

"No, Andy, come back down. You're not good at climbing; you're gonna fall," cried his brother.

"I can too. Watch me." Andy reached for the pail. It tipped, spilling stagnant water all down the front of his shirt. "Oooh, this stinks!" Andy scurried back down.

"You stink! I told you not to do that. Now look at you."

"We need to get you out of that shirt and back home."

Andy unbuttoned his light-blue plaid shirt and tossed it on the ground. He stood with his arms crossed against his chest. "I'm cold."

"No, Reggie. We don't want to leave. Do we?"

"No. I want to stay, but I'm cold."

Freddy began unbuttoning his bright-red shirt. "Here, you can wear mine. I have an undershirt on."

"Thanks," Andy said as he buttoned the shirt and tucked it into his shorts.

Back up in the open-air rooms with tall stone walls and arched window openings, the boys went back to sword fighting. Reggie leaned against the wall closest to the street and watched.

The twins stopped playing. "Reggie, I have to pee," Freddy whined as he held himself and jumped from side to side.

"Not a problem, little man," Reggie said as he walked over to where the twins were standing. "Go over there in the brush and do it."

"I don't want you to watch."

"Okay, we won't. Come on, my good knight; let's stand over by that wall."

Reggie turned when he heard a twig snap behind him. "Hey, what are you doing here? I thought you were—" Reggie felt a beesting and then nothing.

Andy saw what happened but wasn't quick enough to get away. He was grabbed from behind and lifted off the ground. At that moment, Freddy climbed back in the large open room to see Reggie lying on the ground and Andy kicking and struggling against the man in the wheelchair.

"Run! Run—dungeon!" Andy shouted.

"It doesn't matter. Andy can't get away. He's too afraid of falling," the man said.

Andy recognized the wheelchair guy's voice. This was bad. He had to get away. He remembered the lessons in self-defense that Reggie taught them. He was still holding his sword. Andy used all this strength and shoved the hilt of the sword into the man's groin. The man yelled and bent over but didn't let go. Andy remembered the vulnerable parts of the body they had learned from Reggie. With wheelchair man bent over, Andy could possibly reach his throat. Andy lunged to the side, and with his right elbow, he jabbed the guy's throat. The bad guy let out a loud cough and let one arm go to reach his throat. It gave Andy just enough time to give the bad guy one more hit to the groin and run. Andy forgot his fear of falling and ran as fast as he could toward the catacombs. He entered the passage, while the sound of heavy steps was getting closer. If he could only run fast enough to make two turns and climb the short wall, he'd reach the dungeon.

"You got away!" Freddy hugged his brother.

"Shhh." Andy put his hand to his mouth. Then Freddy did the same.

They huddled together in the corner of the small space. They could hear the bad guy searching the catacombs. "You're in here. I saw you come in. You can't get out without me seeing you. Snakes like cool dark places, you know. This island has lots of snakes and big spiders too."

Freddy suddenly recognized the man's voice. His eyes widened. Andy nodded that he too knew who it was. He motioned for Freddy to remain quiet.

"Do you know how these snakes operate? They wait until they can strike. Then they begin wrapping themselves around you. Inch by inch until their long smooth body has itself around your neck and then it squeezes."

The boys had seen enough Batman movies to know what he was doing. Higgins calls it mind games. The bad guy tries to get into your head and use your fears to make you slip up. Andy slowly shook his head at his brother, indicating that he shouldn't listen. Freddy nodded affirmative. They waited for what seemed like hours. Then off in the distance, they heard the faint sound of sirens. So did he, and he took off at a run.

"Andy, Freddy, where are you?" Travis shouted.

"It's okay, boys; it's safe to come out," Logan hollered.

The twins crawled down from their hiding place and ran through the catacombs to the rooms above and into their dad's arms.

Reggie was put onto a gurney, and four men carried it through the ruins to a waiting ambulance.

"Is he dead? Did he kill him with that thing he put in Reggie's neck?" Andy asked.

"You saw that?" Travis asked.

"Yeah. He stabbed Reggie with one of those needle things in his neck and then Reggie fell down."

"Hey, guys. Don't leave yet," Logan shouted to the medical person and firemen. "I think I know what happened to him." Logan turned to Andy and Freddy. "Don't worry. Reggie will be fine. He's just going to have one nasty headache."

"Dad, how did you know how to find us?" Andy asked.

"Reggie must have known what was happening. He managed to press his panic button before he passed out."

One of Higgins's rules is every member of his security always wear a panic button. When pressed, it sends a signal to the command center but also alerts everyone else wearing a device.

"Freddy looked around. "Where is Mom and Higgins?"

"Something happened out at Aunt Millie's. She called Higgins for help, and your mom went with him. She was afraid that Aunt Millie might have fallen or something," Travis explained.

"Dad, why would Stanley try to hurt us?"

CHAPTER SEVENTY-FIVE

"I wonder what happened! Did Aunt Millie say she was hurt? How did she sound on the phone?" Olivia asked Higgins as he drove the minivan down Aunt Millie's long driveway.

"She sounded more frightened than anything. And I can't imagine that old bird being afraid of anything." Higgins parked, and they both walked over to the steps leading up to the front porch. Olivia was nearly to the top when the small device that Higgins always wore clipped to his belt next to his pager chirped. He read the message on the screen. "It's Reggie's panic button. Something must have happened at the ruins. We need to get over there."

Olivia feared something happened to one of the twins, probably Andy; he could be so clumsy. She ran down the steps and jumped in the car. Higgins turned the minivan around and headed down the drive.

"What about Aunt Millie?" Olivia worried that she may be lying on the floor in pain or something.

"As soon as we know what's going on, we'll head back. See if you can reach her on your mobile?"

Olivia grabbed the phone out of her tote bag, pulled up the antenna, and pressed Aunt Millie's number on speed dial. "It can't get a signal."

"Keep trying."

"I'll call Travis." She pressed number one on speed dial. Olivia was relieved to hear his mobile phone ringing.

"Hello? Livy, is that you?"

"Travis, what's going on? Higgins got a panic signal from Reggie."

"I have the boys; we are heading back . . . static . . . Stanley . . . static." Then the call dropped.

Olivia tried the number again. "No signal. But he said he has the boys, and they are heading back. Then I had nothing but static until he said Stanley."

Higgins pulled over to the side on Ward Road and stopped. "No point in going any further if they have left and are on their way back. But we should have seen them. This is the only road that leads back to Long Point from the ruins, which is across from the cemetery."

"Unless they continued on down Division to town for some reason."

"Okay, I'll drop you off at Aunt Millie's and swing by Long Point. After I find out what's going on, I'll be back and help with whatever she needs. Maybe you won't even need me."

"Sounds like a plan. Call me at her house and let me know the boys are all right. I wonder what Stanley wanted?"

Higgins stopped at the foot of Aunt Millie's front steps. "Want me to come in and check things out?"

"No, I'd rather you find out what the panic button thing was about, and let me know how Andy and Freddy are."

"All right." Higgins pulled his panic button from around his neck and handed it to her. "Just in case you need it."

Olivia glanced up at the sign that hung from the ornate fretwork that decorated the old Victorian: *The Vines.* She put the device in the pocket of her pants. She got a weird feeling in her gut as she climbed the steps. Her inner voice was screaming for her to stop. It was only jitters because Higgins wasn't at her side. But this was Aunt Millie's. What could possibly happen to her out here?

She opened the screen door and entered the front hall. "Aunt Millie, I'm here." There was no answer. Olivia glanced at the stairway. "Are you upstairs? Please answer me. Have you fallen?" Nothing. Olivia looked in the front parlor. It was empty, no Aunt Millie lying on the floor unconscious. She headed down the hallway to the rear of the house and checked the bathroom along the way. She knew accidents happen in the bathroom all the time, but this one was empty. "Aunt Millie?" Olivia called out once more on her way to the kitchen. No response. She opened the kitchen door and stopped.

Aunt Millie stood in the center of the room. The woman standing behind her had one hand over mouth and the other held a knife to Aunt Millie's throat.

"Emma?" Only she didn't look like the housekeeper Emma. This woman wore slim white slacks and a soft floral-print top with spaghetti straps. Her long hair fell in waves around her shoulders. New, white Nike's finished the look—the look of a summer tourist at the glacial grooves. Olivia's blood turned to ice. Her heart raced. "What is this about?" Although she had a damn good idea it was all about HELIOSmm-88.

"Oh my dear, you have made this *so* difficult. Right from the very beginning. You could have been killed."

Those words, "Oh my dear." Olivia would never forget those words and the voice that had said them—Mabel Polanski.

"Toss your bag on the floor—now!"

Higgins. His last words to her rang in her head—"*Just in case you need it.*" Olivia eased the tote bag off her right shoulder and, at the same time, slid her left hand into her pocket and pressed the button.

"Mabel Polanski, or whatever your real name is, this woman has nothing to do with me and what you want. Let her go."

"My name is whatever it needs to be. And you are wrong, Aunt Millie is *very* important. She's the reason I got you here without your bodyguard, Higgins. I'm sure you have him off searching for your son Freddy in his red shirt. Don't worry. Stanley has him. He will keep him safe as long as his mother cooperates."

Olivia's brain raced. How could Stanley have Freddy? No one can tell them apart—except she had explained it all to Emma. That Freddy always wore bright colors. That Andy was hesitant to run on uneven ground. But how would they know he was wearing a red shirt today? Olivia also remembered Emma and Stanley's shocked faces when they came home early the other day to get the boats. Emma was having a pool day and Stanley looked like he had just stepped off the cover of *GQ* magazine.

"Your face, dear Olivia, mirrors your thoughts. I would stay away from poker games if I were you. You will find, in that monstrous tote bag you carry, a tube of lipstick that isn't your brand."

"So, you've heard everything we've said since I arrived."

"Oh, before that. It began with that little accident with Mabel Polanski who put the tiny little bug in your handbag. Our people are much more advanced than yours when it comes to espionage gadgets. War changing technology like your HELIOS—not so much. Unfortunately, for us, you often left your bag on the pool table, and we'd lose you for hours."

Olivia realized they had been living with two of the Russian super-spies. The ghost operatives that didn't exist. She needed to be smarter, at least until Higgins and his team arrived.

"So, if you've been listening, then you know how Aunt Millie gets dizzy. We try to have someone, even the boys, with her at all times in case she falls." Olivia saw Aunt Millie open her eyes wide and try to speak. Emma's hand tightened over her mouth.

"Emma, I get it. Russia needs me to turn over HELIOS to you. So, you kidnap my son for leverage."

"You're not stupid. I give you that."

"But you are being stupid by holding Aunt Millie as long as you have." Olivia paused a beat. "Making a hundred-year-old, frail woman stand ridged like that, and with a knife to her throat. Why, with her history of getting dizzy and falling—why, she could have a spell at any moment. Then she falls and you lose your balance and, bang—you are no longer in control."

Olivia knew she needed to keep the situation on a calm level until the guys got there. "Let her go. I'll cooperate. This will be over, and you go on to your next spy assignment."

Emma frowned. Her eyes scanned the room. She seemed to be thinking about her options. She lowered the knife and stepped away from Aunt Millie. "Okay. Nothing heroic. The old lady stays where she is. And you, my dear, come with me to the front door. Stanley will be picking us up in your lovely Lincoln."

Olivia watched Aunt Millie step back and move to the antique Hoosier cabinet.

"What are you doing, old lady? I said stay where you were."

"I'm getting dizzy. I have to hold on to something."

Emma set the knife on the kitchen table and picked up her white leather purse and removed a handgun. "I hear Stanley. Move it." Emma pointed the gun at Olivia's back. "Now!"

Olivia began walking to the hall doorway.

"Excuse me, Emma. But I'm having a problem," Aunt Millie said. "Livy, to the wall!"

Olivia and Emma both turned at the same time. Emma gasped, and Olivia jumped toward the wall.

The rifle went off and nearly shot off Emma's arm. Her handgun flew back and landed in the hallway as Higgins, Logan, and Lorenzo rushed into the room with guns pointed.

Everyone stopped and stared at Aunt Millie standing next to the Hoosier with an older model rifle in hand.

"No one messes with me or my family." Aunt Millie looked at Olivia. "And just for the record—I don't get dizzy; I hardly ever fall—and I'm ninety-six."

Olivia laughed. "I know. But you must admit, my comments got her attention."

"Wow. Our very own Annie Oakley. Remind me to add you to our security team." Higgins chuckled. "Logan, please remove whoever this is. She's bleeding all over Aunt Millie's floor." He glanced up at the hole in the wall. "I'll send Nick over to fix that."

"One of her names is Mabel Polanski," Olivia informed everyone.

"Stanley has Freddy. I'm sure he's off this fucking island by now," Emma said victoriously.

"Actually, no. Freddy is home with his brother. And Stanley is being held by the Kelleys Island police chief." Higgins gave a heartfelt smile to Olivia. "The ticket person at the ferry dock recognized Olivia's Lincoln, and Freddy sleeping on the back seat, but she didn't recognize the driver. She directed him to a lane that wasn't being used and called Chief Monroe."

Olivia walked over to Aunt Millie and wrapped her arms around her. "Thank you. You probably saved my life, and, in turn, probably saved HELIOS, which will soon be keeping our country safe."

"You're my family now."

"And you will always be my auntie." Olivia gave her a squeeze.

"We had better go. You have a husband and two sons, who are waiting for you to return to Long Point," Higgins said as he picked up her tote bag off the floor. He noticed the blood spatter on the side. "Will you feel safe here alone, Aunt Millie? You can come back to Long Point if you'd like."

"Of course, I feel safe here." She raised the old rifle a few inches. "I've got Bertha here with me. Together we watch over The Vines."

CHAPTER SEVENTY-SIX

The reuniting of mother and her sons was a joyous occasion for everyone. Andy and Freddy gave her a minute-by-minute story of their adventure at the Monarch ruins. Reggie participated in the story while sitting at the kitchen table with an ice bag pressed against his forehead. And Olivia recounted the bravery of Aunt Millie.

"I can't believe it. I let Stanley take me out with a needle, and Aunt Millie shoots a Russian spy after being held with a knife at her throat."

"So, the Russians have been after HELIOS since the one they first stole didn't work," Sarah said as she massaged her special seasoning into two slabs of ribs.

"Our group of spies, Mabel Polanski, the Burnsides, and Uri Kozlov are all highly trained and use their talents of disguise and ability to adjust to every situation to become invisible. They had every base covered, from monitoring Travis while here, on Long Point, and listening to phone calls at the Captain's House to watching Olivia and William in Virginia and DC," Higgins recapped.

"We didn't find any bugs at the house," Travis reminded everyone.

"The Burnsides removed them as soon as they arrived," Higgins explained. "Uri Kozlov must have somehow gotten in or placed a device on the Hummer."

"And my photos showed the spies watching us," Andy pointed out.

"Speaking of watching, what about our treasurer hunter?" Olivia asked.

"I have no new information. But he's still on the front burner. I don't want to break this up; however, I need to head over to the police station to interview Stanley Burnside, or whatever his real name is," Higgins said as he got up from the table and headed for the back door.

"I need to chill. If you need me, I'll be in the library." Olivia glanced over at her tote bag sitting on the counter next to the sink. "Sarah, dump everything out of that thing and burn it. I'd rather use a plastic shopping bag."

Half an hour later, Sarah entered the library to find Olivia sitting in her favorite chair, with Andy and Freddy in her lap. "I brought you some chamomile tea. I thought it might sooth stretched nerves."

"Thank you. I'm sure it will do the trick."

"Is that a pipe you're holding?"

"It belonged to the general. I find it calming—like the sweet scent of tobacco in here."

Sarah inhaled deeply. "If you say so. I'll be putting the ribs on soon. Dinner will be shortly after five on the picnic tables."

"We won't be late." Funny that she seemed to be the only one who noticed the tobacco scent.

After dinner, the guys helped Sarah clear the table. Olivia grabbed her glass and the bottle of Merlot and entered the kitchen. She held up the bottle for Sarah to see. "After you're done, bring your glass and join me on the porch at the end of the main hallway. I've had Travis and Nick put two comfortable chairs and a small glass table out there."

In response, Sarah gave one of her brilliant smiles and nodded.

Out on the porch, Olivia set the wine bottle on the table and settled back in the chair. She wanted to put her feet up. She wanted a couple of the chaise lounges that lined the pool at the Captain's House. She rested her head back against the chair and closed her eyes. She'd almost been kidnapped that day. Freddy *had* been kidnapped. Russian spies had been living in her house.

"Olivia?" Sarah whispered.

"Oh, Sarah, I must have dozed off. Please, have a seat." She waited until Sarah was comfortably seated and her glass filled. "I've missed our evening chats by the pool. I thought this might work."

"It is a beautiful night. Unlike Marblehead, we may be able to actually see the sun set, or at least part of it."

Olivia inhaled deeply. "Sarah, it just doesn't get much better than this."

Sarah thought about that for a moment, then turned her head to face Olivia. "Do you mean that?"

"What? That it is nice out here tonight."

"That's not what you said. You said it doesn't get much better than this."

"Yes. No. I don't know what I meant." Olivia thought about all that had taken place at Aunt Millie's. How much did her life really mean? Was it the cost of a state-of-the-art machine—a machine that puts our Navy above all others? Was that the life she wanted? There would always be a Russia or China lurking in the wings. She'd believed that she had done everything in her power to protect her sons' lives since the day they were born. But it didn't work—not this time.

"I feel safe here. Andy and Freddy love it here. I think Travis loves it here. Higgins and his team like it. The only thing they want is an elevator—I do too."

"I got a call today from the JCPenney delivery service. The mattresses, bedding, and towels I ordered for the guys will be delivered tomorrow."

"Wonderful. Higgins plans to have Logan and Lorenzo take shifts staying out here."

The rays of the setting sun glistened on the calm water. The *Livy VI* rested comfortably at the pier.

"I bet you are looking forward to getting back to Marblehead. I'm sure the boys are missing the pool. And I need to make a trip to the grocery store in Port Clinton, and I have a growing list for Walmart."

Olivia looked out over the lake and the setting sun. "No, I don't think I want to go back yet. I can't get the image out of my head of Russian spies living in our house."

Travis had been standing just inside the door, listening. He stepped onto the porch. "Hello, ladies, it's a beautiful night. The boys have Reggie in a heated game of Monopoly, and Nick is getting ready to head home."

"And I have things I want to get done in the kitchen. Travis, the chair is all yours." Sarah picked up her wine glass and stood. She hesitated at the door and looked back at Olivia. Her world was suddenly crashing down around her, and all the money in the world couldn't help.

"How are you holding up?" Travis asked.

"Okay—I guess. The boys seem to have bounced back. I'm glad Reggie is well enough to play with them. I think having that normalcy is important."

"What about you? Are you ready to get back to normal?"

"I'm not sure I know what that is." The setting sun turned the water gold. "Travis, would you mind if we stayed here another night?"

CHAPTER SEVENTY-SEVEN

At seven, the next morning, everyone except the twins was sitting at the kitchen table with coffee and much conversation. Lorenzo and Logan had taken shifts at the monitor and on the tower roof. They both claimed another great night and had slept well. Reggie was almost back to normal with only a mild headache. Higgins got back late after catching the last ferry back to the island.

"Stanley isn't talking—yet. The FBI is picking him up today. Emma was taken yesterday to Magruder Hospital in Port Clinton for her gunshot wound. She won't be doing any shooting with that hand for quite some time. I figured, since I wasn't getting anywhere with Stanley, perhaps their apartment over the garage would talk to me—it sure did. They had a very impressive surveillance system set up in the bedroom, suitcases full of disguises, and lots of cash—thousands of dollars. I also found a post office box key. What do you want to bet it belongs to Emily Elfin?"

"Great news, Higgins. What happens next?" Travis asked. Hoping they would need to stay away from the house for a few more days.

"I'm meeting the FBI from the Cleveland office to do a thorough sweep of both the house and garage, which, of course, includes the apartment above. I'm afraid that could take a day or two. I'm happy to bring whatever you need back with me."

"Thank you, but Benjamin and I must run into Port Clinton today. We will stop by the house. The boys need more clothes, and I'm sure the rest of us do as well."

"Okay with me, but be sure to check in with the senior agent when you get there."

Sarah was down to a few eggs and less than half of a gallon of milk but a lot of bread. She served French toast and bacon for breakfast.

Everyone scattered after they had finished eating, leaving Olivia with the boys while they finished off the last pieces of French toast. She had one last cup of coffee, while Andy and Freddy dressed for an outing with Reggie in the Gator. Nick was bringing a new propeller for the Zodiac, and he and Travis were going to work on that.

"I'll be around, Sarah. Not sure where, but in the house." Olivia grabbed the shopping bag containing the items from her tote bag and headed for the library. "Good morning, Horatio," she said while dropping the bag on the pool table. She tried sitting but couldn't get comfortable. She tried reading but couldn't concentrate. She then got up and left the room.

Olivia wandered from room to room until she noticed that the Monopoly game was still in progress. One player had lots of money stacked neatly in piles—that would be Andy. One player just had a pile of money—that would be Freddy. The last player was close to being bankrupt. Olivia noticed the pieces representing the players had been swapped out for objects the twins had found. She picked up what looked like a brass button; it looked military. She set it back down on Reading Railroad. Next was a piece of blue sea glass; it resided in Jail. The last piece intrigued her the most. It looked and felt like a round coin of some kind. The markings weren't very clear. She put the coin in her pocket and placed a piece of red sea glass on the coin's spot—Park Place. She decided to keep the button as well and replaced it with a nicely veined skipping stone. She would ask the boys about them later.

Olivia wandered from room to room until she reached the tower, where she found Higgins.

"Exploring? You might end up finding this a favorite. It's mine."

She looked in all four directions. "I feel free—like a bird looking down on the world. I feel in control—because I see everything, but they don't necessarily see me—the watcher. A place where the wind blows the cobwebs of the mind away."

Higgins turned to Olivia, looking deep into her soul. "You get it."

She glanced over at the roof, knowing what lay hidden below. Bent Tree Cottage still had secrets.

Some force seemed to pull Olivia back to the library. Andy and Freddy were playing a hide-and-seek game when she entered. She remembered the two items in her pocket. She removed them and placed them in the palm of her hand. "Hey, boys. Do you know where you found these?"

"Those are our Monopoly pieces."

"I know, Andy. But where did you find them?"

"In the secret place."

"Can you show it to me?"

"Sure."

Both boys walked over to the firewood box, opened the door, and walked in. "You have to come here to see."

Olivia went over and bent down to see where Andy was pointing. She watched as he pulled out a brick at about his eye level in the chimney wall.

"The brick was loose, and we pulled it the rest of the way out. Freddy put his hand inside. It was only those two things inside."

"Do you mind if I show these to your dad and Higgins?"

"Sure. Maybe they know what they are," Andy agreed.

A few minutes later, Olivia heard Travis and Higgins talking in the main entrance hall. "Excuse me, but could the two of you come in here for a moment? The boys have something to show you."

After both men were inside the library, Olivia closed the door behind them. She then opened her hand to reveal the two objects. "The boys found these hidden behind a loose brick in the fireplace wall."

After close examination, the two men came up with the same thoughts—a button and a coin. "I have a large lighted magnifying glass in the office. How about we take a better look in there?" Travis suggested.

Travis placed the glass on the desk and turned on the light. "Gee, Dad, this would be great to look at our fossils." He ran next door and chose a rock from their collection. "Here, Dad, let's see what this fossil looks like under the lighted glass."

Travis moved the rock back and forth until the image was clear. "Wow. That is so cool. Can we look at this any time we want?"

"How about you let Reggie use it with you?"

"Okay," the twins shouted as they ran out of the office to find Reggie.

Travis held the button under the glass. "It's military, all right. But I don't have a clue how old it is."

Olivia looked at the button. "Man, this looks familiar. But no, I can't place it either. How about the coin?"

Travis placed it with the better side up. "Looks old. I think it might be a woman's profile and a crown."

"Let me look at that." Olivia bent over the lighted glass. "I'd know that profile anywhere—that's Queen Victoria." Olivia took the coin and stood. "Follow me." Then she headed for the bathroom. Travis and Higgins watched as Olivia took a washcloth and ran the coin under warm water while she rubbed it with the cloth. The dirt washed away, leaving shiny gold.

"Could this possibly be a coin from the lost shipment of British gold?"

"The button. Travis, go get it. Let's wash that too."

Less than a minute later, he returned with the button. Olivia washed it the same way. "It's brass, and I know where I've seen it. We're going to the library."

Once inside, Higgins locked the door. Olivia walked over to the mantel and held the button up to the portrait. "They are the same. We have one of General Horatio Buchanan's buttons from his uniform—and a British gold coin."

"Could our treasurer hunter's theory be correct? Our general stole one of the shipments of gold? Where is it?"

"We know, from the photos I saw at Aunt Millie's, that we are standing in the general's cabin. The Whitakers bought Long Point from him and then built The Pines to live in while this was being built. I've researched the cabin, but not this house."

"I have all the documents, and you won't find any answers there. I mostly know *how* the house was built and the finances. I haven't found anything about *why* it was built to these mammoth proportions. Or why I can't change it."

"So, the boys found one loose brick. Maybe there are more." Travis considered his only option. "Higgins, find Nick. We need tools. Hammers, sledgehammer, shovel, pry bars, and big flashlights."

"What do you plan to do with all these tools?"

"Tear this room apart if we have to. This monster of a house is hiding something, and that man is at the root of it," Travis said as he pointed to the portrait above the fireplace.

Higgins and Nick returned with all the tools Travis had asked for and more. Higgins had filled Nick in on what was going on, and they managed to get everything into the library without being seen. Reggie and the boys were still at the point, Benjamin and Uncle Clem were directing the brush crew, Logan and Lorenzo were checking out possible camera locations on the property, and Sarah was preparing lunch.

"Let's examine the inside of the two firewood boxes first, since that is where the boys found the loose brick," Travis suggested.

Half an hour later, Nick and Travis exited the firewood boxes. They both agreed that the storage compartments were solid, no more loose bricks.

Someone tried to open the door. "Anyone in there? Olivia? Lunch in ten," Sarah said in a raised voice.

"Thanks, Sarah. Travis, Nick, and Higgins are with me. We'll see you in ten minutes."

"Okay. We break for lunch. Travis, do you have a key for this lock?" Higgins asked.

"Yep. In my office. I'll get it."

Conversation during lunch was difficult for the four future room-wreckers. They were the only ones not discussing what they had done that morning and what was planned for the afternoon, but Sarah seemed to be the only who noticed the four's lack of participation. And were the first to finish their meals and excuse themselves from the table.

Back in the library, Higgins locked the door, while Travis and Nick discussed how to proceed.

Olivia sat in her favorite chair and tried to remember the times when the twins played in the room while she was there. She loved the library and didn't want to see it torn apart. Although it might be fun to watch the cabin emerge, the only thoughts Olivia had now were of how annoying it was to listen to the boys jumping up and down in the short closets.

She got up and went over to the space on the left side of the fireplace. She ducked and went inside. Once in, she mimicked the sound of her sons jumping up and down. "Nick, Travis, this floor gives a little. Like there might be a hollow space underneath."

"Come out and I'll check," Nick said as he picked up a pry bar and hammer.

He tapped with the hammer. "You're right. It does sound hollow." He used the pry bar to loosen, then pulled up a couple of boards. "Whew! Smells bad," Nick complained as he pulled up another couple of boards. "Travis, hand me the flashlight. I'd rather see what we have before I remove any more boards."

Travis handed him the largest of the three that Nick and Higgins had brought.

Holding onto the handle, Nick directed the beam straight down. "It's a cave." He got down on his stomach and lowered his arm into the cavity, then focused the light further into the space. "It's a big cave. I can't see the end."

They each took a turn looking into the cave. "We need a ladder. A long ladder," Higgins said.

"There is one on the back wall of the barn. I don't know how long it is."

"Livy, you stay here and keep the door locked. The three of us will look for the ladder."

A few minutes later, they returned with an old wooden ladder. "We think it will hold Travis; he's the lightest, unless you want to try to go down, Olivia," Nick joked.

"Funny. How about I watch from above?"

It took some maneuvering to get the ladder down, and they all agreed it wouldn't be coming back up. Travis made it down safely, then Nick and Higgins. They each had a flashlight.

"I don't see any chest full of gold, but look—there's stuff at the very end."

Olivia lost sight of them as they moved further into the cave. She heard the words "Shit—holy crap—what the hell?" All three appeared at the base of the ladder and began climbing. Nick was the last to emerge and closed the firewood box door.

"What did you find?" Olivia asked excitedly.

"Bodies. Lots of bodies," Higgins stated.

CHAPTER SEVENTY-EIGHT

Four hours later, everyone in the household plus the police were in the library and down in the cave. The coroner and several of his team from Toledo were in the cave taking pictures of the remains—mostly bones and clothing. A forensics team was sweeping the floor and walls for any signs of gold or precious metals. More scientists were on the way. Between the people and the floodlights and all the electrical equipment, it looked like a movie set. The pool table had been moved to the side, along with the furniture. Travis, Nick, Olivia, and Higgins were sitting in the living room with Aunt Millie.

"Now, I know why Bent Tree Cottage can never be altered or torn down—the Whitakers had a huge secret to keep hidden. I wonder if James Whitaker III knew about the cave. It didn't sound like it when we met, and he turned over all the documents."

"I was very young when I started listening to what grown-ups were talking about. Especially when it pertained to something that sounded important," Aunt Millie said. "I don't have many photos of this house. I think the Whitakers were private people and didn't have much to do with us islanders. But I know the stone was quarried and cut here. But they didn't employ islanders to lay the stone or anything else."

"That matches what I found in the ledgers. Stone was listed as purchased from the Kelleys Island Lime & Transport Company."

"I believe I have a photo somewhere showing a building used to house the workers. I couldn't tell you where it was located, though." Aunt Millie appeared to be searching her mind for some long-lost memory. "Yes, the Whitakers built the structure away from this site, and it was torn down after the house was finished. Some said it became an eyesore for their fine friends. The family had a large yacht that brought the workers from Cleveland. All were immigrants. I remember my pap complaining that not one of the bunch could speak a word of English. After the house and garage were completed, they were all sent back home to Cleveland."

"Maybe we'll find some evidence of the foundation during the brush clearing," Nick surmised.

Higgins stood. "I'm going upstairs and call a friend at the Cleveland Plain Dealer and have her do a search of Bent Tree Cottage, Long Point, and Kelleys Island—see what comes up on microfiche."

"Why?" Travis asked.

"Playing a hunch" was all he said as he walked into the main entrance hall and took the steps two at a time.

Olivia began connecting the dots. "I have a theory. What if there was a connection between General Buchanan and the Whitakers's————family or friends? They know or think they know about a shipment of gold that falls into Horatio's hands. Horatio agrees to sell Long Point to the Whitakers before his death. The Whitakers now have the gold that is stashed in the cave under the cabin. To stop any further talk about the cabin and make it go away, so to speak, they build their house around the cabin, giving them access to the gold."

"Then who are the guys in the cave?" Travis asked.

"Maybe the soldiers who were delivering the gold from Canada to Richmond," Olivia guessed. "But that would make Horatio a murderer." There had to be another scenario; her general was not a murderer.

Chief Bobby Monroe poked his head around the door. "Excuse me. I only want to let you know everyone is leaving. The remains have been carefully removed and will be taken to a special lab at the University of Toledo for possible identification and cause of death. You've got your house back, but please stay out of the cave at least until we get the okay from the scientific teams."

"Bobby, dear, could you please drop me off at my house? That way I don't have to bother any of the Tanner family—they have been through so much today."

The Kelleys Island police chief glanced at Nick and Travis and rolled his eyes. "Of course, Aunt Millie, I'd be happy to." He reached down and gave her his arm. She patted it as he guided her to the front door.

Travis got out of his chair and took a few steps toward the hallway. "Bobby, that door doesn't—"

After opening the front door for Aunt Millie, Chief Monroe followed her through and gently pulled it shut behind him.

"What the hell just happened?" Nick asked. "How did he just walk over and open the door?"

"Don't know. I just don't know." Travis couldn't think about a sticky door that didn't stick now. He went back and sat down next to Olivia. She certainly didn't seem concerned—there was almost a glow about her.

A calming feeling washed over Olivia. She knew who fixed the door. General Horatio Buchanan was turning over Bent Tree Cottage to its new family.

"The Whitakers did everything in their power to keep Bent Tree Cottage quiet and forgotten, and in only three months, I'll have it front-page news."

"Well, Travis, I must admit our life together is interesting. I had Russian spies living in my house, and you had human remains under yours."

EPILOGUE

Higgins's contact at the Cleveland Plain Dealer found an article dated October 10, 1902. Describing the tragic accident that killed ten passengers aboard Cleveland industrialist James Whitaker I's yacht, Mr. Whitaker had housed stonemasons and highly skilled European craftsmen to build his mansion on Kelleys Island, called Bent Tree Cottage. The family's new summer home had recently been completed, and the construction workers were returning to their homes in Cleveland. Tragedy struck when one of the two boilers malfunctioned and exploded. The yacht sank in the middle of Lake Erie, and no bodies were recovered. Fortunately, none of the Whitaker family were on board at the time.

The forensic findings were that the ten men, found in the cave, were of European origin and had died of gunshot wounds to the head and chest. A gold coin matching the one found by the twins was found wedged inside the heel of one man's boot. Knowing what he was now looking for, Travis was able to match the names of ten workers who were paid twice the amount of the other fifty tradesmen beginning after their first month of employment, during the years 1901–1902. The men were given a proper burial in the Kelleys Island Cemetery. Olivia had a head-stone made from limestone that had been mined at the Kelleys Island Lime & Transport Company. Each of the men's names was carved by local stonemasons.

Roof repairs were made, and the original skylight above the stained glass ceiling in the library was cleaned and once again gave life to the room below. After exhaustive testing had been completed in the cave, it was determined that gold had indeed been stored there. No further gold coins were found, and Olivia had Andy and Freddy's preserved in a special glass box, which they kept on their dresser to remind them of their adventure.

The bungalow called "The Pines" was renovated as a guest-house, or for any full-time estate manager they may have in the future. The barn was restored and equipped for the comfort of Andy's pony, Robin; and Freddy's pony, Joker. The twins are now asking Mom for a dog—and a schooner.

The point has been cleaned up and become the family's favorite swimming beach. It's Long Point's only beach, and the wharf has been dredged for the perfect diving platform.

Emma and Stanley are now living under tight security at Quantico. Higgins was certain their true identities would never be known, since the Russian government would claim they didn't exist. Through encrypted communications found in the apart-ment the Burnsides were using over the garage, the Campbells were rescued by the Dade County Swat Team from an abandoned fishery in the Everglades. The Tanner family flew down to per-sonally bring them back home. The Campbells claimed they had had enough of Florida to last a lifetime.

Olivia never went back to the Captain's House, at least not to live. She couldn't get over the fact that two Russian spies had so easily infiltrated her home and their lives. She and Travis planned to turn it into the bed-and-breakfast that had been her original plan when she bought it.

The Tanner family unanimously voted to make Bent Tree Cottage their summer home. Higgins and his team are creating a security center that would rival NASA. There is now a high-speed elevator conveniently located for the security center and the tower's spiral staircase. Sarah is already making plans for their annual Christmas open house. She will leave the logistics to Olivia of how to get all of the off-islanders to Long Point in the dead of winter. The ballroom would hold its own for one day of the year, and the beautiful oak front door opens to receive guests.

Olivia still talks to General Horatio Buchanan whenever she is in the library. She still holds his pipe when troubled and swears he smiles. She has brought the poolside chaise lounge chairs from the Captain's House so she and Sarah can have their after-dinner chats while watching the ever-changing Lake Erie. Next summer she plans to put in a pool for the boys. Olivia had a custom mattress made for the oversize bed in the master suite.

Olivia, along with Reggie and the boys, continue their island history sessions over tea at Aunt Millie's.

Sarah designed her dream kitchen along with an outdoor kitchen and patio for dining alfresco. The Harrisons and the Campbells together will be taking care of Bent Tree Cottage and the family that lives there.

Lorenzo will be picking up Aunt Millie in the middle of November so she may join the Tanner family for Thanksgiving. Olivia and Sarah hope to convince their favorite aunt to remain at Fairfield until the family returns to Kelleys Island for the 1994 summer season.

ACKNOWLEDGEMENTS

First and foremost, I want to thank my daughter, Marianne Blystone, for her unending support, her encouragement and for believing in me and the stories I have to tell. Secondly, I must thank Polly Sue Poppy who works tirelessly to clean up my drafts and pushes me to expand myself as a writer.

Although a work of fiction, Bent Tree Cottage practically wrote itself. Kelleys Island is an amazing island full of history and incredibly beautiful landscapes. The idea of the book came to me after meeting Jackie and Gary Finger, (a native of Kelleys) back in October of 2016, when Jackie adopted a horse named Stormy Dude from CANTER Ohio, which I am the Executive Director. I couldn't believe that a Thoroughbred ex-racehorse was going to be living on Kelleys Island. I had explored Kelleys in my younger years and the whole concept intrigued me. So, as an author of mystery/suspense the inevitable happened––a story began percolating in my head. A couple of years ago, Polly and I decided to visit Stormy Dude at Jackie's farm and tour the island. I fell in love with Kelleys all over again and the story evolved.

Being part of the Tanner Family series, I embellished A LOT!! The bones of Kelleys Island, or should I say *stone*, is there, but names have been changed and Aunt Millies stories are just that, stories that popped into my head which I wove around actual places. The houses: Bent Tree Cottage, The Pines, The Vines and Captain's House do not exist except in my head.

I want to thank everyone at the North Shore State Park visitors center who made Kelleys history come alive. I intend to spend more time on Kelleys Island in the future digging up a new plot for Andy and Freddy Tanner as they turn thirteen.

AUTHOR BIO

Pamela Ann Cleverly grew up in Cleveland, Ohio with stories suddenly popping up in her head when needed to settle her three younger brothers' rowdy behavior, or her own boredom.

Years later with the adult responsibilities of being a wife, mother and moving to Toronto, Ontario the stories stopped.

Fast-forward twenty-three years and back in Cleveland, Pamela suddenly found another story in her head. So she began writing and hasn't stopped.

She writes her stories from the rolling hills of northeastern Ohio with her two tiny Yorkshire Terriers, Hemingway and Peluche, nestled on her lap.

www.ingramcontent.com/pod-product-compliance
Lightning Source LLC
Chambersburg PA
CBHW072335020726
47506CB00004B/891